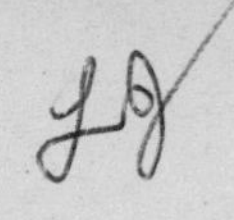

HUNGRY FOR REVENGE

One bitch is dead.

I'm not sorry.

I've done everything I can, used every method available, and yet I'm still an unknown face. I can barely see myself in the mirror anymore.

I am no one. They've made me no one.

I'm dissolving from sight, little by little.

But now I'll have my revenge. I find it is no great heartbreak to kill them.

I hate them. I hate them all.

But as they disappear into a hazy forever where they can never hurt me again, I keep their treasures close to me.

Now, as I stand in quiet reflection, naked, eyes closed, sensing a fire smoldering in the secret core of myself, I crush the envelope in my hand and feel a sexual thrill at its resistance.

There are hazards ahead. Annette was brazen and stupid. She talked and talked and talked. She took one of my treasures.

And Coby Rendell found it. Looked inside. She heard more than she should have. She sees more than she lets on.

She knows too much already.

In my mind there is a list of names.

And Coby's has risen to the top like a cresting wave.

Something will have to be done.

Something soon . . .

Books by Nancy Bush

CANDY APPLE RED

ELECTRIC BLUE

ULTRAVIOLET

WICKED GAME

UNSEEN

BLIND SPOT

WICKED LIES

HUSH

Published by Kensington Publishing Corporation

Hush

NANCY
BUSH

ZEBRA BOOKS
KENSINGTON PUBLISHING CORP.
http://www.kensingtonbooks.com

ZEBRA BOOKS are published by

Kensington Publishing Corp.
119 West 40th Street
New York, NY 10018

Copyright © 2011 by Nancy Bush

All rights reserved. No part of this book may be reproduced in any form or by any means without the prior written consent of the Publisher, excepting brief quotes used in reviews.

If you purchased this book without a cover you should be aware that this book is stolen property. It was reported as "unsold and destroyed" to the Publisher and neither the Author nor the Publisher has received any payment for this "stripped book."

All Kensington titles, imprints and distributed lines are available at special quantity discounts for bulk purchases for sales promotion, premiums, fund-raising, educational or institutional use.

Special book excerpts or customized printings can also be created to fit specific needs. For details, write or phone the office of the Kensington Special Sales Manager: Attn. Special Sales Department. Kensington Publishing Corp., 119 West 40th Street, New York, NY 10018. Phone: 1-800-221-2647.

Zebra and the Z logo Reg. U.S. Pat. & TM Off.

ISBN-13: 978-1-4201-0342-7
ISBN-10: 1-4201-0342-3

First Printing: July 2011

10 9 8 7 6 5 4 3 2 1

Printed in the United States of America

Prologue

Twelve years ago . . .

The last few minutes of Lucas Moore's life were spent in self-reflection.

Lucas was a surfer-dude type with long, blondish hair and a lean body, and at seventeen was, indeed, a surfer. He was also a lover. He liked girls and he had girlfriends, maybe one particular girlfriend, but things were getting kind of confusing in that department and he wasn't sure what to think. Especially with the particular group of girls he hung with. Their problems made him feel uncomfortable inside. He hadn't meant to hear all the secrets they told. He didn't want to know.

Maybe it was time to bail on all of 'em and move on.

It was night. Dark. A thin moon skimmed in and out of clouds as he trudged along the beach away from the party. He found a rickety wooden staircase that led up to the bluffs way, way above. This wasn't his beach. No waves, man. Just sand and smelly beach stuff.

He didn't much like it here. Was antsy to leave.

It was cold and he tucked the collar of his shirt closer to his neck: He was barefoot, having left his shoes back at the campfire. He wore a pair of ragged jeans and no briefs.

He never wore 'em. He'd had sex once tonight, unexpectedly, and had a couple of other "maybe" chances still out there and wasn't sure what to do about that. Sex was good. Sex was great.

But there were all these *problems*. . . .

He wasn't made for problems. He was made for earth and waves and sky. Big waves that roared toward you like griffins from another world. When they reached you, you climbed on their backs and rode them like the flying beasts they were. Conquered them. Flew with them, and while you were there you were in a better world, a world where earth and gravity and sound didn't exist. It was just you and air and moisture and the roar of power! The board beneath your feet was barely a sensation, didn't even exist.

But he wasn't on a surfboard now. He was trudging away from the girls and their secrets and the campfire and all the *problems*. He was finding his peace.

Now he crested the top of the bluff and could feel his pounding heart from the exertion. Jesus, what a long way up. Placing a hand over his chest, he closed his eyes and zenned. His thoughts expanded in all directions and then slowly coalesced and came back to him.

Okay, the girls had their problems. But maybe a little more sex wasn't such a bad thing. He liked women, liked feeling himself moving inside them . . . as long as they didn't howl and screech and claw like they were freaked out. Some guys got off on that, but Lucas liked a smooth ride with minimal stress, just sensation, the way nature intended.

Looking around, he squinted in the moon's uncertain light. He wasn't familiar with this bluff, either. The stairs he'd climbed ran upward and eastward, cutting into the hillside so that when he'd reached the top he was about a hundred feet inland from the western point of the bluff. Below, this jut of land cut through the beach like the prow of a ship, splitting it in half, reaching past the sand and into a rocky shoal that bubbled and frothed at the base like a cauldron.

Lucas considered. The whole area looked like private property, but he could see through the darkness that there was a trail on the other side of the gravel drive where he stood, a trail that meandered down toward the west, back the direction he'd come, and it was littered with wrappers and beer cans. If he followed it, he might reach the "prow" of this ship.

So thinking, he crossed the drive to the trail and headed west again. The trail's existence suggested trespassers like him didn't give a rat's ass who owned the property and just traveled it as they saw fit. That was fine with him. He wound toward the ocean, which he could hear but not see, and wished he'd brought a beer with him.

Nearing the edge of the bluff, he slowed his steps. There was no guardrail here. No safety net. The rocks and tide pools sat three hundred feet below. Carefully, he walked to the very edge and stared into the inky night. Faint moonlight illuminated the ruffled edges of the waves to the north. Below him was blackness.

He closed his eyes and soaked in the moment. He loved the feel of the stiff breeze against his forearms where he'd rolled back his shirt.

A noise to his left. A whisper.

Lucas cocked an ear but didn't move. He wasn't alone.

Slowly, he turned. In the grass to his right, a bare human leg. Moving.

"Hey, man . . ." he said apologetically. He wasn't the only one getting some tonight.

And then the leg jumped up and a figure leapt in front of him.

"Oh, Jesus," Lucas said, surprised.

The figure raced toward him and Lucas automatically recoiled.

And that's when it happened. The ground beneath his foot shimmied. He was still feet from the cliff's edge but a chunk of dirt and sand suddenly gave way.

One moment he was processing; the next he was falling through a black sky.

The next he smashed onto a bed of large stones, landing faceup.

He looked up at the smiling moon, which tore through the clouds at that very moment and shone down on him lovingly.

His last conscious thought was: *This really sucks. . . .*

Chapter 1

The night Lucas Moore died, we were all telling secrets.

Bam! Coby Rendell's front tire hit a bump and wrenched her arms as she fought her steering wheel. Her dark blue Nissan Sentra slew sideways, nearly heading into the large ditch on the right side of the highway. Her heart raced. Gripping the wheel with white knuckles, she was peering through the driving rain and wind and wondered for the billionth time why she'd agreed to this madness. Why? Why? She didn't want to go to the beach tonight, and she certainly didn't want to go to her stepmother's birthday party.

But sometimes, you just had to do what you had to do.

Setting her jaw, she felt her pulse start to slow as the car straightened out and the tires kept spinning, driving her west to the Pacific coast and the beach house where her father and stepmother and other party attendees would be. Another hour or so and she would be there. Back to the scene of the crime, so to speak.

"Were you with Lucas Moore, Miss Rendell?" the detective had asked her that day. A serious man in his late forties at the time, just beginning to develop a paunch, Detective Fred Clausen with the Tillamook County Sheriff's

Department was interviewing them all in Coby's father's beach house.

We wanted to be. All of us girls. He was that *guy. That surfer dude with a slow smile, lean body, great abs, and muscular legs. Long, brown, sun-bleached hair to his shoulders and a way of pulling you close and kissing you that made your knees quake.*

But she didn't say that to the detective then. No, no. And she hadn't say it to anyone since. She'd been seventeen when Lucas fell from the cliff and into the ocean, seventeen when she'd witnessed his body floating in the water, his long hair drifting along the tide pools, skin cobalt blue, limbs broken. The image was burned into her brain and now, at twenty-nine, she could see him just as clearly and remember the fear and grief and horror.

"Tell me what happened, in your own words," Detective Clausen had said, as he had to several of the other girls, and Coby, sitting at one of the dining room chairs in a halo of weak June sunlight that filtered through the clouds, had looked through the picture window toward the ocean, shivering like she had ague. It was her turn to talk. Her turn to tell all. But she couldn't.

"I don't know where to start," she said, her lips quivering.

"You all went to the campfire," he reminded her.

Now the car lurched again and Coby held tight to the wheel, frowning. Something was wrong. Glancing at the fir trees lining Highway 26, she realized that Halfway There, a diner tucked in the Coast Range between the Oregon coastline and the Willamette Valley, would be on her right in about five more miles.

All she had to do was make it.

She should have left work earlier. It was a Saturday, not even a regular workday at Jacoby, Jacoby, and Rosenthal. But she'd met with a client, a woman in the throes of a divorce who didn't see the money pit she was about to fall into, as Coby's job was to guide JJ&R clients to their new financial reality. This woman hadn't taken the news well, as most didn't, and she'd been late in leaving, the November daylight disappearing by four thirty P.M.

Now, with a feeling of intense relief, she saw the lights of Halfway There appear before her, the diner's logo of a half-empty, half-full glass flashing away against the darkening sky in neon green, beckoning travelers to their door as its "water" filled and emptied, filled and emptied.

Coby turned into the lot and managed to avoid the worst of the potholes, pulling up beside an older, once-red Chrysler sedan, its now faded pink exterior being pummeled by the drowning rain. Stuffing her rain hat on her head, she stepped out in cowboy boots and jeans; she'd managed to change at work before she took off for the coast, which should have been two hours away in decent weather, at least three in this.

Her right front tire looked okay from what she could see. It wasn't completely dark, but the cloud cover made everything seem later than it was. She tried to see the axle and thought it looked bent a little, but who could tell? The rain was torrential.

Mumbling invectives to herself, she pushed into the diner, dripping water from her raincoat onto the well-worn indoor/outdoor carpeting of the vestibule between the outside and inside doors. Sweeping off her hat, she shook the rain from it, then pushed through the inner door, catching the eye of a wise-eyed waitress who was stacking empty plates onto a large tray from one of the tables.

"Sit anywhere," she said. "Someone'll be right with ya."

Coby looked around and chose a booth in the corner with a window to the parking lot and road. She watched a semi rush by, its headlights cutting a swath through the gathering twilight, water shooting from its tires in a flat stream, spraying into Halfway There's parking lot.

"Nice night, huh." The waitress, her name tag reading Helen, appeared with her notepad and poised pencil.

"Just coffee," Coby said.

"Honey, you sure? Look at that weather. Wherever you're goin', it's gonna be a while. I can't interest you in a nice piece of apple pie?"

"I'm trying to make dinner at the beach," she said with a shake of her head.

"What part?"

"Just north of Deception Bay."

She snorted. "Better take somethin' to go, then. 'Cause you're gonna be hungry before you get there."

Stuffing her pad into a pocket, Helen headed behind the bar to grab the glass coffeepot and a mug and, as she was returning with both, a man behind the counter looked up and yelled, "Hell!"

"Yeah, Gary. That's my name, don't wear it out," she called over her shoulder.

"This order's been here for ten minutes!"

"Now, that's a darn lie," she said calmly. "Let me get this lady her coffee and then I'll take the order. Don't have a hemorrhage, for God's sake."

She shook her head as she placed the mug and a small pitcher of cream in front of Coby, pointing to the sugar packets with one hand as she poured the coffee with the other. She left, muttering under her breath.

Coby used the cream and stirred it into her drink. She wasn't worried about the weather. She was worried about her car but was going to give it the old college try. She wanted to get there, if for no other reason than to get out of this weather and into somewhere warm.

But she didn't want to stay the night. Please, God, no. Her father and stepmother were having a party—her stepmother's birthday party—and there would be lots of people. Coby planned to stay for an hour or so and then head home.

She glanced at the rain squiggling down the windows. Well, at least that had been the plan. Maybe she would be looking for a motel, if she ever got to the beach.

The beach . . .

Tell me what happened, in your own words.

She didn't want to think back. She didn't want to relive a past she was trying really, really hard to put aside forever. But it was not to be, apparently, and giving in, Coby closed her eyes and thought back to the night that had changed the lives of everyone there. . . .

June 14: Just after school was out at the end of junior year

Coby had been seventeen—well, at the time all the girls were either seventeen or eighteen. None of them had wanted to be at the beach party where it had all started. They weren't even really friends, and they never had been. It was just that their dads had formed friendships back when the girls were all in grade school and they'd never gotten the memo that their daughters didn't care whether they hung out together or not.

But the beach trip happened anyway. And so there they were, sitting in a circle on the sand around the sputtering flames of a campfire that was feeding on driftwood and the pilfered sticks from a broken-down laurel hedge near Coby's dad's beachfront home. They'd added some leftover brown paper grocery bags that they'd discovered stacked on shelves in the garage to use as kindling, and now the fire smoked and crackled and burned their eyes.

They were seated directly on the sand. June sand. Coby

could feel the damp and chilling cold seep through the bottom of her capris. She wished she'd worn jeans. Even with the fire's warmth she shivered—they all shivered—and they stared at each other through drifting smoke that the wind occasionally, gleefully, snatched away and then tossed back into their faces, rife with sand. Several of the girls had pulled their sleeping bags around themselves like blankets, and the collective thought on their minds was whether they really, really, really wanted to spend the night on the beach or go back to the house where it was warm and light.

But nobody wanted to be the one to wuss out first. There was some strange need to prove something to each other that no one was copping to. They'd told themselves they were here to have fun. F.U.N. So, maybe they weren't the best of friends. So, maybe they didn't even really like or know each other. It didn't matter. They'd been on soccer teams and softball teams and participated in student body functions and pep rallies together and they'd weathered the years of grade school, junior high, and now high school together. And though it was their fathers who'd bonded in those early years, forming a group of Dads and Daughters, organizing trips and functions for them all, clinging to their male-bonding while the girls drifted further and further away from their second-grade selves, the girls let it all happen and went along with it. They had determined, by tacit understanding, that they could keep up the facade for their dads' sakes by handling this beach trip and even pretending they were having a good time. Maybe they even would.

The fact was they were facing their senior year. The last year of high school before they would all be launched into adulthood where a whole new horizon awaited them. For some, it might be a tragedy, but for Coby it was all she'd been waiting for: the beginning of a welcome future where she could shake off the sticky remnants of her youth and run toward something totally new and fabulous.

She was lost in happy thoughts about this unwritten future when Genevieve Knapp slowly stood up across the campfire from Coby, her right hand cupping the flame of a candle that she held in her left. Coby regarded her suspiciously. What the hell was this? Genevieve was cool, blond, and one of the most outspoken of their group, and the way she was standing regally, chin jutted out, did not inspire confidence. Coby glanced to her left, to petite Ellen Marshall, and they exchanged a worried look.

"It's time to play Pass the Candle," Genevieve intoned. She gazed in turn at each of them seated in the circle around the ragged campfire that had been dug into a pit in the sand. With the wind snatching at her hair and the smoke funneling around her, she looked like some kind of spectral being arisen from the ashes.

Pass the Candle? Coby didn't much like the sound of that.

One of the girls, Dana Sainer, a small, birdlike brunette, coughed several times and waved away the smoke. She blinked up at Genevieve. "What?" she asked.

"Yeah, what?" Rhiannon Gallworth cut in. "What does that mean?" Rhiannon had dark eyes and pale skin and a doelike look about her that was belied by her sharp chin and faintly militant manner.

"Yeah," Coby said, not to be outdone.

"We've all known each other since forever, but do we really know each other?" Genevieve asked, in lieu of answering directly. "Everyone has secrets. Some we can't wait to tell. Some we never want anyone to know. This is about those secrets that are buried deep. Each of us needs to tell one now. Our deepest, darkest secret. And once told, it never leaves the circle of this group."

"Like, oh, sure," Coby sputtered, half laughing. She expected all the others to go along with her on this, but no one said a word. They all looked at each other, or the fire, or the ground, or the ocean, its dull roar a constant background noise.

Overhead there was a crescent moon and stars glimmered, as if offering their own comments. Coby looked skyward herself, thinking, *Good God,* before the wind tossed more sand into her eyes, forcing her to turn away.

She didn't want to do this. She wanted to run away screaming, right now. Surreptitiously, she threw a glance at her watch and wondered when she could legitimately leave, but it was too dark to read the tiny clock face.

Rhiannon's brows were lifted in disbelief, but it was Wynona Greer, whose dishwater brown pageboy locks fell across her cheeks, obscuring her features except for the tip of her sharp nose, who demanded belligerently, "Oh, yeah? Well, who's going to start? You?"

"I'll be last," Genevieve answered, and there was something about the way she said it that made Coby think she possessed some big secret, or at least thought she did, and wanted to wait to spring it on all of them. But that was kind of Genevieve's way. High drama, even when there was none. Especially when there was none, actually.

Wynona repeated, "So, who's going to start, then?"

"I will."

They all looked in the direction of the determined voice of Yvette Deneuve. Yvette was one of five sisters dubbed the "Ette sisters" by their friends and classmates because the sisters' first names all ended with *ette*: Nicholette, Annette, Yvette, Juliet, and Suzette, in that order. All of them were dark-haired and dark-eyed with mocha-colored smooth skin, a gift from their French father, Jean-Claude Deneuve, one of the dads currently back at the beach house and best friend to Coby's own dad, Dave Rendell. They were all staying at Coby's family's beach house—now her father's house, since the divorce—and back at that house Coby's sister, Faith, and Yvette's sister Annette Deneuve, both a year older than the group on the beach, were hanging out together. In fact, Jean-Claude had brought all of his daughters, except Nicholette, the eldest, and Coby suddenly, fervently wished she'd stayed back at the house with the rest of the Ettes.

But Genevieve had been insistent, so here they were.

Now Yvette took the candle. Her dark hair was held back in a ponytail and the candle's uncertain light cast deep shadows, hollowing out her cheeks. "I've kept this secret for years. I've never told anyone." She inhaled and exhaled several times, as if seriously considering backing down, then said quickly, "I had sex with a nineteen-year-old neighborhood friend when I was thirteen."

Coby's brows lifted in spite of herself. *Whoa. That sure sounds like statutory rape. Thirteen?*

"You mean like sex, sex?" Wynona asked, looking scandalized. "Or just a blow job or something?"

"You want an anatomy lesson?" Yvette demanded. "Yeah, sex, sex. Like in you can get pregnant from it. That kind of sex. Jesus." With that she thrust the candle to McKenna Forrester, who was seated on Yvette's left, then sat back down, frowning, her arms wrapped around her knees, her chin resting on them.

It was clear to Coby that Yvette was already regretting her revelation, and she totally understood. Coby had no idea what she herself was going to say. What the hell! She didn't have any deep, dark secrets. But McKenna was only two people to Coby's right, so that meant that after McKenna, then Ellen, it would be Coby's turn.

Maybe I should just run away now!

Wynona threw Yvette a *look*. Her father, Donald Greer, was the vice principal at their high school, and Wynona had always been the goody-two-shoes type, even looking that way with her pageboy and conservative clothes. It sort of surprised Coby that Wynona seemed to think a blow job was somewhere further down the sex scale from going all the way. As far as Coby was concerned, she didn't want any part of any kind of sex unless that sex was with either Lucas Moore or Danner Lockwood. Danner was a few years older than Coby, long out of Rutherford High, and didn't know she was even alive. His brother, Jarrod Lockwood, was in Coby's class, but he was just a friend and Coby didn't feel the same way about him as Danner. But Danner was about as attainable as a movie star, where Lucas Moore, her other crush, was a classmate and kinda available. He'd made out with practically all of the girls in this group at one time or another. Currently he was hooked up with Rhiannon, but with Lucas, who knew?

McKenna stood up slowly. She wore camouflage pants and a T-shirt and her short, dark hair was covered by a baseball cap. She dressed like a boy and was androgynous enough to make them all wonder if she was gay. The fact that the issue was unaddressed showed how little they all really knew about each other. McKenna cleared her throat several times and Coby wondered if they were about to have that question finally answered. "I don't want to do this," she said.

"Oh, come on, McKenna," Genevieve cajoled. "Yvette spoke the truth. You can't do the same?"

McKenna pressed her lips together, thought hard for a moment, then suddenly burst out, "I wrecked the car when I was fifteen and my brother took the blame for me. I shouldn't have been driving alone. Mom and Dad still don't know. I don't think we woulda got the insurance money if they reported me, and we didn't have the money to fix the car otherwise. I owe my brother big-time." Quickly, she sat back down and handed the candle to Ellen, who cupped the wildly jumping flame until it smoothed out.

Coby glanced sideways at Ellen, who carefully uncupped her hand but didn't stand up. Everyone in the group stared at the mesmerizing flame.

Ellen said in a hypnotic voice, "I had an abortion."

Coby's lips parted in pure shock and it was all she could do to keep from jerking around to stare directly at her. *Ellen?* Petite blond, blue-eyed Ellen, who was the quietest of the group? Coby knew next to nothing about her other than her parents were divorced, like hers, and she lived with her dad.

But an abortion?

"It was a guy I met last summer," Ellen went on in a barely audible voice. "Summer camp. We hung out and . . ." She trailed off and deep silence lasted for about five seconds, then she added, "I had it done right before school started last year."

"I thought you went out for cross country last fall," Wynona said breathlessly. "How'd you do that?"

"That was the year before," Ellen answered, lips tight. "Last year I couldn't."

She carefully passed the candle to Coby, who gazed at it with an escalating heart rate. She had nothing to say. *Nothing!* Her parents were divorced and her dad had won the beach house, while her mom got the Portland Heights home that looked over the city. But the whole divorce thing had been a fairly businesslike transaction, it seemed to Coby, who, though she hated the fact that they'd split, sort of got it that they'd just moved emotionally apart from each other. Coby had one older sister, Faith, who was a bit of a goody-two-shoes like Wynona, so there was no drama there. The rest of her extended family weren't scandalmongers, either. Well, except for Great-uncle Harold, the lech, who'd laid a couple of disgusting kisses on Coby's and Faith's lips—yuck!—and had made kissing attempts with any other female within reach, but Uncle

Harold had died a few years earlier with no serious incidents to report, so he was out.

So, no . . . there was nothing, really. Coby wildly thought back to the night she'd shared some rotgut wine with her best friend, Willa, and they'd both puked in the backyard. But last year Willa had moved to the East Coast, and what could have been a long road of merry transgressions and exploits together had left Coby pretty much alone and partnerless in crime.

The girls were all looking at her expectantly. She was annoyed to see her hand tremble slightly as she stood up. But one thing she wasn't, was a wimp. So if this campfire required a story, she would come up with one.

If you don't have anything bad to say about anybody, make up something.

"I caught my father in bed with another woman before my parents' divorce was final," she announced, the lie tasting bad on her tongue.

"Daddy Dave?" Genevieve said with a squinty look. "You caught Daddy Dave with another woman?"

"I don't believe it," Yvette stated flatly.

Coby was instantly pissed off. "Why am *I* the liar?"

"Because your dad's just a really good guy," Yvette said on a huge sigh accompanied by major eye-rolling and a switch of her ponytail. "We all know it. That's why we're here, isn't it? Because Daddy Dave wanted to get together with my dad, his best bud?"

"Well, it's true," Coby insisted stubbornly, passing the candle on to Dana Sainer, who stood up to take it from her. Coby sat down hard. Even though she'd made the whole thing up out of a tiny incident where she'd caught her father at a café with a woman she hadn't recognized—a coworker, it turned out later—during the final stages of the divorce, Coby was bugged that they didn't believe her. It was a dumb game. Dumb, dumb, dumb!

Dana smoothed her short, dark hair away from her eyes with her free hand, stared into the candle's flame for a long moment, then looked around at their faces, one by one, as if memorizing them. "Well, I'm . . . I've had an eating disorder as long as I can remember."

McKenna pulled off her baseball cap, waved it at Dana, then stuck it back on her head and declared in a bored tone, "You're supposed to tell a *secret*."

"That's a secret! A big secret! I've never told anyone before!" she sputtered. "Well, except Genevieve . . ." She glanced at their leader with a dark scowl.

"It's no secret. *Everyone* knows." This was from Rhiannon, who swiped the candle from Dana with such speed that its flame flickered out.

"Damn it," Genevieve muttered, grabbing the candle from Rhiannon and holding it toward the fire. Flames reached for her, swallowing up the wick and half the candle. "Jesus, that's hot!" Genevieve jerked her hand back, then, more carefully, managed to relight the wick before handing the candle back to Rhiannon, whose doelike eyes refracted the firelight.

"I wasn't done," Dana declared huffily. "I've been fighting bulimia for years. And anorexia. It's nothing to laugh at. You have no idea!"

Yvette sighed loudly. "We're not laughing. It's just that you wear it like a badge of honor."

"I do not."

"Yeah," Yvette argued back. "You kinda do."

Dana's mouth dropped open but before she could take it further, Genevieve broke in, "It's just that you haven't exactly kept your eating disorder a secret. We've all caught you puking at least once."

"Well, excuse me for having a real problem!" Dana plopped down on her butt and stared fixedly at the burning sticks of wood, fighting tears.

"They're all real problems," Coby said, trying to placate, still feeling guilty about her lie and feeling the weight of Ellen's revelation as if it had blanketed their whole group. And though she felt sorry for Dana, being put on the spot and all, Yvette and Genevieve weren't wrong: Dana liked having something that made her special, in this case her anorexia and bulimia.

"Go ahead," Genevieve urged Rhiannon, who was still standing with the candle, tendrils of her dark hair being teased by the growing wind. Rhiannon's large eyes seemed to swallow up her face.

"My mom's an alcoholic," she said. "I mean hard-core. If there's nothing else, she goes for the vanilla extract. Anything. One time I called nine-one-one when she wouldn't wake up. Scared me to death. I even kinda wonder what she's doing right now, but my brothers are with her, so maybe she's okay. My dad doesn't talk to her anymore at all. He's seeing somebody else. I've met her. She's nice."

"Aren't your parents still married?" Ellen ventured cautiously.

"Some marriage." Rhiannon shrugged. "They don't even like each other anymore." She gazed toward the ocean, and to Coby the crashing waves suddenly sounded loud and angry. "Hard to believe they were ever in love." Rhiannon looked wistful for a moment, then a small smile played on her lips.

"Like you and Lucas?" Wynona guessed, sounding faintly jealous.

"Well, yeah," she said, glancing around as if daring anyone else to argue the point.

Lucas doesn't love her, Coby thought, a bit envious herself that the blondish surfer-dude was currently spending more time with Rhiannon than any of the rest of them.

Rhiannon gestured for Wynona to stand up, and she did so reluctantly. Rhiannon handed her the candle, then retook her seat while Wynona stared at the jumping flame for a moment, lost in thought. Then she lifted her chin. "I've never told anybody this. No one. My parents, I think have guessed, but I've never said a word." She plucked at her pageboy with her free hand. "You know I was on the swim team? Last year? But I'm not this year. I used to belong to this private swim club and we used the pool over by Tualatin. The swim coach there was known for coaching winners. He and I had private sessions." She started breathing faster and Coby felt the hairs on her arms lift. "And when we were in the pool he helped me out a time or two, and there were a few times his hands kinda grazed me. Down there. And at first I thought it was just random-like, but then one time I was heading for the locker room and we were alone and he was following after me and I turned around . . ." Her voice trailed off for a moment. "And then he was right there and I didn't know what to do. He pressed me against the lockers and kissed me, and then his hand was inside my swimsuit and—"

"*Holy shit*, Greer!" a male voice yelled from deep in the darkness outside their circle. "Coach Renfro *felt you up*?"

Half the girls gave an aborted scream as guys from their class suddenly burst into the light of their campfire. Wynona's knees gave out and she sank down. The candle slipped from her grasp, rolling into the campfire. Genevieve scrambled for the candle as Coby shot Wynona a worried look and the boys swarmed into view.

Lucas Moore stepped forward first, his sexy, shoulder-length hair tousled and moving in the wind, his gaze searching for someone.

But it wasn't his voice they'd heard. That loud question came from Kirk Grassi, who showed himself next, his hair pulled into a long, black ponytail, his guitar over his shoulder, his smile flashing, his eyes zeroing in on Wynona as he repeated, "Holy shit, Greer!"

"You morons!" Genevieve blasted, infuriated at the interruption. She'd caught the candle before it was engulfed in the fire and was now dusting off her hands.

Lucas frowned. "Sorry we barged in."

Rhiannon ran straight at him and he seemed surprised by the show of affection, as it took him a moment to wrap his arms around her. *Good,* Coby thought, as unrepentant as the rest of them in hoping the Lucas/Rhiannon thing would burn out.

Other guys from their class emerged from the darkness and collectively blew a raspberry in Genevieve's direction. They'd clearly planned on busting their party, and Coby was pretty sure she could put the blame at Rhiannon's feet, as she was totally wrapped up in Lucas.

"Oh, for God's sake, relax," Vic Franzen told Genevieve, spreading his hands. He was the heaviest of the group, with a shape just short of portly and a mean way of directing negative attention toward anyone else, maybe because he was the butt of so many jokes himself. He was hefting two six-packs of beer and he lifted them up so all the girls could see. "We brought alkee-hol."

Coby inwardly sighed, knowing she wouldn't be able to escape without serious ridicule now. Genevieve pressed her lips together and looked ready to explode. The rest of the guys found places around the campfire: Jarrod Lockwood, Galen Torres, Theo Rivers, and Paul Lessington. Jarrod had long hair like Kirk's, or more accurately, Kirk had followed Jarrod's lead as they both played guitar and jammed together; the two friends dreamed of being in a band one day. Galen was Hispanic with a look faintly like Ricky Martin; Theo had short hair, almost a buzz cut, and a hard body from regular workouts; and Paul was a tall stringbean with a pronounced Adam's apple.

Coby saw Jarrod Lockwood coming her way. He held a large brown paper bag, and he sat down next to Coby and dug the bag into the sand between them, forcing Ellen to move over to make room. Inside the bag was a bottle of vodka and one of bourbon. "Paul's got the mixer," Jarrod said.

Paul Lessington pulled a large plastic bottle of Sprite and a stack of plastic glasses from inside another bag. He was on the school's basketball team, if he didn't get caught for this indiscretion and find himself ineligible.

Coby didn't know how she felt about the booze, but she was in no mood to be called names for refusing to join in. She glanced at Rhiannon, who hesitated but then accepted a beer, and given what she'd just shared about her family history, Coby thought she understood why. If Rhiannon was joining in, so would Coby, and in truth, all she wanted to do herself was escape, and so she ended up with a full eight-ounce tumbler of mostly vodka with a splash of Sprite and settled herself into the party.

Jarrod whispered into Coby's ear, "Telling secrets?" Like his older brother, he was tall, dark, and handsome. But Danner Lockwood, three years older, was the man of her dreams—quietly observant and a bit of a loner—while Jarrod was more of an exhibitionist whose scripted appearance and guitar playing seemed designed to win him female attention.

She looked over at Lucas, who was now half lying on the ground beside Rhiannon, stroking her hair and smiling into her eyes. "Not really," she said to Jarrod, sort of depressed that Rhiannon and Lucas's relationship was now looking like the real deal.

"Oh, come on. What was your secret?" Jarrod teased Coby.

"I didn't have one," she said truthfully, earning her the evil eye from Wynona, who was still recovering from being overheard.

"Yes, you did. We all did," Wynona snapped.

"Who invited you?" Genevieve suddenly demanded of all of the guys. "Huh? Who invited you?"

"Jesus, Knapp. PMS, why don't you." Kirk Grassi yawned and added, "Your ass is tight enough to hold water."

There were sniggers from the rest of the guys and Genevieve scoured them all with a baleful look. "We were having a *private* meeting," she said with a bit of acid.

"I'll say," Vic Franzen said. He burped heartily and lifted his beer can in a salute to himself. "Greer there was telling how she and Coach Renfro did the dirty." He gave Wynona some hip action to emphasize his point.

Wynona's face was pale, deep circles beneath her eyes. "It wasn't Coach Renfro."

"Sure it was," Vic said.

"It wasn't!" she declared.

"There's nobody else," he responded.

"Shut the fuck up," McKenna told him coolly.

"Sure thing, lesbo." Vic smirked and looked around for support from the rest of his buds, but they had collectively cast their eyes aside, not willing to get into that dogfight.

Ellen said in a near whisper to Coby, "Maybe we should go back."

"Maybe we should all have another drink," Kirk suggested, looking straight at Ellen.

Coby glanced over at Wynona, who seemed shrunken in on herself. She thought how she would feel if the guys had appeared when she was telling her supposedly most private, deepest, darkest secret. Or Ellen. What would have happened if they'd heard about her abortion? Or of Yvette having sex at thirteen?

Some secrets just shouldn't be shared with a group, she concluded, and it was her last serious thought of the evening before the effects of alcohol took over and they all let go of their annoyance over the boys' intrusion and settled in to party.

Chapter 2

Coby paid for her coffee, jammed her rain hat on her head, and stepped back through Halfway There's vestibule into the miserable weather outside. If this current November storm was any indication, the winter ahead was going to be a doozy.

Hurrying through the rain, she paused to look at her axle, couldn't tell anything more, jumped in her car, and switched on the ignition. Tossing her hat into the passenger seat, she snapped the seat belt, then slowly backed out onto the highway again. She eased the accelerator down and was gratified when the car seemed to be holding its own, not straying to the right as it had been. She held her breath, expelled it, then held it again, for several miles, and when nothing worse happened decided that maybe the car had been pulling to the right because of the wind and rain, that the pothole she'd banged through hadn't damaged the axle. Anyway, she would go on that assumption until she found out differently. She just would drive more slowly than she wanted, which was practically a prerequisite anyway given the shitty weather.

Her mind tumbled back to that long-ago beach party as if it were stuck in a groove. Every time she drove to the coast her brain traveled this same path, some times worse than others, like tonight.

The day following that fateful night of the campfire, Lucas Moore's body was found floating in the surf. He'd fallen from a cliff above onto rocks below, and the waves had dragged him into the ocean and then back to the tide pools where he'd gotten hung up, his arms and legs and hair pulled and pushed by the ebb and flow of the water. All the girls were devastated. Not just because one of their group had died, because it was Lucas. *Lucas!* Who seemed touched by the gods. That morning they were wailing and screaming and pulling at their hair, even fainting, in grief and denial, and when Detective Clausen showed up it was a melee.

Tell me what happened, in your own words.

She'd told Clausen about the beach party, how they'd been sitting around a campfire, just talking, bonding as good friends do. The words were ashes in her mouth but she would rather cut her tongue out than tell their secrets. If someone else did, so be it, but it wouldn't be Coby.

But no one did.

And then she told the detective about the guys showing up with alcohol and how they'd all imbibed. That she would confess because it could have been the reason Lucas died, and she knew Wynona would not be able to keep that secret. She'd had a few drinks herself, but her father was still the vice principal. The shit was going to hit the fan in more ways than one, so Coby spilled about their drinking with no serious regrets.

She and Clausen were together in the den, the room he chose to conduct interviews so they could have a modicum of privacy. Not everyone wanted to talk to the detective; well, no one did, actually. But they were called in one by one, so Coby related what she knew, keeping the secrets they'd told around the campfire to herself. She realized even through her grief and fear that Clausen was just doing his duty, gathering the facts. She sensed he didn't think there had been foul play, but he needed to talk to them all to fill out an accident report.

Of course, the fact that they were all drinking became a significant factor later on, and there was serious talk from the authorities about going after whoever had supplied the alcohol. Then it was learned the guys had stolen the beer and vodka from their own parents' houses, and the horrified dads of the girls heard this and looked shattered. No one knew exactly what to do. Eventually, the boys' parents all heard about what happened and their punishment was meted out in varying degrees of harshness, depending on who those parents were. Jarrod's parents were divorced and he lived with his father, who grounded him until January. His older brother, Danner, was away at college, presumably, and Coby didn't learn till later what he thought of it, which was that his little brother and his friends were boneheads who should have taken better care of their friend. Lucas's parents were also divorced, each spouse remarried, and they, though heartbroken and miserable, blamed their son as much as anyone for drinking and didn't try to go after anyone for retribution.

Coby was up front about her own drinking, but she was quiet about Pass the Candle. She also neglected to mention that Lucas Moore had kissed more than one girl that night. She didn't say that after Rhiannon fell asleep, he moved over to talk to some of the others and found himself kissing Genevieve and Dana, and yes, even Coby herself, later on. She didn't point out that drinking alcohol made a convenient excuse for why they wanted and planned to kiss Lucas, even though they knew he was with Rhiannon; that being under the influence was a means to claim they didn't know what they were doing later, in case Rhiannon found out.

In the end Lucas Moore's death was ruled an accident. It was decided he fell from the edge of an unstable cliff above the ocean, impaired by alcohol consumption, and died of massive trauma to his head. Even when the lab work came back and his blood alcohol level was .00, no one wanted to believe it was anything more. So he hadn't been drinking. So what? Then the accomplished surfer/athlete had simply fallen to his death.

Accidents happen.

"You didn't see him after he left your campfire?" Detective Clausen asked at the end of Coby's questioning.

"No."

A lie. She had seen him. Briefly. While fuzzy-headed. Late in the night when she took a stumbling walk to the ocean and stood with her bare feet in the water, numbed by the cold, and Lucas appeared beside her and raised his arms skyward and howled like a wolf. When he turned her way, his mouth a slash of white in the moonlight, she just wanted to crush her mouth on his.

"Isn't this great?" he'd said, tossing an arm to encompass the black ocean with its white ruffled waves.

"I think I'm drunk," Coby responded, to which he laughed and reached out for her hands, rubbing them between his as he felt how cold they were. She looked up at him, seeing a little double. "Where's Rhiannon?"

"Oh, you know." He inclined his head in the general direction from where they'd come. And then he pulled her forward and kissed her on the lips. She felt the heat on her mouth when the rest of her skin was cold, and the whole thing was cool and sweet, and kinda felt like a dream.

Pulling away reluctantly, she said, "You're a bad boyfriend."

"I like you," he said, and kissed her again.

Vaguely she remembered somebody breaking them apart. Jarrod, maybe? Although it seemed more like Paul

Lessington. And then in one of those snapshots that stood out later, a sharp memory surfacing from the drunken haze, she recalled seeing Lucas kissing Genevieve sometime later during the night.

She'd been right: He was a bad boyfriend. A bad, bad boyfriend.

But she didn't tell Detective Clausen any of that. She told him about the guys and the alcohol but revealed as little as she could about Lucas himself. It just seemed wrong and unimportant. He'd fallen. It was sad and horrifying and a total loss, but he'd simply fallen.

Twelve years . . .

Twelve years since then.

Now Coby flexed her hands on the steering wheel of her Sentra and drew a deep breath. The road to the coast was dark, wet, slippery, and lonely, and she was driving with careful control, slowing to almost a crawl around the blind corners and snaking curves. She was in a hurry, but hurrying could get you killed on this stretch of two-lane highway, even without a bent axle.

A lot of things could get you killed.

Twelve years.

She seemed destined to dwell in the past tonight, and why not? It wasn't just that she was going to the beach. For the first time in years she was going to be seeing many of the players from that fateful night: guys, girls, even dads. This was not a reunion she was looking forward to, and if there were any way she could have gotten out of it, she would have.

But she was stuck. Almost as powerless as she'd been all those years ago when they'd foolishly played Pass the Candle and the guys had invaded their secret meeting and the next morning Lucas Moore's body had been discovered floating in the surf, his long hair tangled with seaweed, his surfer-boy good looks reduced to chilling purplish skin and cobalt blue lips.

Now, cautiously lifting a hand from the wheel, she ran it pensively through her auburn shoulder-length hair, brushing out leftover rain that had found its way beneath her hat. She'd spent these twelve years trying desperately to forget about Lucas Moore and Pass the Candle and a whole lot of other things. She hadn't learned her lesson with Lucas, either. A few years after graduation she'd run into Danner Lockwood, her other secret fantasy, and had gone out of her way to get him to notice her. He had, too; in that she'd succeeded. But what she'd hoped was a fabulous romance had been a fling. She'd been infatuated, even more so with Danner than with fickle Lucas. And for a time Danner had been sort of interested in her, too, but then the relationship had died beneath them.

And later, another tragedy: Rhiannon Gallworth, Lucas's supposed girlfriend, fell from a hiking trail to her death shortly after graduating from college.

Slam! The car suddenly jerked sideways again and Coby quickly grabbed the wheel hard with both hands as the Nissan shuddered and shimmied toward the side ditch, its back wheel having squarely hit the pothole she'd tried to miss. Carefully she guided it back onto the road, hoping she hadn't screwed the damn thing up even further.

"Good God," she murmured, her heart still racing. Six o'clock at the end of November. It had been dark since four thirty and the rain was a black, unrelenting curtain. At this rate she would be lucky to get to the beach house in one piece.

Swallowing, she waited a dozen more miles while the Nissan's wheels spun on the wet tarmac and her headlights split the dark road ahead before allowing herself to uneasily revisit the past again. Rhiannon's death, so similar to Lucas's, at least in manner, had led some of their group to speculate that they were both suicides. A kind of lover's leap where the first couldn't find a will to live, and the second couldn't live without the first.

Coby didn't believe it for a moment. Lucas's death was an accident. Period. She was still going with that. He'd fallen from a rocky cliff to the rocks below.

An accident, nothing more.

Like Rhiannon's, years later.

Both accidents.

Unless . . . ?

Coby clamped down on the thought before it could fully materialize. No. Nope. Nada. She was not going to start that nightmare again. Lucas Moore's death had been ruled an accident, and Rhiannon's was just an unhappy coincidence. Whatever happened, happened. Nothing more to say.

But at Rhiannon's memorial service, where Coby had seen the whole gang again, or at least those still living in the area, she'd allowed some doubts to creep in; she hadn't been able to keep them out. How could they both die so young? she'd asked herself. How could there be two accidents where they both fell? Was there something cosmic involved here, or were their deaths the work of a murderer?

McKenna had been the only one to dare ask such a question. When they were outside the service, standing on the steps of the church, watching the sea of family members drift out, she'd voiced the thought on everyone's mind: "Two too many accidents for my taste." Then she left, heading for a waiting motorcycle to roar away and out of Coby's life.

Coby had gone on to finish her undergraduate studies at Portland State University, earning a degree in business. She'd taken a job at a law firm while she considered going on to graduate school and working toward an MBA, or maybe applying for law school. But she'd found a niche for herself at Jacoby, Jacoby, and Rosenthal, a prestigious downtown Portland law firm, and had never changed course. Her firm dealt mainly in divorce and custody issues, and as an offshoot, the establishment of financial health for the firm's clients. That's where Coby came in. She was a case manager, which meant she was the one who counseled the newly divorced into understanding their financial situation as it was in its current state, not as it had been. She was the one who had to break the bad news time and again, the news that though their client might have ended up with the house, mortgage free, that real estate they now owned—generally a huge property, for JJ&R clients tended to be among the wealthiest in the city—was a money-sucking albatross around their neck that would drain them of every penny within two years' time, given the cost of property taxes and upkeep, yada, yada, yada. Coby was the one who advised them they would need to sell and hopefully buy something they could afford, something more modest. She was the one who pointed out in black and white that their previous lifestyle, the way they had lived, *their world*, was over.

It was a bitch of a job, really, but she was good at it. Understanding, but firm, impervious to the abuse they sometimes threw at her as she often became the target for their anger and frustration instead of their ex, the perceived block to their ultimate happiness. Coby wouldn't say she was used to it; she'd actually had a paperweight tossed at her once by a hysterical client, who ended up checking into a hospital for a few days directly afterward for "exhaustion." But she'd grown a pretty hard crust over the years and felt she could handle most anything thrown her way, so to speak, at least at work.

That afternoon she had just finished a particularly grueling meeting with a woman who had cried bitterly into a tissue the whole time, Saturday being the only time she could arrange to see Coby as she felt she did not need counseling and had only grudgingly agreed to the meeting because her lawyer, the firm's Joe Hamlin, had insisted.

"But I'm getting the house free and clear," she'd declared frostily for about the fifth time. "He *left* me for that tattooed *whore*! I made him give me the house, and it's worth a fortune!"

"Yes," Coby agreed.

"We sank every penny into the house over the years. Every fucking penny. It's all we had, and now it's mine!"

"The house is worth a lot," Coby agreed.

"And I'm keeping it! We're in the worst recession in decades! Nothing's selling. I'm not some stupid bimbo, you know. I'm aware of what's going on," she pointed out, her perfectly coiffed hair shivering a bit, echoing her outrage. "I am not selling until the market recovers!"

Her name was Shannon Pontifica, and she and her ex had bargained to the last cent over the palatial mansion located in Dunthorpe, one of the most tony areas just outside of Portland. Shannon had waived a suggestion of higher alimony in order to keep the house, a proposition Coby had tried to dissuade her from, to no avail. No amount of explaining the difference between cash versus equity had filtered through her stubbornness and attachment to the real estate. Shannon didn't want to look at the fact that she was giving up cold, hard cash in the name of some nebulous value an appraiser would guess at, on a property she didn't intend to sell anyway. The end result? She was basically broke. She had no income apart from the reduced alimony, which wouldn't come close to covering the cost of her home's upkeep. She had to sell or lose the property.

"Take a moment to look at this," Coby told her, sliding a spreadsheet across the desk in her direction, then glancing surreptitiously at the clock, knowing she had that two-hour drive to the beach ahead of her while rain was already peppering the windows behind her with increasing force. Late fall weather. Cold as the arctic. Wetter than wet.

Shannon, early forties, blond, trim, good-looking, although lines were etching in her face from setting her jaw and glaring at everyone and everything through icy blue eyes, mulishly would not drop her gaze to the figures before her. But in her expression a faint but growing panic was developing. She'd made a choice and the choice had been based on emotion rather than the cold, hard truth. She knew it now, but it was too late for a "do-over." She had to work with what she had.

Coby didn't love being the bearer of bad news, even when it was advice the client sorely needed. But someone had to do it, and Coby was the one. She'd developed into the job because she was a natural born fixer. She was a sounding board for the lawyers, a cool head, a troubleshooter, and often times the "detective" who uncovered the information the other side was hiding. She could often discern what was really going on behind the "he said, she said" dialogue that developed between opposing sides. From receptionist-cum-secretary-cum-possible soon-to-be law student, she'd become an integral cog of the firm's machinery that was crucial in holding it together, a piece no one knew was even missing until Coby filled the space.

She hadn't intended for things to turn out this way, but there it was.

In a cool but firm voice she warned Shannon, "The house is only valuable to you if you sell it and walk away with the equity."

"I won't get enough. I won't."

"You have the appraisal," Coby reminded her. "Your property is valued somewhere around three million dollars in today's market. That's a lot of money."

"I *know* it's a lot of money. That's why I got the house! It's my money!"

"But it's trapped. You can't keep feeding the house for long. It will swallow you up."

"I won't lose it!" she declared stubbornly.

"I understand how you feel, but it won't alter the facts. The sooner you sell, the sooner you stop putting money into the house, the sooner you can access the property's equity."

The lines between her eyes deepened ever further. "You act like I have no choice!"

For an answer, Coby dropped her gaze to the spreadsheet caught somewhere on the desk between them. The numbers were on the conservative side, but they were unrelenting. By the middle of next year, maybe sooner, Shannon would lose her house and all the equity it represented.

It took another twenty minutes of quiet insistence for Shannon to finally buckle and accept what Coby was telling her, a truth she already knew herself but couldn't even look at. The Kleenex box on Coby's desk was nearly depleted by the time she plucked out the last tissue and pressed it to her red, swollen eyes.

"God damn it, he screwed me again, didn't he?" she said on a hiccup.

Technically, she'd done it to herself, but Coby decided it might be counterproductive to say so. "You have a lot of money coming your way. You just have to take the steps to get it."

"Fine." Shannon jumped to her feet and stuffed her clutch purse under her arm. A designer label that must have cost her a small fortune. "The fucker!" she muttered as a final salvo, then slammed out of the office.

Ten minutes later Coby had changed into her jeans, shirt, and boots, tossed her raincoat and hat in the back of the Sentra, and was driving to the beach, an eye on the approaching storm, wondering if she should have put more in her overnight bag before her meeting with Shannon. She did not want to spend the night, but that decision might be taken from her. This was a duty to perform, nothing more. She was headed for her stepmother's birthday party at the beach house her father still owned. There were so many reasons she didn't want to go, but she had little choice in the matter. Her plan was to show up, eat dinner, suffer through some small talk, then turn around and drive back to Portland and her rented condo in the Pearl District.

Still, as the sky grew darker, she wished she'd tossed in more toiletries beyond her toothbrush and comb. This storm had its hooks in the area, and she was driving straight into it.

Now she powered on through long miles and driving rain, her windshield wipers working overtime. Sometimes the rain sloshed over her windshield like she was going through a car wash. At this rate, mudslides would form in the mountains where the trees had been clear cut. Luckily or unluckily, depending on how you looked at it, the road she was on was bordered by Douglas firs, their roots dug deep into the ground. Their presence might help her escape mudslides, but she had to watch out for falling limbs.

Finally she was over the Coast Range and cruising toward Highway 101, which wound down the coastline from Washington state, through Oregon and then California. A glance at her watch: 6:30 P.M. The rain was still raging but she could relax a bit, knowing she was through the most treacherous part of the trip.

The car seemed to be handling itself. Another half hour and she would be there.

Turning south onto Highway 101, Coby flicked a look to the west and the black area beyond that was the Pacific Ocean, indiscernible through the storm as anything but a continued blackness that stretched to an equally black horizon.

The beach house was only sixteen miles away.

In a few minutes she would be there. She'd tried, over the years, not to let the events of that night ruin the place for her, but in essence, they had. She shied away from trips to the beach, often finding a way to say no to a weekend with her dad and sister. She couldn't help it. The place held too many unresolved issues, too many uncomfortable memories.

Were you with Lucas Moore, Miss Rendell?

No. Yes. Sort of. . . .

Bringing alcohol to the party had changed the tenor of the evening, which wasn't all bad, considering it got them away from talking about the secrets that were spilled that night. Coby sipped her drink and listened to the guys talk louder and louder as their consumption increased and watched as Lucas and Rhiannon snuggled deep into her sleeping bag. The other girls noticed, too, though everyone pretended to be oblivious. Man-slut that he was, Lucas was adorable, and Coby leaned back in the sand and saw the stars blur and spin overhead.

"C'mon, Wynona," Kirk Grassi coaxed, his speech beginning to slur. "Quit lyin'. It's Coach Renfro, isn't it? You got down with him, huh."

"She went down on him, y'mean," Vic said. Coby turned her head and squinted an eye at him. He was grinning like an ogre.

"Shut up," she told him.

Wynona sputtered, "It wasn't Coach Renfro! It wasn't anybody!"

"Yeah, sure," Theo muttered from the other side of Ellen.

"I told you!" Wynona sobbed. "You're such bastards! All of you!"

"Who was it, then?" Kirk demanded.

Coby realized Kirk and the others had dismissed, or not heard, the part about using the Tualatin pool and assumed

Wynona was talking about the Rutherford High swim instructor, Coach Renfro. It would be a simple matter to put together, probably, if they had all the information. She had to find a way to keep them from learning anything more about any of them, but her head wasn't tracking as well as it should.

"You can all go to hell!" Genevieve spat between her teeth. She'd been drinking, too, and now stood up and swayed a bit on her feet. Her face, normally so cool and careful, was stretched with fury.

"Stop talking," Yvette complained.

"This isn't good," Jarrod said. He staggered to his feet and left Coby to walk to where Genevieve was planting her feet in an effort to keep her balance. "Let's just chill."

"Leave me alone," Wynona told Kirk. "Just leave me the hell alone!"

"Well, excuse me, bitches." Kirk lay on the sand and stared up at the sky, much like Coby.

Theo, who'd wriggled in between Ellen and McKenna, gave them each another beer. Ellen was already sipping vodka and Sprite, so she started alternating with swigs of beer, which made Coby shudder a little inside. McKenna took her longneck in silence, her face hard. She hadn't decided whether to accept the boys or not.

"Dana," Jarrod said, holding up a beer from Paul Lessington's sack. "Here." He lightly tossed it to her. Coby turned her head to see Dana fumble it before setting it down into the sand immediately. Then she pulled back her hands as if she'd touched cooties, looking around to see who noticed.

No one cared. Lucas and Rhiannon were wrestling in their sleeping bag. Yvette was watching them through half-closed eyes, sipping at her vodka drink. Genevieve still looked like she wanted to kill someone, and as the alcohol took further effect she subsided into angry silence.

Wynona made some hiccuping sounds, on the verge of crying. Having left Coby, Jarrod stayed close to Genevieve, and Coby, finding that oddly funny, kept lifting her head to sip her own Sprite and vodka until she had a really nice buzz going. She didn't plan on getting sick again, like she had with Willa, so she was trying to pace herself. Ellen, seeming to sense Coby was a friend, moved closer until her side was nearly pressed against her. Coby didn't move, recognizing that Ellen needed a friend, and McKenna, still smarting over the "lesbo" comment, glared at Kirk between gulps of beer, but Kirk was blotto by then and impervious. Galen, Paul, and Theo were trying to catch up with Kirk as fast as possible while Dana kept refusing all drinks, declaring there were too many calories in alcohol.

"There are four calories per gram in carbohydrates, but there are seven in alcohol," Dana stated with certainty. "Seven! That's almost as many calories as are in fat, which is *nine*!"

"You're a freak," Vic Franzen told her, then belched loud enough to wake the dead. Paul and Galen shared a glance over their longnecks, as if Vic bugged them, too, which warmed Coby's heart a little.

With an effort, Coby squinted a look at her watch, but Yvette caught her. "Got a hot date, Rendell?" she accused.

"With the sandman." She hiccupped, found that funny, and laughed. "I'm beat."

"You can't leave," Genevieve told her.

That did it. She'd been vacillating whether to stay or leave, but Genevieve's arrogance just plain pissed her off. Coby deliberately dug her now-empty cup into the sand, then clambered to her feet, swaying a little as she dusted off the back of her pants. Ellen jumped to her feet, also, and Theo followed suit and asked her if she wanted to walk along the edge of the surf. Ellen looked flummoxed for a moment, then happily surprised, and she strolled away with him.

"Aww, come on," Vic said, wrapping Coby in a bear hug as she tried to back up and get away.

"Leggo," she muttered.

"Stay," McKenna said, and it was more a plea than an order.

"Don't leave us," Wynona begged.

Well, hell. They actually wanted her to stay. Lifting her hands in surrender, Coby sank back down and picked up her empty cup again, which Jarrod promptly came over and filled, and wondered if she could manage to spend the night on the beach with them after all.

"So, Wynona's a sex mermaid," Vic said, circling back to the topic they'd already declared taboo.

"Jesus, Vic." This from Jarrod.

"I just wanna know what else they were talkin' about," Vic defended himself.

"Wouldn't you like to know!" snapped Dana.

"Yeah, I would. That's why I asked." He made a face at her.

"It was private," Genevieve said sternly.

"Hey, c'mon, we got no secrets," Vic said. "You all know about Theo knocking up that girl from Gresham."

Everyone looked toward the waves where Theo and Ellen had wandered off.

"He didn't knock her up," Paul Lessington corrected him flatly. "Get your facts straight, man."

There was a groan from Kirk as he sat up again, swiping at the sand that was sticking to his cheek. "He knocked her up," he disagreed with Paul. Then, "Gimme a beer, Lockwood." Jarrod tossed him a longneck, which he bobbled a bit then caught. "The bitch said so."

"Everybody's a bitch, aren't they?" Coby pointed out,

glaring at him. Well, at least it felt like she was glaring. She was kinda tipsy. Definitely, definitely tipsy.

"That's right," Kirk said.

"Well, she lied about Theo," Paul insisted, throwing both Kirk and Vic a dark look. "Imagine that, the little ho lied. She screwed half the school and then some, then said Theo was the dad."

"So she's a bitch and a ho. Do you even know this girl?" McKenna demanded. "Jesus, I'm sick of guys name-calling and making judgment calls! We're always hos, sluts, bitches . . . or worse."

"Well, *you* sure don't have to worry about getting that kind of reputation, do you?" Vic pointed out with a snicker.

McKenna marched up to him and for a moment Coby thought they might actually come to blows. McKenna looked ready to grab him by the throat and Vic, for all his boasting, was shocked and maybe a little scared. McKenna might be a girl, but she was a good-sized girl and she was bristling with fury and intent.

"You're all fucking idiots," Yvette declared in a voice that could cut glass. She let her gaze slide over the guys. "No wonder college guys look so good. You're all like junior high losers."

"About the age you first got interested in dick?" Kirk said, throwing her a sly glance. "No judgment here," he said, before Yvette could react. "Just sayin'."

The girls all froze and looked at each other. *They'd overheard? The guys had overheard? How much did they overhear?*

Genevieve scooped up some sand and threw it at Kirk. "Get out!" she screamed.

"Hey!" he protested.

"Get out, get out, get out!"

"I didn't hear yours," Kirk protested.

"Get—the—fuck—out!" Genevieve was in a froth, and Coby was with her completely.

"Whose did you hear?" McKenna asked cautiously.

"We were here awhile, just listening," Jarrod admitted.

"Oh, don't be such a girl," Kirk accused him.

Coby threw a glance toward where Ellen and Theo had gone, but there was no sign of them. Her head felt fuzzy and her tongue thick. Nevertheless, she declared, "You can't eavesdrop on our privacy, throw it in our faces, and then think we want to hang around with you creeps."

"Creeps," Vic repeated, laughing.

"Assholes, then," Coby stated firmly.

Lucas stuck a head out of Rhiannon's sleeping bag, his hair mussed, his face flushed. "You're ruining my mojo," he declared, extricating himself with an effort from the bag.

Rhiannon instantly protested. "You didn't do anything. It was Kirk and Vic!"

"We all overheard your confessions," Lucas said, looking at the other guys, who didn't deny it.

"You didn't overhear mine," Genevieve said with a snarl to Kirk. "Because I didn't get a chance to tell it. You wanna hear it? Since you barged in and never gave me a chance to tell it? I'll tell it."

"Hey!" Kirk was pissed. "We didn't know you were gonna be tellin' big secrets."

"Gen, come on," Jarrod said, trying to placate her.

"No. You might as well all know what a bitch I am, too. Here it is: I made out with my sister's boyfriend. She cried and cried when I told her what I did, but I didn't care. I wanted to take him from her, and I did."

"You don't have a sister," Rhiannon argued, her hands still on Lucas's arm, trying to get him to stay.

"My stepsister, then. I call her my sister. I wanted her boyfriend and I took him from her."

"How are you and your sister now?" Dana asked, frowning.

"Not good." Gen shrugged.

Coby found herself wondering if Genevieve was lying. She was just one of those people who couldn't face losing, even in a contest about who could tell the most horrendous secret about herself. Did she have a stepsister? "Was your dad married before?" Coby asked.

Genevieve turned away, as if she were deaf and said instead, "I just wanted him."

"I'm going down to the ocean," Lucas said, completely free of the bag now. He slipped his feet into flip-flops, then thought better of it and took them off again before heading barefoot across the cold sand to the waves.

"Hurry back!" Rhiannon called after him, looking sort of annoyed. She seemed torn between following him and getting back in the sleeping bag.

Yvette watched Lucas's disappearing form, then jumped to her feet and followed him. "I'll be right back," she said.

"Fuckin' A," Rhiannon muttered, furious. She took two steps after her, then stopped and said to Galen, "Give me a drink."

Galen complied, pouring her another vodka and Sprite, and gallantly getting up to hand it to her. Rhiannon muttered something about Lucas being a man-slut, and Genevieve, who'd popped up to her feet as well when Yvette tore after Lucas like a homing pigeon, said, "Yvette's a horny whore."

"Whoa," McKenna said.

"Well, it's true," Gen declared.

Vic said, "I'd give her a ride."

Paul half laughed. "She wants Lucas. They all do."

"That bitch better not sleep with my man," Rhiannon warned through tight lips.

Coby, swirling a bit, listened to their words with half an ear. Outside of their ring she heard something else. Turning, she strained to see through the dark night. Was that a moving figure? Lucas or Yvette, maybe? Ellen and Theo?

Genevieve said with a snarl, "Lucas is too smart to put his dick in her overused crotch."

"She did start pretty young," Galen burst out as if he couldn't help himself.

"She sure did," Genevieve agreed, suddenly not bothered in the least by further evidence of the boys' eavesdropping.

Jarrod groaned and shook his head. "Gen, shut up. Sit down. Have a drink." He grabbed her hand and tugged on it, pulling her back down beside him, though she was reluctant to give in. "Who gives a shit? Let's have some fun."

And with that he found his guitar, settled it over his shoulder, returned to Genevieve's side, and started lightly strumming, silently inviting everyone to relax and stop ripping at each other.

Coby, after a moment, did just that, determining she would leave the group once they were all settled in. Her last thought before falling asleep herself was that Lucas Moore might be a man-slut, but he was good-looking and boyishly sexy and they all sure liked kissing him.

Chapter 3

Jarrod's guitar playing did the trick; everyone settled down around the campfire and into their sleeping bags. The evening grew later and the beach got colder and Coby let alcohol keep her there long after she was ready to leave. She nodded off for a while, distantly aware of the other kids continuing to argue loudly for a while, but she lost track of the gist of it and didn't much care anyway.

Late in the night, she climbed from her bag, looking around at the humps of bodies in other sleeping bags, unable to tell who was who. Some of the guys must've gotten in with the girls because it didn't seem like there were the right number of bags for every individual. She thought about heading straight to the beach house, but she stumbled toward the water instead, and that's when she had her moment with Lucas.

Thinking about it now, she was pretty sure it was Jarrod who'd broken up that tête-à-tête, but she really couldn't say for sure. Later still, as she was sneaking away from the party, sleeping bag in hand, she'd caught sight of Lucas and Genevieve *really* going at it. They were down the beach, standing up, pressed against each other, their hands all over each other and, as if sensing her, they slowly moved away, farther south. As if that hadn't been enough, when she turned northward she interrupted Theo and Ellen, who were humping frantically behind a huge piece of driftwood. Their voices drew her near and as she passed, she glanced over, wondering what she was hearing. She was totally embarrassed upon seeing Theo atop her and hearing Ellen's mewling in the dim moonlight as their bodies moved rhythmically. It didn't take much imagination to understand what they were doing.

After that, she hurried back to the beach house, where she climbed the outside stairway on the side of the house and entered through the front door, which was on the road side, opposite from the beach, allowing her to enter with no one seeing her. She then found the love seat in her dad's study, spread out her sleeping bag, and collapsed inside it. The next morning she woke up late, swimming up from a deep sleep fueled by both exhaustion and alcohol, to a bright morning that hurt her eyes and head.

Loud voices emanated from the main room. Girls' voices. Angry . . . or maybe fearful? Her companions had clearly made it back from the beach sleepover and were now yelling shrilly.

It hurt Coby's ears.

With an effort, she staggered from the den, rubbing her eyes, and worked her way down the hall to the main living room, where her friends and the dads and a couple of the guys were all staring in wide-faced shock.

"Coby!" her dad cried in relief. "You were here?"

"I was in the den." She squinted at them. The light was bright and everyone looked pale and ill.

"We were about to send out a search party!" He hurried toward her and threw his arms around her as if he hadn't seen her in years.

"I came back last night." She gently pulled back from

her father's crushing hug, ran a hand self-consciously through her hair, and asked, "What's going on?"

"It's Lucas," Genevieve said after a moment, her voice raw. Her gaze shifted to Rhiannon, who looked as if she were staring into the yawning gates of hell. "He fell from a cliff into the ocean. He's . . . dead."

"Dead?" Coby repeated, uncomprehending.

"Dead," Rhiannon whispered, fresh tears welling in eyes that looked as if they'd already cried a river. She started sobbing and wailing and Coby realized this was what had woken her up.

"I'm sorry, Bug," her father said, murmuring his favorite nickname for her. "I'm so sorry. The police are on their way and want to talk to all of us. . . ."

Twelve years ago

Now Coby pulled into the gravel drive that led to the same house, still her father's beach house, listening to the crunch beneath the tires, watching the rain pour over her windshield and the trees wave their branches menacingly as she slowed to a stop. Twelve years that felt like a lifetime ago in some ways; like it happened yesterday in others.

Switching off the engine, Coby sat for a moment, her hands still on the steering wheel. She gazed at the familiar beach house and wondered, as she had so many times before, if there was any way she could have stopped the events that happened later that night. It was the same thing she wondered anytime her thoughts touched on the beach and Lucas Moore. If something—if just one thing—were different, maybe there would have been a different ending as well.

But it was what it was, and many other things had happened since, some good, some not so good, some out-and-out tragic. They had all graduated from Rutherford High the following spring and Coby had gone onto college and then her job at Jacoby, Jacoby, and Rosenthal. McKenna was a stand-up comic on the regional circuit and was still single, and Dana had moved to the East Coast, married, and had birthed a passel of children, apparently; at least three by last count. Genevieve Knapp was married also, to Jarrod Lockwood, and they lived in the greater Portland area but were unhappily childless at last report. Ellen was a mystery; living in California, maybe. At least that was the extent of the information that had reached Coby's ears, though she thought McKenna kept in touch with her. Wynona was now a social worker around Portland, unmarried, according to her Facebook page, and uninterested in anyone from Rutherford High, according to her attitude. Rhiannon was gone, the tragedy of their group. She'd attended school in Arizona but had been home for winter break, hiking along a trail above Multnomah Falls, just east of Portland, when the fatal accident occurred.

Coby expelled her breath, feeling that eerie breath of fate brush her nape whenever she thought of unexpected death. Why Lucas? Why Rhiannon? It seemed like there should be some reason, some explanation, for what had happened to them, yet both deaths were accidents. Statistics.

Bad things happen.

She was cocooned inside her car by the rain, and it was a last moment of peace before she had to face the social battle ahead. With a sigh, Coby reluctantly climbed from the car and crunched up the gravel drive, head bent to the dousing rain and ripping wind.

Their last friend, Yvette Deneuve, had turned up pregnant her senior year. She'd delivered her baby boy in mid-March, almost nine months to the day after the beach trip, and that certainly got the rumor mill spinning. But Yvette had yet to tell anyone who the father was, to Coby's knowledge. If she was asked outright, her answer was to walk away and cut that person dead. Everyone had expected her to give up the child for adoption; Yvette just didn't seem like the motherly type. But she fooled them all, keeping her little boy and raising him as a single mom. Like all the rest, Coby had seen next to nothing of her since graduation, though that wasn't true of Yvette's sisters, who were a large part of Coby's life for various reasons, one of them being this party.

As she approached the door, she remembered that Yvette's son's name was Benedict. She would probably see both him and Yvette tonight. Like she would probably see a number of her old high school friends.

Because that's what this birthday party was all about.

Because Coby's stepmother was none other than Annette Deneuve Rendell.

Go figure.

With a studied effort, Coby placed a smile on her face and knocked on the door. Maybe if she was lucky the power would go out and they would all have to abandon the party in search of electricity. Maybe there would be a mudslide that would prevent everyone from getting here. Maybe something would happen to put an end to this craziness. Maybe—

The door flew open, shattering her silent hope.

"Hey there, girlfriend! So good to see you!" Annette declared, oozing with bonhomie as she hugged Coby for all she was worth. "So glad you could come and help usher me into my thirties! Isn't this weather just the worst?"

"Pretty bad," Coby agreed with a smile she hoped looked more natural than it felt.

Annette wore a pair of slim, body-hugging black pants

and a fuzzy white sweater with a boat neck that exposed her collarbones. Her hair was pulled back by a slim black leather headband and she wore silvery earrings that caught the light. She looked young, beautiful, and elegant, and Coby had a mental image of herself: hair flattened in the rain; a tailored dark blue shirt; denim jeans; cowboy boots.

She should have really rethought her wardrobe for this event.

Looking beyond Annette, Coby saw her father standing where the foyer opened to the living room with its picture window and the ocean beyond. Tonight it was just a view of blackness upon blackness. Her father smiled at her uncertainly, and she understood why: Dave Rendell had married Annette Deneuve Rendell seven years earlier, when he was forty-six and she was twenty-three. Annette, Coby's sister Faith's good friend. One of the Ette sisters.

Some things were just plain wrong.

Annette released Coby and they entered together, Annette closing the door behind them with a shiver. "Brrrr," she said. "Cold and wet."

Dave Rendell walked forward and put his arm around his wife's shoulders as he greeted his daughter. "Good to see you, Bug. So glad you came."

"Me, too," she lied. "And happy birthday, Annette."

Annette dimpled. "Thanks. Dave, honey, take Coby's coat." Dave dutifully removed Coby's rain jacket from her shoulders and hung it in the hall closet. Then he gave her a bear hug.

Coby accepted it all. She'd learned over the years that some things needed to just be let go and this was one of them, though it was still a work in progress. Coby, a fixer by nature, really wished she could fix this one. In the beginning she'd tried to reason with her father, pointing out their age difference. She'd been nicely, but firmly, told to stay out of his personal life, and it had been a struggle, no doubt about it. She'd wanted to scream at him: *Annette Deneuve? Twenty-three years younger than you are?*

She still kind of wanted to scream at him, but she managed once again to fight back the urge. Not that he didn't have a point. She sure as hell wouldn't want him interfering with her love life. But twenty-three years younger. Really?

Annette was chattering away about the preparations they'd made for the event. Like all the Ettes, she had an exotic look with a slim physique, mocha-colored skin, hollow cheekbones, shining dark brown hair, and luminous eyes, just as dark. She was a decent person, too, Coby supposed. A hard worker at her father's partnership venture, the boutique hotel known as Lovejoy's in Portland's Nob Hill area—which echoed San Francisco's district of the same name—his partner in the hotel being his good friend, and now father-in-law, Jean-Claude Deneuve.

Annette Deneuve Rendell. Thirty years old today.

"Is Faith coming?" Annette asked Coby a tad anxiously, finally daring an even touchier subject.

"I haven't talked to her." Coby and her sister were close in times of crisis, but they didn't have a lot in common on a daily basis and their general relationship consisted of sporadic phone calls, amusing e-mails, and a line or picture on Facebook from time to time. But if Coby had difficulty with Annette, Faith was, well, not into acceptance at all.

Coby distantly realized that her heart was pounding as if she'd run a marathon. It had been seven years since her father had married Annette, but their romantic relationship had started not long after the beach trip. They'd met during that fateful night, which felt like the end of one life for Coby and the start of another. At the time Annette was eighteen and Dave forty-one. Of course, they kept their mutual attraction secret for a long while for a lot of reasons, the one Dave copped to most often being he wanted more time to pass since he was newly divorced. *Bullshit,* Coby thought, *then and now.* Her father just didn't want to look at the fact that he was seeing a teenager. Couldn't work that into his overall view of himself. A teenager.

Jesus, she thought, feeling the wrongness of it all sweep over her once again. It was not okay for her father to date one of her classmates, no matter whether it was legal or not. It just simply was not okay. And no amount of trying to logically accept it would ever make it okay.

But . . . whatever. A lot of years had passed. A lot of water under the proverbial bridge. She wasn't going to change his mind now. Coby loved him and Daddy Dave was still a good guy, even if his crown was tarnished a bit in his love for a girl only a year older than Coby herself and one the same age as Faith. Coby had mostly kept her real feelings about the union to herself. Mostly. Her sister, her mother, and everyone else except for her friend Willa, who, though she still lived across the country, had become a deep confidante, did not know the extent of Coby's ambivalence. Willa had given the marriage ten years and had wagered a hundred bucks on the outcome. Unfortunately It looked like Coby was going to win that bet.

"Let's get you a drink," Dave said, and Coby walked toward the kitchen across the familiar reddish fir floor of the living room, which had been remodeled and expanded westward to show off a commanding view of the restless Pacific. Tonight she could just make out the ruffling white edges of the waves in the darkness beyond.

The house itself was several short flights of stone stairs above the beach, and apart from the laurel and a few scrub pine trees to the south, there was nothing but sea, sky, and sand. And tonight, shifting, pouring rain and a low, keening wind.

"Hope you brought your suit for the hot tub," Annette

said. She was standing at the sink as Coby entered the kitchen and nodding toward the window and the outside deck. Coby raised her brows as she glanced outside again to the helllish weather and Annette laughed. "JK. Just kidding. How's Cabernet suit you? Red wine makes bad weather better."

"Perfect," Coby said.

Then Coby saw through the window above the sink that Annette wasn't completely kidding about the hot tub. Sunk into the wooden deck on the south side of the house, it was clearly heated and ready, a cloud of steam on its surface spiraling upward through the slanting rain.

Feeling her dad's eyes on her, Coby turned and gave him a smile. He hugged her again, as if he couldn't help himself, wrapping his arms around Coby in another hard squeeze that always seemed to convey the question: Do you still love me? Is this okay? Am I still a good father?

Coby hugged him back before sliding away from his embrace, hoping this time that he would be assured that she was on board with his marriage when she clearly wasn't. She was trying, but it was hard.

"Are we the only ones here?" Coby asked. "I thought I'd be the last one."

"People are having a little trouble in this god-awful weather," Annette said on a sigh. "But a bunch of them are here. Yvette, Juliet, and Benedict are at the store. My dad's watching TV upstairs in his bedroom. Suzette's taking a nap, I think, and Nicholette's on her way with her boyfriend, Cal Ekhardt. Do you know him?"

"I've met him a few times when he's picked Nicholette up." Nicholette, Annette's older sister, was an attorney with Jacoby, Jacoby, and Rosenthal and consequently had become the Ette sister Coby knew best.

"Juliet's guy's on his way, too," Annette added. "Kirk Grassi."

"Kirk Grassi," Coby repeated in surprise.

"Well, she invited him, but I can't really tell whether they're together or not, you know what I mean? And you heard about Suzette and Galen Torres, right? They've been dating for almost a year. Those boys in your class . . . they seem to hook up with my family, don't they?"

Not just the boys, Coby thought, shooting her dad a surreptitious look. "I haven't seen Kirk since high school. He wasn't at Rhiannon's memorial service."

"Yeah . . . I don't know what his deal is. It's going to be kind of like a reunion around here." Annette glanced at Dave, too, and smiled. "Even Mr. Greer is going to be here."

"Donald," Dave said, as if they'd had this discussion before.

"I know, I know. But I'm never going to be able to call him Donald," Annette dismissed. "He was our vice principal, after all."

Coby thought about Wynona's serious-minded father. "Is Wynona invited?"

Annette made a face. "Yes, but she's not coming. Said it was to do with work, and maybe it is, but she's really not interested in any of us."

"I haven't seen her in forever, either," Coby said, more to herself than Annette.

"Social work has made her really hard," she said, grimacing. "It's like helping people has made her totally hate them, does that make sense?"

"She hates the people who victimize children and women," Dave corrected her carefully. "Not the victims."

"Well, she doesn't like any of us much, either," Annette responded, giving Dave a long look. Then to Coby, "You know about her suicide attempts, right?"

"No," Coby admitted, as Dave snapped, "Annette!"

"I'm not trying to gossip," she snapped right back, "but if you don't know the truth you can sure step into a whole big pile of shit without meaning to. Especially when you're talking to someone like Mr. Greer . . . Donald," she corrected herself.

"You shouldn't just announce these things," he said.

"I'm telling Coby. Coby. No one else."

"What happened?" Coby asked, and Dave, annoyed, made a gesture of impatience, handed the opened bottle of Cabernet to Annette, then left the kitchen, as if he couldn't bear listening in any longer.

Annette made a sound of frustration. "Oh, hell. I'm so sick of secrets. I know way too many of them, and keeping a lid on them is like bottling up poison. Eventually the container breaks and the stuff just spills all over everybody. Ugh." She poured them each a glass of ruby red wine. "I'm thirty, and I'm just not going to play that game anymore. That was my birthday promise to myself. Bad secrets need to be laid on the table. What you know can't hurt you as much as what you don't. So, yeah, Wynona made two suicide attempts, one with pills, one by slitting her wrists. Neither effective. I don't want to sound like a complete bitch, but they were cries for help, not a serious attempt to kill herself, and she got a lot of attention. Then she decided to dedicate her life to social work, helping others, but she's not very good at it."

Coby stood with her glass in hand, speechless.

"I am a bitch, aren't I?" Annette said without a bit of remorse. "Maybe the real me is just coming out now." She eyed Coby speculatively. "I've always played by the rules, and it's exhausting! I'm giving myself a pass, starting today. I know you're supposed to keep up a facade, ignore the elephant in the room, sometimes, for the sake of being a nice person or something. Half the time, I just don't know why I should even care." She shrugged. "Anyway, to hell with what everybody else thinks. I don't give a flying fuck anymore."

Dave returned with several more bottles of red from a wine rack in the dining room and, catching the end of her words, appeared embarrassed. Sliding him a look, Annette finished with, "But what do I know? I'm just a kid."

"You're not a kid," Dave said on a sigh.

Annette snorted and, with her drink in hand, headed into the living room, where Coby heard a male voice greet her. Her father, Jean-Claude.

"She's kind of on this new kick," Dave said to Coby with a shake of his head. "I think something happened at the hotel. Somebody convinced her that she wasn't leading a 'real' life unless she was brutally honest. Comes off as rudeness, though."

"You don't have to apologize for her. I don't like keeping secrets, either," Coby said, "but sometimes it's a better plan." She couldn't help thinking back to the night of the campout and felt herself blush as she remembered what she'd said about her own father.

From beyond the kitchen Annette and Jean-Claude had entered into an animated conversation, and by mutual, unspoken agreement, Dave and Coby moved to the living room as well. As if the previous conversation hadn't even occurred, Annette turned an animated face from Jean-Claude and asked Coby, "What would you think about having a little brother or sister?"

Coby automatically shot a look at her father. "Wow."

Dave groaned, but Jean-Claude grinned, his George Clooney good looks engaging. "Oh, don't worry. Annette just loves to fool around. She's kidding, Coby. Not that I would mind being a grandfather again." He had the faintest accent, which only increased his appeal. Coby's father had said on more than one occasion that it was

Jean-Claude's charm that got Lovejoy's name on the map. He was the face of the hotel, which was really a renovated, older apartment building turned into suites and a first-floor bistro that served tea and coffee by day, wine by night.

Dave stated, "Annette's not pregnant."

"No, I'm not," Annette agreed on a sigh. "At least not yet." She shot Dave a mischievous look.

Jean-Claude's teeth flashed white again. "You're making Coby uncomfortable. Try to not be so shocking, my dear." To Coby he said, "All my daughters are smart and beautiful, but a little tweaked, eh?"

"Oh, shut up," Annette told him fondly.

"But you're seriously thinking about having a baby?" Coby asked, feeling breathless. A half sister or brother? Jean-Claude was right: Coby was definitely uncomfortable.

"You don't even like babies," Dave reminded his wife. "You've told me enough times."

"That's not true. I just don't know jack shit about them," Annette admitted. "People try to hand me their baby and I practically freak out. It feels like I'm going to break them. So I keep telling Dave we need to have our own so I won't be such a spaz, but, well, he's not into it. Says he's too old. But it's not about the sperm, is it? It's the egg that counts, and mine are ripe!"

She laughed and leaned into him, giving him a big kiss, her earlier tension dissolved.

"You look a little struck," Annette observed a moment later, her knowing gaze on Coby, her arm still around Dave's waist.

Coby was pretty certain this was territory she really didn't want to travel. Sure, she'd wondered more than a few times if her dad might start another family, especially given Annette's age, but truthfully, the thought kind of horrified her. "I don't know how to feel about that," she admitted. Then, to her dad, though she knew perfectly well, "How old are you again?"

"Too old. Way, way too old. Diapers and babysitters and all those years of school. College . . ." He smiled at her. "Your mom and I used to take turns driving you and your sister around when you were babies to get you to go to sleep."

"Ooh, no. Reminiscing." Annette gave him a slap on the butt. "It's my birthday, so quit it."

"Is Joe coming on his own?" Dave asked Coby, clearly taking Annette's advice and changing the subject.

Coby thought of ten ways she could answer him, then settled for the unvarnished truth. "Joe and I aren't together anymore. We called it quits based on mutual apathy. This last year had been . . . a slow ride downhill."

Joe was Joseph Hamlin, a member of the firm whom Coby worked with often, the member, in fact, who was Shannon Pontifica's lawyer and had set up the meeting between Coby and Shannon for earlier that afternoon. Joe was driven to make partner above all else. He was ten years older than Coby. Divorced. No children. Not looking for any. Coby wasn't exactly sure what she wanted for herself in the future, but she knew she needed to keep her options open and, well, Joe didn't care about options. It was his way or the highway. Early last month she'd chosen the highway, and he'd pretty much shrugged and said have a nice trip.

So much for the power of passion and true love.

She'd worried a little that after their breakup, since they worked at the same firm, things would become awkward and weird. But Joe treated Coby just the same as before they'd dated, and she took a page from his book and treated him the same way. She and Joe just didn't go out for drinks alone anymore, or make plans for dinner, or stay over at each other's places. They saw each other at work every day and smiled and joked and generally kept on keepin' on and that was it.

It was so damned civilized it sometimes made Coby sad.

But if she were really, really honest with herself, she could admit her emotions had never been fully engaged with Joe. She'd been three-quarters of the way there, but she couldn't quite make that final turn. Sometimes she'd asked herself what she was waiting for. True love? Like, oh, sure. That was going to happen.

And then, if she were really, really, *really* honest with herself . . . and if she dug deep into her own secret self and examined her feelings closely, she could admit that she'd never loved Joe. She'd been in love only once with, of all people, Danner Lockwood, her high school crush. She'd had a teen fantasy about Lucas Moore, but she'd had an actual relationship with Danner during her college years, making her one-time dream a reality. And things between them even kinda worked for a while. She'd been thrilled and surprised to actually be with him as a lover and a friend. It was glorious. Absolutely glorious. She loved him and he . . . liked her just fine.

Just. Fine.

And it wasn't enough.

"I'm sorry about Joe," Dave said now, unhappily. "I really liked him."

"Everybody likes Joe," Coby said. "Joe likes Joe pretty well, too," she added with a faint smile.

"Bitchiness," Annette observed with amusement. "I love it."

That made Coby laugh, which surprised all of them. Coby determined that maybe, with enough wine, she might actually have a pretty decent time.

"Well, I'm totally bummed," Annette said on a sigh. "I had it all planned out that you would marry Joe and we would have some kids and then you would have some kids and we'd all hang out together."

"Some things are not meant to be," Coby said. This baby thing was much on Annette's mind, apparently. "I'm picking up some vibes here . . . like maybe you are pregnant and just don't want to tell me yet."

"Oh, I wanna be. I so wanna be." Annette stared straight at Dave. "I've *tried* to be, actually. But somebody's not totally on board yet."

Jean-Claude eyed his friend and partner and said to Dave, "You're not getting any younger, my friend."

"Maybe for my next birthday?" Annette tilted up her chin and gazed at Dave pleadingly.

"I'll be fifty-four," Dave protested.

"One more reason to start today! There. I've said it. I want a baby and I want it now." She turned to Coby. "That's probably more than you ever wanted to know about us."

Coby lifted her hands in surrender.

"Bug, are you sure?" Dave asked her seriously. "I mean, really?"

So they were testing the waters with her, staring at her intently, and though she could tell her father was drag, drag, dragging his feet, it looked like the matter had already been decided. "I don't need to tell you, this isn't about me," Coby said. "Or Faith. Or even Mom. It's about you two."

"Thanks for nothing," Dave said with a faint smile.

"Hey, I'm Switzerland. Totally neutral," Coby responded.

"Sounds like Coby might really like a little brother or sister," Annette suggested.

"I wouldn't go that far. Switzerland," Coby reminded her.

"Don't push, my dear," Jean-Claude told his daughter. "I think you've won this battle."

"More wine?" Coby asked, holding up her empty glass.

"I'll get it." Annette scooped up Coby's glass and headed into the kitchen.

"You're sure it's over with Joe?" her father asked her again.

"Pretty sure."

Coby heard Annette open the oven door, and the scent of warm bread and cheese and baking mushrooms wafted into the living room. There was a moment or two of awkward silence as they all tried to figure out what the conversation would be next.

Finally, her father asked her, "So, how's work?"

"Fine. How's the hotel doing?"

Jean-Claude answered, "Humming along. I would like to get rid of the tearoom completely and just have a wine bar, but people love it."

Dave said with pride, "Annette practically runs the place, though Juliet and Suzette do a nice job running the tearoom and wine bar."

"I'll have to stop by," Coby said, wondering how long it had been. She had a tendency to avoid situations that put her together with her father and Annette.

"Any interesting cases?" Dave asked, looking toward the kitchen as if he already missed his wife. Coby embarked on a story about an acrimonious divorce—no names given—where the wife had run off with her lover and the husband was asking for full custody of the two elementary-school-age children. Coby's firm was representing the wife, and it was a sticky wicket, no doubt. Even Coby had trouble sympathizing with the woman, whose self-involvement was damn near record-breaking, even among Jacoby, Jacoby, and Rosenthal's wealthy and powerful clients. She finished with, "The children want to stay with their dad. He wants the kids and the wife talks like she does, but I don't think her heart's really in it. He'll get the kids and she'll probably win in the alimony department."

"So the kids are merely a bargaining chip for more money. Too bad," Dave said.

Jean-Claude had wandered back to the den and now he returned to catch the last bit. "I should not speak ill of my ex, but she did the same. Wanted my money more than our girls." He shrugged. "But they got the better parent: me."

Annette brought Coby a new glass of wine, then headed toward the front door as they heard voices outside. But the door opened before she could reach it, letting in a cold rush of wind. A moment later Juliet and Yvette Deneuve and a boy of around twelve came into view: Yvette's son. Benedict. Coby smiled a greeting at the sallow-skinned and dark-eyed youth who looked a lot like his mother.

Yvette took one look at Coby and instantly headed her way. She still wore her hair in a ponytail, but her face had grown thinner over the years. She was also wearing jeans, which made Coby feel instantly better.

"Hey," Yvette greeted her, sizing her up. She was a little taller than Annette, a little more voluptuous, and there was a line drawn between her eyes, as if she spent a lot of time scowling.

"Hi, Yvette." Coby greeted her with another forced smile. They'd never been close friends, and that last year of high school had been difficult. No one knew whether to be happy for Yvette and her pregnancy, and Yvette wasn't one to let anyone be close to her.

"You want to meet my son?" Yvette said now. Then, "Benedict, get over here." Dutifully the boy walked over to stand in front of his mother and stare at Coby with a certain amount of suspicion. His eyes were big and round like Yvette's but more hazel than brown. His skin was lighter and his hair was medium brown. Coby found herself trying to see Lucas Moore in him, but it was impossible to say.

"This is Uncle Dave's daughter Coby. She and I used to be friends . . . sort of," Yvette said.

"Hi," Benedict said, sticking out his hand.

Coby bent down and shook it. "Hi, yourself."

"He's not," Yvette said in an expressionless voice.

"What?" Coby looked at her as she straightened and Benedict walked away to plop himself in front of the television.

"He's not Lucas's."

Yvette was nothing if not direct. "I didn't say he was," Coby pointed out.

"I read your mind." Her smile was cool. "It's what you thought. It's what you all thought senior year. Probably still do."

"Well . . . yeah . . . I suppose you're right." This was the kind of thing Coby wanted to avoid. Exactly this. She'd known it was going to be tough seeing Annette and her father fawn all over each other, but she really hadn't wanted to relive the night Lucas died with her old classmates, and yet, here it was.

Yvette was challenging her, and Coby did not want to be challenged.

With a glance toward Benedict, who was absorbed in a video game on the TV, Coby moved closer to Yvette and said in an undertone, "You told us the day we found Lucas that you and he were an item. That he wasn't into Rhiannon and he never had been. That you and he were together, in love, secret boyfriend and girlfriend. You made a point of it. So, yeah, we got the impression Benedict might be Lucas's, but *you* gave that impression to us. On purpose, I might add. Loudly and insistently."

“Whoa.” Yvette’s brows lifted in surprise. She clearly hadn’t expected Coby to be so forthright.

“Yeah.” Coby left her then, clomping across the wood floor in her cowboy boots back toward the kitchen. She was irked and angry. Yvette was just one of those people who liked to be a pain in the ass, and Coby, with a glance outside at the bad weather, thought she might like to spend the night at the beach after all, maybe book a hotel in Cannon Beach or Tillamook, because as the night wore on she sure as hell felt like getting drunk.

Chapter 4

If there was one thing Danner Lockwood hated above all else, it was small talk.

Small. Talk.

All right. That was a bit of hyperbole. There were far, far worse things in this world he hated more. Things worthy of serious hate. Like intent to cause pain, killing for personal gain, abuse of the weak and dependent. He'd seen more than his share of all of that.

But he did hate small talk. Hated listening to it. Hated acting like he knew how to respond to it. Hated being polite.

What he'd like right now was to be having a beer with his homicide partner, Detective Elaine Metzger, mid-forties or fifties, built like a tank, language as salty as the briny sea. Elaine made all the crap of the job seem insignificant. She had gallows humor that kept the worst parts of being a cop bearable and made the best parts enjoyable. She'd survived two marriages and as many divorces and she was all about work, which was fine by Danner, as he was a lot the same way. But she'd just left on two weeks' vacation and it had left him a bit rootless and dissatisfied. In this funk he'd accepted an invitation with his "date," now seated across from him, and he could already tell it was a huge mistake.

Had he really thought this would work?

He smiled at her. She was a nice woman. Someone he'd gone to school with. He watched her mouth and tried to concentrate on her words. The weather? Politics? God, he hoped not. Whether the latest celebrity marriage would end in divorce before or after they had children?

His ears seemed incapable of listening, yet he listened every day to information that would help him solve serious crimes. Just that morning he'd interviewed a man suspected in multiple gang shootings and had learned some key information that had led to the discovery of a cache of guns and ammunition that could put the bastard away for several lifetimes.

But for now, on this late Saturday afternoon, he was seated at a café table in Cannon Beach under a covered porch, thank God, because the rain was streaking from a black sky, the wind was winding up from a low moan to a building shriek, and the approaching storm had sent all but him and his date scurrying inside.

She suddenly looked at him expectantly and he quickly reran her last words through his mind, praying he would remember the gist of her conversation.

Aware of his distraction, she asked, "What'd I just say?"

"Something about your family?"

"Uh-huh. What was it?"

She always talked about her family. There were issues among them that she considered to be a lot bigger than they were. He could have told her he'd seen a lot of families with a whole hell of a lot worse problems, but she wasn't much of a listener, either, so he let it go. "You wish your mother would stop interfering in your affairs."

"Nice try. I wish she showed some interest in my affairs rather than that rat-faced loser with the houndstooth jackets and musky aftershave she's been dating. God, what a loser."

"I thought you said your mother was through with him, and it was too bad, because he at least seemed to care about her."

"I was wrong. They're still together."

Danner reminded her, "You thought he was the one getting used, not your mom, because she was involved in some secret affair, or something?"

"Okay, okay! You do listen. But I was wrong about that, too." She held up her hands and half smiled. "I said as much to Mom and she got really bitchy about it."

"Imagine that."

"Told me I didn't know my ass from a hole in the ground—the PG version of those words, anyway—and that I should mind my own business. There wasn't some secret affair, apparently. But her relationship with Barry is just *wrong*. They're too kissy-smoochy in front of people and that's always a bad sign. Like they're trying to *prove* how happy they are when it's all a big fat lie."

"His name is Barry?" Danner asked.

"Barry," she agreed as if the word tasted bad. She brooded for a moment, gazing out across the sand and toward the restless waves. The ocean was more a low-grade buzz than a roar; the roar was the driving rain and wind that shot in and slapped them with a gleeful snap of water and cold every few minutes. "I wish—"

But he never got to hear what she wished for because a blast of sideways rain shot in and hit them with a *swoosh*, drenching their table.

"Oh, my God!" she cried, jumping from her seat. Her gray sweater-coat was soaked and her black slacks looked wet, too.

"Let's go." Danner was laughing as he followed her inside the restaurant, his own jeans wet from waist to knee, his black cotton sweater soaked across the waist, his black parka easily weathering the blast. They'd ordered coffee for her and a light beer for him, and now he paid and they hurried to her car, a late-model white BMW convertible, the top securely fastened against the elements. She was driving, so now he sank into the passenger seat again and thought of his older, black Jeep Wrangler with its plastic windows, which weren't working as well as they once had, and was glad to be warm and dry.

He was not, however, glad he'd agreed to this fool's errand. He'd agreed to accompany her because he wanted to see Coby Rendell. He'd agreed because his "date" was Faith Rendell, and this birthday party had given him a golden opportunity to see the one woman who'd gotten away, so to speak.

Opportunity. And motive.

"As if Mom's problems aren't enough," Faith was saying with zero enthusiasm, "now I get to wish my stepmother 'Happy Birthday.' Whoopee. Can't wait."

He knew Coby and Faith's father had married Annette Deneuve. He knew all about everything.

Crossing his arms over his chest, Danner laid the seat back, relaxed into the cushions, and closed his eyes.

"It could be a bumpy ride," Faith warned him.

Yes, he thought, *it definitely could.*

They drove to the party.

The doorbell had been ringing constantly as guests arrived at the party and straggled in from the rain and blasting wind. The decibel level had been rising accordingly and Coby, on her third glass of wine, had a pretty good buzz going. She'd learned to pace herself since those early high school days at the campout; maturity was a great thing all around. And she also made certain tonight to eat the hors d'oeuvres as they were passed around.

She decided she didn't much like Yvette. Even though her sister had married Coby's father, she hadn't had much contact with her over the years, which was just as well. Coby had seen Juliet and Suzette sporadically in the time since—they were second to youngest and youngest, in that order—and she was in close contact with Nicholette, of course, since they worked together. But Yvette had been the one who'd been the most reclusive, maybe because of her teen pregnancy, maybe because she was a single mom, maybe because of all the secrets they'd told together, secrets that made them want to run away from each other, secrets that kept them from bonding. Maybe it was Lucas's death. Or maybe it was something else entirely.

Whatever the case, Coby did not feel warm and fuzzy toward Yvette, and the feeling was clearly mutual.

Yvette's eyes were on her son, who was still immersed in his video game, which was right in the center of the action. The boy wore headphones, so the elevator music Coby's dad had put on was all she could hear, but across the TV screen ran explosion after explosion, mega-gunfire, while soldiers keeled over and bodies turned into melting flesh and bone.

"Good God," Coby murmured aloud.

Yvette glanced over at her. "He's eleven," she said. "It's what they do."

Coby didn't comment. She sensed Yvette was spoiling for a fight and she didn't want to be any part of it. But it was just so like Yvette to be unable to let things go; that hadn't changed since high school. Now she moved Coby's way.

"Everyone talks about the teen years," Yvette said, standing next to Coby, her gaze on the back of Benedict's head. "How awful they are. I just didn't think they'd start so early. It's already a battle just to get him to talk to me, and it drives me crazy. Of course we all know I made my share of mistakes," she added. "I was . . . thirteen when I had that affair, as you well know. Benedict's already eleven."

She'd lowered her voice. Her underage affair still wasn't for public knowledge, apparently, which was just fine with Coby. Despite Annette's earlier rant, Coby did believe some secrets were meant to stay that way.

"I didn't mean to piss you off earlier," Yvette said. "You're right . . . I said all that about Lucas and me being together the morning after he died, and it probably wasn't the moment."

"Why did you say it? It wasn't true."

"Wasn't it? We were all kind of into Lucas, weren't we?" Her dark eyes were knowing and the small smile on her lips spoke volumes.

"Yeah, but that day you said you and Lucas were secretly together. None of the rest of us did. We were all freaked out and upset, and you sure didn't help."

Yvette pressed her lips together, then seemed to almost physically shake off the memories. "I wish a lot of things were different, but wishing doesn't really change things. There's a lot of water under the bridge."

"You say Lucas isn't Benedict's father."

"That's right." She eyed Coby cautiously.

"Does Benedict know who his father is?"

"Is that any of your business?"

"Probably not. But you accused me of thinking it was Lucas, so whatever." Coby shrugged. It was bizarre how fast they got back to that night, that conversation, that moment when everything changed. Maybe this was the reason she hadn't seen much of Yvette. Both of them dreaded facing the other.

"Benedict does not know his father," she said shortly. Then, "Weird, huh? Your dad and my sister. Daddy Dave with an eighteen-year-old . . . that was kind of a surprise, wasn't it? Makes my exploits at thirteen not seem so out of line."

"Are you kidding?" Coby couldn't believe her ears. "At least Annette was of legal age when they met."

"It's all just numbers," Yvette murmured.

"Numbers that matter," Coby stated hotly. "You want Benedict in a sexual relationship in two years' time?"

"Jesus, you do work at a law firm, don't you? Relax. I wasn't trying to dis Daddy Dave for having sex with her. He stepped up and married Annette, didn't he? Way to put his money where his mouth was, so to speak."

"What's wrong with you?" Coby demanded. She knew she was feeling the effects of the wine, but too bad.

"Me? Why don't you ask Annette? She's the one acting all high and mighty and ready to tell everybody's secrets. Just because she's frustrated that she can't get pregnant. It bugs the shit out of her that I had Benedict and she's having trouble conceiving."

Coby was taken aback. "I didn't get that impression. She just said she wanted children, and my dad seems to be thinking it over."

"More like he wants out of the marriage than ever having another kid." Yvette tossed back the rest of her wine. "You haven't had kids yet. You don't know what it's like, but your dad does. I'm not saying he doesn't love you, but it can be like jail. Stuck all the time with this responsibility and no one to share it with."

"That's your experience," Coby reminded cautiously. "Not everybody's."

"Touché," Yvette agreed.

They'd been standing a few steps away from Annette and Juliet, who were just heading into the kitchen. Jean-Claude had seated himself next to Benedict and was trying to engage the boy with little success. Dave was talking with Donald Greer, who looked more conservative and out of touch than he had even when he was the vice principal, and McKenna's dad, Big Bob Forrester, towered over the crowd with a large belly to match. Twelve years earlier both Donald Greer and Bob Forrester had been married, but those marriages had since fallen apart and both men had come to the party stag. In fact, the only dad from the campout who was still with his wife was Ellen's father, Ted. Ted and Jan Marshall lived somewhere in northern California, which was where they'd moved just before Ellen's graduation. Hank Sainer, Dana's father, had been single then and now, and had run for local office a time or two since the beach trip. He'd been the mayor of Laurelton and the representative from the district where he lived. Rumor had it that he wanted to be governor of the state, and there was a groundswell of interested people planning to put him there. Coby didn't know if Hank would actually be at this party; it seemed unlikely, but who knew.

Lawrence Knapp, Genevieve's dad, had died from a heart attack several years back, and Rhiannon's father, Winston Gallworth, had never reconciled with Rhiannon's alcoholic mother; he'd been virtually single throughout the years no matter what his marital status was. Though invited, he hadn't attended the campout twelve years earlier and had seemed to let go of the friendships altogether ever since. Coby was pretty sure no one had seen him since the memorial service for his daughter.

"Lucas feels really close tonight," Yvette said quietly, surprising Coby with her change of mood.

"I think about him whenever I come here," Coby admitted.

"I don't like remembering that night. It was just such a bad scene all around."

Coby watched as she wandered over to her son, chastising him for ignoring his grandfather, then ripping the controller from his fingers and turning off his game. Benedict stomped off down the hall and Yvette looked after him with a long-suffering expression on her face.

She didn't want to, but Coby couldn't help recalling how Yvette had acted the morning Lucas Moore's body was found floating in the surf. She'd come in late; it was almost afternoon by the time Yvette appeared, claiming she'd wandered off and fallen asleep and had lost track of time. Everyone at the house, especially Jean-Claude and her sisters, had been completely nuts with worry over what had happened to her. Lucas was dead and where was Yvette?

They were totally pissed as soon as their relief dissipated.

But Yvette was blithely unconcerned, saying she'd simply taken a long walk and decided she was too tired to go back right away. She'd fallen asleep behind a huge driftwood wind block and lost track of time.

No one believed her. No one. But then she was hit with the news of Lucas's death and her face lost all color and she started screaming, "No, no, no! Not Lucas. No! It can't be!"

She was asked whether she'd seen him, by any chance, but she shook her head violently and then stunned them all by suddenly crying, "Lucas . . . we were in love! He was my secret lover. He can't be dead. He can't be!"

She collapsed onto the sofa and into the arms of her father and started sobbing.

"It's not true," Rhiannon said into the moment, as

white-faced as Yvette. She was like a ghost, floating around, but not really in the room. "It's not true. She's lying."

"It's bullshit," Genevieve agreed, glaring daggers at Yvette.

"It's the truth," Yvette wailed. "I'm sorry . . . Rhiannon. I'm sorry. He was going to tell you. He really was."

The guilt of kissing Lucas enveloped Coby, but not so Genevieve, apparently who was just flat-out mad. "You're a liar!" she accused Yvette, standing with clenched fists, her face a mask of fury.

"No . . ." Rhiannon murmured. "No."

Jean-Claude eyed the advancing Genevieve with caution. "Calm down," he said.

Yvette was crying uncontrollably. "We loved each other! We loved each other!"

And then Rhiannon's eyes rolled back and she fainted. Genevieve was closest to her and managed to catch her before she hit the ground, though they both went down and Rhiannon cracked her forehead on the coffee table and went limp. Jean-Claude and Dave jumped to help and Rhiannon was stretched out on the couch while Genevieve moved away, her expression dark.

Ellen, Dana, and Wynona sat in silent shock, as if their brains had gone on stall, which maybe they had. McKenna regarded Yvette narrowly and later conferred with Genevieve, clearly of the same opinion that Yvette was making the whole thing up.

Coby hadn't believed Yvette, either. If Lucas was really her secret boyfriend, if he *really was* . . . then why had he been kissing the rest of them? It was more likely Yvette was just using his death as a means to deflect the spotlight from herself and the probing questions that had rained down on her about where she'd been all night and morning.

Which was almost worse.

"It's true," Yvette kept insisting, wailing it like a siren. "It's true! We were lovers. It's true. It's all true!"

But no amount of declaring that she and Lucas loved each other could convince the rest of them, and by mutual tacit agreement their group chose to ostracize Yvette all senior year. Yes, they were all at fault for wanting Lucas; some of them more than others for actually acting on their desires. But Yvette had taken it to another level, and it was just *so wrong* to lie about Lucas when he couldn't even defend himself!

And then . . . Yvette turned up pregnant. Everyone wanted to ask her who the father was, but no one had the guts. No one wanted to believe that Yvette might have been actually telling the truth. That she and Lucas were an item after all, that the baby was his, that they had been involved in a full-fledged love affair all the while.

No one wanted to believe it, but it was the underlying, unspoken thought that followed them throughout their final year of high school.

And it was still a question today, though Yvette acted like she'd answered it with a big, fat "no."

Now Coby's gaze turned thoughtfully in the direction Benedict had gone. Yvette wasn't around, having moved to the kitchen, and Coby glanced back that way as the doorbell rang again, this time to admit the delivery people from Nona Sofia's, the Cannon Beach restaurant from which Annette had ordered the Italian-themed meal. Large foil-covered pans of food were carried to the table and Annette bustled around directing the arrival of the different pasta dishes, lovely smelling loaves of bread, plates of bruschetta, and a monster bowl of Caesar salad. While she directed, Annette snapped at both her sisters and Suzette and Juliet stepped up to help, though Yvette was noticeably absent.

Coby arranged a stack of white china plates and silverware at one end of the long table without being asked. She recognized the silverware with its embedded "R" as the fine stuff from when she was growing up. Her mother, Leta, had, in her one irrational moment during the divorce, hauled out the huge wooden box of silverware and thrown it at her husband's feet. She declared she was taking back her maiden name and he could have anything and everything that had an "R" on it. Then she looked up and saw Coby standing in the doorway, scared by the crash she'd heard in the kitchen, and without a word Leta pulled herself together and pretended the scene never happened. The rest of their divorce was totally civilized. If they had deeper feelings, they weren't visible to Faith and Coby, and Leta never actually went through with her threat to go back to her maiden name. She was still Leta Rendell, though she was now dating some guy named Barry whom Coby had yet to meet and Faith couldn't stand.

The doorbell rang again and Coby looked around to see who was answering, but she was the nearest. She walked forward and opened the door and found herself face-to-face with her sister, Faith.

And Faith was with Coby's ex, Danner Lockwood.

Chapter 5

Time literally seemed to stand still for Coby. She'd never really believed it could. Had thought that old saying was a fallacy. But when she saw Danner with her sister, it felt like the world stopped for a moment. She heard a rushing in her ears and everything seemed to recede and freeze.

She stared at Danner for what felt like an eternity but was probably only a second before pulling herself together and dragging her gaze to her sister. Faith was wearing a gray sweater-coat, damp and wet as if it had been doused with water, over black slacks, and her short, light brown hair was sparkling with rain.

"Hey, there," Faith greeted her, moving inside and giving Coby a quick hug. "How'd you get door duty?"

"I—just was here." Coby felt slow and stupid.

"Hi, Coby," Danner said, his familiar face breaking into that slow smile that made her pulse race and her mouth go dry.

She couldn't decide how to react. She was shocked to her core. Of all the scenarios she'd run through for this evening, this hadn't been one of them. She felt disembodied as she took Faith's sweater-coat and Danner's black parka and hung them up in the hall closet. Danner seemed to want to talk to her, but Coby found she just couldn't. She managed a few words of greeting and then escaped to the kitchen.

Her heart was pounding as if she'd run a marathon.

What the hell was Faith doing with Danner?

Juliet looked over at her and asked her, "What's wrong?"

When Coby didn't answer Juliet threw a glance toward the living room, clearly wondering what had taken place. She headed to the other room while her sister Suzette gave her a quizzical look. "You look weird," Suzette said.

Coby wasn't certain whether either Juliet or Suzette knew about her past relationship with Danner. She didn't want to talk about it. She couldn't, even if she had. She not only looked weird, she felt weird.

"Are you serving more hors d'oeuvres?" she asked Suzette, glancing down at the array of food on the counter.

"No, you are," Suzette said, thrusting an antipasto tray into Coby's arms. "I don't know what the hell happened to Annette. She was in charge, but I guess she's enjoying her party."

Coby turned to head toward the dining table but Juliet stood in the doorway, blocking her, her brown eyes knowing. "Danner Lockwood's out there with Faith."

Suzette's head snapped up. "Really? I thought she was dating that other guy that Annette talked about. Go find Annette and ask her."

"Hugh," Coby said without expression.

"Hugh Westfall," Juliet said. "But I don't see him out there. She ditch him for Danner?"

Coby didn't want to go there. She sidestepped Juliet and walked into the dining area, studiously avoiding eye contact with anyone in the room. She sensed that Danner and Faith were standing in front of the windows, gazing out toward the dark ocean, and she couldn't stop herself from sliding them a glance. Annette was with them, making sure they each had a glass of wine, talking with them, smiling, being a great host.

God. Damn. It.

Coby wondered at her sister. Really. Really? She decided to bring Coby's old boyfriend to this party, out of all the people she knew? The only guy Coby had ever really cared about?

Really.

"I need another glass of wine," she told Suzette upon reentering the kitchen.

"Should I make it a double?" Suzette asked, lifting two wine goblets up.

Coby inwardly sighed. Clearly, they all knew about her past relationship with Danner. "Thanks, but I'll just drink really fast and come back for a fill-up."

"If any of my sisters went out with my ex, I'd kill her," Suzette said, pouring Coby another glass.

"The night is young," Coby murmured.

One step inside the house—actually *before* his first step inside—Danner had felt a vise grip around his chest that was more emotional than physical. It was a warning sign. An alarm that let him know the precise moment he was making a big mistake. A kind of all-system alert that beat a rhythm inside his head: *Get out, get out, get out!*

But it was too late. He was here. And Coby was here, though she'd disappeared from sight as quickly as she could. He could scarcely blame her. It had been years since their time together, and he hadn't tried hard enough back then to keep things going. He'd let things come to an end. He'd been completely focused on his career in law enforcement and had let Coby Rendell slip away.

He hadn't really known how much she'd mattered until she was gone.

So he'd come to this party to see her again. He'd allowed Faith to talk him into this trip, though it was definitely out of character. He and Faith weren't even all that great of friends. She was just someone he ran into occasionally because she worked in the same downtown area of Portland and they frequented the same bistros and coffee shops. They were acquaintances, ex-schoolmates, though from different classes, and when they'd run across each other about a year earlier they'd become friends. He hadn't known Faith when he was dating Coby. He knew of her, but she had made a point of not visiting her father and Annette and so there weren't any family events where Danner was part of the scene. And Coby didn't much hang out with her father or mother, either, for that matter, so while he and Coby were together Danner's relationship with the Rendells was fairly peripheral.

Meeting Faith, knowing who she was . . . it probably played a big part in why he'd let himself get to know her. Their occasional meeting could be construed as dates, he supposed, but for Danner, really, they were just a means to an end. A way for him to feel connected to Coby even though Faith rarely actually brought up her name.

So when Faith had asked him to join her for her stepmother's thirtieth birthday, her stepmother being one of the Ette sisters and an ex–best friend, he'd thought it over briefly and given her a resounding yes. Faith seemed to believe he was being a good guy, accepting her invitation as a means to help ease the tension that would undoubtedly arise from the situation. Well, yeah, there was a little of that. If he wanted to be kind to himself. But truthfully, his motivation was a lot more selfish. The birthday party was a means to see Coby again. Plain and simple.

And any bullshit he might try to lay on himself wasn't going to work. He knew why he was there. He wanted to see Coby again. He wanted to talk to her. Be with her. See if the old spark was still there.

He could remember the first time she swept across his radar.

He was newly graduated from Portland State in business but considering going into law enforcement. He'd been at the university to pick up some information and she'd walked into the administration building. He'd recognized her a little. Or maybe she just touched a chord somehow, but in any case, she sure as hell knew who he was.

"Hi," she said, intriguing him with the quick, quirky smile that was her trademark. It disarmed. It covered up the fact that she had a piercingly keen intellect. It drew his gaze like a magnet to pink lips a shade too wide that hinted at sensuality.

"I know your brother, Jarrod," she said, sticking out a hand of introduction. "We were classmates."

"I'm Danner," he said, shaking her proffered hand.

"I know. I've seen you around. Upperclassmen and all that. You know them, but they don't know you." She pulled her hand back and glanced at his brochures. "Law enforcement?"

"Thinking about it. Are you enrolled here?"

"Business," she said with a nod.

And that was the beginning of a friendship that spiraled quickly into something more and burned hot and fast and might have turned into something else if he hadn't then joined the Portland Police Department and immersed himself in another world, both business-wise and socially, that left him no time for an interest in anything else. Did he regret letting Coby go? Yep. Did he wonder why he did it? All the time. Did he have an answer? Only a half-assed excuse that was wrapped up in his own parents' misguided union because they'd married too young and then proceeded to make each other's lives, and the lives of their two children, Danner and Jarrod, a living hell.

Or maybe he'd been too young to get serious. Or maybe he'd just not realized what he had. Or maybe he'd just screwed up royally.

To be fair to himself, there had been the Jarrod issue. Though his brother was already with Genevieve by the time Danner hooked up with Coby, there was clearly something that bothered Jarrod about Coby Rendell being Danner's girl. Jarrod had a thing for her that had never been requited, and although Danner shouldn't have cared and didn't, really, it had definitely colored his relationship with his brother. Jarrod was cool and remote when he learned of the relationship and, like the Rendell family, he kept his distance from Coby and Danner.

So Danner let Coby go.

Years passed and, as his star rose career-wise, his romantic encounters took a nosedive, sliding along a downward trajectory that worsened with each passing year. He couldn't maintain a relationship. There was no passion. He seemed to lack the ability to care. If a woman did manage to pique his interest within fifteen minutes, that interest started to wane, and if they managed to get past that decline and actually made it to the bedroom, sex sent him into a full crash and burn. Nothing was satisfactory and he found himself racing to get away as quickly as possible, using any excuse he could think of. He wasn't proud of it, but he didn't know what to do to make things better. He lacked the skills, maybe; the initiative, certainly.

And then he ran into Faith.

She knew enough about his relationship with Coby to recognize Coby and Danner had shared something special, at least for a time. Faith was looking for a friend, not a lover, which suited Danner perfectly. She was still dating Hugh Westfall when they first started meeting, but the relationship was in free fall. After they broke up, Faith used Danner for a sympathetic ear. Hugh wasn't anyone Danner knew, so Faith could malign him up one side and down the other and Danner just let her. Over coffee, or beer, or wine he heard about Hugh Westfall's faults, ad nauseam. Faith's blather was almost soothing to Danner; it allowed him to switch his brain off and just let it wash over him in a wave while he watched her and thought of Coby.

Faith wanted to hear about Danner's forays into the dating scene, but he didn't have a lot of fodder for her. Any hookups he had were short and infrequent. He was all about work, morning, noon, and night. Boring? Yup. But there it was.

When she'd invited him to her stepmother's birthday party, he'd seen the opportunity for what it was, though he'd initially tried to lie to himself.

"I can't go alone to this party," Faith had told him. "It's hard enough dealing with my mom, and I can't have my father grilling me about my love life, which is what he'll do. I don't want to talk about Hugh, but since he got with Annette it seems to be his only focus of conversation with me. Like he's goddamn Cupid. Coby's with Joe, so she's safe, but I had to admit to him that Hugh and I aren't together anymore and it's become this huge problem!"

Joe? Danner had thought with a tightening of his gut. He would have dearly loved to stop Faith right there, but he hadn't been able to.

She swept on, "God, it's annoying. Dad married someone half his age, so he has no credibility at all in talking to me about relationships! I just don't want to deal with it. And then there's Mom. I swear she's just acting out with Barry. She never really wanted the divorce and it's been hell for her. Pure hell. And Dad . . . all these years with . . .

with . . . my best friend. Ex-friend," she amended. "Can you stand it? I can't talk to Annette anymore. I can't even look at her."

He'd nodded. He couldn't get past that Coby was with someone named Joe, but his nod was enough to keep Faith going and eventually, both because he wanted her to shut up and because he wanted to see Coby, he said yes to her invitation.

So here he was.

And Coby was hiding out in the kitchen. From him, probably. He'd seen the look of shock on her face and the way she'd managed to be polite and welcoming to him and Faith, fairly adroitly, he had to admit, before hightailing it out of the room to safety.

To hell with that. If she stayed in the kitchen much longer, he was just going to have to go find her.

"Oh, go out and talk to him," Suzette said. She took Coby's empty glass and exchanged it for a full one.

Coby looked down at her drink. "At this rate I'll be drunk by eight and won't have to."

"Don't you want to?" Suzette asked.

"Hell, no."

"You're not with Joe anymore, are you?"

"Nope."

"I didn't see him here, so I figured."

Juliet cruised back into the room and gazed at them both. "I don't know what Annette expects us to do," she complained. "Why didn't she hire Nona Sofia's to do the serving, too? It's not our job to keep the hors d'oeuvres and drinks coming."

Suzette just shrugged and Juliet seemed to want to say more, but then shook her head and returned to the living room and the party.

Coby pulled her thoughts from Danner with an effort, and that somehow reminded her of Lucas again. Lucas and Rhiannon. And Yvette? How did that fit in?

She stared out the window at the steam rising from the hot tub. Her feelings for Danner were unresolved, and having him here made her feel anxious. Setting her glass down, she pressed her palms to her cheeks and shook off her feelings with an effort.

"You okay?" Suzette asked, holding a tray.

"Peachy."

Suzette left with a shrug, and for a moment Coby was alone in the kitchen. Lucas and Rhiannon. Had they been in love? Had they felt any part of what she'd felt with Danner? Or was it all blue smoke and mirrors?

Rhiannon had hated Yvette with a passion, and from the time of the campout she made no secret about how she felt about Yvette and her pregnancy. That whole senior year Rhiannon's eyes shot daggers at Yvette whenever they passed in the hall. Yet, in a strange way, Yvette's pregnancy sheltered her from some of the worst of Rhiannon's wrath, so it was after Yvette gave birth to Benedict, just before graduation, that Rhiannon actually attacked Yvette outside the gym. Yvette was talking to Kirk Grassi. Maybe she was even flirting a little; Coby wasn't sure. But suddenly there was screaming and hair-pulling and name-calling and it took Vice Principal Donald Greer to separate them, for which he earned a clawing fingernail across his cheek that filled up with blood.

The incident was handled internally by the school and Rhiannon and Yvette received separate counseling and agreed to keep their distance from each other. A few weeks later they all graduated, went their separate ways, and that's the way it basically stayed until Rhiannon died.

Coby heard she'd fallen to her death the Christmas before college graduation. Rhiannon was home for the holidays and had gone hiking with some friends, but she'd taken off ahead of them and slipped off a treacherous ridge. Everyone was shocked and it put a pall over their holiday plans. The memorial service was two days before New Year's. Coby went alone but saw her high school classmates and most of the girls who'd been to the camp-out, though Yvette was a no-show. Her absence caused its own round of speculation. Coby suspected Yvette just hadn't wanted to revisit her own bad behavior. Who would? She was a single mother now, making her way in the world, and probably figured that was hard enough. The rest of the girls didn't want to talk to her anyway. Genevieve sniffed something about Yvette being a piece of work, and everyone else just kept her own counsel.

Coby let her thoughts turn to the other girls who'd been at the campfire and how they'd fared since revealing their deepest, darkest secrets. Dana had apparently gotten her eating disorder under control; at least that's what her last Christmas card suggested as she looked healthy, happy, and pregnant beside her husband and kids. Ellen had taken up with Theo for a while after the beach trip, through most of senior year actually. They broke up just before prom and Theo had ended up going to the dance with the girl from Gresham whose reputation had been so maligned by Vic Franzen and Kirk Grassi. The rumors about that girl's pregnancy had turned out to be just rumors, apparently, because there was no more mention of it, and in the meantime Ellen and her family moved to California. If Annette was correct, Wynona was still dealing with some serious issues that very possibly hearkened back to the sexual abuse by her swim coach. McKenna was still single and performed her comedy all over the Northwest, and Genevieve's dad died and she married Jarrod.

That brought Coby's thoughts back to Danner with a bang. And in that moment the doorbell rang again, and a moment later Coby heard Genevieve's flinty voice and Jarrod's deeper tones.

She picked up her glass of wine again and braved walking into the dining room where Yvette was standing at the end of the table. Coby stopped short and watched as Genevieve and Annette both squealed like teenagers upon seeing each other. They'd become good friends over the years, which was weird, given how Gen had felt about Yvette and probably still did. *But maybe she'd gotten past all that?* Coby thought, sliding Yvette a sideways look. In some ways, Gen and Annette were very much alike: outspoken, leaders, bullheaded, overly confident. Maybe that transcended disliking—hating—your friend's sister.

Coby sensed, rather than saw, Danner and Faith approaching the newcomers, as she wouldn't move her head to see them. But then Danner was shaking his brother's hand and Faith was forced to greet Genevieve warmly, though she couldn't seem to bring herself to thaw for Annette, as she wouldn't deign to even look at her.

Jarrod Lockwood had cut his hair in the intervening years. No more was it overly long, rock-star long. Now it was short, damn near a buzz cut, and as he said hello to his brother and Faith, his eyes searched the room, finally colliding with Coby.

Jarrod Lockwood. Danner Lockwood's younger brother. Genevieve Knapp Lockwood's husband.

Coby swallowed a gulp of wine as Jarrod and Genevieve headed into the room, big smiles of greeting on both of their faces.

"God," Yvette murmured. "The 'It' couple."

That was the first thing Coby could agree with her on though she'd be damned if she'd say so. Jarrod and Gen didn't seem real. Too bright and cheery for words. They *were* the everlasting "It" couple. Genevieve's blond hair was blunt cut at her chin and her body looked hard and lean, as if she worked out every spare moment. She'd thrust a large box into Annette's hands when she'd entered, which made Coby feel guilty for not bringing a gift. She hadn't even thought of it, which said something about their relationship.

"It's enough to make me lose my lunch," Yvette said. She wasn't drinking, had declined every round of drinks that passed by, though now she glanced at Coby's glass as if rethinking that decision.

As Gen and Jarrod bore down on them, Yvette asked, "You think your dad cheats on Annette like he cheated on your mother?"

"I never said he cheated on my mother," Coby said, surprised. Her lie had come back to haunt her all these years later!

"That's what it sounded like to me."

"I was just trying to come up with some big secret because I didn't have one. It wasn't even true."

"Yeah?" Yvette shrugged, skeptical and uncaring.

"Yeah," Coby said, her jaw tight.

"You think it was Vic Franzen who left those notes in our lockers. The prick," Yvette said. "He's not coming tonight, is he?"

"You'd have to ask your sister."

Gen got sidelined by Big Bob, who started bragging about how well McKenna was doing on the comedy circuit. Coby would have liked to hear more about McKenna, but Jarrod had reached her and Yvette by that time. Behind him, Faith had put her hand on Danner's arm and moved him toward the far end of the living room, where they were in a conversation with Jean-Claude.

"Hey, Yvette." Jarrod greeted her but his eyes were on Coby. "Hi, Coby."

"Hi." She smiled.

He might have traded his long hair for a trim above his

ears, but he still had a lazy way of talking that reminded Coby of his older brother.

Yvette gave him the once-over. "You married Genevieve Knapp."

"Yeah, I did."

"Why?"

Jarrod chose to be amused rather than annoyed. "She held a gun to my head and said she'd take out all my friends and family unless I walked her down the aisle."

"Funny." Yvette drifted away, looking bugged.

Jarrod looked at Coby and saw the smile she couldn't contain. "Has she always been such a bitch?" he asked.

"Yes." Coby couldn't contain a small laugh. "How are you, Jarrod?"

"Can't complain." His brown hair and eyes were as she remembered. It was unfair, but Danner's blue ones slid across the screen of her mind. "Economy's shit, but I still have a day job," he went on. "Play guitar at a few places. You should come by sometime."

"I will," she promised automatically. Just like she'd promised to stop by her father's hotel.

"Will you?"

"Yes." She was emphatic.

"Okay. We're at the Cellar in Laurelton for the rest of the month. Friday and Saturday nights." He gave her a sideways look. "Danner was by last weekend."

"Oh?"

"Is he really here with your sister?"

"Looks like it," Coby said.

"Have you talked to him tonight?"

"Nope."

"You still got a thing for him?"

"Good God, no," she assured him quickly. "I just got out of a relationship and I'm not even thinking about that part of my personal life."

He looked at her in a way that called her a liar, but what he said was, "Didn't I see an hors d'oeuvre tray going by? There! Suzette's got a plate of bruschetta."

He tucked his hand around Coby's elbow and started guiding her toward Suzette, who was moving between people and growing closer to Danner and Faith. Coby's footsteps dragged. "I think I'll stay by the table. They're going to be bringing out the lasagna soon."

"I won't make you talk to Danner."

It was Juliet he snagged first, and she gave him a melting look as she held out a tray of stuffed mushrooms. Jarrod grabbed several and handed one to Coby.

"I'll talk to him," Coby assured him. "That's not a problem. He and I are long over," she said. "And it wasn't much to begin with." Coby tossed the mushroom cap in her mouth. It turned out to be burning hot and she started choking.

"Really? Well, here he comes," Jarrod said. "You can tell him that yourself."

She glanced up through tearing eyes to see him bearing down on her, sans Faith.

Chapter 6

Danner reached Coby as she was fighting something caught in her throat. She held a hand up, half laughing, and he asked, "Water?"

"No, I'm okay," she choked out. "Really."

"I think Juliet's trying to kill us," Jarrod said and Juliet, who overheard, swung around.

"I can't help it if they're hot!" she declared.

"I was just giving you shit," he said. "Chill. Kirk'll be here soon."

Juliet moved off, clearly still angry, but Coby's concentration was focused solely on Danner.

He looked . . . good. She liked the black sweater and the casual way he pushed the sleeves up his forearms. She liked the way he smelled, lightly citrus from his aftershave, she remembered. She liked the way his hair curled behind his ear; he was wearing it a bit longer now. He was with the Portland police, and she'd heard along the way that he'd had a meteoric rise within the department. She didn't doubt it. He was just someone who was capable and quietly determined and aware.

She'd loved him. That she knew.

Jarrod said, "When was the last time you two saw each other?"

"About twenty minutes ago," Danner drawled. "When I got here Coby was already here. We said hi."

"I'm guessing it's been a few years," Jarrod said, ignoring him.

"A few," Coby agreed. She'd stopped fighting a cough, *thank you, God.*

Faith was suddenly there, at Danner's side. It rattled Coby though Faith didn't seem fazed in the least. "Got a minute?" she asked Coby. "I'd like to talk to you about something."

And she led Coby away.

Danner watched them head toward a corner by the windows. He stayed back, biding his time. He wanted to be with Coby, but steps had to be taken to ease the path and if Faith wanted to buttonhole her sister for a tête-à-tête, so be it.

With a strange feeling of déjà vu, he remembered this was the house where they were all staying when Lucas Moore fell to his death. Danner had been out of high school by the time the accident occurred, but Jarrod had been at the scene and therefore interviewed by the sheriff's department. Danner recalled his own interest in the case and idly wondered now, as he had then, whether Moore's death was really an accident.

Faith said to Coby, "I wanted to talk to you about Annette. Have you heard about this whole baby thing?"

"Well, yeah."

It was hard for Coby to get Danner out of her head completely. Her attention was shot and she was having trouble keeping track of any conversation. She knew it would be rude to go off by herself, maybe somewhere to the back of the house—the den, her refuge—but she really didn't want to talk to Faith. Or anybody.

But then, dinner was about to be served, so she was kind of stuck.

"What do you think about it?" Faith demanded. "Doesn't it make you just want to scream?"

"I guess."

"You guess? Jesus, Coby. Are you listening to me?" Faith snapped her fingers in front of Coby's face.

"Don't do that," Coby said swiftly. When Faith got on her older-sister high horse it really pissed her off.

"Annette can't have a baby. I can't have a half sibling *thirty years younger than I am*!"

"At the risk of sounding like Dad, it isn't about you."

"Yeah, it is. And it's about you, too. Come on, be on my side for one goddamned time," Faith demanded. "We've got to talk some sense into him. Maybe we can get him away for a few minutes. It's about the only reason I came tonight."

"You brought Danner," Coby said.

"I needed a date. Hugh broke up with me, you know. I wasn't going to come alone."

Like I did, Coby thought, but she didn't say it. And anyway, she heard something in Faith's tone that caught her attention. "You're missing Hugh."

"Of course I am. I thought I was going to marry the asshole!" Faith looked at Coby as if she were totally dense. "Oh, you think I brought Danner like a date? Well, of course you would," she said a moment later, as if talking to herself. "It's not like that. Danner doesn't even hardly date women, from what I can tell. We're friends. He lets me bitch about Hugh and that's it. I'm surprised he accepted my invitation, unless he did it to see you. Maybe you guys can hook up again, at least for some fun, unless you and Joe worked things out?" she asked hopefully.

"No."

She sighed heavily. "I wish one of us was having something work out in the love department. Hugh is such a . . . bastard."

Coby was definitely starting to feel a little more lighthearted. "Why did you two break up?"

"He's a commitment-phobe. I want to make plans. Get married. You know, normal stuff? He just freaks out anytime we talk about it, and now it's over."

Coby nodded sympathetically, but she was selfishly jubilant inside. Faith didn't have any designs on Danner and she doubted he had any on her, either. She looked around the room, seeing Danner talking with Jarrod and Genevieve. She also saw that Annette had put Juliet on table duty and she was currently placing another tray of bruschetta next to a huge Caesar salad in a big silver bowl. The tomato-and-basil-topped crispy baguette slices were disappearing fast, and Coby wondered if Jarrod was going to get his portion before they were gone. Juliet didn't look too happy about helping her sister; her pretty face was set in a scowl.

Faith absently picked up a piece of bruschetta and held it. "But it's the baby thing, Coby. Dad doesn't want it. You can just tell. But Annette just keeps pushing. She'll get herself pregnant whether he agrees to it or not."

"She told me she wants to start trying."

Faith gazed at her in horror. "See?"

"I'm not crazy about the idea, but it's not our call."

"What about Mom?" Faith asked. "Think about her."

"It's not up to Mom, either. Duh," Coby said to her.

"It'll make her crazy. She'll do something crazy. Mark my words. She's not over Dad. Certainly not with Barry." As if recognizing she'd taken the bruschetta, Faith finally bit into it, holding her left hand under her chin to catch any bits of tomato and onion that might drop off. "God, this is good."

Jarrod separated from Danner and Genevieve at that moment and rejoined Coby and Faith, who asked him about his band. He told her about the Cellar and invited her to come by, too. He went on to say that his day job, where he actually made his living, was being in charge of inventory at a regional retail store. Faith seemed interested but Coby's attention drifted. She saw that Danner was now caught in a conversation with Big Bob Forrester, and Genevieve was untangling herself from them both and heading Coby's way as well.

"It's not that much of an intellectual challenge but it lets me stay with the band," Jarrod was saying as Gen sidled up next to him, tucking her arm through his, giving Coby a long look.

"Jarrod was just talking about his job," Coby felt required to say.

"Yeah, well, I work for a title company and in this economy I'm lucky to still have a job," Faith said.

Genevieve looked past them, as if she were waiting for someone better to come through the door. "I used to work for a downtown developer who built office buildings."

"Where do you work now?" Faith asked.

"I don't."

Jarrod said, "Gen's looking for a job," to which Gen's lips pinched together as if she'd bitten into something sour.

Genevieve's father, Lawrence Knapp, had been into commercial real estate before his death, and Coby wondered if he was the "downtown developer" she referred to.

"You have anything to do with Lovejoy's?" Jarrod asked Coby curiously, bringing her back to the moment.

"I'm at Jacoby, Jacoby, and Rosenthal. But Annette works at the hotel, and I think both Juliet and Suzette?"

"Lawrence had some property in the Alphabet District," he said, mentioning his deceased father-in-law. The Alphabet District was another name for the area where Coby's father's and Jean-Claude's hotel was located. "He wanted to develop some apartments into a hotel like Lovejoy's but he was all wrapped up in red tape and then the real estate market just went to shit. He managed to sell the property but he took a loss. Maybe that's what brought on the heart attack."

"No," Gen said coldly. "It was chronic heart disease."

"And investments that went bad," Jarrod kept on.

Coby said quickly, "It's kind of the story for practically everyone who's invested in real estate and needs to sell right away, isn't it?"

"You have some property?" Jarrod asked.

"No, that would be Annette who's inheriting," Faith put in, sweeping an arm to encompass the beach house. "I think the bitch'll get it all."

Coby nearly choked on her drink and Gen sucked in a surprised breath.

"Annette and your father love each other!" Genevieve declared furiously.

"Yeah, well, she was my friend before she was yours," Faith pointed out. "I can call her a bitch if I want to." She turned on her heel and left them, zigzagging through the crowd toward Danner.

Coby wondered if she should ease away from Gen and Jarrod so she could talk to Danner now that she and Faith were done.

"I know she's your sister," Genevieve said, "but she's pretty awful."

"She says what she thinks," Coby answered. "Sometimes it comes out as inappropriate oversharing."

"Glad I don't have a sister," she said heatedly.

"Just a stepsister," Coby responded.

She didn't know why she said it. Another memory from the campout that wouldn't go away.

But Genevieve looked at her blankly. "What do you mean? My parents were still together when my dad died."

"She doesn't have a stepsister," Jarrod added, frowning at Coby as if she'd let him down somehow.

"You said you had a stepsister at the campout," Coby reminded her. "And you stole her boyfriend from her. That's what you said."

Genevieve made a strangled sound that turned into a laugh. "Sorry. Right. That was a lie."

Jarrod said quietly, "Oh, yeah. I forgot that."

"It doesn't matter," Coby said, seeking to change the subject. "Mine was a lie, too."

"I know." Gen looked over at Annette. "The only weird thing Daddy Dave ever did was marry your sister's best friend."

"Where are you living now?" Jarrod asked her, clearly ready to change the subject.

"I rent a condo in Northwest. Not far from Lovejoy's, actually," Coby told him.

"We're living with Gen's mom, Kathy, right now. Took a bath on a house we bought. Couldn't keep that mortgage up, so we had to let it go. Sometimes you just gotta say 'what the fuck,' you know?"

Coby nodded. Danner looked her way and their gazes caught. He inclined his head toward the back of the house and she nodded.

"Where are you staying tonight? Here?" Jarrod asked.

"I'm hoping to go back," Coby admitted.

Gen snorted. "In this weather? Forget it."

"I know." Coby glanced down at her empty glass. The Sand Dune Inn, known as the Dunes, was the closest motel. She'd probably crash there.

"We're at the Dunes," Jarrod said, as if reading her

mind a second time. He glanced over at Genevieve. "Kind of a delayed anniversary trip. We've been married five years already, can you believe it?"

"It happens to the best of us."

"Or the worst of us," Gen murmured.

"You said you just got out of a relationship?" Jarrod made it sound like a question and that's how Coby took it.

"It was a long, slow decline," she admitted.

"How long?"

"A few weeks."

"Wow, that is recent. Who did the breaking up? You?" Jarrod asked.

"It was a mutual decision," she said.

"So he dumped you." Genevieve was knowing.

Coby broke into laughter. "Why does everybody say that?"

"Because that mutual decision stuff is bullshit," Gen declared.

"Sometimes," she agreed.

"Always," she countered.

"I guess I was the one who ended it, then. Not that he's heartbroken," she added lightly.

Jarrod's gaze was frankly appreciative. "I don't know. He might be more heartbroken than you think. I would be."

Genevieve scoured him with a look, but the doorbell rang again and Coby chose the distraction as a means to escape. She hurried to the door, but Annette beat her to it and opened it to Hank Sainer, Dana's father. Dana might be living on the East Coast and unable, and maybe unwilling, to come, but Hank was still one of The Dads. He had a genial smile and though his hair had grayed it was thick and full, and he looked like he worked out. He was tan, too, so he'd either been on a trip or hitting the tanning salons, as the Oregon weather had been dark and gloomy for longer than Coby wanted to remember.

He looked just like a politician.

Dave stepped forward and shook his hand, clapping him heartily on the back, and Big Bob and Jean-Claude stepped up, too. As they were greeting each other, the doorbell chimed again and this time Coby answered it. Kirk Grassi and Galen Torres stood in the rain beyond.

"Hey, Coby," Kirk said.

"Hey, Kirk. Galen . . ."

The two men entered together. Kirk had shaved his head bald and looked harder than he'd been in high school, but he still carried his guitar everywhere. Galen appeared much the same, compact, dark-complected, with a rare smile that was blinding when it appeared, as it did when he spied Suzette. Annette had said they'd been dating a year, and from the way Galen reacted, he seemed to want things to keep on going down that path.

Juliet practically threw down the empty tray she'd been carrying to the kitchen upon seeing Kirk. She gave him a big hug that he seemed to just tolerate, but she was into it. Her eyes scoured the room while she hugged him, scoping out who was watching. Another "It" couple in the making?

Right behind Kirk and Galen was Donald Greer. Ex–vice principal Greer. His hair was thinner and the lines across his forehead, tiny impressions twelve years earlier, were now deeply etched lines. His eyes, behind steel-rimmed glasses, seemed to search the room for errant students even yet, and his lips were a straight line without a hint of curvature. Coby realized Annette wasn't the only one who would have trouble calling him Donald.

Genevieve had moved to greet them and asked Donald, "Is Wynona coming?"

"No," was his short answer, which stopped even bold Genevieve from venturing further.

Coby engaged in small talk with Hank Sainer for a moment. She asked him what his political aspirations currently were and he responded, "You mean after I become governor?" with a wolfish smile.

"Really? That's where you're heading?" Coby asked.

He shrugged, but she suspected it was false modesty. Still, he was charming, in his way, and good-looking—his smile engaging and ever present—and she figured no matter what his qualifications, he would make it pretty far just looking like he did.

"How's Dana?" she asked.

"Married. Happy. Making babies." Something crossed his face and when he saw Coby watching, he added with a self-deprecating shrug, "I have trouble thinking of myself as a grandfather sometimes."

Jean-Claude heard that last bit and said, "You'll get used to it. I've been one for eleven years now. Eleven years!" He grinned and looked around for Benedict, who was at the table carefully tasting some antipasto. The look of horror that chased across his face as he sampled marinated olives made Jean-Claude belly laugh and Hank Sainer smile.

The decibel level was definitely increasing, and Suzette came by with another tray filled with shivering glasses of red wine. As Coby exchanged her empty for a full glass of red, Suzette asked, "Did you know I'm engaged?"

"No. Wow. Congratulations!"

"I wanted to tell you earlier, but Galen wanted to keep it secret a little while longer. But now that he's here, I just thought, oh, hell. What am I waiting for?"

"I'm happy for you," Coby said.

Suzette grew surprisingly sober as she shifted the tray in her hands. "We've talked a little bit about Lucas Moore. Galen told me all about raiding your campout that night, and about Pass the Candle."

"Did he?" Coby's gaze touched on Galen, who was with Kirk and Jarrod, and they were joking around and playing air guitars.

"Yeah, and the notes Vic wrote. He still sees Vic, you know, but Vic's changed a lot. Really."

The notes. Clearly Galen felt Vic was the perpetrator, but Coby, who'd purposely shoved that memory to a distant corner of her mind because it was stupid, distasteful high school stuff, wasn't convinced it was Vic's doing. It just wasn't quite his style. She remembered him as being up front; loud and obnoxious, sure, but when the notes arrived just before high school graduation, slipping into each of the girls' lockers who'd been at the campout, with their "I know who you are and I saw what you did" kind of message, it was the work of someone sneaky and mean-spirited. Coby remembered hers as reading, "Daddy Dave has a wandering cock." She'd been disgusted and mad, but when she'd heard the gist of what some of the other girls' notes had said, she'd swallowed back her anger because her message was one of the least offensive.

Still, they'd stirred up quite a controversy. Genevieve had waved her note for all to see, incensed, offended and ready to fight. "Who did this? One of you assholes!" she yelled at the boys. "And get it right, okay? This isn't even right!"

"What did it say?" Coby asked her later, to which Gen snapped, "He got me confused with Yvette. Thought I was in love with Lucas. Stupid." She glared at Vic Franzen.

"You sure it was Vic?" Coby asked.

"Juliet saw someone slipping a note inside Yvette's locker. She's sure it was Vic."

An accusation Vic Franzen fervently denied, apparently to this day.

Some of the other girls wouldn't even admit they'd received one. Ellen had assured them that she hadn't gotten one, but then she hadn't walked at graduation, either. She left school early, so it was hard to know what the truth was.

"When's the big date?" Coby asked Suzette.

"Haven't really decided yet. Well, actually," she whispered, leaning forward, "we have, but we don't want to step on Annette's birthday celebration." She glanced Galen's way and he caught her eye and smiled. "Maybe we can announce it after she blows out the candles on her cake or something."

Coby couldn't help a stab of envy for their happiness. She remembered Galen as being one of the quietest guys, the most serious. Both he and Paul Lessington had been lieutenants to Kirk Grassi, Jarrod, and Vic Franzen, whereas Theo Rivers had kind of moved in and out of their group, a football player more than a musician. Lucas Moore had also done his own thing.

"If I were you, I wouldn't let Danner Lockwood get away a second time," Suzette pronounced before walking away.

Juliet, who was standing near Coby, her gaze on Kirk, now glanced Coby's way. "But he came here with your sister. . . ."

Chapter 7

Coby watched Danner head down the hallway toward the bedrooms and the den. She said something to Juliet, but her thoughts were chaotic and a moment later she followed after Danner. The den door was ajar as she neared. Pushing it open with her finger, she found him standing in front of the picture of Annette that covered a good portion of the south wall, flanked by oil lamp sconces. Annette was wearing a dark blue dress, the skirt artfully spread around her as she sat on a dark brown velveteen-covered settee, her arms folded over a curved wooden scrolled edge, her beautiful, if slightly frozen, face gazing out at them, smiling faintly.

"It wasn't always this picture," Coby said. "Dad had an old sailing ship on that wall for years."

"I wonder whose idea it was to change it," Danner said.

"Annette's," Coby said with conviction. "And Dad's."

"Faith has a real problem with their marriage." His blue eyes searched her face and Coby fought the sudden speeding up of her pulse.

"It's just always been weird. You know that."

"Yeah."

"Why did you come here with Faith?" Coby heard herself

asking, both appalled and thrilled at her own reckless courage.

"To see you," he said.

"You couldn't just call?" she asked a bit breathlessly.

"Not really."

He smiled and she smiled back. Good . . . God. It took so little to make her feel this way.

And then the lights flickered.

"We'd better eat soon or the power's going to go out and we'll all be stumbling around looking for candles and flashlights," she said.

"I'd say we've only got a matter of minutes before we're rounded up."

"I'd say you're right."

"Can we talk later?" he asked. "After all this is over?"

"Sure."

"Tomorrow? When we're both back in Portland?"

"I'd . . . like that," Coby admitted.

"Danner?"

They both turned toward the voice that sounded from outside the den. Faith's voice. She might not be romantically involved with him, but she was his date for the evening and Coby couldn't help but feel slightly guilty.

For an answer he headed toward Faith's call, brushing by Coby on the way out, squeezing her hand briefly before going to find her sister.

As soon as he was gone Coby collapsed onto the navy blue love seat, which still had the same corduroy cover from twelve years earlier; that hadn't changed. She'd sneaked into this room as soon as she could get away from the campfire, her head swimming from vodka and shocking secrets, and laid her sleeping bag on the love seat and crawled inside, shivering.

Like she was shivering now.

With a feeling of annoyance she rubbed her arms hard,

lost in pleasant thoughts of seeing Danner the next day. *Danner.* Without Faith or Jarrod or anyone else around.

It was amazing.

Feeling absurdly happy, she glanced around the den, noting how little it had changed since that night she'd sneaked away from the campfire to its safe warmth. The giddy smile that had been on her lips since meeting with Danner slowly fell away as her thoughts, as ever, returned to that haunting night.

She hadn't been able to sleep. The couch was too small and she was suffering the effects of too much alcohol. Her mind ran in circles, constantly running over the same unsettling snapshots of the whole evening, returning again and again to review them once more. She'd had enough to drink to only recall snippets of the evening, but she definitely remembered kissing Lucas. But Lucas had also made out with Genevieve; she'd seen that, too. And then he was really supposed to be Rhiannon's boyfriend and it was wrong to cheat on a friend. But was Rhiannon even a friend? And there was cold sand beneath her feet as she ran to the water's edge and threw up. And then Lucas was there . . . no, that was before . . . and someone—Jarrod?—came and broke them up. It was all swirled together, and as soon as she ran it through her mind, she ran it through again. A never-ending, low-grade bad feeling. An anxiety hangover that vied with the real one.

Just before she fell asleep that night, she came back to being with Jarrod. He'd definitely been the one who'd interrupted her and Lucas. Definitely, maybe. But she recalled him asking her if she was all right. "Fine," she'd assured him, swaying a bit on her feet, and there was a dark stain on her pant leg, just below her knee, and a jagged hole in her jeans. She then sensed something trickling down her calf. Blood? Vaguely she remembered slamming her leg into something on the beach, and that reminded her that she'd seen Ellen and Theo humping away behind the huge driftwood log.

And then her mind traveled back to Lucas and circled around again until it returned to her bloody leg. Vaguely she remembered Jarrod sitting her down onto the cold sand once again, pulling up her capris to reveal a gash just below her knee. It was black and ugly in the dim light, but Coby swept Jarrod away from her. She ignored the cut that night, instead going back to the campsite, grabbing her sleeping bag and hauling it back to the house and the den, crashing onto the love seat, and that's when her mind began its incessant circling. Close to dawn she stumbled to the bathroom, puked her guts out again, then returned to the sleeping bag and fell into an exhausted slumber that lasted well into the next day.

It wasn't till after she was back home in Portland that she'd treated the injury to her leg, which had left a small scar just below her kneecap, for when she got up that morning she learned that Lucas Moore was dead, and that stopped everything else.

In this very den, that day, she'd awakened to the sound of high-pitched female voices and strong male ones and loud crying and the phone ringing and ringing and ringing.

"Where the hell is Coby?" Her father's hoarse voice was loud.

"I don't know. I don't know! I told you!" Wynona wailed in response.

"No one's asking you," her father, Donald Greer, stated flatly. "Just stop a moment!"

"And where's Yvette?" Jean-Claude asked in a voice threaded with fear.

"I don't know." Genevieve. Sober and scared.

"They're both missing!" Dana declared, and it was an invitation for more crying and wailing.

Then Ellen said in a quavering voice, "They must be here. They can't be hurt, too."

Hurt, too?

That's when Coby staggered out of the den, feeling flat-out ill, and gazed around the room, lost. "I'm here. I've been in the den. Why? What's happened?"

"Thank God!" Dave cried, running to her, throwing his arms around her, as if she'd been resurrected from the dead.

"What's wrong?" Coby asked, fear skimming through her veins.

"You're all right. You're all right," her father said, pulling away to look at her, then seeing the gash on her knee. "Your leg!"

"I cut it on the beach. . . . It's nothing. I want to know what happened!" she insisted.

A moment of silence, as if no one had an answer.

It was Genevieve who spoke up, her voice heavy with pain. "It's Lucas," she said. She was standing by the kitchen and Rhiannon was on her right, swaying, her doe eyes huge and staring. "He's . . . dead."

"*Dead*." Coby recoiled. "What do you mean?" She couldn't process. "No . . . no . . . that's not true. . . ."

"He fell off a cliff," Dana said. She pointed out the window to the surf. "He's out there right now. Down on the beach." Her voice quavered.

"Where are the guys?" Coby asked.

"What guys?" her father demanded.

"They all left," McKenna said, then explained, "The guys from our class." She was sitting on the living room couch, hunched over, her hands dangling between her knees. "They drove back, I guess. They crashed our party."

"They drove after drinking?" Wynona demanded, shooting a look toward her father, the vice principal. Donald Greer's thin lips grew even thinner.

"I don't know," McKenna murmured and her father, Big Bob, came over to sit beside her.

Hank Sainer, looking like he'd aged ten years in one night, walked to his daughter and put an arm around Dana's shoulders. She leaned into him and started gently crying. Coby looked at Jean-Claude, who was standing in front of the fireplace with his daughters flanking him, Annette and Juliet on one side, Suzette on the other. Nicholette wasn't at the campout and Yvette was nowhere in sight.

"You think something happened to Yvette?" Dana asked tremulously, gazing over her father's shoulder to them.

"No," Hank assured her. "I'm sure she's fine."

"My dad's out there with Lucas," Rhiannon said, looking through the window, her voice barely audible. She seemed fragile and weak, her eyes huge but far away as if she were seeing some other reality.

"Mine, too." McKenna went to stand beside Rhiannon and placed a light hand on her shoulder as they both stared toward the Pacific.

"Well, where the hell is Yvette?" Jean-Claude demanded of Hank, moving restlessly around the room. "Where is she?"

Hearing that Lucas was out there, Coby had walked to the window, as if pulled by an invisible string. She followed McKenna and Rhiannon's gazes and saw, far up the beach, tiny dots of people milling along the beach and surf.

"Looks like the sheriff's department has arrived," Dave said to the girls, coming up behind them.

"Where the hell is she?" Jean-Claude demanded more forcefully.

McKenna muttered suddenly, "I'm going," and headed fast for the front door.

"Stay here!" Dave ordered, but McKenna had flung open the door already and was clambering around the house to the stairs that led to the beach. Rhiannon was on her heels, and Coby, after a heartbeat, took off after them, hearing her father yell at her to stop, too.

"Coby! Coby! Damn it! Get back here!"

But she was outside, glad for the rush of cold air that slapped her face. She gulped it like a liquid. Her stomach was unsteady and she didn't know what she was doing but she couldn't stay at the house.

Lucas . . . Lucas Moore . . . no. She didn't believe he was gone!

McKenna bounded down the sandy wooden steps at the side of the house to the beach below. Rhiannon was behind McKenna and Coby caught up to her at the bottom step. They ran across the sand as if in a footrace, catching McKenna only when she started to slow down a half mile farther, where the group of men waded in the water, their dark green coats glimmering with moisture from the surf and a faint rain. Prisms of color floated through the haze of a shrouded sun.

They were just covering Lucas Moore's body but Coby caught an image, a picture that had been burned into her brain ever since: blue face, blond ocean-soaked hair, purple hands, glassy eyes, torn pants and shirt, ravaged skin.

She turned away and her stomach heaved again but she only threw up bile, holding the back of her hand against her mouth afterward, hearing McKenna's dad, Big Bob, growl, "Get the hell out of here!" and seeing Rhiannon faint dead away, face-first into the tide.

Big Bob and Rhiannon's father, Winston Gallworth, grabbed her and flipped her over. Rhiannon was breathing, dragging air into her lungs while her limbs twitched and her eyeballs moved rapidly back and forth beneath their lids.

"Rhee. Baby," her father whispered brokenly and her eyes snapped open. She looked confused for a moment, then memory rushed back and her face turned red and she began to cry. Big Bob took her from Winston and started carrying her down the beach and back toward the house. McKenna caught Coby's gaze.

"You girls need to head on back, too," one of the deputies told them sternly. Coby shot another glance toward Lucas, but his body was now covered. With a shiver, she and McKenna straggled back together, trailing Big Bob, who was carrying Rhiannon, and Winston Gallworth, Rhiannon's father.

At the beach cottage they were met by an anxious and half-angry Dave, a frantic Jean-Claude, and some of the guys who'd shown up at their door: Jarrod, Vic, and Kirk. McKenna had been mistaken when she said they'd all left, and they looked as stunned and disoriented as the rest of them.

"Lucas was in our car," Jarrod was saying, sounding like he'd already said it more times than anyone wanted to remember. "We were supposed to bring him back. He was in our car. But he wasn't there this morning."

"You were drinking," Jean-Claude snapped. He was normally so calm and relaxed, the one parent they all felt they could go to in times of trouble. But his face was white and tight today.

Where is Yvette?

"We weren't going to drive last night," Kirk said sullenly. "We were going to wait to go back today."

"We slept on the beach," Vic put in, swallowing hard.

"And you didn't see Yvette. None of you have seen Yvette!" Jean-Claude demanded.

They shook their heads and Coby wondered seriously, for the first time, if something had happened to her. Yvette was just so . . . indestructible-seeming. Fear settled like a rock in her chest.

"And Lucas? Where was he?" Jean-Claude demanded of the group as a whole.

"He wandered off," Jarrod answered. "It's what he does. He's kinda that dude, you know? A surfer. Like a loner. Ask Rhiannon."

Everyone turned to look at Rhiannon, who was awake and leaning against her father on the couch. "I wasn't with him," she said tremulously.

Coby glanced at her father, who'd moved to stand by Annette and Juliet. It didn't register at the time but later she realized Dave and Annette had bonded the night before, the beginning of their relationship, though Lucas's death kept them from acting upon their desires for a time. At least that's what Dave told Coby later on when she demanded to know the truth.

"Well, who was with him? Yvette?" Jean-Claude demanded.

"We were all sitting around the campfire and then we just crawled into our sleeping bags and went to bed." This was from Ellen, who'd been sitting in a chair by herself, extremely quiet. Her father hadn't been able to make the trip, so she'd come with Wynona and Donald Greer.

Coby gave her a long look, remembering her and Theo wrestling in a sleeping bag. "Where are Theo and Galen and Paul?" she asked, and Ellen shot her a worried look.

"They drove back. Galen was sober," Kirk added quickly.

"A deputy's coming this way," Dave said, gazing out the window toward the beach.

He didn't say it—maybe he wouldn't have said it—but Coby heard the unspoken comment as if her father had sent out the verbal warning:

You'd better all get your story straight.

And then the deputies arrived. Two members of the

Tillamook County Sheriff's Department, Fred Clausen and Marsha Kirkpatrick. Neither of them pulled any punches and they grilled the girls, guys, and dads alike for several hours, taking turns interviewing them in the den. Jean-Claude's anxiety grew with each passing moment and his other daughters were silent and wide-eyed.

And then Yvette suddenly opened the front door and just breezed in.

Jean-Claude gave a yelp of joy and wrapped her in a bear hug and Yvette blinked in surprise at the crowd of people before her, her gaze focusing on the two members of law enforcement who were just starting to interview the guys. Detective Clausen and Kirk were aimed for the den but Yvette's appearance stopped them.

Yvette's eyes widened and she demanded, "What happened?"

"Lucas is dead," Genevieve said again, and Yvette shook her head violently, as if the image were tearing into her brain.

"No . . . no . . . he's not," she declared. "He's not dead. He can't be. He's not dead."

Hank Sainer said dully, "He fell from the cliff into the rocks."

Yvette burst into tears and then, a few moments later, she wailed that she and Lucas were secret lovers and so began her story, one Coby still had trouble believing was anything more than a fairy tale.

Now, taking a deep breath, Coby shook off the memories once more. Everything had changed. Time had moved on. Lucas's death was an accident. Rhiannon's death was an accident. There was no reason to dwell on any part of the past when there were so many new issues in the present she could fret over. Like Annette wanting a child. Like Faith poaching a bit on Danner. Like Coby wanting to believe she was over him when she'd known deep down she wasn't. Also knowing she'd always wanted to give their relationship another go, and that being with Joe had been merely marking time.

And she was going to get her chance.

Climbing to her feet, she was about to rejoin the party when the door to the den suddenly slammed open and against the opposite wall. Coby stopped short as eleven-year-old Benedict Deneuve barreled into the room, looking as surprised to see Coby as she was to see him.

"Oh . . . sorry . . ." the boy muttered.

Yvette was right behind him. "So, this is where you went to hide," she observed to Coby.

"Excuse me?" Coby was too surprised to take offense.

"I saw Danner Lockwood, too. With your sister."

"Can we go now?" Benedict wheedled, saving Coby from an answer.

"I don't want you playing video games the whole time," Yvette said to him. "Come on, it's time to eat."

"I can't play anyway. There are too many people out there." He gestured to the outer room, where the decibel level was increasing with the consumption of alcohol. "I want to go!"

"After birthday cake," she told him shortly.

"When is that?"

"Right after dinner. Come on." She herded him out of the room and a loud wave of laughter washed over Coby just before the door shut behind them.

It was a pisser having everyone believe Danner was with Faith.

She yanked open the door and reentered the party just as Annette yelled, "Grab a plate. *Mangia!*"

"There you are," Jarrod said to Coby as if he'd been waiting for her.

Danner was standing back from the table and Faith

was at his elbow. Well, fine. There was nothing to do about that.

"You okay?" Jarrod asked, following her gaze.

"Absolutely."

"Need another glass of wine?"

"Not a chance." She'd left hers in the den.

"You sure?"

"Maybe later."

She surreptitiously threw a glance around the room, sizing up the party. People had lined up and were serving themselves. Juliet Deneuve was standing next to Kirk Grassi, an empty serving tray held loosely in one hand as if she'd forgotten its existence. Like Coby, her gaze was moving restlessly around the room to settle on Annette, who was urging people to move to the table and fill their plates.

Coby moved up behind Donald Greer and Genevieve slid in behind her, forcing Jarrod one person back. She said in Coby's ear, "Have you been thinking about that night?"

"Uh . . . yeah. A little."

"Not just Lucas. I mean everything." She exhaled. "But then you've been here lots of times since. This is my first."

"I haven't been here as much as you might think," Coby admitted.

"Like that, huh? Because of that night?"

"And other things."

"Oh, your dad and Annette. I suppose that is a big hurdle."

"A hurdle, anyway."

They both looked over to Annette, who was standing a bit away from the table, overseeing, except that she was staring at something she held in her hands. An envelope? Then Suzette and Galen, plates full, stopped in front of her and

Annette folded up the envelope and tossed on a smile that looked forced. After a moment Suzette and Galen moved on and Annette looked down at the envelope, tight-lipped, then headed down the hallway toward the bedrooms.

"I was too hard on Rhiannon," Genevieve was saying, as if she'd just been waiting to explain herself. "I shouldn't have said those things."

"You were hard on Yvette," Coby said. "We all were."

"Yeah, but don't you remember? I blamed Rhiannon for bringing the boys by telling Lucas where we were and what we were doing."

Coby gave Genevieve a sideways look. It wasn't really like her to place blame on herself, but that's what she seemed intent on doing. On the other hand, she wasn't wrong about her actions, because almost as soon as the deputies had finished their questions and were out the door, she'd turned on Rhiannon and said, "If you hadn't invited the guys, Lucas would still be alive!"

Rhiannon had paled again and swayed on her feet, but she'd stayed upright.

"We were all a little crazy," Coby said now, feeling her way.

"Yeah, well, I shouldn't have said it." Gen paused a moment before adding, "But we were all a little in love with Lucas, weren't we?"

"More like infatuated with."

"Oh, I don't know. Felt more like love."

"We were teenagers," Coby said, picking up a napkin and fork after scooping up lasagna, salad, and bread. "We're forgiven."

"You made out with him that night, too."

Coby didn't answer as she rounded the end of the table and walked away to make room for more diners. She thought about going into the kitchen, too, and looking for seating at the table in the nook, but she was pretty sure all the seats were already taken, so she chose the living room sofa beside Benedict, who was turning scowling at the blank TV into an art form.

Genevieve floated into the room, taking a chair across from Coby and next to Hank Sainer, whose head was bent to Yvette, standing on his right. Genevieve was still looking at Coby in an almost accusing way, which made Coby's cheeks heat, and she was annoyed with herself. Lucas had been a high school crush, nothing more. Genevieve had to know that; she'd felt the same way about him.

Yvette moved to Benedict and said in a voice that was tired of arguing, "Get something to eat! Now!" then she headed to the table herself. Benedict got to his feet reluctantly and followed his mother.

Jarrod, plate in hand, moved to where Genevieve was seated, couldn't find a place to sit, and chose the spot next to Coby.

"Did you talk to Danner?" he asked her.

"I did."

"Everything okay?"

Danner and Faith were just going around the table, filling their plates, and Coby, feeling Genevieve's gaze on her as well as Hank Sainer's, growled with a touch of humor, "Eat your lasagna, Lockwood, and shut up."

Jarrod lifted his fork and napkin in surrender, then tucked into his food. Wanting to turn the attention away from herself, Coby pushed Hank Sainer to talk more about his political ambitions, filling the gaps in the conversation so that she could finish her meal without any more of Jarrod's probing comments.

Kirk Grassi sauntered into the living room, holding a plate. He chose to lean back against the wall and eat standing up. "Where's Juliet?" Genevieve asked him.

"Don't know. Don't care."

"Aren't you living together?"

"I don't check on her every nanosecond like you and Jarrod." He glazed at her blandly.

"You're such an ass," she said.

"You're such a bitch," he responded.

"Stop, please, children. Not in front of the guests." Jarrod was smiling faintly. "They might think you don't like each other."

Genevieve rolled her eyes. "You're friends with him. You and the band. That's our whole connection."

Annette appeared from the hallway, looking serious. Suzette caught up with her and clearly was bubbling over about Galen, but Annette put a hand on her arm and looked past her, her gaze searching through the crowd for someone. Coby glanced back and saw her father meet Annette's gaze and motion for her to come forward.

"It's cake time!" Dave Rendell yelled.

Coby had picked at her lasagna and salad and was glad for the interruption. She got to her feet but Hank Sainer took her plate from her. "I got this," he said with a smile. "For listening to me go on and on."

"Thanks." Coby crowded forward with other guests to ring the now-empty table as Juliet and Suzette were quickly removing the last of the main dishes. Yvette walked out of the kitchen with a stack of dessert plates, her gaze narrowed on Benedict who, having taken a piece of bread, ignoring any kind of vegetable and casserole, was sneaking toward the back hallways and freedom from the adults. She set down the plates and headed after him as Galen Torres carried out a three-tiered white cake with blue flowers cascading down its sides. There were thirty candles flickering away and loops of caramel icing gleamed beneath their uncertain light.

"I can't blow all those out," Annette said.

"Think how many it'd be if they were for Dave!" Big Bob chortled and the crowd laughed.

But Annette was pensive, not really in the moment, and Coby watched her shake her head as if pulling herself together with an effort. As she bent to attempt to blow out the candles on the lowest tier, Coby caught Danner's eyes and they stared at each other a beat. Faith was hovering near his right shoulder, looking somewhat uncertainly at Annette. Coby knew she didn't know how to feel about her one-time friend.

Annette managed to get about half of the candles but the rest of them remained stubbornly lit. It took her two more tries, but then everyone clapped and Dave stepped forward and kissed her and handed her a slim blue box.

"Tiffany's," Genevieve exhaled behind Coby.

"We all like the blue boxes," Suzette said, dimpling and looking adoringly at Galen.

Juliet just stared at it with a locked jaw, her expression an echo of Yvette's, and Yvette was still in pursuit of Benedict.

Annette's hand was poised over the lid. She blinked several times, and Coby wondered what the hell was going on with her. It was like she couldn't keep herself focused even though it was *her* birthday party. Then she untied the ribbon, pulled off the lid, and lifted a necklace with a gleaming sapphire pendant from the puffy cotton within.

Chapter 8

An admiring gasp went around the room like a wave.

"I know how much you like blue," Dave said to Annette gently, taking the necklace from his wife's fingers and slipping it around her neck. It nestled in the hollow of her throat and was surrounded by the fuzzy white sweater, much like it had been nesting within the cotton inside the box.

Annette held a hand to the necklace at her throat, blinking. "Wow," she said, her voice quivering a bit. "It's amazing."

Coby's father chuckled. "You're supposed to say 'my husband's amazing.' Didn't I teach you anything?"

Annette looked at Jean-Claude, then at Juliet and Yvette, who'd reappeared from the back of the house, then Suzette, and finally, Dave. "My husband's amazing," she said, and the group laughed again.

The spell was broken and people started moving around. Coby, whose attention had been fractured by Danner, dragged her attention to the beautiful necklace, cake, festivities. She hung with the women who crowded around Annette to get a closer look.

"Hubba hubba," Yvette said, though her voice was flinty.

McKenna snorted. "So now we know why you're all dressed up while the rest of us didn't get the memo!"

Annette protested, "I didn't know."

"She always dresses like that," Juliet said, though in black slacks and a green silk blouse she was also a few notches up from the lousy weather/beachwear the rest of them were sporting.

Danner and Faith were standing back by the windows as Juliet poured cups of coffee from a silver urn. Suzette held up the cake server and asked how many more plates she should fill, but no one was paying attention to her.

Faith left Danner and came up to Coby. "So, what do you think now?"

"About . . . the party?"

"Annette and Dad. Is it real, or an act?"

"I'm guessing real, based on the necklace," Coby said. "I hope Lovejoy's is doing as well as Dad's making it seem, otherwise he's in a world of financial hurt."

"You always count things up in dollars and cents."

"It's my job." Coby slid her sister a wry look. "And you do it, too."

"I know." Faith gazed at Annette, who was still accepting the admiration of her guests as they went up to her as if in a receiving line to see the necklace and tell her how lucky she was. "They make me kinda sick. I have to be honest. I will not be able to accept a little brother or sister, and it would kill Mom. Just kill her. You know she's at the beach this weekend."

"Mom. You didn't tell me that. Where is she?"

"Up in Seaside, I guess."

"Why this weekend?" Coby demanded. "She knows we're at this party. Is Barry with her?"

"God, I hope not." Faith shuddered. "I don't think she could stand the idea, you know. Annette turning *thirty*. So she just decided to go by herself. I know she wants me to call her, but I'm not going to." Faith turned her gaze to Coby. "Where are you staying tonight?"

"I don't have a place yet. The Dunes, maybe?"

She nodded. "That's where we are."

We? Coby couldn't help wondering, shaken in spite of herself.

At that moment Danner appeared, threading his way through people to Coby and Faith, carrying two glasses of red. Faith looked a little startled, then said, "I hope one of those is mine."

"For you and Coby," Danner said, holding out a glass to each of them. "Unless you're over wine," he said to Coby.

"Nope." She had been, but after Faith's last comment, she wasn't so sure.

Faith took her glass, looking from Danner to Coby. "Hmm . . ." was all she said.

Benedict came through the room in swim trunks and a towel tossed around his neck. Yvette was nowhere to be seen. "Hey, buddy," Jean-Claude said, putting a restraining hand out to his grandson. "You heading to the hot tub?"

"Uh-huh." Benedict tried to ease past the older man's grip.

"Your mom know?"

"She said I could."

Jean-Claude and Coby both shot a look through the front windows at the rushing rain slamming into the windows, pouring down the panes. It wouldn't be much better at the side deck outside the kitchen. Jean-Claude said uncertainly, "Okay, then. I'll find your mom and we'll join you."

Benedict didn't wait. He rushed through the crowd toward the door off the living room deck, threading his way. But Yvette, coming from the kitchen, skirted the table and ran after him. "Benedict!" she screamed. "You're not going in that hot tub!"

"Oh, chill," Kirk Grassi said. "I'll go with him." He put his empty dessert plate on the table along with his drained wineglass.

"You have a suit?" Genevieve asked him, surprised. "You're prepared?"

"I'm going commando," he responded and turned toward the kitchen, apparently hearing Yvette, who was yelling at Benedict to go through the garage to access the hot tub rather than using the glass door off the living room to the front deck, where he was aiming. Benedict reluctantly took his hand off the door lever to the deck that wrapped around the back of the house and was currently getting beaten hard by the weather. The garage entrance was definitely a better idea.

Coby set her glass of wine down to carry a few dirty plates back to the kitchen. She should probably find her cell phone and make a reservation at the Dunes, if there was a reservation to be had. She entered the kitchen and interrupted the end of a tense conversation between Annette and Yvette.

"And what about Dana?" Annette demanded. "The truth's going to come out."

"Just keep your fucking mouth shut!" Yvette shot back. "You were only eighteen when you got involved with Daddy Dave."

"This isn't about me!"

"It's always about you, Annette. Always."

Yvette stormed away as Coby set the plates down on the counter. She threw open the door to the garage, heading toward the hot tub, Coby assumed.

Annette was staring at the envelope she'd had earlier, her face grim. Seeing Coby, she folded it and casually stuffed it behind a napkin holder full of bright blue paper napkins that was sitting on the counter.

"You okay?" Coby asked.

She drew a breath and the necklace glimmered. "Absolutely." Then, "You know what I said earlier about secrets?"

"About telling them, so they can't fester and grow worse?"

"Is that what I said? Sounds better coming from you." Her lips tightened. "What if they've already grown worse? Maybe always were and you just didn't want to look at it, and now . . . they're monstrous."

"You want to tell me something?" Coby asked seriously.

Annette pulled herself together. "Oh . . . God . . . no . . . It's my birthday." She scared up a smile and shook her head. "You're a lot like your dad, y'know? More than Faith. I wish we were all better friends. I know it's been weird for you, and Faith, and I want good things for the future," she added urgently, giving Coby a big hug. A moment later she released Coby and headed back to the main party, but what Coby noticed most was that Annette's whole body had been quivering.

Coby glanced at the envelope whose edge was just barely visible behind the stack of blue napkins. Knowing she was really overstepping her bounds, she simply plucked it out and slipped open the flap.

Inside was a lock of blondish hair.

Then she heard Donald Greer's voice from the main room: "Tillamook's at flood stage, so we're not getting home that way!"

Quickly she stuffed the envelope back, wondering what the hell that curl of hair meant to Annette, as a chorus of excited voices erupted from the other room. Danner appeared in the kitchen aperture. "Are you staying here tonight?" he asked.

"I don't know. I was thinking maybe the Dunes . . . like you and Faith?" From the living room several cell phones started ringing.

"We're in separate rooms," he clarified. "You need one?" He was already pulling out his phone, looking at her questioningly.

"Maybe."

"That was Nicholette!" Jean-Claude yelled loudly. "She and Cal are stuck on Highway 26. There's a mudslide and one car at a time is getting through. They're planning to turn around and go back."

"Yeah, I need a room," Coby said to Danner and he punched in the numbers to the hotel.

Ten minutes later the party exodus was in full swing. Those who didn't have rooms were scrambling to find some. Coby found herself soothing Donald Greer, who seemed almost frantic to get over the pass and back to Portland. "Wynona wanted to come, you know," he said, as he was hoisting a bag over one thin shoulder. "She did. But she was treated badly by your friends." His gray brows were an accusatory line above his eyes. He didn't say, "You, too," but Coby felt it. "She needs to put it all behind her, but until she faces you all, she won't be able to. I told her to come with me, but she wouldn't. And now she's waiting for me. To report that's it all okay. I have to be back tonight."

"You're going to have a long wait on Highway 26, and they've closed the roads south," Coby said.

"Then I'll go through Astoria and circle around the top on 30."

They'd turned on the news and it didn't look good anywhere. Coby wanted to tell Donald as much, but his jaw and mind were set, so she let it go.

She turned, caught a glimpse of Danner talking with Jarrod and Genevieve, and suddenly the lights went out, plunging them into total darkness.

"Damn it," Donald said.

"I'll light the candles that are still on the cake," Hank Sainer's disembodied voice said from somewhere near the table. He flicked a lighter and touched the flame to each wick. Watery light, waving like tiny sparklers, filled the darkness.

"We're outta here," Big Bob's voice boomed as he and McKenna opened the front door, letting in a rush of wet, rain-soaked air.

"I'll help get you on the road," Danner's voice answered.

"I'm going, too," Donald Greer said, nearer to Coby, and fumbled his way toward the door with Coby at his heels.

A wet towel suddenly slapped her and she stopped short, making out Benedict's eely form moving past her. "Need some light?" she asked him.

"No." He slipped down the hall and toward the bedrooms, less affected than the rest of them by their near blindness.

Coby's eyes slowly adjusted and she could make out blacker shapes against black and dark gray ones. It took another twenty minutes before the brave or foolhardy or just plain desperate were all in their cars and ready to attempt the trek back. The dome light inside Big Bob's truck cab came on, blasting both him and McKenna into relief.

Donald Greer had found his sedan, and his balding pate shone beneath his interior light as well. A grim man with a sour expression who still blamed Coby and her friends for Wynona's problems, though surely he knew by now they stemmed from the sexual abuse she'd suffered from her swim coach?

Suddenly a wild shriek rent the night air. A screaming woman. Over and over again!

Everyone froze, a tableau in black and gray and white dome light.

Coby shuddered at the fear in the woman's scream.

Then, "Annette! It's Annette!"

It was Suzette's voice. Shrieking.

"Oh, my God! It's Annette," she said again, her voice receding as if she were running away.

Bodies rushed back into the house, crowding toward the kitchen. But Suzette wasn't there. They swarmed through the rooms and Coby found herself with a crush that moved through the garage to the outside.

And that's where Suzette was. Standing by the hot tub. Pointing to the white sweater floating in the bubbling water. The white sweater was attached to a body. Annette's body.

It was Danner who leapt into the water and turned over Annette's body in the foaming froth.

Her eyes were open. A glint in the beam from the flashlight held in Coby's sister Faith's hand.

Suzette was blubbering. "Oh, God, oh, God, oh, God . . ."

Dave and Jean-Claude grabbed Annette from Danner and dragged her to the deck. Danner started immediate CPR. Suzette was crying and crying.

"Where's Yvette?" Jean-Claude demanded, his voice shaking. "Juliet?"

"I'm here," Juliet said, her voice charged with fear.

No answer from Yvette.

"Danner . . . ?" Faith asked, the question they all wanted to know, but he wouldn't quit working on Annette.

"Don't let her die," Jean-Claude begged.

More minutes passed. Danner kept it up. Finally Jarrod put a hand on his brother's back. "She's gone?" Jarrod asked.

Danner wouldn't stop. He kept at it for what felt like an eternity as rain fell on their sodden group and the wind slapped them in the face.

Finally, slowly, Danner sat back on his heels. "She's gone," he said.

And Suzette started wailing again.

Hours later the power still hadn't come back on, but the Tillamook County Sheriff's Department had sent a man over who'd brought battery-operated outdoor lamps that lit up the scene on the outside deck like daylight. Annette's body had been covered by a tarp while everyone but Dave, who refused to leave his dead wife's side, waited inside the dark house.

Coby was in a state of suspended animation. Shock, she supposed, but she couldn't logic herself out of it. She sat in a chair by the fire, which hadn't been lit earlier because Dave had assumed, rightfully so, that the party guests would emit enough body heat to keep the room toasty and the fire would be too much. Now, however, it was crackling merrily away, in tandem with the wild, blythe weather beyond the windows and juxtaposed against the unnatural quiet of the room's occupants. Galen Torres was tending the fire as if it were the only thing he lived for.

Danner was wearing a pair of his brother's pants and a sweatshirt from his own pack. He hadn't brought a second pair of pants, expecting to be one night at the coast, not planning a fully clothed dip into the hot tub. He was talking to Deputy Burghsmith, who was interrupted constantly on his walkie by other members of his department who were scattered around the region dealing with other crises, most brought on by the storm.

The county coroner was on his way, but it wasn't going to be soon. Dave was finally urged inside by Jean-Claude, who was equally shattered, and the two men sat on the couch in shared shock. Juliet hovered near her father, looking scared, and Suzette paced from Galen at the fire, to Juliet and her father, to the kitchen, and back again. Yvette was with Benedict in the back den.

Rousing herself, Coby walked to the kitchen, which was lit by several flashlights. She encountered Suzette and suggested, “Can we heat some water on the gas stove and make some more coffee? Dad usually keeps some instant on hand.”

“Uh . . . uh . . .” She kept tucking an imaginary strand of hair behind her ear. “Um . . . it’s in the pantry? It’s . . . over there. . . .”

“I know the house,” Coby assured her. “I’ll take care of it.”

As soon as Suzette paced away, Coby went to the napkin holder and looked for the envelope Annette had tucked there. The space was empty.

Coby set about making the coffee, her concentration intense. A voice behind her said, “You know it doesn’t require a surgeon’s skill.”

It was Jarrod.

“It does for me right now,” she said.

“Let me help.”

He collected the cups, newly put in the dishwasher, and rinsed them out and started drying them. Coby glanced his way and realized someone had pulled down the shade over the window that looked onto the deck and hot tub.

“Coby?” It was Danner’s voice.

She looked up as she was spooning instant coffee into cups.

“The deputy wants to have a word with everyone before we all leave. Would you mind helping me round them up? It looks like an accidental drowning. He just wants to write down their contact information, mostly.”

“Sure.”

“I’ll take it from here,” Jarrod said, sliding the cups his way.

Genevieve and Juliet were the first people Coby encountered outside the kitchen and Coby told them what the deputy wanted. They lined up dutifully but with some trepidation, like kids for an obligatory trip to the school nurse. Meanwhile Danner was alerting Jean-Claude, Big Bob, McKenna, and Donald Greer.

Coby found Hank Sainer standing by the windows, his gaze focused outward to the restless black sea and driving weather. "Deputy Burghsmith wants to talk to all of us and get our contact information. They're over there."

He dragged his gaze away to see the forming line. Kirk Grassi and Galen Torres were at the end, a big gap between them and Donald Greer, as if they had no intention of actually moving forward. Juliet, who was finished with Burghsmith, squeezed between them and curled herself around Kirk, as if needing his body warmth.

"Tell the sheriff's department to call me," Hank said in a near-unrecognizable voice. Coby looked into his eyes, which were sunken pools of dull blue, and there was a stretched look about him, as if he'd looked into the depths of hell.

"He needs a phone number. And your address."

He wanted to argue; she could see it in the determination around his mouth. But he nodded curtly and Coby left him in search of Yvette and Benedict.

She found them not in the den, but in a back bedroom that the boy and Yvette were obviously sharing. She told Yvette what Burghsmith wanted, and like Hank, Yvette tried to get out of it, but when Coby insisted it was no big interrogation, she finally consented, dragging Benedict with her.

Eventually they all spoke to the deputy, who finished about the time the coroner's wagon pulled up. Everyone moved to the far end of the living room while Annette's body was loaded into the back; no one wanted to watch. Dave had to sign some papers and looked worse for wear when he was done. Burghsmith, after leaving them with two of the battery-operated lights, took the remaining one and headed toward the wagon. They were followed out by Big Bob, McKenna, and Donald Greer, who climbed back in their vehicles and drove off. Kirk Grassi announced Annette's death had knocked the drunk right out of him, and taking out his keys, looked to Galen, who'd driven from the city with him, silently asking him if they were ready to leave.

Suzette stopped her incessant pacing and ran to Galen, who had straightened but was still looking into the fire. She latched onto his arm. "He's not going with you. He can't leave! He's with me! Aren't you?" She turned beseechingly to him.

"Of course." He patted her arm but looked uncomfortable.

"Then pull up a square of carpet," Kirk declared. "'Cause that's where you're gonna be racking. I'm outta here."

"Galen and I are engaged!" Suzette burst out. "We wanted to tell you all after dinner. We just never had the chance."

Jarrod and Genevieve, who were getting ready to leave as well, both stopped short in surprise. "When did that happen?" Jarrod asked Galen.

"Musta been after him and Juliet," Kirk said, his eyes boring holes through Galen, who looked as if too much information was bombarding him.

"You know that's not true," Suzette said. "Juliet wasn't with Galen. Stop talking like this. I just can't listen to your guy shit right now." And tears rushed down her cheeks.

"We are engaged," Galen confirmed, holding her close. "I love Suzette and she loves me. I'm staying, Kirk."

The firelight gleamed orange against Kirk's bald head as he lifted his shoulders and walked off, heading out the door without another word. Juliet, who'd heard the whole conversation, turned away, her shoulders slumped.

Jean-Claude roused himself enough to come over and shake Galen's hand, but it was clear he wasn't in the moment.

Coby sat down beside her father in the spot Jean-Claude had vacated. "Hey," she said.

"Hey, Bug." His eyes were red and his voice raspy.

She collected his hand in hers and said softly, "Oh, Dad. I'm so sorry."

He couldn't talk, just patted her hand, swallowing. Faith came over and said, "Dad, we're all going to the Dunes tonight. You wanna come?"

"I . . . don't think so."

"We could be with you," she pressed. "You need family tonight."

"Annette was my family," he said in a woeful voice.

"Come on, Dad. I'll pack your things."

"No, Faith. I'm staying. Jean-Claude's here, and Juliet and Suzette." He trailed off, then seemed to dust the cobwebs out of his head. "And Yvette and Benedict."

"And Galen," Suzette reminded him.

Dave just nodded absently, already removed from the conversation. But then he surprised Coby by turning to her and pleading, "Will you stay here tonight?"

"Well . . . sure. I could sleep in the den, unless it's taken?"

"It's yours," Jean-Claude told her.

Coby slid her eyes to Danner, who nodded that he would take care of canceling her room.

"Okay, I'm just going to say it," Genevieve suddenly spoke up. She'd been exceptionally quiet for her throughout the whole evening, but Coby suspected it was just that she was so shattered. "I don't think Annette's death was an accident."

Chapter 9

"What the fuck," Jarrod breathed, gazing at her as if she'd grown horns.

Genevieve turned on him, an outlet for her anger. "Well, what the hell was she doing out there? You think she just *fell in*?"

"Benedict was out there, too. She was probably watching him," Suzette burbled, sounding like she was drowning in her own tears. "Maybe she slipped."

"Benedict was clearly already out of the tub." Genevieve shot her down. "Nobody saw anything. Why was she there? To meet someone? She didn't just go out to enjoy the weather!"

"Is that what you told Deputy Burghsmith when he was here?" Danner asked neutrally. Coby shot him a look, feeling a bit of a chill at the subtle change in his persona, the cop coming through.

"Of course not. I didn't want him to stay any longer. But something's wrong here! You all know it," Genevieve insisted.

"Why would anyone kill her?" Juliet demanded. Since Kirk had left she'd hovered by her father. "She didn't have any enemies. Everyone loved her!"

"Except my mother," Faith said, smiling faintly. Coby knew in Faith's strange way that she was trying to lighten the mood, but her words only made Coby uncomfortable.

"She had secrets she was going to tell," Genevieve dropped the bomb. "She couldn't keep them any longer."

"What secrets?" Everyone turned to see Yvette standing in the hallway, glaring at Genevieve. She'd mostly burrowed herself into her bedroom with Benedict since Annette's body was discovered but had apparently decided to join the group now that the deputy was gone.

"If I knew, I would tell," Genevieve declared fervently. "But that's why she's dead. That's why someone killed her. All she could talk about was how she needed to tell those secrets. How they had to be finally out in the open because they were festering. She was all about it tonight, wasn't she?" she demanded, staring at Coby.

Everyone turned to Coby, who felt the heat of their combined gazes like a wall of fire. Luckily, the uncertain illumination from the battery-operated lights made her feel less exposed.

"She was talking about secrets," Coby admitted. "She said they were poisonous and the truth needed to come out."

"What secrets?" Jarrod asked.

"We don't know!" Genevieve snapped back, glaring at him. "Open your ears, for God's sake. That's why I'm asking Coby!"

Yvette, Suzette, and Juliet were all looking at Coby, and she said, "She didn't tell me anything other than what she said to Genevieve. She seemed kind of militant about it, like she wanted the secrets revealed and the reasons for them dealt with, but she didn't say what they were. She just wanted to move on."

"From what?" Suzette asked, her dark eyes huge in her small face. She and Juliet were a lot alike, the most delicate of the Ette sisters, wiry and small-boned. But Juliet's hair was a shade or two lighter than Suzette's dark brown, and her manner was more direct and showed more conviction than Suzette's emotional demeanor. Of course she was overwrought now, but Coby knew enough about the Ettes from their older sister, Nicholette, to have a pretty clear picture.

"From whatever it was that killed her," Genevieve decreed.

Dave said tiredly, "It was an accident. That's all. A goddamn accident." He wiped a hand over his face. "She's not here anymore." He said it like he was testing its validity. "She's gone."

"Where's her necklace?" Suzette suddenly asked, her head popping up as if pulled by a string. "Where's the sapphire pendant?"

"Probably at the coroner's office," Dave said, waving a hand as if swatting a fly, clearly uncaring.

"It wasn't on her," Danner said. "I gave her CPR and it wasn't on her."

"Where is it?" Juliet asked.

"The killer took it?" Genevieve suggested, but she didn't sound like she liked that angle. "Maybe that's why she was killed. For the necklace."

"Jesus." Dave Rendell got to his feet and Coby stood with him, a little afraid that he might keel over. "I'm going to my room," he stated, and he left them standing in the living room.

"Are you ready to go?" Faith asked Danner.

He nodded and his eyes searched out Coby for a long moment.

Jarrod said, "We'll follow you."

They gathered their belongings and headed for the door. Coby walked them out to their cars. "Thanks for getting me the room even if I couldn't use it," she said to Danner.

"What's your cell number?" he asked her. His own cell

phone was in his hand and as Coby gave him her number, he punched it into his permanent caller list. Faith, Jarrod, and Genevieve were waiting for him, heads bent against the incessant rain, but Danner hesitated. "What's your take on Annette's death?"

"You mean, do I think it's murder? No."

"What if it is?" he asked.

"Is there something you're not telling me?"

"No." He shook his head. "But two accidental deaths in the same small piece of geography, involving the same group of people, seems kind of remarkable."

"Lucas died twelve years ago."

"Uh-huh."

"Danner!" Faith called, starting to head back their way.

"I'll see you in Portland," he said to Coby, then he turned to jog out to meet Faith and climb into her car.

"So Annette Fucking Bitch Deneuve Rendell is dead," Kirk Grassi said aloud as his wipers smacked across the Toyota 4x4's front windshield. He was in a mild state of shock. For all his bravado, he didn't do well with death. Lucas's floating body, a lot of years ago, still preyed on his inner vision. Now Annette, also floating. At least she'd been facedown in the tub when he'd looked. He'd turned away before Danner Lockwood could roll her over.

And he was glad he hadn't seen Rhiannon at the bottom of that canyon, or whatever.

With an effort, he pushed thoughts of dead Annette aside. He kinda had that blasting memory of water-covered limbs and a white, fur-matted sweater and bubbles in her slacks that made her butt kinda lift up pressed into his brain, and he was determined to squelch it quick.

He hadn't really hated Annette, but she was one bossy bitch who had all kinds of things to say about him to Juliet after they'd hooked up. Like she knew anything about him or what he thought! He'd made it clear to Annette that she should keep her nose out of his business, but she'd just looked down on him and gossiped about him to Genevieve, a loud, equally bossy clone of her. He supposed now that would all come out, which made him want to shit-can his relationship with Juliet altogether, not that it was much more than sex anyway.

He'd never intended on fighting the mudslide or floods or whatever other shit Mother Nature was throwing at them in an effort to get back to Portland. Fuck it. He wasn't going that way. His buds, Paul and Vic, were in Seaside where he and Galen—the pussy-whipped ass—had planned to meet them after the party that Juliet had wheedled him into going to. He never woulda listened to her, except Jarrod was going to be there. Jarrod, his partner. Without Jarrod there was no band, and no matter how much bass guitar Kirk threw down, he wasn't as good at lead as Jarrod. Just fucking wasn't. And though Kirk was the man with the beautiful bald head and rock-hard abs—Jarrod hadn't had the balls to go with the look, so he sported that dipshit clipped hair because Genevieve the screecher missed his long locks—Kirk just couldn't sing with the conviction of his friend, and without Jarrod, the band was fucking nowhere.

It pissed Kirk off no end. He was like Daughtry, a bald rocker, but definitely better-looking. He had perfected a way of talking hard and meeting a woman's gaze that just had them creaming their jeans for him. Even so, it was Jarrod who could really get the girls, and he fucking didn't even care! Did. Not. Care. The moron had married Genevieve Knapp. The worst of those bitches. And why? Because he really had a thing for Coby Rendell but she passed him over for his big brother? So he settled for the screecher?

It went something like that, for sure, though Jarrod wouldn't cop to it, of course.

But it sucked big-time.

Annette's floating body crossed the screen of Kirk's mind and he blinked his eyes hard several times, willing it away, as he pulled into the parking lot of the Seventh Heaven Inn, a dive that sometimes hired a band for a gig in their dusty bar. That's how Kirk knew them, and how he'd gotten a deal for him and his friends, a room with a fold-out couch. Their band, Split Decision, had played at the Seven once or twice, back when they called themselves Intent to Kill. Kirk had loved that name, but Jarrod said it got in the way of bookings 'cause they sounded too gang-like. Utter bullshit, but Jarrod was the man.

The man.

Kirk sniffed as he climbed from the cab. Behind Jarrod's back sometimes he jokingly referred to their band as Jarrod and the Pacemakers, ripping off the name Gerry and the Pacemakers, a British group from the sixties with the hit "Ferry Cross the Mersey," which was some English bullshit that didn't make sense unless you knew the Mersey was the name of a river, but okay, it was a big, big hit at the time. Anyway, Kirk liked to call them Jarrod and the Pacemakers in a kinda derogatory way whenever he was pissed at Jarrod, which was a lot, but the other morons in the band, Ryan and Spence, had never even fucking heard of the group so they stared at him like, "Duh?" whenever he said it, in fact whenever he said anything clever, which pissed him off no end some more. Stupid idiots thought "pacemaker" had something to do with the heart, and Kirk wasn't going to give them all a lesson on music; they were supposed to be musicians.

He didn't have much use for Ryan and Spence outside of the band. They played keyboard and drums, respectively, and that, as they say, was fucking that. No, tonight

Kirk was meeting his real friends, Paul and Vic, and he was meeting them on his own 'cause Galen was a pussy and Jarrod was married and a worse pussy.

The Seven was an L-shaped motel currently a scary aqua color with Levitz reject furniture in the rooms and a girl at the desk who constantly sucked on lollipops in a way that should have been sexy but bothered Kirk. She was young, maybe sixteen or seventeen, with huge eyes rimmed in black liner, and he kinda thought she might think she was all that, but Jesus, if she wasn't one of those spooky kids from a horror movie that suddenly grinned with filed, spiky teeth, she was close enough to count.

Kirk passed by the neon-lighted office and saw the back of her head as he hefted his bag on his shoulder and followed the fluorescent-lit concrete walkway to room twenty-three. He heard the tinny sound of a television as he turned the knob only to find it locked. Banging loudly on the panels, he was about to yell when Paul opened the door.

"Jesus. Turn that down," Kirk said, throwing a hand at the TV. "I got something to tell ya."

"Was Jarrod there?" Vic Franzen asked. He'd lost weight since high school, but he was still kind of an asshole, which appealed to Kirk in an indefinable way.

"Yeah, he was there. With the bitch."

"How was Juliet?" Paul asked, and there was almost a smirk in his voice. He knew Kirk didn't really care about her and somehow found it funny, which irked him in another indefinable way.

"She was—uh—distraught," Kirk stated, flinging his bag on the only bed, bumping into Paul's duffel, which tumbled over the edge. "You got the floor, buddy," he told him.

"Hell, no!"

"Or the couch. 'Cept you're too tall, so Vic's got it."

"It's a fold-out," Paul declared. "I'll take it."

"And have that bar in the middle of your back all night?" Vic said. "Be my guest. The floor's fine. I've got a bag."

"Why was Juliet *distraught*?" Paul mimicked Kirk's tone.

"No reason." Kirk flopped onto the bed, staring at the ceiling, struggling with watery Annette invading his thoughts. "Unless you count the fact that her sister drowned in the hot tub."

The two other men hesitated a moment, then Vic laughed shortly. "I hope it was Yvette."

"It was Annette."

Now Paul and Vic exchanged a look. "What the hell, man," Vic said. "What are you talking about?"

"I'm talking about Annette being dead! Slipping in the fucking hot tub and *dying*! Inhaling water instead of air! That's what I'm talking about."

"You're serious?" Paul asked cautiously. Kirk had a really twisted sense of humor at the best of times. Then, "This some kinda joke thing about Lucas?"

Kirk swore swiftly and pungently. "Yeah, it's a fucking joke. I said Annette drowned so that we could all talk about Lucas again. Get in touch with our pain and grief. Makes a lot of sense."

"Well . . . God . . ." Paul drew a breath, beginning to believe.

Vic wasn't so sure. "You're a sick fuck," he told Kirk, who leapt off the bed and shoved him with all his strength. The heavier man slipped backward, stumbled over Paul's bag, and fell on his butt, hard. He jumped up quick, fists ready. He didn't want to fight Kirk; that wasn't part of their hierarchy, but sometimes one quick pop to the face, Jesus . . . he could live with that.

But Kirk was breathing hard, not from exertion, from emotion. "I'm telling you, Annette's dead. Suzette found her and started screaming and we all ran to look and there she was. Had to call the sheriff and they showed up and slammed the body into the back of a van and took her away."

"You're fucking serious?" Vic yelled, holding up his hands as if to ward off the truth.

"As a heart attack," Kirk muttered, sinking back onto the bed, all energy depleted. He couldn't help thinking about pacemakers and those morons Ryan and Spence and he suddenly felt like bawling like a baby and it was all he could do to turn over on his side and block his ears to the cries of shock and surprise from his friends.

Coby made up the sofa in the den with sheets, blankets, and pillows from the hall closet, working in the dark. Then she lay on her back, her hands behind her head, feeling her heart pound hard and deep as if she were on the last miles of a marathon. The window was a square of gray, more "less black" than any real indication of light. She figured they could be out of power for days, the way this storm was raging, and given what she already knew about the road conditions and getting around the area, it didn't look like Tillamook PUD would be able to fix the problem anytime soon. Idly she wondered if the Dunes had power; probably a generator if nothing else. She half wished she'd gone with Faith and Danner, but her father's request had been something she couldn't deny.

Underlying these thoughts was the strange, frozen realization that Annette Deneuve Rendell was dead. Gone. Forever. Her evil stepmother who wasn't really so evil, but who Coby had wished, at the very least, would go *poof!* and disappear. Coby was still struggling to believe it. She'd witnessed Annette's body. Watched as it was taken out on a gurney. Imagined it being tucked into the coroner's van, the doors slammed shut behind it and then gone.

But it didn't feel real.

Yet.

Neither had Lucas's death. Her mind's eye traveled to him. His body. Cobalt blue color beneath his skin. Blue. Like Annette's favorite color. Blue, from lack of oxygen. Two accidental deaths that occurred from asphyxiation. Lucas had fallen, but it was drowning that had actually killed him, according to the final report.

Tell me what happened, in your own words.

She inhaled hard and squeezed her eyes closed even more. Didn't want to think about it. Couldn't help it.

Did she think there was more to these two accidental deaths? Did she?

The night Lucas died they'd played Pass the Candle, the guys had crashed the party, most of them had drunk alcohol, and they'd hooked up with each other, or not, and fallen asleep and woken up the next day to learn Lucas had fallen from a cliff to his death. At the time Coby had told Detective Clausen a truncated version of the events, but she was clueless and scared and grief-stricken and Clausen closed his notebook on her and went on to someone else.

Yvette's story was the only one that had further detail. Clausen talked to her in a separate room, but Jean-Claude was with her and when the interview was done, neither he nor Yvette had any compunction about keeping things secret. After Clausen left Jean-Claude urged Yvette to tell the rest of them where she'd been all night and she did so in a quiet, clear voice that Coby thought later sounded rehearsed.

In essence, Yvette said she'd wandered away from their group late in the night. And yes, Lucas Moore was with her. They went to the overlook just south of the area known as Bancroft Bluff, an expensive housing development built on an unstable cliff where the million-dollar-plus houses were slipping off their foundations and basically uninsurable. Beyond the bluff was a jut of land called simply the Overlook. It was a viewpoint during the day for those in the know, as it was down a private road, not made for public use, and it was a meeting place at night for anyone who wanted privacy and secrecy. Another mile down the beach was the small town of Deception Bay, and if the Overlook was ever raided, you might be able to make a desperate scramble down the cliff to the beach and get away.

But it was a sharp drop off the edge. A tumble to the rocks below for those who were not cautious. A place to die for Lucas Moore.

"I wasn't there when he fell," Yvette said. "We were talking, arguing, about Rhiannon mostly . . ." She waved a hand. "And other girls. I wanted everyone to know about us. I loved him. He loved me. But he wouldn't do it. Was so afraid . . ." She let her voice trail off, and looked away, setting her suddenly quivering jaw. "I just left him there. Walked down the highway for a while. These people tried to pick me up. An older man and woman. They were scared for me, walking alone. I refused to get in the car and went down to the beach. There was a big piece of driftwood that I crawled behind. I just curled up and lay there on the sand, cold. I didn't care. I just wanted him to be honest! I was sick of pretending!"

"It's all right," Jean-Claude said to his daughter soothingly. Like everyone else, she couldn't quite get it that Lucas was gone.

"He fell," she said, as if trying out the words. "He just . . . fell."

No one knew what to believe about Yvette's story. Coby realized Yvette had witnesses that she was alone, should she need them: the couple in the car. But she hadn't needed them. Lucas, as Yvette said, just fell.

And then the last year of high school began, and Yvette gave birth to Benedict in March, and Vic, or someone else, stuck notes in their lockers, and they graduated and went on to college and the rest of their lives.

And Rhiannon died . . . and now Annette.

Was it all random? Or did some of what Genevieve had suggested tonight, even if it was half-hysterical, ring true?

Annette had been adamant that she was going to tell secrets. Were they the kind of secrets that could expose something? Something so big that killing Annette seemed like a good option? An option they took advantage of?

No way. No . . . no way. That was just too unbelievable.

But . . .

What did Annette know? What, if anything, did it have to do with the lock of hair in the envelope? Should she tell someone about that? Like Danner? Was she, Coby, just being spooked by three unrelated deaths of people she knew?

"Danner," she said aloud. Almost with relief, she turned her mind to him. He was a feel-good. A happy place to go.

She concentrated on what he looked like: the dark, slightly unruly hair; flashing, if rare, smile; blue eyes; lean body; low-riding jeans, especially when they were his brother's. Strong hands. Strong manner. Indefinable sexiness that came at Coby like pheromones, filling her senses.

Troubled, but with images of Danner flooding through her mind, she finally fell into a fitful sleep.

One bitch is dead.

I'm not sorry.

I've done everything I can, used every method available,

and yet I'm still an unknown face. I can barely see myself in the mirror anymore.

I am no one. They've made me no one.

I'm dissolving from sight, little by little.

But now I'll have my revenge. I find it is no great heartbreak to kill them. Even those I've loved . . . especially those I've loved. They never, ever do what they should! They continually disappoint me.

I hate them.

I hate them all.

But as they disappear into a hazy forever where they can never hurt me again, I keep their treasures close to me.

Now, as I stand in quiet reflection, naked, eyes closed, sensing a fire smoldering in the secret core of myself, I crush the envelope in my hand and feel a sexual thrill at its resistance.

There are hazards ahead. Annette was brazen and stupid. She talked and talked and talked. She took one of my treasures.

And Coby Rendell found it. Looked inside. She heard more than she should have. She sees more than she lets on.

She knows too much already.

In my mind there is a list of names.

Coby's has risen to the top like a cresting wave.

Something will have to be done.

Something soon.

Fucking. Bitch.

Chapter 10

The power came on at 4:37 A.M. and blasted the house with light and the rumble of the electric furnace. Coby's eyes flew open and she nearly blinded herself. She'd unwittingly left the light on in the den.

Throwing back the covers, she struggled to her feet. She'd fallen asleep in her jeans, blouse, and socks; she had no other clothes except what she'd worn to work.

Her father poked his head into the hall as she came from the den. They stared at each other a moment. His eyes were red-rimmed and the skin on his face sagged. Was his hair grayer? Because of Annette's death? Or had she simply not noticed until now?

"I'm just going to turn the lights off," she told him.

He nodded. "Thanks, Bug."

He closed the door behind him as Suzette appeared in the hallway, shivering in a nightgown, her hands clutching a short Windbreaker close, using it as a robe. Galen came out of the bedroom as well, in jeans and an unbuttoned shirt, his dark hair tousled.

Juliet's door opened next. She looked out solemnly. "Coby?"

"Turning off the lights," she told them all, heading for

the living room, which was only illuminated by a floor lamp, then the adjunct dining room, which was flooded by can lights. She snapped off the switches and walked through one of the two archways into the kitchen where plates were stacked, some rinsed, some not, and the disposable aluminum pans that held the lasagna had been rinsed, crushed, and balled up, ready for the recycle bin. What was left of the cake had been moved to the table in the nook and now the blue icing flowers looked unnatural and artificial. Some had been smashed and smeared into the frosting.

Everything looked used and forgotten.

The coffee urn was on a side shelf. Coby checked it. Half-full from before the loss of power. It was decaf and had no punch, but she poured herself a cup and put it in the microwave for a minute, watching the timer run down the seconds.

Jean-Claude suddenly appeared in the aperture. "Got any more of that?"

"It's decaf."

He shrugged and Coby readied another cup. When hers came out of the microwave, she inserted his. When the microwave dinged again, she handed him his cup and they both sat down at the nook table, facing the wilting cake.

Jean-Claude's normally dark skin had lost color. Grayed. Like her father's hair. Tragedy. Shock. They could physically affect people. Coby briefly wondered what she looked like, then decided she didn't want to know.

"What happened?" he asked, but it was a rhetorical question.

Coby cupped her mug with her hands, absorbing its warmth. "Are you the only one who got up?"

He nodded. "I haven't slept."

Coby wanted to ask if Yvette had even stirred but decided against it. What did it matter. Yvette had a preteen son who might have witnessed his aunt's dead body, and she needed to do whatever was best for Benedict.

"I'm sorry," Coby said, inadequately.

"I talked to Nicholette for over an hour. I was trying to console her, but I think she was consoling me." His smile was heartbreaking. "I have five daughters, and Nicholette's a father's dream. Smart, assured, a lawyer at your firm." Jean-Claude faintly smiled. "Juliet's always been focused and I think she's the prettiest, though I'd never say so in front of her. She kinda likes the boys."

Coby nodded. He needed to talk and she had no problem listening.

"Suzette's the sweetest. The youngest and the sweetest. The most naive," he conceded as if Coby had posed the thought. "Yvette's determined. She can do anything she wants—and does. I always thought she could blast through a mountain by sheer personality, y'know?"

"I do," Coby said.

"But Annette was my girl." His voice faded to a ragged whisper. "I could count on her. I knew her thoughts because they were mine, too. Did you know that she ran everything at Lovejoy's? Everything. The personnel. The reservations. The tearoom. The books. There was no part of it she didn't oversee. Who's going to do that now? Nobody can. Not like Annette."

Coby placed one hand over his. She could have told him that since both Suzette and Juliet already worked at Lovejoy's, maybe one or both could step up to the overseer position. She could have mentioned that though Faith worked at a title company, she wasn't exactly married to her job and had always served in managerial roles. She could have offered her own services, temporarily, if need be.

But Jean-Claude was just talking. Rambling. Beginning to grieve. So instead, she just sipped her coffee and kept quiet as he went on about Annette, coming up with moments from her childhood, little scenarios that he wanted to share with someone, and Coby was the only one about.

About an hour into his reminiscing he suddenly stopped short. "Oh, my God. I haven't even thought of Miriam. I need to call her. She is their mother."

It was almost six. The rising sun was lifting the darkness by degrees and the wind had slowed to a steady breeze. Rain still fell from the heavens but it was coming down in a drizzle rather than a downpour, at least for the moment. Not exactly the calm after the storm, but close.

Jean-Claude left to find his cell phone and returned a few moments later, holding it aloft for Coby to see. "No signal now."

"Would you like to use mine?" Coby asked. "It's pretty good here, usually."

"Do you mind?"

For an answer she went to retrieve her cell, glad to see that she had both battery life and a moderate signal. She handed it to Jean-Claude, who stood for a moment by the living room windows, staring through them in silence. Then he made a sound of discovery and punched in the phone number. "I hardly know it by heart," he explained to Coby as he waited for Miriam to answer. "The problem with a call list."

"I know." Thinking he might want privacy, she retreated to the kitchen and reheated another cup of coffee. As she waited for the microwave to do its thing, she noticed the shade over the window that looked over the back deck and hot tub was once again lifted. Probably happened after Annette's body was discovered. Someone wanted to look out.

She wondered why it had been pulled down. It hadn't been that way when she first arrived. And she was pretty sure it was up when Benedict was in the hot tub; Yvette would have kept a close eye on him. For all her faults, she loved her son and she wasn't the type to trust him to be safe. Jean-Claude had called her determined. Coby kinda thought she was a control freak, but then so was Genevieve, and maybe she suffered a little from that herself.

She heard Jean-Claude click off, and he came into the kitchen and handed her the phone, his expressive eyes looking bruised. "She is hysterical," he said in a clipped voice. "I wish I could be kinder, but it's mostly drama. Her own daughter's death is just another excuse to be a drama queen."

"Maybe it's how she copes," Coby said, trying to soothe.

"I wish." His faint smile again.

Her father came into the room and glanced around, as if everything were unfamiliar to him. Slowly he focused on Coby's cup of coffee, though he didn't say anything.

Squaring her shoulders, she prepared herself for what was going to be a long day and said, "Let me make a fresh pot of regular," and she got up from the nook table.

Danner stood on the balcony of his room at the Dunes in his brother's jeans and nothing else, facing the ocean. He was pretty much sand-blasted and rain-scoured by the elements, and the precipitation soaked him to the bone. The sun had risen in the east and the western horizon's curtain of night was just beginning to lift. Today was going to be one of those dark ones, like the kind that came in the dead of winter.

Well, it was almost that already.

He walked back inside and slammed the sliding glass door shut. He could feel sand mixed in with the water on his skin. The Dunes overlooked dunes all right, and what were dunes but just big mounds of sand?

It hadn't been the smartest move to stand outside; he didn't have any extra pants. But he didn't really give a damn.

Stripping down, he ran through the shower, turning the

water as hot as it would go, but of course the hotel had one of those temperature regulators so he couldn't scald his skin like he wanted to, like he often did when his mind was full of too many questions with too few answers.

Twenty minutes later he pulled on his briefs and his brother's wet pants again, making a face as the thick, wet denim chilled his skin. Jarrod's pants were wet, but they weren't as bad as his own. Those were stuffed in his duffel bag, thoroughly soaked and smelling of chlorine.

Jarrod's shirt was still okay and he yanked it over his head, running his hands through his hair and looking at himself in the mirror. Dark hair. Five o'clock shadow. Blue eyes that regarded him soberly.

He didn't like the way this was going. Annette accidentally dying in the hot tub on her thirtieth birthday? He was going to wait for the facts, but his skepticism was huge and he half believed already that foul play was at work here.

But then, he was a homicide detective. He felt that way a lot.

Currently, there was a case at work; several, actually, that were tugging at his attention all the time. They hung below the surface of his consciousness and popped out a thought every once in awhile. Sometimes that thought was like a *kapow!* An answer to some niggling issue he couldn't resolve. More often the thought was just another question. Questions upon questions upon questions. The kinds with no answers, and maybe no rhyme or reason.

The case that had been his primary focus was a home invasion where the wife and daughter were killed in an attempted robbery and extortion gone bad. The husband had been tied up in the basement and knocked out cold. Persons unknown had escaped without being seen and there was no DNA evidence, not much evidence at all, actually. When the husband came to, he admitted being forced to take money out of their savings account to pay off the two men who had held them hostage. There was no sign of the money, no sign of the getaway car, no sign of anything.

The two women were killed by bullet wounds to the head. The mother with a blast to the back of the skull. The daughter suffered two shots. One in the neck, one closer to her crown. Neither woman had been tied up and they fell where they were shot. The gun was a 9mm Glock owned by the husband and used . . . on the spur of the moment? It was nowhere to be found now and the husband said the doers had taken it with them.

The case bothered Danner because it just didn't hang together. The wife was not sexually abused. She didn't struggle. Had simply turned her back to the doer and let him blast a bullet into her head. She was shot first, in the bedroom. Then the daughter must have appeared at the house unexpectedly and walked in on something. She'd been grocery shopping, and there was produce scattered across the floor, celery and carrots and a couple of avocados. She'd walked through the front door, seen something, then turned on her heel and sprinted. She was shot at a full run.

The wife's murder looked premeditated. The daughter's an unfortunate moment of bad timing.

Danner had examined all the evidence and he just didn't like it. Why them? Why their house? They didn't have a lot of money. They weren't high profile. They were a nice, middle-class family in a two-story house that was starting to get that worn-down look.

The husband had taken out their life savings and given it to them. About three thousand dollars total. There was a bank video that showed him nervously taking the money. He said there were two men, one in his twenties, one more like forty-five to fifty.

It was an awful lot like the Petit case in Connecticut a few years earlier. Maybe too much . . . ?

And there was no evidence anywhere. No footprints, fingerprints, pieces of fabric, saliva, whatever the hell the CSI team wanted.

Could the husband be lying?

All the pieces ran through his head as he shaved, but he couldn't scare up anything new that on second or third or fourth examination might seem odd or new. His thoughts were at that second level of consciousness still. Nothing was really surfacing. No *kapow.*

Of course, his brain was more involved with the events of the night before. Annette's death. Lucas Moore's death about a decade ago with all the same players.

Coby Rendell.

His jaw quirked in the semblance of a smile. Okay. She was in his thoughts. Pushing a lot of other stuff aside, stuff he really needed to get to. Was he really going to try again? He wanted to. No question about it.

He had images of her stuck in his mind: the way she bent her head to listen to something Jarrod was saying, the tilt at the corner of her eyes, the green-brown swirl of color in their depths, the serious mouth and self-deprecating smile. Her slim body and firm breasts. Her even teeth and a nose with a decided bump, the result of a fight with her sister where Faith threw a handheld phone receiver at her and it caught her just wrong. A flaw she'd worried about but that Danner thought added character. Something he'd told her once; something she didn't believe.

He dragged his thoughts to the home invasion case again, couldn't keep his brain on it. Considered Annette Rendell and wondered if his brother's wife had something there in her insistence that Annette's death wasn't an accident. Genevieve was loud and bullish by nature, but she wasn't prone to flights of fancy. She had her feet on the ground, to a fault sometimes, maybe. She'd said it because she believed it. She and Annette were good friends, had become that way over the past few years. They shared things, and Gen, though undoubtedly sick with shock and grief, believed there was something about Annette's death that warranted looking into. Not that it was Danner's job. But something did feel off, and there was no question there were more than a few deaths within this small circle of friends.

He was curious as hell what the sheriff's department would come up with.

And if they do determine her death wasn't an accident?

Danner looked at his reflection in the mirror. If it wasn't an accident, then maybe Lucas Moore's wasn't either. Maybe there was some kind of link.

He was just having a hell of a time believing it was all happenstance.

Kirk slammed his bag in his 4x4 and woulda headed out but a guy from the Seven's office waved him over. Frowning, Kirk wondered what the hell this was. The room was a comp. That was the deal.

"Room twenty-three? Ya got some incidentals," the guy told him. "And I don't see no credit card."

"I'm with Split Decision. The room's a comp."

The guy yawned hugely, showing teeth that needed a trip to the dentist's office, tout suite. "But there was some pizza delivered and charged to the room."

"No, there wasn't." Kirk denied it, but he remembered the box he'd seen outside the door of room twenty-four. Had Paul and Vic ordered it and then stuffed the evidence aside so Kirk wouldn't notice?

"Yep. There was."

Kirk stared at the guy. At least it wasn't the girl with the black-rimmed eyes and no soul, but this guy was only a couple of levels higher up the "worthless pieces of shit" meter.

"Ya got a card?" the guy asked him.

Yeah, he had a credit card, but it was damn near at the limit and he needed a little bit of breathing room in case of emergencies. The band worked on the underground. Free this, free that, or a wad of crumpled bills. It worked for him and even Jarrod, who, though he liked to play by the rules, turned a blind eye.

"How much is it?" Kirk asked, reaching for his wallet and the cash inside.

"Forty bucks."

"You're shitting me!"

"Two large ones, man. Maximum Meat pizzas ain't cheap. You can check with Bill." He waved an arm over toward the nearby pizzeria, which looked tired in the gray morning light. "He brought 'em over and put 'em on the room. It's kind of a deal we got going with them."

"My friends are still in the room," Kirk snapped, shoving his money away. "They ate the pizza. They can pay for it." Why the fuck had he tried to work this out anyway? It was their problem, not his.

"Old man Dyer ain't gonna like it if they don't pony up." The kid gave Kirk a knowing eye.

Kirk couldn't afford to piss off Dyer and break his relationship with the man. The Seven might not be much, but word got out if bands took advantage and/or cheated—and that word would hit the circuit, for damn sure—and that, as they say, would be the end of that.

And right there Kirk Grassi had an epiphany. He wasn't living the life he was meant to. He was supposed to be somebody. Somebody famous and have a lot of cars and sex with blondes with big kahunas and drink really expensive shit and stuff. This penny-ante crap wasn't for him. He needed more, before he ended facedown in some E. coli–infested hot tub at his next birthday.

"Fuck 'em," he said as he threw down two twenties and stalked back to his truck.

Things were gonna change, starting today.

Coby went on automatic pilot, organizing breakfast, cleaning the house, helping her father contact the sheriff's department and coroner's office. She hoped to be on her way over the mountains by noon but knew that was a pipe dream unless her father surfaced from his fugue state of grief and recognized that everyone had a life to get back to, including him.

But she was wrong. By eleven Dave Rendell was turning the corner and asked Coby humbly if she would mind just staying a few hours longer? He'd be ready to go himself by then, and maybe they could drive back at the same time?

Faith and Danner stopped by as Jean-Claude and Yvette and Benedict were packing up. Juliet was almost ready and Suzette and Galen kept looking at each other, then at everybody else, then back at each other, as if they hadn't decided quite what to do.

Danner pulled Coby aside, motioning for her to follow him into the kitchen while Faith sank down on the couch beside Dave who, though now saying all the right things, couldn't seem to get his legs moving forward.

"How's your dad?" Danner asked when they were out of earshot.

She shrugged. "You've seen him. What do you think?"

"Shock. Grief. He's struggling to take it in." He paused, then asked, "Has the necklace turned up?"

"Not so far. Maybe it's at the medical examiner's office?"

He shook his head. "If they'd have found it, you'd

already know. Genevieve said Annette was determined to stop keeping secrets and that she told you the same."

"That's right."

"What's your impression on that?"

"I don't know. She never explained herself," Coby said. "I got the impression it was just something she couldn't keep secret any longer. Maybe something she'd held inside for a while, years maybe."

"If you had to make a guess?"

Coby found herself staring at him, realizing this was cop mode, something she really hadn't seen before. He'd been new at the job when they were dating. A recruit, then an officer, then it was over. That was eight years ago, and now he was a detective. "Well . . . I guess I would say it had something to do with her personal life. My dad thought it was something that happened at work. Somebody telling her she wasn't leading a real life unless she was brutally honest, and maybe that set her off, but the issue itself . . . the secret? Her passion made me feel like it was personal."

"She works at the hotel?"

"At Lovejoy's. She's, like, the general manager. My dad and Jean-Claude are the business owners but they aren't as involved in the day-to-day running of the hotel as Annette is . . . was."

"You feel the secret Annette planned to reveal was about a personal issue," Danner reiterated. "Maybe about someone she knows personally."

"Something about someone. That was my impression. Yes."

"Someone that she knew well?" he pressed.

"I didn't get that exactly. She was vague. Maybe . . ."

"What?"

Coby closed her eyes a moment, giving herself time to think. She did have some impressions. She did have some information. But Annette's death wasn't a homicide—at least it hadn't been ruled one yet.

As if reading her mind, he said, "Maybe there's an investigation about to start, maybe there isn't. But I wanted to get your impressions right now. Just in case."

"You think Genevieve's right. That Annette was murdered."

Danner seemed about to say yes, but then responded instead, "She drowned in a hot tub with all her clothes on. Nice clothes. And she was wearing a sapphire pendant necklace that she'd just been given for her birthday. If it was an accident, then Annette slipped and fell into the water and died."

"It could have happened that way," Coby said slowly.

"Could've," he agreed. "Maybe that's just what it was. Annette accidentally drowns in a hot tub on her thirtieth birthday just after she's been given an expensive gift, which is now missing."

"Or misplaced."

Danner gave her a sideways look. She didn't know why she was defending the idea that it was an accident; she had suspicions herself. But she didn't want to think someone had actually killed Annette. That opened the door to a lot of other possibilities she just didn't want to face.

"I want to be in front of this thing, not behind it, just in case," Danner told her. "It's not my jurisdiction, but that doesn't matter to me if someone killed her."

They were speaking quietly. People still hadn't completely left. Coby could hear Yvette yelling at Benedict to get the lead out.

"I don't want to talk out of turn," Coby said. "I don't know what to think. But Annette was kind of rabid about the whole secret thing when I first got here, like something had just set her off."

"Who was here then?"

"Mostly her sisters, except Nicholette, who never made it. Jean-Claude. My dad. Benedict."

"Then?"

Coby lifted her shoulders. "More people came. I can't remember in what order. Everybody got here who was coming. And sometime in there, Annette was . . . distracted."

"Distracted?"

"She wasn't in the moment. Was only listening with half an ear. I remember wondering what she was thinking about. She had an envelope in her hand that she was holding tight to. I glanced at it, she saw me looking, so she crumpled it up, as if it were trash, except I knew it wasn't. I think she wanted me to forget I'd seen it." Coby hesitated, but Danner was too perceptive.

"You looked in the envelope?" he asked, reading her.

"Right after dinner I was talking to Annette in the kitchen and she still had it, and then she tucked it behind the napkin holder. I picked it up and glanced inside, then put it back."

"And?"

"It was a lock of blond hair. Blondish, I guess, with some light brown in it."

"Hair," he repeated.

Coby glanced again toward the holder with its blue napkins. "I put the envelope back and later it was gone."

"You think this lock of hair had something to do with her compulsion to tell an old secret?"

"Actually, no," Coby said, surprising herself a bit. "She was all about telling the secret, or secrets, earlier, but after she got the envelope, that's when she was distracted. Kind of like it derailed her."

"Whose hair do you think it is?"

"Oh, God, I don't know."

"Sometimes first impressions are the best ones we ever get."

Coby thought that over. "I don't know, but I don't think the envelope was Annette's. I think she found it somewhere, in someone else's possession, and it bothered her. It was just something she stumbled upon and it kind of took the air out of her balloon in that she wasn't so crazy about telling secrets."

"So someone else had this lock of hair with them."

"Yeah . . . maybe . . ."

"Maybe it was a part of the secret that she didn't expect to find?" Danner suggested.

He was gazing at her hard. It distracted her momentarily and she was a little annoyed at how fast her pulse was starting to race. Pulling away from his mesmerizing blue eyes, her gaze fell on the open window shade.

"The shade," she said. "It was down when we found Annette. Then it was up later. It seemed odd, because Benedict was out in the hot tub and Yvette was watching him from inside and I saw her keeping an eye on him through the window and at that time the shade was obviously up. But it was down when we all rushed in just after Suzette started screaming. I noticed it."

"You're thinking someone deliberately lowered it to hide anyone's view of the deck and hot tub?"

"You have a way of putting words in my mouth."

"Am I wrong?" he asked.

"I guess not."

Danner's attention was on the window, too. "It was loud. No one heard anything. With the shade down, you wouldn't be able to see any part of that portion of the deck."

"I really don't think it's murder," Coby said, though it was the beginning of a lie. "I just noticed the shade and wondered about it."

At that moment Juliet stepped into the kitchen, white-faced. "I'm sorry. I overheard you two talking. You think someone killed Annette!"

"A possibility, that's all," Danner assured her.

"I put the shade down," she told them. "It was me. Kirk was getting into the hot tub naked and I just . . . pulled the shade down. Yvette was embarrassed, too, so she went out to get Benedict after Kirk got in the tub."

"Mystery solved," Coby said, feeling relieved. "Thanks," she told Juliet, who gave them each a searching look before leaving the kitchen. Turning to Danner, she gave him a "see?" look. "Everything's probably totally explainable. I feel like a mean gossip even talking about this."

"It's how the truth gets learned," he said, unrepentant.

"What good are impressions, anyway? Don't you need facts to make a case, not someone's idea of what happened?"

"In a court of law," Danner agreed. "But investigations run on hunches and impressions and then corroborating evidence."

She nodded.

"I'm going to call you as soon as we're back in Portland," he said. "We'll know more soon and I'd like to sift through some thoughts together."

They walked back into the living room where Faith, who'd apparently finally convinced their father to pack up, as he was nowhere to be seen, was hovering near the kitchen door and had to move away quickly when Danner and Coby came through. Danner talked a little more to Juliet, then tried to engage Yvette and failed, had a few words with Jean-Claude, Suzette, and Galen, and then gave it up. Coby wasn't trying to look for hidden agendas, but she kinda thought Danner might be just going through the motions with them, that maybe there was a teeny part of him that had interviewed her so thoroughly because he'd wanted to be in her company.

Well, at least she could hope.

Everyone slowly left. Jean-Claude was first, then Coby watched Danner and Faith depart in her sister's white BMW. Yvette and Benedict took off a few minutes later, and Suzette and Galen finally got their act together and climbed into her compact Ford and followed after them.

It was thirty minutes later before Dave was ready to leave, and he and Coby argued over how they were going back. He and Annette had come together in her black Lexus sedan and Dave planned to drive back on his own with Coby following. It wasn't ideal, but he was adamant, so Coby waited on her father, who was just checking the lights, taking his time as he seemed to be standing in each room for long minutes, reviewing each one, as if reliving some memory, probably of him and Annette, before he closed each door.

Finally Coby stepped out the front door with Dave locking it behind her before he headed to the garage. It was then she realized Juliet was still standing outside her own sedan, a silver Mercedes from a decade past, or two, holding an umbrella to keep off the rain. Seeing Coby, she sidestepped mud puddles and crossed to her. "I wanted to talk to you. I don't know if you're right," she said. "About Annette. But if you are . . ." She slid her jaw to one side, thinking hard. "Like you said, you don't want to spread gossip, but if it means uncovering something that helps?"

"What did you see?" Coby asked.

"Oh, nothing. Nothing!" It was as if her question shocked Juliet back to the present. "Really. Nothing. I . . . maybe you should talk to Yvette, though? Annette was arguing with her." As if she couldn't bear even revealing that tidbit, she hurried back to her car.

Coby thought about it. She'd seen Annette and Yvette arguing, too. Something about Dana Sainer Bracco. What was it they'd said, exactly?

Annette: "And what about Dana? The truth's going to come out."

Yvette: "Just keep your fucking mouth shut! You were only eighteen when you got involved with Daddy Dave."

Annette: "This isn't about me!"

Yvette: "It's always about you, Annette. Always."

"Well, huh," Coby said aloud, watching Juliet's Mercedes drive off through the cloudy gray afternoon.

Chapter 11

Joe Hamlin followed on Coby's heels as she walked into her office, but she was unaware of his presence. When she reached for the door to close it behind her, his hand stopped her and, surprised, she half gasped, then saw who it was.

"Got a minute?" he asked.

No. "Sure," she said, circling her desk and seating herself in her chair. She grasped the desktop and pulled herself forward, trying not to be annoyed at his familiar ways.

Joe leaned a shoulder against the now-closed office door. He had a casual way of presenting himself that made it look like he was relaxed and engaged, but she knew him well enough to realize his brain was running along avenue after avenue, working toward his next goal, whatever that might be.

"You got through to Shannon on Saturday," he said with a note of admiration. "Good job."

Her meeting with Shannon felt like a lifetime ago. It *was* a lifetime ago in that so much had happened between Saturday night and Monday morning. "Thanks," she said to Joe, her mind on other issues. Danner hadn't called her yet, but she sensed he would soon, maybe today.

When Joe didn't immediately leave or say more, she lifted her brows. "Something else?"

Straightening, he ran a smoothing hand over his tie, a courtroom move. "I heard on the news about your stepmother. You were there when she accidentally drowned. Jesus, how did that happen?"

"The authorities are trying to figure that out." She'd had a message from Nicholette the night before, a voice mail left on her phone that sounded scattered and didn't make a lot of sense. Coby called her back and got her voice mail in return, so she'd just left a message saying Nicholette could call her back or they would see each other on Monday. They hadn't reconnected yet.

"Are you okay?" Joe's dark eyes were probing as he came forward, bending down a bit to look directly into her eyes.

"Not really."

"What a shock. On her birthday, right? Her actual birthday?"

"You writing a book, Joe?"

He looked like she'd slapped him. "Just trying to be sympathetic, babe."

"Don't really feel like talking about it . . . babe." Unconsciously, she crossed her arms over her chest.

"Coby, come on. You hated her and now she's gone. That's gotta be screwing with you, at some level."

"I didn't hate her," she denied heatedly. "I didn't love her. And I really didn't love that she was married to my dad, but I didn't hate her. You want to know what I feel? Confusion, mostly. And a need for answers. Like there must be a reason, or something, that this happened, when I know there isn't."

"You really don't want to talk about it," he said on a note of discovery.

She mentally counted to five. "No."

"All right." He headed for the door, pausing with his hand on the knob. "How's Faith doing?"

"She's okay. My dad? Not so much. Thanks for asking."

He laughed. "I absolutely adore you when you're bitchy." Then he was out the door and cheerily onto other Joe Hamlin business.

She shook her head in wonder. He was so completely wrong for her. Why had it taken her nearly a year and a half to figure that out?

Did Annette accidentally drown? Did she?

Pushing that thought aside, she pulled out a file on one of Nicholette's clients, the next one she needed to work on. The divorce case concerned a man who swore, swore, swore that he'd never cheated on his wife against all evidence to the contrary. Nicholette had tended to believe him, but that was kind of her way. If her clients were telling the truth, she could do the best for them, but if she thought they were lying, she wasn't good at giving it her all. If she believed in them, she could work with them.

Coby was more cynical. She thought the guy was a lying piece of shit, but he was a JJ&R client, so she would try her best to level with him about what this divorce was going to mean in dollars and cents.

She'd half expected Nicholette to beg off work today; the family undoubtedly had preparations to make for Annette's memorial service. But half an hour later Nicholette knocked on Coby's office door, ducking her head inside as Coby called, "Come in."

Nicholette Deneuve Ennis, the oldest of the Ette sisters, looked the worse for wear. She normally wore her dark hair tucked into a bun that emphasized her cheekbones and made her brown eyes seem huge in her face. It was an austere look that somehow had a touch of vulnerability, too. Like Joe, her way of being worked in the courtroom. Nicholette inspired confidence but also seemed human. Coby could vouch for the human aspect; sometimes she felt Nicholette's emotions overrode her sense of going in for the kill. And yes, in life, that was a good thing; in the courtroom, not so much. Upon occasion Coby felt compelled to confer with Nicholette when the court was in recess and remind her of the firm's overall goal: to win the case for their client.

Nicholette's eyes were heavily made up and Coby could see the puffiness beneath the eyeliner and mascara. "I wasn't going to come in but I wanted to see you," Nicholette said. She sank into one of the client chairs, her whole body collapsing as if it were made of Jell-O.

"How are you?" Coby asked her.

"Better than Suzette, who's crying all the time. Not as good as Yvette, who's made of stone, which we all knew anyway. Juliet doesn't seem to know how to feel, flipping back and forth. And Dad's a wreck. How's Dave?"

Coby just shook her head. "He went back to his condo in the Pearl. I think he's even at Lovejoy's today."

"Dad's going there, too." Nicholette shook her head. "Why? Neither of them is going to get anything done at work. We need to plan the memorial service."

"Who's in charge at Lovejoy's, with Annette not there?"

"They have an assistant manager. I can't think of his name." She sighed. "Dad told me, but my brain's mush. It's lucky that Suzette and Juliet are basically minions and don't have to make decisions. They're not worth anything either right now. No one is. God . . . I just can't believe it." She inhaled heavily and blew out the air slowly. "You know how you wonder weird things? I mean, we were so frustrated with the mudslide that we just stopped at Halfway There and stayed in one of their rooms, but if I'd kept coming . . . I don't know . . . maybe there would have been a different ending? Just one thing different, you know?"

Coby felt a frisson slide down her back. Nicholette was echoing how she still felt about Lucas's death. "I thought you turned around and went home," Coby said.

"No, we got through the damn mudslide as it was happening, ended up on the west side of it. But the whole road was so unstable that they closed it for hours and we were stuck. Cal was totally frustrated. We had to fight for a room at Halfway There 'cause a lot of people had the same idea we did. It was hours before they opened the road to the beach and even longer till they cleared the mudslide itself." She made a face. "I just told my dad we were turning around because Cal was . . . done."

Coby had met Nicholette's boyfriend, Cal Eckhardt, on several occasions and had found him silent and unsmiling. She could imagine what it would be like if he were "done."

"I might stop by the hotel at lunch," Coby said. "See how they're doing." She'd promised her father she'd pop in sometime. She just hadn't expected it to be so soon.

"Good," Nicholette said. "I hear you got through to Shannon Pontifica. Nice job."

"The figures were there in black and white."

"Don't be humble. They could've been printed on the insides of Shannon's eyelids and she still wouldn't have seen them without your help. What do you think about Mr. Webber?" she asked, referring to the file Coby had splayed on her desk.

As diplomatically as she could, Coby said, "I'm not sure he's being entirely truthful about his economic situation."

"His wife's out for blood."

"Yeah, well, he's got one woman claiming she was his

mistress and another who's been calling the office," Coby reminded her. Nicholette grimaced, as she'd been ducking the woman's calls. "He needs to settle with the wife unless he wants a Tiger Woods debacle on his hands. It might not be the same media sensation, but it's going to play pretty ugly in the courtroom."

"You're right." Nicholette pressed her lips together. "I wanted to believe him. He seemed so genuine."

"I know."

"I'll talk to him." She placed her hands on the arms of the chair and resolutely pushed herself to her feet. "I'll probably be sending him to you for a consultation."

Coby nodded. *Terrific*, she thought as Nicholette left.

Three hours later Coby was just grabbing her purse and getting ready to go to Lovejoy's when her cell phone rang. Normally, she didn't answer it during office hours, but this time she shot the screen a glance. It was her father.

"Hi, Dad," she answered. "I was coming—"

"She was murdered! My God! She was murdered, Coby! They've ruled it a homicide," he broke in. "Someone held her head underwater and deliberately killed her! *They killed her.*"

Coby was stunned to have her fears suddenly turned to reality. "Oh, Dad," she murmured.

"Who? Who would do that?" he asked, lost. "Who?"

"I don't know. I'm coming to Lovejoy's. Wait for me. I'll be there in ten minutes."

She hurried to the elevator and slammed her palm on the Down button, waiting for the car that would take her to the building's parking lot. She could scarcely think. She felt disembodied, somehow. Removed from the truth that she'd feared deep in her soul.

Her father's voice circled her brain: *Someone held her head underwater and deliberately killed her.*

* * *

Lieutenant Draden stepped into the squad room and glanced around at the desks slammed up against each other, ignoring the buzz of telephone conversation and the grumbles and odors of the two perps currently being booked. He caught Danner's eye and gave an almost imperceptible nod. Danner nodded back to indicate he'd received the message and would be heading to the lieutenant's office soon.

Detective Joshua Celek, cherubic, perpetually cheery and still somewhat naive, was saying, "There's just no evidence. Nobody to pin it on."

Danner had been sitting at his desk, lost in thought, listening to Celek with half an ear about the home invasion and homicide case they were working on. Even though Celek had been with the department for almost five years, he wasn't really the critical thinker Danner would have liked. Nor was he particularly intuitive, another quality that elevated the department drones to higher levels. He'd been with robbery, moved up to homicide, and was now kind of straddling both, as were most of the detectives given the current cutbacks, but in Danner's opinion, he wasn't up to homicide yet. The job required something more than Celek possessed, and though the man wore slacks and open-necked shirts, Danner always visualized him in high-water pants and horizontal striped T-shirts, like a kid from the fifties. Celek was over thirty but you'd never know it.

Danner longed for Elaine to get back from vacation. He could use a heavy dose of her acerbic wit and an even heavier one of her unflinching look at the seedy side of life. She could pick up a rock and look at the slime beneath without the slightest queasiness or need to look away. She was tough, but also intuitive, and her determination and persistence tended to open up cases and create results.

Celek was a nice guy and, well, that was about it.

Pushing back his chair, Danner headed toward Draden's glass-walled office, ignoring Celek's, "Hey, where you going?" figuring the answer would be self-evident.

One more minute of listening to his stumped review of the ugly home invasion and homicide might send Danner over the edge.

Draden was seated at his desk as Danner closed the door behind him. The lieutenant was affectionately known as Drano because of his craggy face and hangdog expression, as if he were drained of life, which was a complete misnomer as the man was savvy and acute and filled with more energy than his persona revealed.

"Sheriff O'Halloran called from Tillamook County," the lieutenant informed him. "Your drowning accident now looks like homicide."

Danner stood stock still. He'd known it. There were just times you could tell. "I'd like to talk to the sheriff."

"He wants to talk to you, too, since you were friends with the victim."

"Acquaintances."

"Give O'Halloran a call. Sounds like he wants an in-depth interview."

"Maybe I could help in the investigation," Danner suggested, his mind already churning ahead.

Lieutenant Draden gave him a look. "First, I think you gotta clear yourself off the suspect list," he said dryly. "O'Halloran sounded—tense."

"Yeah?"

"A lot of people at that party, and nobody saw anything? O'Halloran didn't say it, but there's bound to be someone holding something back. Someone you probably know personally."

Danner nodded.

"Can Celek handle the Lloyd case by himself?" Drano

asked, referring to the home invasion. Danner's hesitation prompted the lieutenant to add, "Okay. No surprise. Just don't give this Tillamook County case all your time, Lockwood."

"I won't."

"When's Metzger returning?"

"The end of next week," Danner said.

The lieutenant swore softly under his breath, looked through the glass walls of his office at Celek, then shot a glance at Danner's shuttered face. "Keep in close contact," he said, basically giving Danner carte blanche to investigate on his own.

"Got it." But his attention had already moved on to Annette's homicide, and as he walked back to his desk and telephone, it was Coby Rendell who was on his mind. He planned to see her. Directly after he took a trip to Tillamook for a face-to-face with Sheriff O'Halloran.

Genevieve stood at her kitchen window, staring out at her rhododendrons, their brilliant fuchsia blossoms being hammered by the rain. Water was pooling in the yard; the grass was practically underwater. Only a few extra-long blades were pointed up through the brown, dirty flood of precipitation.

Genevieve sighed, her thoughts dark. Why was she the only one who thought Annette had been murdered? Even Jarrod acted like she was half crazy, infuriating her. And this place—this house! It wasn't even really her house. It was her mother's. After her father's heart attack Kathy Knapp sold the family home and bought a house that was smaller and more affordable. She was a real estate agent who'd weathered the economic downturn better than some, and only by the timing of Genevieve's father's death; if he'd lived a few more years her mother would have probably taken a loss on the sale. Of course, Lawrence's death hadn't saved Gen and Jarrod from losing their own home. They'd kept their place with its exorbitant interest rate and had taken out a home equity loan to boot. They hadn't meant to borrow up on the second, but they had, and then *boom*. Everything went to shit. Gone. Their house underwater. No equity. Owing more than the home's worth and letting it go back to the bank. They'd moved in with Kathy while they got back on their feet, whatever that meant, since the way things were going, there was no way to get back on their feet. Jarrod needed a real job for that, not some menial inventory checking that earned him a pauper's paycheck.

Genevieve liked nice things. She could admit that . . . had no problem admitting that . . . was proud of it, in point of fact. That was just one of the things she and Annette had in common, an appreciation of the finer things. It was why she'd chosen Jarrod Lockwood, who was a business major with winning ways and therefore a bright future. How was she supposed to know he was never going to give up that damn guitar? He'd cut his hair and put on a dress shirt and tie, but the guitar held him in a grip as strong as a drug addiction.

It wasn't fair, the way things had turned out. She'd really thought that Jarrod's job at Our House was a temporary position, a stepping stone to something bigger. But all he still did was make sure the candlesticks, and settees, and crystal, and bedroom sets, and bath linens, and mixers and every other goddamn thing was in its rightful place or sold. Still! That's all he did.

And play that fucking guitar.

After her father's death Genevieve began feeling anxious; she'd always thought there was something *there* for her, something he'd put aside for her. But it turned out Lawrence Knapp wasn't the investor everyone thought he was, apparently. When Jarrod lost his parents in quick succession—

his father of lung cancer, his mother to basic inattention to her own health after her husband's death—Gen kind of expected something financial to come their way, but again, no such luck. The Lockwoods were part of the vast middle-income group that was currently slip-sliding into lower-income and maybe even downright poor. There was no money left for Jarrod and Danner after their deaths, and therefore, certainly nothing for Genevieve.

She thought now about her father, feeling ambivalent, if she were kind to herself. In reality she was hurt and pissed off. How could he leave her like this? How could he?

Her father had been a lawyer and she'd grown up an overindulged only child; she could admit that. But she'd done everything right, hadn't she? She'd gone to college, married a good guy, and started a real estate career of her own. Her mom had always wanted her daughter to join her in the business, and Genevieve had. Her mother had then planned to start their own real estate firm, Knapp and Knapp; Kathy never seemed to accept Lockwood as Genevieve's last name.

But, of course, about the time they were making plans for their company, the real estate market tanked. Forget the new business, Genevieve couldn't make a single sale to save her soul after that. She started looking around for other work and found nothing. Annette, bless her well-meaning but deluded soul, had offered Gen a job at Lovejoy's in the tearoom, somewhere in the menial range of Suzette and Juliet's jobs, and Gen had told her politely, but firmly, "No, thank you."

So Jarrod worked at Our House and Genevieve tried to get a job in marketing until she'd been turned down enough times to be completely disheartened. Besides, she didn't really want to work, though she pretended to be pounding the pavement every day. Jarrod played with his band, Split Decision, whenever they could get a gig, but the economic downturn had taken its toll there, too: they hadn't been getting as many gigs as before, and the ones they did involved long-distance traveling for not much cash.

Money was tight.

It just wasn't fair.

Now Genevieve heard her mother on the phone in the third bedroom, her office, sounding cheery and upbeat to some potential client. It made her angry, her mother's positive attitude. What the fuck was she thinking? Everything was shit, shit, shit.

As if determined to make Genevieve's mood darker, Kathy appeared a few moments later and gave her daughter a big smile. At sixty, she was still slim and attractive, with blond-gray hair, bleached a bit but natural-looking. She could pass for fifty, easily, but didn't seem to care, which also pissed Genevieve off.

"So, what did the doctor say?" Kathy asked, pulling a mug down from the cupboard, pouring herself a cup of cold decaf coffee that was still sitting in the pot, and sticking the mug in the microwave.

"What do you think he said?"

"Oh, honey. What are you going to do?"

Genevieve stared at her mother in frustration. Kathy knew Genevieve was having trouble conceiving, and her concern grated on Gen's nerves. "What can I do? I can't afford IVF. You know that. And it doesn't look like I can have a baby any other way, although other women seem to barely brush up against a penis and they get pregnant. Why can't I?"

"You're sure it's not Jarrod?" Kathy asked, blowing across the top of her coffee cup to cool the now nearly boiling liquid.

It was all Genevieve could do to keep from blowing her top. "It's me, Mom. *Me.* I'm the one whose parts aren't working. It's my uterus. My ovaries. My goddamn cervix! I'm flawed. Broken. I don't know if in vitro would work even if I had the money. Probably not!"

"But if you had the money, you'd try, right?"

"Jesus, Mom. Yes!"

Kathy nodded and wisely walked away before Gen could bite her head off further. She felt a small pang of guilt. Her mom just wanted to help, but there was no helping this situation.

If only her father had lived . . . if only Jarrod had a decent-paying job . . . if only there were a pot of gold delivered to her front door. . . .

She thought about Annette again and felt a pang of grief mixed with envy. Her husband had given her that sapphire pendant necklace for her birthday. What had Jarrod gotten her when she turned twenty-nine? He'd taken her to a special restaurant on her special night. It was sweet, she could admit it, and they'd made passionate love later that night, giddy with the hundred-dollar bottle of Dom Perignon he'd splurged on. But then they'd got in a big fight where she'd begged him to grow his hair out again and he'd accused her of trying to turn him into Lucas Moore.

Well . . . that had certainly stopped the breath in her throat.

Lucas Moore . . .

Now Genevieve tilted her head back, closing her eyes, remembering. Lucas . . . lovely, lovely Lucas. She'd lain right down on the sand with him atop her that night. They'd made out furiously earlier, standing up, and had been seen by the likes of Coby Rendell. Lucas had made out with some of the other girls, too. It was kind of his way. Like he liked having a Lothario rep. But he'd met Genevieve later and she'd let him lie atop her on the sand. It was cold as hell but she wanted him. In fact, she begged him to hurry in case Rhiannon or someone else came looking for them. He'd been almost reluctant, which had surprised her because he was the kind of lazy, sexy guy who took whatever came his way. But called to task, at the moment of true desire, he'd paused, poised above her, unwilling to enter her completely though she was raking her hands along his back, grabbing his buttocks and squirming like a bitch in heat beneath him.

"Come on," she'd urged in his ear, biting delicately.

She'd done *it* before, once, with that college guy who'd so impressed her dad, a law student with a huge ego and roving hands. He'd pressed Gen up against the door to her father's den, then held his hand over her mouth as he pushed inside her hard, groaning like a wild man while she was half-smothered. Her dad and mom had been out to dinner, briefly, and he'd practically slammed her up against the wall as soon as their car turned out of the driveway. Gen had thought about using it as her secret the night of the campout but she'd been a little embarrassed. She'd just *hated* it, the way his tongue nearly strangled her and he flopped around on her and shoved himself inside too fast, hurting her. But it wasn't cool to hate sex. No self-respecting high school girl hated sex.

And anyway, she knew she wouldn't hate sex with Lucas. She wanted him. Wanted him with that kind of hot, wet desire they talked about in the male magazines she'd purchased from the Plaid Pantry down the street in a desperate attempt to connect with her inner slut.

But Lucas Moore made her feel that way by just looking at him. That chest . . . those abs . . . that back . . . that hair! That night she ran her hands through it, reveling in the long, silky strands. When she kept thrusting her hips up at him, arching her back, and moaning like she was going to die, he couldn't hold back and finally drove into her, gasping her name, and Genevieve finally got what the big deal about sex was. She felt thrilled, thrilled to her core, that he was inside her.

But it was over way too soon. He suddenly stiffened, groaned, "God . . . no," and spilled his seed inside her. As cold as it was outside on the beach, as uncomfortable as the sand was that crept around her own clothes, which she'd thrown down for a blanket, she was warm inside. Glowing. Hot.

Afterward, she was afraid she might be pregnant. Kinda hoping, too. But that night she brushed back his hair and soothed, "It's all right. It's all right. All right . . ."

They were both kinda drunk, but not that drunk. "Jesus, it's not all right," Lucas muttered. He pulled out of her quickly and she gasped with the cold, groping for her underwear, dragging them on and feeling sand. But she didn't care. She really just wanted him to make love to her again, and she tried to hold on to him but he was on his feet, pulling on his jeans, which he'd worn commando style, something she found wildly sexy, something she still tried to get Jarrod to do upon occasion, though he seldom did.

But then the next school year it was Yvette who was pregnant, not Genevieve. Yvette who declared she and Lucas Moore were in love! The lying slut. Lucas wasn't with her that night, unless he left Genevieve on the sand and went straight into her arms, which he didn't, because Gen talked him into having a second go after he'd gone back to the camp and scored them each a couple more vodka and Sprites. The second time took longer and wasn't quite as good, but Genevieve didn't care. Then Lucas told her to go back and get in her sleeping bag and he would be back in a few minutes, but no one could know.

So she did. And Jarrod Lockwood was asleep in a bag next to hers, which she thought was totally terrific. Great cover. He'd moved from being near Coby Rendell to being near Genevieve and she was all about it. She hadn't known at the time that Coby had already picked up her bag and hightailed it back to the beach house.

So she lay on her back and stared up at the stars, shivering with the cold that had seeped in, but she was smiling.

Lucas is mine! she thought before falling into a hard sleep that was really more like a half-drunken coma.

Then the next morning when she woke up there was no Lucas. And no Yvette. And no Coby. And Theo and Ellen had moved outside their circle because they'd obviously been doing it all night, which kinda half pissed Genevieve off. *She* was the one who'd fucked her brains out. *She* was the one who'd been with Lucas Moore! She was the one who'd finally figured out what the big deal was about sex, sex, sex! She didn't want Ellen to have that crown. The slut. Hadn't she learned anything from her *abortion*?

But then Lucas was dead.

Even now Genevieve felt an internal quiver of dread and disbelief, remembering how she'd felt when she'd learned. What had happened? How could he possibly be dead?

And now Annette.

And Rhiannon, in between.

Rhee, Gen thought guiltily. She'd tried to become Rhee's friend, for a while. Rhiannon was Lucas's accepted girlfriend and though it was kind of a lie, Gen gravitated to her. Wanted to be near her. Like it made Lucas seem still a little bit more alive. 'Cause Rhiannon didn't want to give up his memory one little bit. Uh-uh. Anytime you saw her, she relived the whole Lucas Moore part of her life, like it was the absolute epitome, and maybe it was. Her alcoholic mom just got worse and worse and even Rhee's brothers gave up on her. Rhiannon stayed with her, always trying to find a cure, but it never happened. She died shortly after

Rhee's accident and it seemed to Gen like everybody left in the family, Mr. Gallworth and his three sons, breathed a collective sigh of relief.

But without Rhiannon, Lucas faded away. Genevieve had married Jarrod by that time and she bullishly focused on developing a new life with him. She tried. She really, really did, especially in the beginning, but God help her, Lucas's image kept intruding. It wasn't that she constantly wanted to remember him; far from it. But she did wish Jarrod would indulge her fantasies just a teensy little bit and try to be more like him. Why couldn't he grow his hair out again? Was it really too much to ask? And couldn't he act just a little less willing to screw his wife, like he was having second thoughts? A little role-playing when she ran her fingers through his hair and dragged his mouth to her hungry one, instead of the gentle lovemaking he thought she liked?

What she wanted was to wrap her legs around him, tangle her fingers in his hair, and throw back her head and grunt with desire.

Except his hair was short. Fucking short.

And he was sweet and self-deprecating and a tender lover, which should have made everything better but didn't. Didn't!

But a baby—that would make her feel better. She could forget Lucas, forget everything if she just had a baby. Annette had felt the same way, but she probably didn't have the same female problems as Gen. She just couldn't get Daddy Dave to go for it.

Gen looked out at the embattled rhododendrons and scowled.

It just wasn't fair.

Chapter 12

Lovejoy's was an apartment building that rambled over half a block of prime real estate, erected at the turn of the last century when the Victorian style was all the rage. It had been converted to a hotel in the early 1980s with the original house rearranged into an office, reception desk, and small tearoom during the day, wine bar at night, and there were several rooms in the back reconfigured as hotel rooms with handicap access. There were no elevators. Guests found their way to the adjoining apartments via covered outdoor stairways and walkways. The room decor was straight out of the Victorian era with ornate filigree, heavy maroon velvet curtains held back by gold ropes, lots of delicate china tchotchkes and crystal chandeliers. The plumbing and electricity had been completely overhauled throughout the sixties, seventies, and eighties, and by the time Lawrence Knapp brought the property to the attention of Jean-Claude Deneuve and Dave Rendell, all that really remained to do was find financing, easy enough during the time the sale was made.

Lovejoy's was also one of the only hotels available in the coveted Alphabet District of Portland; the more modern chain hotels were north, toward Thurman, where you could find your Hiltons and Holiday Inns.

When her father was buying into Lovejoy's, Coby was finishing college and trying to get over the fact he was marrying Annette Deneuve. She paid little attention to the negotiations. Faith, too, had practically clapped her hands over her ears and run screaming from the idea of anything their father was doing. He'd always been involved in finance, at some level, and as far as Coby knew, had been nothing less than brilliant in his job. When the bottom fell out of the real estate market in late 2007, he and Jean-Claude were already well-established in Lovejoy's and Dave had long moved from the financial sector. Jean-Claude had been in the hotel business all his life, working for some of the large chains. Lovejoy's was the first foray on his own, but he brought valuable experience to the partnership. With Dave's money and financial acumen and Jean-Claude's on-the-job experience, they formed an enterprising partnership. Annette as general manager was a no-brainer.

The hotel had a deal with a small parking structure across the street; they were all small in Portland's Nob Hill. For an exorbitant fee you could park your car there, exorbitant being the going rate in the area. Coby pulled in, checked the hourly fee, and shuddered. But it was either the lot or driving around forever trying to secure a parking spot, like San Francisco's Nob Hill in more ways than one.

From the street, Lovejoy's presented a large three-story home complete with two flanking Victorian turrets and a huge, double front door thick with beveled glass windows that ran from another beveled-glass transom above to a brass kick plate below. Coby climbed the five-step stoop, looked through those windows, and was rewarded with a watery view of a hotel lobby complete with mahogany desk and paneling and a dark red carpet with a gold fleur-de-lis pattern.

Inside, a young man stood at the reception desk. He wore a black jacket and slacks and a white shirt with a maroon tie. His near-black hair was slicked down and wet-looking, on purpose, Coby felt. The look made his pale skin seem downright ashen. He had large gray eyes, a mouth with pressed lips, and a harried expression on his face.

"May I help you?" he asked in a tone that suggested he really didn't have the time. Coby read the dull brass tag on his jacket lapel that read "William Johnson, Assistant Manager," the one whose name Nicholette could not remember.

"I'm Coby Rendell. My father is expecting me?"

He blinked several times, processing. "Oh. Oh, okay. Yes, yes. Mr. Rendell is in the back office. I'll go get him."

He left the front desk and hurried through a carved door that led to a back room. Coby leaned an arm on the counter and gazed around with new eyes. She didn't know what Lovejoy's was worth, but she could hazard a guess. And it must be doing a healthy business, as her father had bought his wife a sapphire pendant necklace that looked, and undoubtedly was, expensive.

His wife—whose death had been ruled a homicide.

And where was that necklace now?

Dave came out from the back room and met his daughter with another bear hug. "Bug," he said brokenly.

"Dad, I—" She cut herself off when she recognized the woman who'd followed him, a few steps behind, from the inner sanctum. "Mom?" she questioned, not hiding her surprise.

"Hi, honey." Leta Rendell smiled at her daughter. She was fifty-four, newly trim, as if working out was a daily routine—Barry's influence?—and her hair, always short, was now shoulder length and tucked in at her chin. She looked ten years younger than the last time Coby had seen her, which was . . . well, a few months ago now.

"What are you doing here?" Coby asked her.

"Well, your dad needed someone," she said, as if Coby were truly dense.

"I know, but . . . how did you learn . . ." She turned to her father. "Did you tell her?"

He spread his hands. "I'm a wreck. I can't believe any of this! Leta came by and I told her when she got here."

"It's shocking," Leta responded, pulling in her shoulders and shivering. "Murder. Really? It feels so . . . melodramatic."

Coby was just staring at her mother. As far as she knew, they didn't have anything to do with each other, but here they were, acting as if it were the most natural thing in the world for her to "be there" for him.

"She comes by a lot," Dave added, seeing Coby's face.

"Really?" Coby questioned.

"She heard about what happened to Annette from Faith," Dave said.

"Not from you," Leta chided Coby gently.

Coby had never had the close relationship with her mother that Faith had; she'd been more of a daddy's girl, though that had certainly suffered since his marriage to someone of her own generation.

"When Faith told me I called your father immediately," Leta said. "Not that she was murdered, of course, but that she died on her birthday. I'm speechless. I mean, it's just shocking."

Coby said to her father, "How are you, really? This is shocking. Mom's right about that. I'm not sure I even believe it all. Who called you? Someone from the sheriff's department?"

"Actually, the TCSD sent that same detective, the one

that came to the house after your friend Lucas's death. Clausen. He came to the hotel after he found I wasn't home. You always hear about that, you know? The police coming to your door with bad news. Only this time I already knew she was dead, I just didn't know someone had purposely killed her."

He looked about to break down, so Coby quickly asked, "What did Detective Clausen say, exactly?"

Jean-Claude joined them from the back room, his face gray. He almost looked worse than Dave, but then Annette was his daughter.

"He said that her fingernails were broken on her right hand," Dave said in a quiet voice, as if he could barely get the words out. "They think she was underwater and trying to grab hold of the side of the tub, but that someone held her down. There are marks on her neck, bruises from someone's fingers. They believe she was purposely drowned."

Coby felt a chill at her father's careful recitation. She glanced at Leta, who was nodding and had reached out to place a hand on his arm. "Was Mom here when Clausen came by?" Coby asked.

Leta answered, "He was just leaving when I got here. I saw him getting into his squad car. Is that what you call it? A squad car? With the sheriff's department?"

"Did he ask you any questions?" Coby asked, turning to her father.

"He asked a lot of questions," Jean-Claude put in. "Where we were when her body was discovered. What happened just before. Why didn't anyone see anything. It was rude."

"They just want to know what happened," Dave said on a sigh. "So do I."

"We all do," Leta agreed swiftly.

"It was rude," Jean-Claude reiterated. He closed his

eyes, shook his head, then walked like an old, old man back through the door into the inner office.

Coby's cell phone rang. She almost didn't glance at it; work knew where she was, so it wouldn't be them, and she didn't care about anyone else. But she did look, wondering. It was a number she didn't recognize.

"Excuse me a moment," she said, taking a few steps away. "Coby Rendell."

"It's Danner." His familiar voice reached across to her. "You got a minute?"

"I'm with my dad at Lovejoy's. I know Annette's death has been ruled a homicide."

"Ahh . . . can I see you?"

"Like, today?"

"Like now," he admitted. "I'm driving to Tillamook to meet with the sheriff about Annette's death. I was going to call you tonight, but I thought maybe we could squeeze in some time before I leave."

"Well . . . can you meet me at my office?" Coby asked. "I'm heading back to work. JJ&R's in the Clatsop building."

"I know it. I'll meet you there."

"There's a coffee shop in the lobby. Cuppa Joe."

"Good," he said. "I'll be there in twenty."

Coby clicked off her phone, then returned to where her father and mother were still standing in the lobby. At one time she'd wanted them to get back together more than anything, but under the circumstances it was a little unsettling to see them so comfortable with each other. When had that happened?

"Was that Joe?" Leta asked, which stopped Coby cold for a moment.

"I'll tell her," Dave said.

Coby shot him a quick smile. "Thanks, Dad." And then she headed out.

* * *

Cuppa Joe was a coffee spot with a couple of satellite shops, seeking to find a niche in Portland's saturated high-end coffee market. Someone once said you could throw a quarter from anyplace on a downtown street and hit a Starbucks, which had been true once, though the company's expansion had slowed during the recession, like everything else.

In the downtown building that housed Jacoby, Jacoby, and Rosenthal, Cuppa Joe had scarlet pendent lights hanging over an L-shaped blond wood counter where two baristas worked a steady stream of customers. Postage stamp–sized tables were scattered across the floor on the north side of the lobby. The south side was a bank of elevators that led to the upper floors.

Danner beat Coby to Cuppa Joe, and he walked to the "ordering" barista and asked for a plain black coffee. He grabbed one of the chairs at an empty table near the revolving front door and sprawled into it. He clearly remembered meeting Coby at a coffee shop soon after they'd started dating and watching the tip of her tongue try to reach a bit of foam on her upper lip. He'd itched to reach over and wipe it off, but at the time he and Coby had been too new into their relationship, so he'd kept his hands to himself.

Now she burst through the revolving doors, checking her watch. Seeing him, she asked, "Do you mind waiting? I need to just check in upstairs and see if there's anything waiting for me."

"I'm okay." He just needed to be in Tillamook before five o'clock. It took two hours to get to the coast, although they were still cleaning up damage from Saturday night's storm and the drive could take longer. In any event, he was good till two, and as it was just coming up on 1 P.M. he had some time.

Coby was back in ten minutes. She beelined to the counter and Danner got up to pay, which she absolutely refused. "This isn't a date," she told him a bit crisply. "I've got it."

He wanted to pay. That was all. He sat back down and watched as she ordered a black coffee and a croissant. "Lunch," she said as she sat across from him.

"That isn't even breakfast."

"It's kind of both today," she admitted.

"No latte?" he said, a little disappointed.

"Gave 'em up," she said. "Kind of indulgent."

"Indulgent?" he repeated, now really disappointed. "What happened to you?"

That seemed to stop her. "What do you mean?"

"The Coby Rendell I remember still had room for fun. Even if it was just foam from a latte."

He saw a bit of color climb up her neck. "I still have room for fun," she said, sounding offended. Danner kept his expression neutral and Coby flicked him a skeptical look. "You called me to talk about my stepmother's murder," she reminded him carefully.

Danner nodded, wondering dryly when he'd discovered that murder was often a safer topic than personal issues. What did that say about him? "I take it the TCSD contacted your father?"

"Detective Clausen came to Lovejoy's to deliver the news. Fred Clausen," she said. "I remember him from the last time we had the sheriff's department at our beach house, when Lucas Moore died. Jarrod was there, too."

"I remember."

"But Lucas's death was an accident. He fell from the cliff to the rocks below Bancroft Bluff."

"It was ruled an accident."

"Yes," she said, definitely.

"And there's no reason to think the two deaths are connected."

"Other than proximity? And some of the same cast of characters?"

He shrugged. "I have a lot of trouble with coincidence."

Coby took a swift sip of her coffee and nibbled on the croissant. "I don't know what I think," she admitted, and Danner felt that was the first unedited thing she'd said since they sat down.

"Tell me about Annette's party. From start to finish."

"Like I already did at the beach house?"

"You've had time to think about it since we talked. I bet you've thought of a few more things. That's kind of the way these things go. And now we know it's homicide. We're no longer trying to make it something it's not."

"Why me?" she asked. "There were a lot of people there."

"I know you," he answered. "I like you. I trust your insight. I can get to the others later, but I wanted to see you today. I've—missed you."

Coby felt like she'd been thrown into a time warp. Danner was so *the same.* And it was in a good way, and she'd missed it, too, and now she just wanted to lay her head on the table and cry and she didn't have a clue why.

Instead, she swallowed a piece of croissant that felt like it was sticking in her throat and told him about her Saturday from start to finish, everything she could remember, from racing out of the meeting with a JJ&R client, to the worry over her tire and stopping at the Halfway There, to the moment when she, like everyone else, ran to the back deck and saw Annette floating facedown in the bubbling hot tub.

"And then Juliet left in her Mercedes and I followed my dad's car back to his condo, and I drove to my own place, parked, walked inside, and sat down at the table and had a glass of water. I don't know how long I sat there, but I went straight to bed after that. I got up this morning and went to work."

He was watching her, an engaged listener. She'd expected him to take notes, or something, he simply listened.

"Did you think it was strange that Juliet said Yvette was embarrassed over Kirk being naked?" he asked.

"Uh . . ." She smiled quizzically. "That's what you want to know?"

"It just seemed like you thought it was weird. Your expression, when you brought it up, like you remembered and it caught your attention."

"Well, you're right," she admitted. "I never think of Yvette's being embarrassed. She's just not built that way. But she might have been pissed off and Juliet put a nice spin on it. Juliet was the one who was embarrassed. Kirk's her boyfriend, I guess."

"What do you think she meant that you should talk to Yvette?"

"I don't know."

"Do you think she was worried that it was a homicide, and that Yvette might know something? Be involved, possibly?"

Coby spread her hands. "Maybe she was referring to an argument that Yvette had with Annette. I heard her mention Dana. Like Dana Sainer . . . um . . . her married name is Bracco. Dana was one of the friends at the campout."

"Hank Sainer's daughter?"

"Yep."

"But she wasn't there on Saturday."

"No, she lives on the East Coast. None of us have seen her in years."

Now he did take out a small spiral notebook, flip it open, and write down some thoughts. "Anything else in that argument?"

"Annette said it was all going to come out and Yvette snapped back at her, and she said it wasn't about her, and Yvette responded that it was always about her."

"What do you think that meant?" he asked, his blue eyes searching hers.

It made it hard for her to keep her mind on what they were talking about. Her attention just felt fractured. "Um . . . you know, I thought it was about something Yvette had done, and Yvette was pissed at her and just made that last comment because they were sisters and were just letting each other have it."

"Think it had to do with the big secret Annette wanted to see the light of day?"

"I thought it had to do with Benedict's father, actually," Coby said now, realizing. "I thought maybe she was talking about Lucas, but I don't know what Dana had to do with that unless maybe she knows the truth and was going to finally tell."

"You think Lucas was Benedict's father?"

"Yvette practically said so, the night of the campout. She said they were lovers. But at Annette's party she made a point of telling me that wasn't the truth. We were talking and I swear she brought it up just so she could tell me Benedict was *not* Lucas's."

Danner mulled that over. "If Dana knows, and Yvette sees it's what you suspect as well, it's not much of a motive to go after Annette. Everybody already knows."

Coby shrugged. "Maybe Annette had incontrovertible proof."

"Big word," Danner said with a smile.

"I work in a law office."

And for some reason that made them both laugh, a sudden release of tension. Then Danner said, "Still, given the circumstances, would it really be a reason to kill your own sister?"

Coby thought about it and slowly shook her head. "No. It wouldn't be. So it must be something else. I can see Yvette being totally pissed off and getting in a shoving match, maybe even hitting, but to hold Annette underwater?"

"Rage can sweep you away," Danner mused, but she could tell he wasn't wild about that motive either.

Glancing at her watch, Coby said reluctantly, "I have to get back to work."

Danner nodded. "I've got to get on the road to Tillamook."

They both stood up. There was an awkward moment where they almost shook hands, and then he simply gathered her in his arms and hugged her.

"I'll be back tonight," he said lightly. "I'm just exchanging information with the TCSD."

"Not your jurisdiction," Coby said.

"Not my jurisdiction," he agreed, then sketched a goodbye as he headed out the revolving doors.

"Be still my beating heart," Coby muttered to herself through clenched teeth. Damn, but he had a hold on her. After all this time. After all this wasted time.

It really kind of pissed her off.

Sometimes things just didn't work out the way they should.

In Yvette's case, they never worked out as they should. She'd spent her life scratching and fighting for everything she'd earned. Nicholette had been blessed with being first and Daddy's favorite. Annette had been smart and cagey, with a mind like a chess player, always two or five or ten moves ahead. Juliet was a pain in the ass, really. Always skulking around and watching for an opportunity to shine the light on herself, usually at someone else's expense. And she couldn't keep her legs together, either. Was always lying down for some guy whom she deemed the coolest of the moment. Sure, it was Kirk Grassi now, but Yvette had it on good authority that she'd slept with Theo and Paul and maybe even Vic—*puke!*—a time or two. Did Kirk know? Did he care? He'd certainly cut a swath through their group, as well.

But of all her sisters, Suzette was the one who made Yvette want to rip her face off. Her sweetness, her naivete, was a complete act. Suzette had set her sights on Galen with a bulldog's determination. For whatever reason, she found him perfect for her means. Her job at Lovejoy's was a stepping stone; she'd been planning Annette's demise for a long time. Yvette had overheard the sugar-coated poison Suzette had bandied about. To the Lovejoy's staff, whenever there was a problem: "Oh, Annette said she'd take care of that. It didn't get done?" To the hotel guests, when their needs weren't met: "I'll be sure and let our general manager, Annette Rendell, know." And then Suzette conveniently forgot to mention the issue until the guest was screaming on the phone at a confused Annette.

Yvette never intervened. Why should she? Annette was a know-it-all who thought she was always right. Let Suzette screw things up for her. Annette could use a distraction 'cause she sure as hell wanted to mess things up for Yvette.

Who was she to blab secrets about their family, huh? Who was she?

Now Yvette stood behind the couch of her apartment with its rented Danish modern furniture, gazing down at her son's dark head, wanting to pull Benedict into her arms and squeeze him hard, protect him from the shit that was coming their way.

Controlling herself, she yanked her cell phone from her purse and checked the time. If she didn't leave soon she'd be late for work. She was on the afternoon and evening shift at Xavier's, a steak house in Laurelton, west of Portland, a popular spot with the commuters heading home after a day in the city. A place to meet the wife, the business associate, off duty, so to speak, the mistress and/or a possible new hookup. Yvette had been propositioned by the best of them. She wasn't friendly. She was sultry, kind of smoky, definitely walking on the dark side. It was a persona that was half-natural/half-designed. It got her good tips and an occasional date, but for all her bad-girl vibe, she'd become about as chaste and dried-up as an old nun.

There was only one man for her, and she couldn't have him anymore.

"Juanita will be here soon," Yvette said to Benedict, who had come home from school and flopped himself in front of the television with hardly more than three words.

He grunted an answer. He didn't like having a babysitter anymore, and Yvette kind of understood. But she was under fire these days, a situation that made her gnash her teeth, and she couldn't afford anything—any little thing—that might portray her as an unfit parent.

Thank you, Annette-fucking-Rendell.

She flipped open the shades to the front kitchen window, which offered a view of the parking lot. If Juanita was late, Yvette was going to kill the charming Mexican babysitter. The woman was just so goddamned happy!

It was too irritating for words.

Now, brooding, Yvette thought back to that last fight with Annette.

"You can't leave him in the hot tub by himself," Annette snapped, tossing a towel around Benedict.

"Take a chill pill," Kirk drawled, lounging in the tub. The bubbles didn't cover his floating penis, which sent Annette into overdrive. She toweled Benedict off with enough energy to take off his top layer of skin, and the boy ran to Yvette's arms. But Yvette was deep-down angry at Annette, and after wrapping the towel more securely, she sent Benedict inside, intending to have it out with her sister.

By then Kirk had suffered enough of Annette's rough tongue as well. He climbed out of the tub, shot her a stiff middle finger, then tucked a towel around his waist and sauntered back inside the house.

"You're going to lose Benedict," Annette said, lifting her chin.

"Shut up," Yvette told her. She could see the sapphire necklace glint in the light from the kitchen window. Otherwise it was dark as sin outside, and though the rain was little more than a mist at that particular moment, it was cold, damp, and uncomfortable.

"You've had ample warning," Annette went on. "You've done a piss-poor job of raising him, and I'll be the first one to say so in court!"

"Stay away from me and Benedict!" Yvette's fury, barely below the surface at the best of times, ran over in a froth of indignation.

"I'm sick of lying for everybody. You're done, Yvette. As of now."

And Annette had stood there in triumph, with her expensive white sweater, and her expensive sapphire necklace, and her planted feet, crossed arms, and tilted chin.

Yvette lost it. Just lost it. Without thinking she barreled into her and knocked her into the hot tub. It was all she could do not to jump in after her and rip her hair out by the roots!

Annette was sputtering, stunned, her face blank. Sitting in the tub, she lifted a hand to her head in slow motion, as if testing for a wound. Yvette just didn't care. She circled the hot tub and headed back through the garage and into the house, dimly aware that her sister was sinking into the water.

She remembered hoping the bitch would drown.

And she had.

And now?

The doorbell rang, saving her from an answer.

She let in the chattering Juanita, then rotely gave her son a hurried kiss good-bye before heading out the door to her job.

Chapter 13

The Tillamook County Sheriff's Department was in the center of the town of Tillamook, located along a stretch of land between the south and north lanes of Highway 101. Danner pulled his Wrangler into the back lot, which was, on a good day, filled with large mud puddles and on a day like today, and after the wild, weekend weather, was pretty much a crater-filled mess with lakes of water bisected by narrow isthmuses of graveled land.

Danner sloshed through the puddles and around a cement walkway to the front entrance. He was met by a scowling black woman in a uniform with a tag that read, "Johnson."

He showed his badge and said, "Sheriff O'Halloran's expecting me."

The scowl never lifted and he suspected it was a perpetual expression. But she pointed out the way around a long counter to a hallway that led into the back of the building and the inner sanctum. Danner walked by a back door he'd noticed from the parking lot that he'd bypassed because it clearly said "No Entrance" and was undoubtedly meant to be used only by members of the department.

He ran directly into Fred Clausen, the heavyset, middle-aged detective who'd taken over at Dave Rendell's beach house. Clausen recognized Danner, too, and shook hands with him. "Meeting with the sheriff," Clausen said, a statement more than a question, but Danner nodded as he followed the man down the rest of the hall and into a small office with a window that looked west onto the southbound lanes of 101 and a diner across the street with a carved wooden sign that read "Joanie's" in a script that looked straight out of the thirties.

Sheriff Sean O'Halloran was a white-haired, blue-eyed, sixtyish man with a hearty manner and crushing handshake. "You were at the Rendell party," he said. "You know these people, then?"

"Some of them," Danner agreed, taking a chair.

"The victim?"

"Not well."

"Why don't you bring us up to speed?" O'Halloran suggested as Clausen took the seat next to Danner and Danner gave them a quick recap of his own history at Rutherford High with people at the party; Annette's relationship to Dave Rendell, Coby's father; and the relationships of the Ette sisters with each other and their father, Jean-Claude Deneuve. What he didn't bring up was Lucas Moore's death twelve years earlier, which involved a lot of the same players, but Fred Clausen took care of that.

"Second time I've been to that house 'cause of a death," Clausen said, and O'Halloran, who'd clearly been prepped, frowned at his detective.

"The first death was an accident," the sheriff said.

Clausen nodded. "I told Gilmore I wanted a copy of the report on the kid's death."

"Gilmore's the M.E.?" Danner asked.

"Been here since the dawn of time," O'Halloran said.

"Even longer than me. Is he getting it to you?" he asked Clausen.

"Like a snail," Clausen said.

"I'll try to speed him up," the sheriff responded.

There was silence in the room for a moment, each of them involved in his own thoughts, and Danner said, "I'd like a look at the Lucas Moore file."

"That's his name," Clausen said with a swift nod of his head, like a mental snapping of his fingers.

"Thanks."

O'Halloran said grimly, "I want some paper on all these people at the party. Get me some financials, phone records, work information . . . and yeah, hell, let's take a look at the Moore file again and mark the ones who were there twelve years ago and now. Maybe the kid's death was an accident, maybe there's something we missed. Something from then that set up this homicide now."

"Want me to do some interviews?" Danner asked.

"You weren't there when the Moore kid died, were you?" the sheriff asked.

He shook his head.

"Your brother was, though," Clausen said, which gave Danner a cold feeling in the pit of his stomach.

"Yep."

"Yeah, what the hell." O'Halloran inhaled and exhaled heavily. "The Rendell death could be something all on its own. Most likely is. But we'll look at both cases and Lockwood, talk to your friends. You could be in it up to your hairy eyeballs, if you try to protect them." He half smiled.

"I won't hold back."

"Huh." O'Halloran didn't sound completely convinced. "Your lieutenant thinks you'll do the job. Said you were an asset. Are you an asset?"

"Yes."

"Then do some interviews. Keep in contact with Clausen or me. We'll be doing some, too."

Danner shook hands with both men again as he got up to leave. At the door, he said, "So, when you get the Moore file, you mind scanning and e-mailing it to me?"

Clausen nodded. "What do you think you'll find?"

"Most likely nothing."

"We'll send it," O'Halloran said, sounding like the interview was over.

"Moore's COD was head trauma," Danner said, getting to his feet.

"Drowning," Clausen responded.

"Drowning?"

"I talked to Gilmore about it this morning. He said it was a combination of both, but it looked like the head bleed was slow enough that he drowned first. Flipped himself over somehow after the blow to the back of the head from the fall. Went facedown in the water and drowned."

"Any chance he was pushed from the cliff?"

"Never found any reason to think so," Clausen allowed.

Danner nodded. It would be a stretch to believe there was some grand conspiracy that had followed this group from one murder to another. Better to assume a more straightforward crime: that Annette was killed by person or persons unknown, period.

And if it happened to play out differently, and Lucas Moore's death was somehow in there as well, then they could take an alternate route.

Coby was leaving the building, eyeing the rain outside and shrugging into her coat with its fake-fur-lined hood, when her sister came through the revolving door, dripping water from her purple raincoat. Faith tossed back her hood and said, "Ugh. This weather's a nightmare. Are you done for the day? Can I talk to you about Mom and Dad?"

"Ugh, back at 'cha," Coby said. "Yeah, I was going to call you."

"What's going on with them?" she demanded. "I thought they never talked to each other!"

Coby looked around the lobby and Cuppa Joe, then said, "Come back upstairs to my office where it's a little more private."

"Good idea."

Ten minutes later, Faith was seated in one of Coby's client chairs, running her fingers through her hair and making a face at the water left on her hands from the rain. "I need to talk to you about a few things," she said, feeling the water between her fingers, her expression grim. "For starters, Danner Lockwood."

"Yeah?"

"Something stirring between you two?"

"Not yet. Why?"

"I know I acted like I didn't really care before, but I do think I want to date him."

Coby couldn't hide her shock and Faith started chuckling. "Oh, God, you should see your face. No, Coby. I'm not interested in him like that. I could be, maybe. He's cute. A little dangerous. But he's more your type. And he's way better for you than Joe, but then anybody is."

Coby took a moment to pull herself together, then said, "I thought you liked Joe."

"Joe's a brass-plated asshole," Faith said. "One of Hugh's favorite expressions, and I've adopted it." She sighed. "Oh, let's call it what it is. I still love Hugh. If I even know how to love, which is questionable, but if I have it in me, that's what I'm feeling for him."

"What happened with Hugh?" Coby asked, too relieved that Faith wasn't really interested in Danner to be as bugged as she might be.

"I don't know. He got working hard. Was out of town a

lot and I started watching a lot of bad TV and spending nights home alone. And then it was just sort of gone."

"Pick up the damn phone and call him. Or text him. Communicate."

"You just want me to leave Danner alone," she said, but she was just jerking Coby's chain. Then she exhaled a long breath. "What about Mom and Dad? I don't get it. Are they *seeing* each other?"

"Hell, no. Dad just lost Annette. *Just* lost her."

She shook her head. "If it weren't for the necklace, I would really wonder. I'm wondering anyway."

"Dad loved Annette," Coby insisted. "He's a wreck. You've seen him."

"Yeah, okay. I just . . . think he still loves Mom, too." She lifted her shoulders, daring Coby to convince her otherwise.

"You know Annette was murdered, right?" Coby asked her sister.

"Yes. I heard from Dad and Mom."

"There's going to be an investigation," Coby warned.

"I'm not going to blab my worries to the police about my mother. And don't you, either! See Danner Lockwood all you want, but keep your mouth shut about this. He's the law."

"Oh, for God's sake, Faith. Dad had nothing to do with Annette's death. That's ridiculous. How many times do I have to say it? He loved Annette. Really loved her."

"And Mom?" Faith asked, her eyes serious.

"Mom wasn't at the party," Coby declared.

"But she was in Seaside. Without Barry."

"Faith—" Coby cut herself off, her patience ripped apart. "You're making a whole deal out of the fact that Mom and Dad are nice to each other. Stop it. Mom would never hurt anybody, let alone kill them. Drown them. If she'd been around the beach house, somebody would have seen her. Whoever killed Annette was on-site. They just chose an opportunity when the rest of us were busy and distracted. Juliet shut the blinds and it left the back deck virtually out of view."

"Somebody could have come through the side door of the garage and then out the back door to the deck. No one would have seen them."

"At that precise moment! And where would they park, huh?" Coby demanded. "They'd have to be down the street because the whole driveway was packed with cars."

"You've thought about this," Faith said.

"Well, yes, of course. I want to know who killed Annette."

"I don't." Faith was sure on that. "Any one of us could be next."

"Oh, first Mom's a homicidal killer and now we've got a maniac out there ready to pick us off one by one."

Faith got to her feet, running her hand through her hair again and fluffing out the short, dark waves. "God, my hair's still wet. Unbelievable."

"Anything else?" Coby asked, watching her sister prepare to leave.

"I just want you to be really careful what you say to Danner. That's all."

"I'm not worried about talking to him. We're all okay."

"Are we?" she asked, then slipped out the door.

Annette's murder was one of the top stories on the local news. That night Coby turned on the set as soon as she entered her condo and stopped short to listen to the newscasters. Pauline Kirby from Channel Seven was making Annette's death sound like a salacious mystery, focusing on the missing sapphire pendant necklace.

Detective Clausen's face came on the screen as Pauline

asked, "Do the police feel robbery is the motive for Mrs. Rendell's murder?"

"It's a possibility," he said.

Robbery. Coby didn't hear the rest of the interview as her mind churned over that one. She hadn't considered robbery. Sure, the necklace was missing, and the killer most likely took it, but she'd just assumed Annette's death was related to something else.

Was that the influence of Lucas's death? And Rhiannon's? And a feeling that Annette had a big secret someone didn't want her to share? Could her murder have been just for the necklace?

No. No way. She just didn't believe it. She'd been the background investigator in more than a few divorce cases for the firm, and she knew a little about the reasons for secrecy. There was a money factor, for sure, but oftentimes the bigger emotional issues ruled the day. Clear heads didn't prevail. Anger and revenge and retribution were often at play, and Coby would bet her bottom dollar that some underlying factor along those lines was the motive for Annette's murder as well.

She had changed into sweats when her cell phone buzzed, and this time she recognized Danner's number. "Hi," she said.

"Hi, yourself. I'm on my way back," he told her. "Can I pick up a pizza or something and meet you at your place?"

She had a moment of feeling she should play hard to get. A moment of remembering how much his loss of interest and affection had tormented her. But it was a long time ago and she wanted to see him, and even her older sister had practically given her her blessing.

As long as she didn't tell Detective Lockwood too much.

"I kind of like those gourmet kinds. With sun-dried tomatoes and gorgonzola cheese and kale, or something," she said.

"Since when? I thought you liked pepperoni," he said.

"Well, yeah. That, too."

"Give me your address and I'll be there within the hour."

She rattled it off and managed a small smile. She didn't like gourmet pizza much. She was a purist along the meat, cheese, and tomato-base kind. She'd just been kind of testing him.

And Danner had remembered.

Xavier's was rocking and rolling with the early after-work crowd. Yvette wore a black tank top, short black skirt, black tights, and hooker shoes with heels that would kill her legs within the hour. She changed shoes during the night several times, because she'd learned that when she walked away, men's eyes followed her ass and calves and the view couldn't be ruined by a pair of sensible shoes if she wanted the big tips. She had decent breasts, but it was her backside that raked in the bucks.

The bar was made of zebra wood in a black and tan striped design and it gleamed like glass. The bartender, Rocky, was filling an order for three dirty martinis, and Yvette took a moment to watch his fast-moving hands squeeze the juice out of the olives into each glass. She personally hated martinis. She wasn't much on alcohol of any kind.

She picked up the tray and sauntered back to the table with the three young bucks in their designer suits. They'd already loosened their ties and were giving her their best smiles and winks. One of them had the audacity to place a hand lightly on her hip as he got up from the blood-red leather banquet.

She said a few words, struggled to drag up a smile, then left before things could get dicier.

When was the last time you had sex? she asked herself. *Enjoyed a man's touch?*

She wasn't entirely sure, but it was a long time ago; she knew that much.

And there was a time . . . even longer ago . . . when sex was all she could think about. With *him.* The fucking bastard. The only man she'd ever really loved. And no, it wasn't Lucas Moore, and she regretted ever letting those dimwits from the campfire even think so. But it had been a great cover-up, hadn't it? Of course she'd earned herself Rhiannon's wrath, and Genevieve's, since Genevieve had aligned herself with Rhiannon right after that weekend. Like all of a sudden they were best buds. And then Genevieve had aligned herself with Annette. God, how she hated Annette. And Genevieve.

She shook her head. Annette was dead. No use hating her anymore. Annette couldn't hurt her anymore.

But there were other problems brewing: Benedict's father wanted to take him away from her. After all these years of practically ignoring that he had a child!

Well, she wasn't going to let it happen.

She would kill him before she let it happen.

Kill him.

And she would mean to kill him. Not just let it happen, like it had happened to Annette. Like it had apparently happened to Lucas. And Rhiannon.

"Wake up," the bartender snapped at her.

Yvette jerked awake from her reverie. "Is my order up?"

"Those guys in the corner want to get their knobs polished. I told 'em your legs were clamped tight together. But they're big tippers."

Yvette looked at the middle-aged men in the corner who were desperately trying to hang on to their hair. Their eyes were all over her. "You pimping me out, Rocky?"

"I'm just sayin'."

Could she do that? Have sex with someone she didn't really care about just to get a big tip? Be a whore? If she had enough money she might be able to fight off the fucking bastard in court.

But she would have to have sex with one or some or all of them, and looking at them made Yvette's stomach feel queasy. "Sorry," she bit out to Dean, picking up a tray full of cosmos for the giddy secretaries and office assistants in a large booth near the door who thought every damn thing was a screech-fest riot, but who kept their eyes carefully watching the door for every new male arrival.

Nope. She couldn't do it.

She was just going to have to kill him.

And that would require a plan, something she was good at making.

Chapter 14

Danner was as good as his word; he knocked on Coby's door about an hour after his call. She let him in and the aroma of hot cheese and pepperoni followed him along with a rush of cold wind, as her condo was a town house with its own small stoop. Quickly, closing the door, she directed him to put the pizza down on her tiny table and he did so, then shed his overcoat, which Coby took and hung on a peg on the inside hook of her coat closet, leaving the door open because his coat was soaking wet.

"You got a towel to put under that?" he asked, frowning.

"A dish towel." She grabbed one from her counter and laid it under his coat while he took off his boots and set them on the small tile entryway.

Then they looked at each other. Danner's dark hair was damp and drops of water glistened like silver beads. She was still in her work clothes, a black skirt and jacket, but had taken off her shoes so she was sock-footed, and it gave her a serious height disadvantage.

"I've got Diet Cokes, water, or skim milk. And a bottle of red wine."

"How about water and wine?" he suggested.

"Sounds good."

She pulled out the wine opener and he took it from her while she grabbed plates, napkins, and a couple of forks. She placed her items on the table, then gathered two goblets and Danner poured them each a glass while she filled two tumblers from a pitcher in her refrigerator.

Then they sat down and each collected a slice of pizza. Three bites in, Danner said, "How many years has it been?"

Since we were together. . . . She could have pretended to misunderstand, could have played coy, but it wasn't her way and she couldn't see how that would get her anywhere she wanted to be. "Eight. But who's counting?"

"It doesn't feel like eight. Feels more like . . . seven and a half."

She laughed. "You're only here now because you've got a murder to solve."

"I didn't know there was going to be a homicide when I agreed to escort Faith to the party," he pointed out.

"Why did you?"

"Are you asking if Faith and I are something more than friends?"

"Faith stopped by today and made it clear that's not the case."

"Huh." He finished his slice of pizza and leaned back in the chair, cradling his wine goblet in one hand. "My ego's taken a hit. I thought she kinda had a thing for me."

"She said you weren't over me and decided to step aside."

He froze as he sat. "She did not."

Coby fought a smile. "Okay, that might have been a lie." She bit into her pizza, eyes dancing.

A slow smile spread across his lips. "You're more sure of yourself than you used to be."

"I'm a heck of a lot older. Eight years, to be exact. Although it only feels like seven and a half."

"I kinda want to kiss you," he said.

"Wait till I get rid of the marinara sauce." She set down her slice of pizza, picked up her napkin, wiped her lips, then gazed at him expectantly.

Danner got up and came around the table, looked down at her a moment, touched his hand under her chin, then leaned down and pressed his lips to hers with more urgency than she'd expected. She felt the surprising softness of his mouth and the hardness of the pressure and experienced a jolt of inner awareness that left her breathless when he pulled back.

He looked at her a moment, then retook his seat, grabbing another piece of pizza. Holding it up to bite, he paused, his gaze locked with hers.

They stared at each other a long moment. Coby was rattled and she hadn't expected to be. She'd been keeping it light on purpose, teasing and challenging a little, sure, but wow. She hardly knew where to go next.

"I should have tried harder to keep things going back then," he said.

Coby nodded slowly.

"Why didn't I?" he asked.

"Because you were young, immature, and unaware what a catch I was?"

"I might have just been stupid," he said.

"Okay," she said.

"You didn't have to agree so fast." He grinned and took a swallow of wine.

"I might have been a little needy," she said, to which he shook his head determinedly.

"I'd like to let you take some of the heat, because right now I'm thinking of all the time wasted and kinda pissed off, but it's all my fault."

"Well . . ."

"And with that magnanimous gesture, I want things to start again right now, and I don't want to wait for some grace period of getting to know each other and wasting any more time and all that. I just don't have the patience for it."

"You just want to jump over the preliminaries and head to the bedroom right now?" Coby suggested.

"Well, yeah, actually. If you're so inclined." He gave her a hopeful look, which made her smile turn into a grin. "But I suspect you might need a little more time," he added, feeling her out. "Maybe an hour or two."

"Maybe an hour or two."

Danner finished another slice but Coby found herself breathless and unable to eat more than one. She wrapped the extra slices in foil and put them in the refrigerator. Then they carried their wine to the living room, where she sat on the love seat, her feet tucked beneath her, and Danner sank into her side chair and crossed his ankles on the chair's matching ottoman.

"In all seriousness, I want to know what happened to Annette," Coby told him. She'd been feeling giddy with all the bantering and promise of the beginning of a renewed relationship, but she didn't want to get ahead of herself. She'd worked hard to find who she was. Caution was the word of the day.

"I confess I wasn't paying close attention the other night. I was more focused on you," Danner admitted, "but thinking back, it did feel like something was going on. Something below the surface with Annette."

"She was upset with Yvette."

"Something to do with Dana Sainer."

"That's what it sounded like," Coby said, and they went over the conversation Coby had overheard between Annette and Yvette.

By the time they'd reviewed everything Danner was seated beside her on the love seat, stretching his legs toward the beat-up coffee table that Coby assured him was also used as an ottoman more often than not. His hands were behind his head. "Tell me something I don't know."

"What?" Coby asked, unsure what he meant.

"Tell me something I don't know about Annette, the people at the party, her friends, someone who could be her enemy. Anything. Something you haven't said before."

"I'm kinda tapped out."

"Something."

She peered at him. "Is this some kind of new detective interview technique?"

"Absolutely. We learn it in detective school."

Though he was joking, he was serious at another level. Coby gave his question some thought. "Annette was my sister's age, but you know that. They were classmates. They were at the beach the night of Lucas Moore's death, but they stayed back at the house while the girls in my grade were out around the campfire."

"They never left the house."

"As far as I know. They were with the dads and the other Ette sisters, Juliette and Suzette."

"Who was at the campout?"

"The eight of us: Genevieve, Rhiannon, Yvette, Dana, McKenna, Ellen, Wynona, and me."

"And then some of the guys from your class crashed your party?"

She nodded. She'd told him a little bit about the campout years before, and he'd heard some from Jarrod. Lucas's death had been one of those things that rocked Rutherford High.

"The campout was separate from what was going on at the beach house with Annette and Faith and everyone else."

"Yep. It was just supposed to be some of the girls from my class. When the guys showed up, it was Wynona's turn and they wouldn't let up on her."

"Her turn?" Danner questioned.

Coby caught herself up short. She'd never revealed the nature of the secrets they'd shared. None of them had, as far as she knew. "She was telling a private secret and they overheard. They teased her about it until she was in tears."

"Oh."

"It was crappy high school stuff, but some of the secrets were intense."

"Can you tell me Wynona's secret?" he asked.

"It doesn't have anything to do with Lucas's death. Certainly nothing to do with Annette's."

"Okay."

Now he was looking at her and she turned away from his scrutiny. It was all so far away it felt . . . almost silly . . . embarrassing, really. But were those secrets hers to share now?

"Look, I don't want to rat out my friends. The others who were there. But I'll say this, we were playing Pass the Candle, where we tell our innermost, deepest, darkest secret when the candle gets passed to us. The guys overheard Wynona's secret and teased her mercilessly, and I heard from Annette that Wynona has attempted suicide, twice, and it could be related to her secret and it getting out that night."

"Annette told you that? When?"

"At the party."

"But she didn't go to the original campout. She was at the beach house. So who told her about Wynona?"

"Yvette, I guess," Coby said slowly. "But Wynona's story was kind of the one that wasn't a secret any longer, since the boys knew. Although they overheard some other ones, too."

"What was yours? Can you tell me?"

"Um . . . mine was a lie." She related what she'd said about her dad. "I couldn't come up with anything and the other girls were baring their souls. It was Genevieve's idea and we all joined in. And then, at the end of school, we all got these notes shoved in our lockers that made it clear someone had overheard all our secrets. Genevieve was pissed. We all were."

"You got a note, too?"

"Yep."

"All of you got them?"

"Well, yeah. I guess so. I didn't take a poll at the time, but it seemed like it. Juliet thought she saw Vic Franzen putting one in Yvette's locker, but he's always denied he was the culprit."

"Did any of you compare your notes?"

"We told each other what they said, if that's what you mean. They had to do with the secrets we revealed that night."

Danner asked, "Did you see the notes themselves?"

"I saw mine . . . and Dana's, I think. I just wanted them to go away. I got rid of mine as soon as possible. Burned it, actually. It felt creepy to have it around."

"So, it's possible that not everybody got one."

Coby took a sip of wine, thought about that. "Ellen wasn't at school. She'd moved. So she didn't get one. Why?"

"Maybe one of the other girls was the perpetrator."

Coby shook her head. "No way. I'm inclined to think it was one of the guys. Maybe it was Vic Franzen. He was always trying to work his way further up the hierarchy of the guy's group. Looking for ways to be cooler."

"Shoving notes in a locker just doesn't sound like a guy thing to do," Danner pointed out. "It's kind of girly."

Coby hadn't thought of it in those terms. "Possibly," she conceded. "What does this have to do with Annette?"

"Nothing, maybe. You said she was adamant about bringing secrets out into the open. Sounds like a lot of secrets started that night."

Coby had an instant mental memory of the campfire, recalling her own anxiety. "We were never the best of friends," she admitted. "The dads were friends. They're the ones who kept the group going, and we were just putting in our time. When Genevieve suggested Pass the Candle, we all went with it, not because we wanted to, or at least I didn't. We just were stuck together and kind of wasting time. And then the guys came and things changed."

"Who were the guys?"

"Jarrod, as you know. Kirk Grassi, Vic, Theo Rivers, Paul Lessington." She thought a moment. "Oh, and Galen Torres, and Lucas."

"Lucas was dating Rhiannon at the time," Danner said. "And she died a few years later."

He sounded like he was trying to remember, so Coby said, "She fell from a hiking trail."

He nodded. "I remember thinking it was a hell of a coincidence that they died the same way."

"Yeah . . ." Coby was pensive.

He gave her a look. "What?"

"I was just thinking . . . the night Lucas died. The night of the campout . . ." She exhaled. "We all kind of had a crush on him. I kissed him," she admitted sheepishly. "And I saw him with Genevieve, too. Lucas was . . . not committed to any relationship and we all knew it. All of us except Rhiannon, maybe. Or maybe she did know, but she always insisted she was his girlfriend. But the next day, when Lucas was dead, Yvette announced that *she* and Lucas were secret boyfriend and girlfriend. She got into it with Rhiannon, who was a wreck. We all were. Yvette was convincing, though, and we all knew Lucas played around, so I think everyone assumed Lucas was Benedict's father. I know I did. But Yvette told me straight out at Annette's birthday party that he wasn't."

"You asked her?"

"More like she attacked me with the facts."

He absorbed that a moment, then said, "It all keeps circling back to Yvette."

"Yes," Coby said, nodding. "It does."

"Two accidental deaths. Lucas and Rhiannon. And then a murder. Annette Rendell. Lucas was Yvette's secret boyfriend, and therefore the other woman in the Lucas/Rhiannon/Yvette triangle, and Annette was Yvette's sister, with a big secret she was about to reveal."

"Maybe Annette learned that Lucas *is* Benedict's father," Coby suggested.

"Worth committing homicide of your own sister over?"

"No," Coby admitted. "But Yvette and Annette didn't get along. None of the Ette sisters seem to get along with Yvette, from what I can tell."

Danner checked his watch, then reluctantly sat up. "I'll go see Yvette later this week. I'm involved with another homicide at work, a home invasion, that's my real job."

"The one that's been on the news? Where the wife and daughter were killed and the husband/father was shot?"

"That's the one. Do you know what day Annette's memorial service is?"

"Wednesday or Thursday. I haven't heard for sure."

"Okay. I'll see you then." Her surprise must have showed on her face because he leaned toward her and kissed her once, hard. "I'm going to give you time to think this over."

"This?"

"This," he agreed, getting to his feet.

"Oh. All right."

He smiled at her disappointment as he collected his now nearly dry jacket from the closet door peg. "There's somebody out there with something to hide. Something they may have killed for. Be careful."

"I will be."

"See you at the memorial service."

He left and Coby gazed after him longingly. He was right, of course. Rushing into things never worked. She just hoped this delay wasn't a method to keep her at arm's length. Sure, he seemed to be all about starting again. Sure, it had been terrific playing around with each other. But she'd opened her heart too fast, too big to him once before and she couldn't afford to do it again.

Fool me once, shame on you. Fool me twice, shame on me.

"I hate that saying," she said aloud.

The squad room was just short of a madhouse when Danner stopped in around 10 P.M. Thanksgiving was still a couple of weeks away, but a pre-Thanksgiving party had turned into a brawl, apparently, and a number of drunken partygoers had resisted attempts by the police to slow down the raucous partying, which ended with beer bottles and the like being thrown at the officers; never a good idea.

Danner ducked around a handcuffed woman swaying on her feet at a nearby desk and headed to his own. He fervently wished Elaine were back, and was both annoyed and resigned to see that Joshua Celek was still around, his freckled cherubic face pulled into a frown of consternation.

"Curtis was here," he said to Danner. "He wanted to talk to you."

Detective Trey Curtis was a homicide detective who'd been pulled onto gang detail for the last few months, and it looked like it might become a full-time position. Danner wondered what the hell he could possibly want with him.

"Where's he now?" Danner asked Celek.

"Around. What are you doing here? Thought you were in Tillamook."

He said it with a kind of sniff, like he thought Danner was trying to escape working on the Lloyd home invasion. "I'm waiting for a file from the TCSD."

"Ah . . ."

Ignoring him, Danner signed onto his computer terminal and checked his e-mail. The scanned file was there and he quickly sent it to the printer. He didn't want to spend any more time at the station tonight than necessary, and he left the squad room at a fast walk down the hall to the copy center. The printer was spitting out pages at a quick clip and he checked to see they were the report from the Tillamook County Medical Examiner. Dr. Jeffrey Gilmore's name was attached to the file, so Danner waited until all the pages were out and then gathered them and stuck them under the stapler. He was just smacking the top of the stapler with his fist when Curtis stuck his head inside.

"Got a minute?" the dark-haired detective asked. He was lean and gruff and had a reputation for getting the job done.

"Sure."

Danner followed Curtis down another hall to an open room, away from the action in the squad room. It was an interrogation room not in current use. Curtis flipped on the lights.

"Got some questions for me?" Danner asked, half-amused, half-curious.

"Just wanted to get away from the squirrels," he said, referring to the drunken brawlers being charged in the squad room. "You're working on the Lloyd case, and I know Drano gave you the okay for that Deception Bay homicide, too. I wanted to know if I could take Celek off your hands for a while."

"Not a problem," Danner assured him.

"We've got some burglaries that I think he'd be better suited for," Curtis explained. "The clubs are trying to blame the gangs, which only pisses them off. But the jobs are small time, amateurish. Mostly equipment theft. Not really in my gangs' scope, if you know what I mean."

"Not drugs and prostitution?"

"You got it," Curtis said.

"What kind of clubs are getting hit?"

"Nightclubs with local bands, mostly, around Portland, Beaverton, Laurelton, Gresham."

Local bands . . . Danner couldn't help but think of his brother, but he kept that thought to himself. Instead, he said magnanimously, "As far as I'm concerned, you can have Celek as long as you want."

Curtis tipped his dark head and grinned slyly. "Like that, is it?"

"He does the job just fine," Danner said diplomatically.

"Just not like Metzger would. I hear you. When is she coming back?"

"End of next week."

Curtis nodded. "If you need help on the Lloyd investigation, tell Drano I'm available."

"It'll never happen. You're too good at what you do."

"Yeah. Shit. You're right." He tapped the jamb of the door as a good-bye and left.

Danner took his scanned file back toward his desk, the noise level increasing with every footfall that drew him closer to the squad room. As he entered, he determined this was not the place to get anything done tonight, so he went down to the parking lot, jumped into his Wrangler, and tried to stay within the speed limit on his drive toward his apartment in Laurelton, the westernmost community outside Portland on Highway 26.

His apartment was a renovated bungalow, taken over by developers at the height of the real estate boom in 2005 and turned into condos that sold like hotcakes at first, then went into short sales and foreclosure, and now were rented out by disheartened owners. Danner had moved from an apartment about ten blocks away whose walls were tissue-paper thin, but it had been all he felt he could afford at the time. He'd socked his money away and when the opportunity arose to sign a two-year-lease at the bungalow, he took it. Now he pulled into the central carport and walked down a narrow concrete sidewalk to the door of his unit. He stepped inside, flipped on the light, wished he had a dog, like always, and tossed the file on the peninsula of solid granite that jutted on an angle from the cabinets, separating the kitchen from the living room.

He had two bar stools, fake black leather with arms, and he sank into one now like it was a Barcalounger. Flipping open the file, he had to blink several times because Coby Rendell's face seemed to be superimposed on everything he was looking at. Recognizing his own idiocy, he allowed himself a few moments to review the evening they'd spent together and then, with a smile on his lips, he dragged his attention to the file's contents.

Twenty minutes later he felt that awareness that always grabbed him like a cold hand on the back of the neck.

Among the pages was a small, typewritten observation at the bottom of a page that listed the condition of the body.

Stubs of hair at victim's crown. Section missing.

He heard his own voice: "You looked in the envelope?"

And Coby: "It was a lock of blond hair. Blondish, I guess, with some light brown in it."

He stared unseeingly across the bar and into his own kitchen.

The question was: when had that lock of Lucas's hair been taken? Postmortem? Or had someone snipped it off as a souvenir?

* * *

Rituals. Rites. I will see all the bitches soon, those that remain.

Once upon a time they were the royalty of the school.

I'm always with them, though they don't know it. Annette would have betrayed me, and when the opportunity arose, I had to kill her. Her gurgling death was necessary.

I always do what is necessary.

I saved Lucas from a life not worth living. He was staring at the sky, broken. His beauty fading. If he had lived, he would have not been the same. I turned him over and pressed his face into the cold salt water.

And I took care of that other bitch, that outsider, with her big lips and thrusting thighs who dared to poach from me, taking what wasn't hers. I found the means to crush her throat.

But when I see the realm from Rutherford High, I will decide who dies first.

Coby, I whisper to myself. Soon. . . .

Chapter 15

The memorial service for Annette took place on Wednesday on a dry, windswept November afternoon with leaves being whirled around in small eddies in the parking lot and mud puddles slowly drying in the respite of two full days without rain.

Coby held the collar of her coat close as she skirted the remaining puddles and headed to the door of Cramer House, a hall in Northwest Portland that had once been an Elks Lodge but had been taken over, renovated, and was now an event destination. She'd worn a black skirt, a pale blue sweater, and a black raincoat that hid everything and offered another layer of warmth.

Jean-Claude, Suzette, Juliet and Nicholette, and Nicholette's daughter, Paige, were standing just inside the double doors, greeting people as they entered an anteroom that led into a larger room with a stage on one end. Dave was a few steps farther inside, and after murmuring condolences to the Deneuves, Coby slipped into her dad's arms as he gave her a heartfelt hug.

Yvette and Benedict were nowhere to be seen.

Faith appeared a few moments later and also hugged

their father, then Coby and Faith found a couple of chairs toward the rear of the room where they had a bit of privacy.

"Do you know I had to talk Mom out of coming," Faith said.

Coby shook her head in disbelief. "She didn't like Annette. At all."

"What the hell is going on with them?" Faith muttered, glancing back to Dave.

"I'm pretty sure I don't want to know," Coby murmured.

McKenna and Big Bob Forrester came in together and squeezed in a few rows ahead of Faith and Coby, McKenna giving Coby a quick smile of acknowledgment. And behind them, something of a surprise: Donald Greer with Wynona. Wynona wore a long brown wool coat, her face as cold and rigid as a gravestone. If she saw Coby she gave no sign of it.

Annette's voice suddenly clamored inside Coby's head as if she were speaking to her again: *Wynona made two suicide attempts, one with pills, one by slitting her wrists. Neither effective. I don't want to sound like a complete bitch, but they were cries for help, not a serious attempt to kill herself, and she got a lot of attention. Then she decided to dedicate her life to social work, helping others, but she's not very good at it.*

"What's the matter with you?" Faith whispered to Coby.

"Nothing."

Just before the Deneuves took their seats Yvette blew in, Benedict in tow. Yvette wore a black turtleneck, black jeans, and black boots; Benedict was in a navy sports jacket over blue jeans. He wore a red tie and yanked at his collar with two fingers, looking about as uncomfortable as any eleven-year-old could.

Surreptitiously, Coby glanced around for Danner. She'd seen Jarrod and Genevieve arrive, but if Danner was on the premises, he was keeping a low profile. Settling in, she drew a breath and waited for the service to begin.

Danner drove with controlled urgency toward Cramer House, aware that he would likely miss the opening remarks and/or prayer. He'd planned on calling Coby and seeing if she needed a ride, but things had started running at work almost from the moment Danner, and then Lieutenant Drano, had okayed Celek to move to burglary and leave Danner on the Lloyd home invasion/homicide case on his own. Things were coming together fast now, a snowball rolling down a hill with increasing speed. He was counting the hours until Elaine Metzger returned, but in the meantime those hours were flying by, leaving him no time for the Deneuve homicide or much of anything else.

He'd had to put off seeing Coby and he had yet to tell her about the swatch of hair that seemed like it might be Lucas Moore's. He'd called Clausen with the information and he'd said simply, "Huh," and that pretty much was how Danner felt, too.

Huh.

Meanwhile, inconsistencies in the Lloyd case had started coming together and the picture that was developing wasn't pretty. Mrs. Lloyd had been shot in the back of the head in her bedroom, unresisting, while downstairs, shortly thereafter, Mr. Jarvis Lloyd was shot in the arm and smacked hard against the head with what appeared to be the missing 9mm. The daughter, appearing apparently unexpectedly, had taken two bullets as she turned and tried to run out the front door from which she'd arrived. She'd died on the entry floor.

Jarvis Lloyd's version was that he'd been unconscious at the time of his daughter's killing and only came to when the house was full of police. When he was told what happened, he broke down and tried to prevent the EMTs from taking his daughter's body from the house. He'd never been able to do more than weep every time Danner, or Celek, or the officers who'd first arrived at the scene spoke to him.

Police had canvassed the area, asking if anyone heard or saw anything that might give them a clue to the perpetrators. The Lloyd house was on a quiet tree-lined street on Portland's east side, a neighborhood that was currently going through a gentrification with Victorian and Craftsman style homes being beautifully restored. Most of the residents were young urban professionals and weren't home at three o'clock in the afternoon. Lloyd was there to take his wife to the doctor for ongoing treatments for breast cancer.

Lloyd said two Hispanic men burst through the door, shouting in Spanish, that one shot at him straight on and the other must have attacked him and knocked him out. He didn't remember anything past the sound of the shot and burst of pain in his arm. He didn't know they'd killed his wife, or his daughter, until he was told at the hospital by the police.

Danner had first interviewed the man at the hospital after he'd had surgery on his arm. Jarvis wept and wiped his eyes and said next to nothing, and when Danner remarked, "Your wife must have heard the shot, but she just stayed in the bedroom and let the killer shoot her in the back of the head."

"She was in her bedroom, getting ready," Jarvis said. "That's where she was."

"But she didn't run. She didn't try to come to your aid. It looks like she was seated at her makeup desk and let the killer walk in, get behind her, and shoot her. Looks like she just toppled off the chair."

"She was getting ready," he said again, starting to blubber.

Danner didn't press the issue at that time. Maybe Mrs. Lloyd had just froze at the sound of the shot. Maybe.

Lloyd couldn't talk about his daughter at all. His lower jaw trembled and his eyes were wild and he cried silently or made hiccupping noises. His grief was real.

Danner had tried to talk through his thoughts with Joshua Celek, but Celek didn't quite get the process, so he gave up. He'd taken the trip last weekend with Faith to kind of step away from the investigation for a few hours, clear his head, and look how that had turned out.

But then, an unexpected break in the case: the deaf woman who lived catty-corner from the Lloyds had seen someone on the street she didn't recognize near the time of the killings. She might be deaf, but she was one helluva nosy neighbor and she kept her binoculars up to her eyes at almost all hours, hiding within the third-story bedroom of her house, watching the world go by in a perfect audio void. Had it not been for Mrs. Berney, the killer would not have been seen.

But Mrs. Berney was new to the street. She'd moved into her daughter and son-in-law's house the previous month and quickly made herself the neighborhood watch-dog, albeit a silent one. One of the street cops discovered her by accident when he was interviewing the son-in-law, who hadn't even bothered to mention that his mother-in-law lived to spy.

She told the officer she'd seen the woman who flew out of the Lloyd house. Had described her black wool coat and boots and baseball cap. A strange choice for a woman who was dressed as nicely as this one, the baseball cap, Mrs. Berney said with a sniff, unless she had something to hide. Mrs. Berney had noted the time and date and written it on the back of an envelope, just in case.

When Danner interviewed the older woman, her daughter took him aside and said that her mother was having mental issues and might be making the whole thing up. She was wont to write notes and squiggles and concoct elaborate plots.

But the crime scene techs had lifted a woman's boot print from outside the front door that hadn't matched any of the mother's or daughter's footwear, and Danner thought maybe Mrs. Berney was sharper than people gave her credit for. Not that a good defense attorney couldn't use Mrs. Berney's suspect mental capacity against her in a court of law, but Danner didn't intend to go that direction.

He chose to keep interviewing Jarvis Lloyd, whose attitude went into a sharp decline when the police started looking through his personal records. How could they think he could be involved in the death of his beloved Angie? His only child? He loved her more than life itself. If he could, he would trade places with her.

Danner responded that he believed him. But he also felt Jarvis was a first-class bastard who had set up the murder of his wife and then run into problems when his partner in crime, the woman in the baseball hat, killed the wife but then took out the daughter, too, when Angie unexpectedly showed up at home and caught the female killer with her father. Angie turned to run but was shot twice, and then the killer simply stepped over her, walked out the front door, and left.

To be seen by Mrs. Berney.

Lloyd was beside himself. Sobbing and shuddering or silently staring with horror-stretched eyes, as if he had looked into the bowels of hell. Maybe he had. If he was as guilty as Danner believed, he'd killed his wife and his beloved daughter.

Danner had put more pressure on the man this week. Subtly, at first, but closer and closer to the bone as they got nearer to Lloyd giving it all up. Jarvis had a lawyer who was scrambling to keep control, but the man was disintegrating. Sooner, hopefully, than later, he would give up the name of the killer and then the whole thing would be over.

The only progress he'd made on Annette's murder was to phone Yvette and talk to her. She'd been hostile and unwilling, and pretty much told him to fuck off. She said she'd spoken to Detective Clausen and that's all she was going to do.

Now Danner wheeled into the lot, checked his watch, ground his teeth, and then hurried hatless through a faint rain to the front door. He let himself in and opened one side of a pair of double doors, then slipped inside the main room and found a place to stand in the back, behind the row of pews.

Pushing the Lloyd murder and Yvette's objurgation to a corner of his mind, he searched the room for a glimpse of Coby.

The crowd slowly quieted and someone coughed as Coby stared toward the front of the room, her mind full of uncomfortable memories of Annette's floating body. She wondered vaguely about the necklace, and the envelope with its lock of hair, and why Annette had mentioned Dana in a way that incensed Yvette.

Her attention sharpened as her father walked to the front of the room and up several steps to a raised dais.

"Thank you for coming," he said. "Annette would have appreciated it." A long pause and then, sounding almost apologetic, he said, "I did love her. It's no secret we had a pretty big age gap, but she was . . . a wonderful partner. I'm going to miss her." He paused a moment, collecting himself, then invited anyone else to come up and say a few words. Jean-Claude took him up on his word and shared stories from Annette's youth that were funny and touching, but once in front of the group he couldn't seem to let go of the spotlight.

Coby let herself have a moment of remembrance of her evening eating pizza with Danner, then she reluctantly moved from that to her meeting with Rhys Webber, Nicholette's unfaithful client with the myriad girlfriends. Coby had tried to tell the man to settle with his ex-wife, give her what she was asking for because it wasn't all that much in the larger scheme of things and it would prevent them going to court and him having to air his dirty laundry. But Rhys had practically laughed at her. He wanted to screw his ex-wife financially like he'd screwed every other woman who'd crossed his path. He wouldn't listen to Coby, so she told him in no uncertain terms that he was making a mistake, which pissed him off big-time. He was into domination over women; he didn't take it well when one of them talked *sense* to him.

From Webber she thought about her friend Willa, whom she'd called the previous night. She'd wanted to fill Willa in on everything that had happened, but they had just begun discussing Annette's murder when one of Willa's children started wailing as if her life were over. In reality she'd simply been bopped on the head by her sister with a plush toy. The emotional hurt was huge, however, and Willa had needed to play parent. She'd begged off, asking for a rain check, but Coby suspected maybe Willa didn't really have the time or even interest in her affairs that she'd hoped for.

The one thing Willa did say, however, after she'd explained about overhearing the argument between Yvette and Annette, was, "Why don't you call this Dana person? See if she can tell you something, since it doesn't sound like Yvette will talk to you."

Coby had mulled that over and finally sent Dana an

e-mail asking for her current phone number. Dana had responded with a number with a Southern California area code, and last night, when Coby called her, she'd been clearly mystified by Coby's sudden need to connect.

"I heard about Annette Deneuve," she said. "Is that why you're calling me?"

"You heard she was murdered?"

"Dad said so. He's totally shaken up."

Coby remembered how white-faced Hank Sainer had looked after Annette's death. She wondered if she'd looked the same. Easing into the conversation, Coby brought up a few things from high school, but Dana wasn't in the mood to be coerced.

"Just tell me why you're calling, really," she said. "Does this have something to do with the campout?"

"The campout? No. It's about Annette. She was my stepmother," Coby reminded her, since Dana had referred to her by her maiden name. "And she was talking to me at her birthday party about secrets. How they needed to be brought to the light, so to speak, so they didn't have so much power. She gave me the impression she was about to reveal something big. Or at least something she thought was big."

"Like when I admitted my eating disorders?" Dana suggested coolly.

"A little like that, yeah," Coby said, not backing down. "But then later I heard Annette arguing with Yvette and she brought up your name. She said, 'And what about Dana? The truth's going to come out.'"

"What truth?" Dana asked.

"I guess that's what I'm asking you. You don't have a clue what they were talking about?"

"Look, I told you all about my anorexia and bulimia at the campout. I've got things kind of under control now and I've got my kids and I'm happy, but back then I was in real pain. And all of you gave me this ho-hum attitude, like my problem didn't even count! That it wasn't *secret* enough, or maybe I just wasn't cool enough for the rest of you. I don't know what the hell Annette was talking about. Are you sure she mentioned me? I'm in recovery from my eating disorders, and the truth about that was aired long ago, so, no, there's no other secret about me. Certainly nothing Yvette would care about."

"It's just what I heard."

"Maybe you heard wrong," Dana stated flatly.

Coby hadn't been able to learn anything further and shortly afterward Dana found a reason to hang up, which was something of a relief. Coby didn't believe Annette had been talking about Dana's eating disorder; it wasn't even a secret when Dana had thought it was a secret!

Maybe the thing to do was ask Yvette and see if she would tell her anything. Maybe Danner would bring it up when he interviewed her, or maybe he already had, Coby thought with a sudden jolt back to the present. If Danner had mentioned it to Yvette, Yvette could be seething over Coby's eavesdropping and just waiting, now, for a moment to pounce on her about it.

Well, okay, she told herself. If that happened, she would be prepared, at least, and maybe she could actually learn something. Not that it would be pleasant. Talking to Yvette was never pleasant.

Jean-Claude finally wound down and then Suzette said how much she was already missing her sister and shed a few tears, and then Nicholette and Juliet added a few words, then Genevieve walked to the front. She gazed across the top of their heads and said, "Annette was my friend. We knew each other a little bit in high school, but we really connected later. The last few years she's really been a help to me, an inspiration. I treasured her friendship, and I want to know what happened to her. We all do."

With that she found her seat again and Coby shot a sideways glance at Yvette, who sat like a statue while Benedict fidgeted beside her.

When no one else rose to speak, Dave stood and announced that refreshments were now available in the basement and the crowd slowly dispersed and trooped downstairs. There were hors d'oeuvres and wine, and tiny pastries and tea and coffee from the Lovejoy's tearoom/wine bar. Coby chose coffee and a tea cake and was just leaving the serving table when she saw Danner standing next to one of the bistro tables set up around the room, his gaze on her as Jarrod spoke in his left ear.

Her heart kicked and she lifted her coffee cup in acknowledgment. Then she found a spot at another bistro table opposite the white cloth–covered serving tables laden with food and drink. She'd barely set her cup down when Faith found her and crowded close to her. Before Faith could say more than, "I'm glad that's over," Yvette strode up to them, her expression dark.

"You sicced your boyfriend on me," she said to Coby.

"Um . . . you mean Danner Lockwood?" Coby asked.

"He *interviewed* me," Yvette said through a tight jaw. "I don't care for you meddling in my affairs. You must think you're some kind of detective, but leave it to the professionals. And I don't count Danner Lockwood in that. As far as I'm concerned, he's worse than his brother. Leave me and Benedict alone. We're grieving, too, y'know. Annette was my sister, and I don't care that you overheard us arguing! I loved her. I wish she were here right now!" At that she pressed her lips together as if she were afraid she might blurt out more.

Faith said flatly, "Don't feel so special. The police grilled our dad, too. I imagine we'll all hear from them eventually, won't we?"

"Stay away from me," Yvette warned Coby, then turned abruptly away and joined Benedict near the serving table.

"She's sure fun, isn't she?" Faith murmured, stealing Coby's tea cake and biting into it. "Is Danner really investigating Annette's murder?"

"He's helping out," Coby said. Then, "Dad didn't tell me he was grilled."

"I may have overstated that a bit. But they did talk to him. Of course they would. That's what police do."

"When he talked to Clausen?"

"That guy from the Tillamook County Sheriff's Department." Faith lifted an uncaring shoulder.

"Yeah. Him."

"I guess so. Ask Dad. I wouldn't have said anything, but she really bugged me. What a self-serving bitch." Faith finished off Coby's tea cake. "So, what argument did you overhear between Annette and the bitch?"

"They were arguing about the truth coming out, and I told Danner. He said he was going to interview Yvette, among others, and he must've said something to her and she knew where it came from."

"She caught you eavesdropping. Shame on you." Faith grinned. "I wonder what truth she was talking about."

Danner arrived at their table at that moment. Faith lifted a brow and gave Coby a look that said, *Be careful what you say.*

Ignoring her, Coby told Danner what had just transpired with Yvette, finishing with, "She's not the most forthcoming."

"She's prickly," he agreed.

Coby added, "Faith said Detective Clausen grilled my dad about Annette's homicide."

"It's usual," he said.

Faith said dryly, "It's always the spouse, isn't it? That's where you go first."

"A lot of times," Danner admitted.

"But not this time," Coby said in her father's defense. "Someone else killed Annette. I don't think Dad was anywhere near that hot tub."

"That's the problem, though," Faith said. "None of us really knows who was where, unless we were with them at the exact moment Annette was drowned, and when was that exact moment?" As if she couldn't help herself, Faith moved her gaze toward their father, and Coby could practically read her sister's mind, could sense the niggling doubt inside.

Danner said, "If your father wanted to kill his wife, I'm pretty sure he would have chosen a different scenario rather than a huge party where the chance of getting caught was so big."

"Good point," Coby said with relief. "Why would anyone choose the party?"

Danner answered, "Sudden opportunity? Could be a crime of passion. Things happen."

"That doesn't help Dad," Faith said. "I don't even want to speculate anymore." With that, she left them and went to join Dave and Jean-Claude, Suzette and Galen, and Nicholette, who were all standing together.

Danner said, "I got the M.E.'s report on Lucas Moore's death. A small section of his hair had been sheared off."

Coby looked at him. "What? *Hair?*" Then, "Are you saying what I think you're saying?"

"There's no way of knowing whether Moore's hair was the lock you saw in the envelope."

"But if it was Lucas's hair, if someone was *saving* it all these years . . . and Annette found out about it . . ." She glanced around the room, staring at the people she'd gone to school with and their fathers through new eyes. "Flat-out creepy."

"I thought I might mention it to some people," Danner said. "See what kind of reaction pops up."

"Is there a connection?" Coby asked. "Between Annette's death and Lucas's? *Is there?*"

"What we know is a chunk of Lucas Moore's hair was cut from the crown of his head. Whether it was postmortem, I don't know."

"Someone at the party had that envelope. Annette was distracted as soon as she had it in her hands," Coby said.

"But *after* she said she was going to tell secrets."

Coby nodded. "Yeah."

"So, that was something else."

"I guess so," Coby said, unwilling to completely let that go. This seemed so big, yet maybe she was making connections too soon.

"It sounds like whatever she was arguing with Yvette about wasn't the lock of hair in the envelope," Danner said.

They both turned and looked at Yvette, who'd collected Benedict and was saying her good-byes to her sisters and father. Feeling their gazes on her, she glanced over. Her face tightened and she gave them the cold shoulder on her way out.

Seeing Danner with Coby, Jarrod headed their way and Genevieve ended her conversation with McKenna to follow after him. As if they'd been invited to the party, Kirk Grassi, Paul Lessington, and Vic Franzen came over in a group, as well. Coby was a little surprised they'd all showed; it wasn't their kind of event.

Kirk spoke up before anyone could say anything, "We're at the Cellar this weekend. Come and see us."

This was apparently meant for Coby, as he was looking at her. "I'd like to," she said.

"Friday night," Kirk said and slid a look toward Danner.

"You dating?" he asked him. "Or just checking out the suspects?"

"Are we all suspects?" Gen demanded with a frown.

"Sure," Kirk said. "Paul and Vic, too. They were at the beach that night. In Seaside. I joined up with them."

"Jesus, Grassi," Vic protested. "God damn it."

Kirk turned up his palms. "If I'm lying, I'm dying."

"We weren't anywhere near the party," Paul said, flushing angrily.

"Well, let's just all make ourselves look guilty," Kirk said in a singsong voice.

Danner said tightly, "Let's go outside and talk."

"What's wrong with here?" Kirk demanded.

"Don't be such an ass," Coby told him tightly, which surprised everyone because generally it was Gen who got in people's faces. "It's a memorial service," she pointed out.

"Good going," Genevieve said admiringly as they all moved toward the exit, stopping to say their good-byes to Dave and the Deneuve family.

Chapter 16

The wind had picked up while they were inside and Coby watched as it whipped at Danner's hair, tossing it into his eyes. He had gone down the front of the steps and into the parking lot. Jarrod, Genevieve, Kirk, Paul, and Vic had followed him, creating an impromptu meeting near Danner's Wrangler. Suzette, Galen, Nicholette with Paige, Juliet, and a couple of the dads, Hank Sainer and Donald Greer, had apparently taken the others' exodus as a sign to do the same and were a few steps back, looking like they wanted to join in. Wynona stayed on the front porch of Cramer Hall but was looking their way, her dark hair waving around her face like Medusa's snakes.

Or maybe it was just the dark scowl on her face that gave Coby that impression. There was no need to be fanciful, Coby reminded herself.

Coby was standing near Genevieve as Danner said, "If you haven't heard yet, Annette's death is being treated as a homicide."

"God." Gen inhaled sharply and Coby slid her a glance.

"You're kidding." Vic's jaw dropped.

"It's gotta be a mistake," Jarrod said, but his eyes were on his wife, who'd already posed the idea of murder.

"Who did it?" Gen demanded, ignoring her husband.

"We're working on figuring it out," Danner said. "I'm helping out with the Tillamook County Sheriff's Department. Some of you may have already spoken to Detective Clausen or someone else from the TCSD. There are a few theories being tossed out. Nothing concrete, so far. I'm open to listen to anything, so if you know something, talk to me. Even if you just think you know something."

"The police must have some favorite theory," Genevieve insisted.

Nicholette handed Paige her keys and said, "Go to the car. I'll be right there."

Paige gave her a look from expressive dark brown eyes that said she resented being shunted out of the way, then dutifully headed across the parking lot. "Big ears," Nicholette said by way of explanation.

Danner pulled out some business cards and handed them out. "I'm available on my cell. If you want to talk, let's make it a different venue."

Kirk complained, "Come on, man. Give us something. We want to help, but who would want to kill her? If you have any theories, throw 'em at us!"

Danner's gaze was turned toward Wynona and the Cramer House porch. Big Bob and McKenna had stopped to say a few words to her and they turned their faces toward the parking lot group. Danner seemed to come to a mental decision, saying, "The night of her party Annette said she was going to reveal a secret. If anyone knows what that secret might be, now would be a good time to share it. She also had an envelope with a lock of hair inside that seemed to disturb her."

"I saw her with an envelope," Kirk said. "Didn't know it was a lock of hair. Whose is it?"

"Hasn't been determined," Danner said.

"But you have an idea, don't you?" This was from Juliet, who'd stepped within earshot along with the rest of her group from the memorial service. Now she gazed at Danner with a kind of dawning horror and repeated Kirk's question,"Whose is it?"

Danner shook his head. "The envelope disappeared the night of Annette's death, so we really don't know."

"Like the necklace?" Jarrod asked, eyebrows raised.

"You make it all sound like a conspiracy," Nicholette said, wrapping her coat closer around her.

"Vic and I weren't there," Paul put in again, with some urgency.

"Shut up." Kirk flicked a glance of annoyance at him. "No one's saying you did it, okay? All right, then whose hair do you *think* it is?" he asked Danner, and when he didn't reply, he turned his attention to Coby. "You know, don't you?"

"No. Of course not." She shook her head.

"Why 'of course not'?" Suzette asked. "You and Annette were talking away that night."

"She said she wanted to bring a secret to light," Coby defended herself. "She didn't mention the envelope."

"How do you know what was in the envelope?" Genevieve demanded of Danner. "Who saw it?"

"I did," Coby admitted. "I saw the way Annette was acting after she found it and when she put it down for a moment I looked inside. I thought it was . . . I don't know. I thought it might explain what she'd been talking about."

"You were snooping."

They all turned at the sound of Faith's voice, but she was looking at Coby and smiling. "She's always been a closet Nancy Drew," Faith said to the group at large as she joined them. "Dad's getting ready to leave," she added.

"I'll be there in a minute," Coby said, but Faith didn't seem to be in any hurry to return, either.

"So?" Kirk demanded of Coby. "You found the hair and told Detective Lockwood. Bet you've got some kind of theory."

"Here comes Jean-Claude," Faith murmured.

He was walking like an old man, coming toward them slowly, his shoulders stooped, to meet up with three of his daughters. Suzette stepped forward and tucked her arm through his, giving him a bright smile that nevertheless was filled with anxiety.

"Have you figured out who hurt my girl yet?" Jean-Claude asked Danner.

"Annette had an envelope with a lock of hair," Nicholette told him. "She was carrying it around the night she was killed." She quickly brought him up to date on what was being discussed.

"The lock of hair might not have anything to do with Annette's death," Suzette said hurriedly. "I don't even believe she was killed. It was an accident. It had to be! No one wanted to harm Annette."

Jean-Claude patted her arm in a distracted way, then bowled them over by saying, "Annette told me about the lock of hair. She said she thought it was from that boy who died. Lucas Moore."

"Daddy!" Juliette was shocked.

In the same moment, Suzette cried, "That's stupid! I don't believe it!"

"It's what she said," Jean-Claude responded wearily. "Some of her last words to me."

That stopped them all cold. Coby watched as her father next headed down the steps, heading their way, one of the last of the mourners to leave the hall. But her mind was whirling. How had Annette made that connection? Did she know something more? Was that her secret? She and

Danner had arrived at that theory only after Annette's death had made them think about Lucas having died in the same area, with some of the same people around.

Dave Rendell hesitated a moment, as if unsure at the last minute that he wanted to join their assembly, but then Faith stepped briskly toward him and he was compelled to come with her. By now Big Bob and McKenna had moved on and Wynona was nowhere to be seen.

"Where did Annette get the envelope?" Coby asked Jean-Claude.

"She didn't say," he answered. "She told me she didn't know what to do. She was deeply bothered. I told her not to put so much emphasis on it. She didn't really know anything."

"It's all conjecture," Jarrod agreed, looking uncomfortable.

Genevieve asked Danner, "Is that your theory, then? That the two deaths are connected? That maybe Lucas's death *wasn't* an accident?" Her whole body was shivering inside her full-length tan wool coat. It wasn't that cold, and Coby could only conclude she was shaking from emotion.

Nicholette said, her gaze toward her car, "All I care about is finding who killed my sister and why. Why? Maybe the police are making too much of this and it really was an accident."

Dave said tonelessly, "She was trying to claw her way out and someone held her head down. I'd call that murder." A small silence held them in its grip. Jean-Claude put a hand on Dave's shoulder and Dave seemed to shake himself back to the present. He turned to Faith and said, "I think I'm ready to head out now." For a moment it looked like Faith was going to protest, then the two of them moved off, toward the end of the lot and Faith's white BMW, having apparently come together.

Danner said as a means of closure, "Think of anything else, just call me."

"It can't have been Lucas's hair," Genevieve muttered. "Where did it come from? It can't have been his!"

Hank Sainer, who'd been listening in silence until now, asked, "Has anyone seen Yvette?"

Jean-Claude's eyes were on Faith's and Dave's retreating forms but now he jerked his attention to Hank. "She left," he stated flatly. "She took her son home."

Hank's brows lifted at Jean-Claude's tone. "I thought . . . since the rest of your daughters are here . . ."

Juliet heaved an exaggerated sigh. "Yvette doesn't really play by the rules. She never liked Annette all that much. She doesn't like anybody."

Jean-Claude blinked at her in surprise and Suzette seized the moment, saying quickly, "Oh, you all know Yvette. She likes to act so tough. You can't make more of it than it is."

"Nobody's suggesting Yvette killed Annette," Nicholette said, taking a few steps in the direction of her car, getting ready to go. When they all stared at her, she said, "You were all thinking it. Believe me, Yvette's got her problems, but she was an Ette. We don't kill each other."

"Nicholette . . ." Suzette murmured, blushing a bit.

Ignoring her, Nicholette said to Coby, "I hope you're helping out Detective Lockwood." She lifted a hand in good-bye and said to the group, "Coby's good, you know. At figuring things out. The firm would practically sink without her."

"Nicholette sure loves the last word," Juliet said coolly.

Coby felt the group's collective gaze turn to her. Suzette moved closer into Galen's arms. Seeing them, Juliet sidled closer to Kirk, but his dark eyes were assessing Coby. He turned to Danner. "That true? Is she helping you find the killer?"

"I'd like everybody's help," Danner said.

"Bullshit answer. You guys have teamed up." Kirk snorted. "Fine. Figure out who drowned her. I sure as hell don't have any answers." With that he took off, and after half a beat Paul and Vic followed him.

Donald Greer spoke up for the first time. Clearing his throat, he intoned in his vice principal voice, "We're all upset. Piling on the drama, perhaps. If we think of anything, we'll be sure and let you know, Danner . . . Detective Lockwood." His smile was faint. "Sometimes it's hard to look at you all as adults."

The rest of them took his words as a cue to leave. Coby fell in step with Danner on the way to her Nissan, then felt a cold shock when she saw that Wynona was standing beside her car.

"Who's that?" Danner asked.

"Wynona Greer. Donald's daughter."

"Maybe I should come with you," he said, undoubtedly wary of Wynona's stony expression and frozen manner.

"No, it's okay," Coby said. "I'll check in with you later."

She peeled off from Danner. Reaching her car, she asked Wynona, "You waiting for me?"

For a moment Wynona looked like she wanted to deny the obvious, maybe even to bolt, but then she seemed to think better of it and said, "I overheard some of what you were talking about."

"Yeah?"

"It always goes back to that night, doesn't it?" Wynona said with a trace of bitterness. "Lucas's hair, and all that."

"We don't know that the hair is—" Coby began, but Wynona waved her off.

"Jean-Claude said Annette thought it was Lucas's. She

must've thought that for a reason, so I'm sure it is his hair. Somebody's kept it all these years. Some sicko from that night. I mean, I'm sorry Annette's dead and all. I really am, even though she could say some hurtful things." She glanced toward her dad, who was standing by his vehicle, a Chevrolet sedan, and waiting for Wynona, looking somewhat anxious that she was talking to Coby. "You know my dad is friends with Jean-Claude, too," she said, as if Coby had questioned her. "I've hung around the Ette sisters more than I'd like. Yvette's a bitch, but Annette was . . . so judgmental. And then Juliet and Suzette . . ." She shrugged. "Anyway, it just all goes back to that night. Certainly screwed me up. I'm sure Annette told you about my problems."

Coby hardly knew what to say. "I just want to know who killed her."

"Yvette would be my guess," Wynona said.

"Nicholette doesn't think so."

Wynona snorted. "You heard Juliet. Yvette hated her. Annette could be so bold. Nothing was off-limits. She would just zing you with stuff. Give her a few drinks and there were no holds barred. She certainly let me know that she thought I didn't really try to kill myself. That both of my suicide attempts failed because I wasn't serious. That I was just looking for attention. I imagine that's what you think, too."

Coby said truthfully, "I think any suicide attempt is real. I don't care what the reason is."

Wynona regarded her silently for a moment. Coby got the feeling Annette wasn't the only judgmental one. "Okay," she said after several tense beats. Then, "I'll say it again: if you're looking for Annette's killer, it's Yvette. Annette must have learned something about Yvette and she was going to tell everybody about it. That was Annette's way. And Yvette's totally unstable." She smiled faintly. "Maybe it takes one to know one. So maybe Annette was going to name Benedict's father, or maybe it was something else. Either way, my money's on Yvette, no matter what Nicholette says. Believe me, the Ettes aren't that close. They'd kill each other over the right thing."

"Wynona!" Donald's voice reached them across the parking lot and Wynona headed his way.

Coby climbed into the car and sat a moment at the wheel. In her rearview she watched Donald and Wynona leave the parking lot.

Rap, rap, rap!

She jumped about a foot at the sound against her driver's window. "Jesus," she murmured, seeing Hank Sainer outside. She switched on the ignition, then pressed the button to roll down the window.

She looked at him expectantly, and he pressed his lips together, as if he were regretting the need to say anything. "Mr. Sainer?" she asked.

"Hank. Please. I'd like to talk to you, Coby."

"About . . . . Annette?" she asked carefully.

"Could we meet next week? Maybe Monday? I'll come to your office. Does that work?"

"You sure you don't want to talk to Danner?"

"No, this isn't . . . no." He smiled tightly.

"I spoke with Dana a few days ago," she said.

"I know." He nodded several times. "She told me. She was seriously thinking of coming to the memorial service, but it's a long flight. So, I'll see you Monday?"

"Just call and let me know what time," Coby said. "I could have a meeting."

"Okay." He straightened, knocked his knuckles on the hood of her car a couple of times, then strode quickly away to a silver Land Rover.

Huh, Coby thought. Maybe this had something to do with Dana instead of Annette.

Danner drove back to the station, lost in thought, some about his impressions from the memorial service, some about Coby. Most about Coby. But as he entered the squad room, his attention was brought back to the Lloyd case with a bang as Jarvis Lloyd was sitting in the chair beside Danner's desk, bent over to where his forehead nearly touched his knees, weeping silently while Celek looked on uncomfortably and Lieutenant Draden—Drano—stood in his office doorway, frowning. As soon as they saw Danner, they both broke into action: Drano signaling for him to come inside his office; Celek, relieved, grabbing his coat, ready to make a quick exit.

Danner avoided Jarvis for the moment and stepped across the lieutenant's threshold while Drano quietly closed the door behind them. In a hushed voice, he said, "He's been like that for thirty minutes. Just walked in, asked for you. We pointed him to your desk and he sat down and that's what we've got. We were calling you but just kept getting voice mail." There was a note of censure in his voice.

"I was at the Rendell memorial service." Danner slipped his cell from his pocket and quickly switched it back on.

"You got any idea what this is about?"

"His girlfriend is my guess." Danner went on, "I think we've got a woman killer on this one, based on the neighbor's ID. My guess is Jarvis was seeing her romantically. Then somebody—one of them—decided to kill the wife, maybe because Jarvis wanted this new woman? Maybe because his wife's illness was draining his finances? There are a number of possibilities, but they probably concern this unknown woman killer. Maybe the whole thing was her idea. In any case, it looks like Jarvis is ready to crack."

Drano nodded, eyeing Jarvis through the glass walls of his office. "How many women execution-style killers do you know?"

"Not many who would coldly shoot another woman in the back of the head," Danner admitted. "Then shoot the daughter as she was trying to escape. Although I don't think that was part of the script."

"Think the daughter's what this is all about?" He inclined his head, indicating Jarvis Lloyd's current breakdown.

"Yeah. I'll take him to an interrogation room."

"Be sure and ask him if he wants a lawyer."

"Way ahead of you," Danner said grimly, and he went out to talk to the sobbing man.

Coby sat at her desk a moment, decompressing. She'd returned to work after the memorial service, but she could scarcely keep her mind on the job. It was an effort to get anything done, and finally she just packed it in and went home.

At her town house, she called her father. She wanted to check up on him and also see if he could tell her more about his interview with Clausen from the sheriff's department. He let her know that it wasn't as bad as it had been made out. It had mainly been an informal questioning, basically a recounting of the events of the night.

"Are you worried about me?" Dave finally asked as Coby kept probing. "Bug, it's okay. I feel like I'm moving through quicksand, but I'm dealing with it. It's really helped having Jean-Claude and Annette's sisters around. We're all . . . getting through it."

"And Mom."

"Yeah, Leta's been great." His voice warmed. "That's her, though. She's always known what to do, especially in crises. You and your sister got that from her." Coby could hear the sad smile in his voice. "Love you all," he said, then hung up as if he were getting choked up and didn't want to lose it on the phone.

Coby went to bed that night in a state of mild uneasiness. There had been strange vibes at the memorial service, culminating with Wynona's belief that Yvette had killed her sister and Hank Sainer's mysterious need to have a meeting with her. It also didn't help that her father, though definitely grieving, seemed to be leaning on his ex-wife, Coby's mother, for support.

And then Lucas Moore's hair, if it was his hair—she kinda thought it was his hair—and so what did that mean?

It meant someone had cut it from his head and saved it for twelve years. That's what it meant.

So what—who—were they dealing with? A killer from the past who had struck again? That didn't make sense . . . did it? Or had someone sheared off a hunk of Lucas's hair after he was dead?

Coby shuddered. She'd been there that night. At the campfire. On the beach. Kissing Lucas . . . touching him . . . running her hands through his hair . . . watching him across the firelight. For that matter, so had Genevieve. And probably Rhiannon . . . and Yvette . . . and maybe a few others. If Lucas had been missing a chunk of hair, it would have been noticed. *She* would have noticed. But Lucas's hair had hung straight and smooth from a center part. It was all there throughout the evening. She was certain of it.

So, the lock had been taken later, sometime after Lucas left the campfire that last time. And sometime before his body was taken away and catalogued by the medical examiner.

Who? Who could have done it?

And how could it have anything to do with Annette's death?

A long time later Coby fell asleep, but her fragmented dreams were of Dana Sainer, who kept telling her that she had it wrong. It wasn't about her. She was fine now. Her eating disorder under control.

"No matter what my father says to you Monday, it's not about me," Dream Dana told her. "You've got it wrong."

Souvenirs. That's what they call them. Mere trinkets. Memorabilia. Sentimental reminders.

I carefully lift the curl of Lucas Moore's hair from the envelope and smile at the touch of it on my hand. It burns like a coal.

Too bad that bitch found it. She suspected it was mine and she wasn't going to give up until she learned the truth.

I had to silence her.

Had to.

And Coby . . . ready to play detective.

I look at her and see how wrong I once was about her, about all of them, as it turns out.

Once I adored them . . . now I just want them dead.

Dead and gone.

I know where Coby lives. I know where she works.

I know. . . .

Chapter 17

On Thursday, Coby met with Nicholette to discuss Rhys Webber and gave her the bad news: Webber wasn't going to do anything his lawyer—Nicholette—suggested and therefore was going to have a very public, very expensive divorce. Every woman he'd ever slept with was bound to speak up and try for her moment in the spotlight; they'd all learned from the Tiger Woods debacle. Everyone except Webber, that is.

"He's not the type to listen," Coby told Nicholette. "Ever."

Nicholette sighed, nodded, and ostensibly went back to the drawing board with her client. Coby had other things to think about, Danner being the top of her list, although Annette's murder and its maybe connection to Lucas Moore was running a close second, if it wasn't a dead heat.

Faith called in the afternoon and said she was meeting Hugh for dinner. She sounded excited, but like she was trying to tamp it down, and Coby felt a faint twinge of envy. She and her sister were communicating more since Annette's death, maybe because they'd been linked again through Danner, in a strange way. For that Coby was glad, but she felt unsettled and unable to concentrate on much of anything and sensed this would continue until there was some resolution to Annette's murder.

At the close of work, she grabbed up her cell phone and checked her list of saved telephone numbers. Some of them were old, old, old. She'd plugged them in from a contact list she kept online of family and friends from the past, some never called even once, most seldom phoned. Like most people, she called about three of the numbers steadily. A bunch more on an irregular basis. Most never, or almost never.

Dana Sainer Bracco was one of the latter, as were most of her so-called friends from the campout, and Coby made a face as she ran by her number. No help there. Of the other girls from their group, only Genevieve, Yvette, and McKenna had been at both Annette's birthday party and the campout, and she planned to talk with them more. But in the interest of thoroughness, she was going to contact all the girls who'd been around the campfire the night Lucas died, if she could reach them. Maybe there was no connection between the two deaths; she believed the sheriff's department considered them independent even if Danner was exploring the idea they were linked. But there was that lock of hair that Jean-Claude had said Annette believed was Lucas's, so there was something weird there.

And then Wynona had pointed her in Yvette's direction. Could that be true? Could Yvette have really killed her sister? Could she be the one who'd taken a swatch of Lucas Moore's hair and kept it all these years? That just didn't sound like her. Yvette was about the least sentimental type of person Coby could imagine.

Or could Yvette have killed Annette and someone else took Lucas's hair, and Annette just happened to find the lock that night?

Coby shook her head, slightly boggled. Too many questions and not enough answers. It was time to check with the other girls who'd been at the original campout. She didn't have Ellen's number, but she thought she remembered that McKenna had kept in contact with her. If she checked with McKenna, she might be able to scare up a contact for Ellen.

She thought briefly of Kirk, Paul, and Vic, who had all been at the campout and also at the beach last weekend; Paul and Vic in Seaside while Kirk was at Annette's party. They would resent any interference by Coby; they already resented Danner. And she really didn't want to contact them unless she had to.

And then there was Jarrod . . . and Genevieve.

And maybe your own father?

"And Leta was at the beach, too, that night," Coby said aloud, a little taken aback at how angry her voice sounded.

Sighing, she grabbed her coat and headed out.

Glancing at the squad room clock, Danner stifled a yawn and wondered if he had the energy to talk to Jarvis Lloyd anymore. They'd spent a long night together that hadn't amounted to much, as it turned out, and by the morning Lloyd had been sent home, as the ADA hadn't found enough evidence to hold the man on anything useful.

"He needs to give us a name," Charisse Werner told Danner when she breezed in bright and efficient after Danner's all-nighter with Lloyd, which hadn't produced much more than Lloyd telling him again and again and again, "She took me over. She just took me over!" Then more weeping. Then, "She took me over. She took me over!"

"Find out who 'she' is," Charisse decreed, when brought up to date with the interview, "and then bring her in. Sounds like this jerk is in it up to his hairline, but get me something concrete."

There was a discussion with Drano about whether to place the man on a twenty-four-hour hold, but the general consensus was to cut him loose and see what happened next. The supposed doer, whoever she was, wasn't one of the numbers listed on Jarvis Lloyd's phone records. Maybe Lloyd contacted her with a temporary cell phone, but they hadn't found one on his person or premises.

"He's close to a complete breakdown," Danner told Charisse. "He should be in a hospital."

"Send him home," the ADA answered, sounding as heartless as her reputation would suggest. "If she's his lover, then associating with her got his family killed."

On that, Charisse had a point. During his interview with the man, Danner had brought up Lloyd's wife's name and his daughter's, and it was the latter that had sent the man into a crying jag that seemed damn near endless. Twenty-year-old Angie Lloyd was Jarvis's "little girl" and he couldn't think about her without breaking down.

"Keep an eye on him," Charisse told Danner flatly. She was a no-nonsense redhead—fake color, he was pretty sure—whip thin, with a hard chin and gray eyes and amazing breasts—fake size, he was certain—and a penchant for tight suits with short skirts. She had nice legs, though a little on the skinny side, and designer shoes that looked about as comfortable as thumbscrews.

Lloyd was released and Danner spent the next couple of hours making notes on his thoughts. He headed home midday and managed to catch about four hours of sleep before he got a call from Celek, who'd been assigned babysitting duty on Lloyd, telling Danner that Jarvis had stumbled out of the house, disheveled and seemingly disoriented, and walked about seven blocks to the MAX line and taken the train into the city, where he alighted on Burnside and found his way south to a hotel with guest suites and a lobby bar in a *Casablanca* style.

"He's just sitting at the bar, nursing a drink," Celek reported.

"Waiting for someone at three P.M.?" Danner asked.

"I guess."

"Has he made you?"

"No." Celek was offended.

"Okay."

Danner ran through the shower and drove back to the station. Celek called him when he was halfway there. "He's on his way home again."

"No one met him at the bar?" Danner asked.

"Uh-uh."

"How does he seem?"

"Beaten down."

Suicidal? Danner veered off course and headed straight to Lloyd's house. He passed Celek coming the other way and jerked his thumb in the direction of Jarvis's place. He didn't have time to talk. He arrived in time to catch a glimpse of the man entering his garage and closing the door behind him.

Danner idled across the street. Through the line of narrow windows on the garage door he saw the light switch off. Lowering his window, he thought he could hear Lloyd's car's engine running.

He hesitated, waiting, hoping the garage door would go up and Lloyd would back out.

Nothing happened.

"Shit."

Danner leapt from the Wrangler, which was double-parked, its own engine running. He sprinted across the street. If Lloyd was intent on killing himself with carbon monoxide, he was sure as hell gonna stop him if he could.

The door was locked. Frantically looking around, Danner found a small tree limb and banged it down on the door handle with all his might, stomping against the door panels with his foot until the wood around the lock splintered and he was inside. He leapt over the hood of the car to the driver's side where Lloyd's feet were sticking out of the door. He was lying on the seats. Eyes closed. Unconscious. Danner held his breath and yanked Jarvis from the car. The open door was letting in air, but he didn't trust himself to breathe until he had hauled Lloyd's limp body five feet from the door and laid him on the damp grass in front of his house.

Celek was there, big-eyed, gulping.

Lloyd half came to, groaning. Danner wanted to slap the man silly but restrained himself with an effort. Bastard. Getting his family killed.

"Tell me her name," Danner growled at him. His fists were bunched in the man's shirt and he wanted to yank him to his feet.

"I don't . . . know. . . ." His eyes rolled around.

"Tell me her name!"

"I don't know it! I don't." He started sobbing again. "I thought I did. But I don't. I called her Sheila, but I don't think that's who she is. She took me over! I didn't know. . . . I didn't know!"

And with that he collapsed into unconsciousness again.

Celek said uneasily, "Lockwood?"

"Call nine-one-one," Danner grunted in disgust.

"Oh, man . . ." Celek put his cell phone to his ear and took a few steps back but watched Danner with a worried eye.

"I'm not gonna kill him," Danner muttered to the freckle-faced Celek. "I don't want him dead. Yet."

He went back inside the garage and turned off the car's engine, and he heard the sirens as he stepped outside again. The EMTs appeared within minutes and started Lloyd on oxygen.

"Is he okay?" Celek asked them.

The taller of the two EMTs answered, "He's breathing, but he should be coming around by now." He frowned. "Did he take something else?"

"Probably," Danner growled. "He wanted to kill himself pretty badly, I imagine. He was in the garage when I got here."

"He was in his house until about forty-five minutes ago," Celek said. "I was outside."

"We need to pump his stomach," the second EMT said.

"Gotta get him outa here," the taller one answered tersely, and they loaded Lloyd into the back of the ambulance and took off, sirens screaming.

Celek stared after them. "Maybe he did know I was following him," he said guiltily.

Danner drew a deep breath, deeply furious with Jarvis Lloyd, but it wasn't Celek's fault. "He came to us," Danner reminded the younger man. "He probably already had this in mind. He just couldn't quite confess last night. Whether he made you or not doesn't really matter."

Celek shot him a grateful look. "Thanks."

Danner shrugged. "Truth." They walked to their respective vehicles, Danner's mind on Lloyd's trip to the bar. Whom had he planned to meet this afternoon? To Celek, he asked, "How's that burglary case coming? With the nightclub venues?"

"Nothing new. But most of 'em have happened on weekends, so maybe something will break soon."

Danner nodded and climbed into the Wrangler. Time to check out the *Casablanca* bar and see if he could learn something.

"He was drinking water," the bartender told Danner half an hour later when he caught up with him inside Rick's—no surprise there, considering the motif.

"Just water?"

He nodded. "Said he was waiting for someone. Guess they never showed."

A waitress wearing all black except for a silver sequined headband around her forehead said, "He took a couple pills."

"When?" Danner demanded.

"Right before he left. What's wrong with him? He was like the saddest guy on the planet."

"He got involved with the wrong woman," Danner told her. "Maybe he was trying to meet her today. Have you ever seen him before?"

The bartender and waitress both shook their heads. "If he came at night, you'd have to check with Len," the waitress said. "He's on at six."

Danner checked his watch. Getting close to it, but there was still some time. "I'll do that."

He drove back to the station and called ADA Charisse Werner and told her that Jarvis Lloyd was in the hospital after a suicide attempt, then, needing a shower and shave, headed back to his apartment.

Hank Sainer stood in front of the wide windows of his rented condo on Portland's south waterfront and watched a storm move in from the west and pour buckets of precipitation onto the Willamette River, which slowly rolled by thirty floors below. The day had disintegrated into a dark, sodden mess that matched his mood as his mind was on his political career and all the choices he'd made that had brought him to this place, this precipice, this end.

He'd struggled for years to hide his past and had been surprisingly successful. He'd even loved and lost a beautiful, politically connected woman whose father had rained money down on him and his endeavors even though the man was a staunch Republican and Hank was a Democrat. A middle-of-the-road Democrat, though, so a man Geri's dad could accept. He'd expected Hank to marry Geri and start a family, but that wasn't in Hank's plan. Hank had loved Geri and had wanted to marry her, but things had gone sideways.

Geri, though Hank had believed she was past the baby-having time, as his daughter Dana called it, wanted to have a child of her own. Hank reminded her that he was a grandfather—Dana had two daughters of her own, Sage and Sara—and that he had no interest in starting another family at this late date. His refusal had not been received well and Geri ended their relationship soon afterward. Sometime later her daddy's money and goodwill dried up as well.

He'd been more heartbroken than he'd expected to be. And in those hours, weeks, and months of self-reflection that followed, he'd come to some hard truths. His political career, the one baby he'd truly cared for and tended to, to the exclusion of almost everything else—and that included his own daughter—was stagnating. Partly because he'd lost some enthusiasm himself; partly because a deep secret, a career-ending mistake, was boring its way out from the locked place he'd kept it safe in for so long.

It was just one of those things that was bound to finally happen. And though Hank had feared it for years—the public exposure, the scandal—he had come to terms with things and honestly didn't give a damn any longer.

So he'd decided to take action. Face the dragon head-on and slay it, if he could.

But then . . . Annette was murdered.

Now Hank closed his eyes, feeling his heart hammering in his chest. He rubbed a hand over his chin, willing away the sense of guilt. He hadn't known she would kill her. He hadn't known she was that desperate.

He turned from the window and walked jerkily across the expanse of gray carpet, unable to stand his own company. The place was decorated in the midcentury modern style, Geri's taste, all whites and grays and chrome with a wet bar behind a pair of sliding doors that would have made the Rat Pack proud. Hank didn't notice. If he was committing political suicide, he was going to do it now, before things got worse.

Plucking his cell phone from his pocket, he punched in a number that was not on his call list, surprised when the call was picked up.

"I know you killed her," he said. Then tacked on the lie, "I was there. Watching. You just didn't know it."

The voice squawked in fury on the other end.

"I don't care," he said. "I'm tired of waiting. I'm tired of hiding. It's over." For a half moment he thought about delivering a further ultimatum, but the message was already understood.

When the voice blasted on, he simply snapped the cell phone shut.

He would wait until Monday. One more long weekend. He would talk to Coby Rendell and tell her what he knew.

And then, as the story broke, he would make himself

watch that bitch of a reporter, Pauline Kirby, as she both shredded his political life and opened the way to a whole new one for him. He'd gone on one miserable date with Pauline, a nadir in his dating career, though she'd had some interest in him. His demise would surely warm the cockles of her cold, shrunken heart, but it also would let him rise from the ashes like a phoenix.

Just before six Danner phoned Coby and his call went directly to voice mail. Figured. He found cell phones slightly amusing, as the person he was calling so seldom seemed to pick up. Screening? Maybe. Or just plain who the hell cares to answer.

He thought of a ton of things he could say: why he'd been so hard to reach; how frustrated he was that he couldn't work on Annette's homicide; how much he looked forward to seeing her. But when her voice mail beeped, he asked simply, "Do you know Dooley's?" then gave her the address of the downtown bar frequented by the men in blue. "Can you meet me there tomorrow, after work? I've been buried, but I want to see you. About six? Let me know. Thanks."

It wasn't much of a message, really, considering there was this thrumming thing going on between them, an engine starting to rev. He was purposely holding back after being at her place the other night. He'd wanted so much and been a bit alarmed at his own desire. There had been a lot of really going nowhere nights these last few years, and he didn't want any of that with Coby. Not that it ever had been, but he wasn't taking any chances that his own jaded ways might jump up and bite him in the ass.

Still . . . the thought of seeing her brought a quickening to his pulse.

With an effort, he corralled his galloping thoughts.

There was much to do. Starting with Len, the bartender at Rick's.

Dooley's . . . tomorrow after work. . . .

Coby saved the message, then clicked off voice mail. "Tomorrow," she repeated, wishing it were today.

She stopped by a deli on the drive home and picked up two different types of salad, salsa fiesta and spinach, and a baguette loaf. At home she settled in with a full plate, a glass of white wine, and the television remote. Turning on the news, she ate her dinner and watched the flickering images on the screen, but her mind wouldn't engage.

Checking the time, she put down her half-finished plate and picked up her cell phone, scrolling through the numbers until she found one for McKenna. She reached McKenna's voice mail, which gave her the times and place of McKenna's next appearances on Friday and Saturday nights at the Joker in southeast Portland. When the beep came, Coby was trying to write down the address and momentarily lost focus. "Uh . . . McKenna, it's Coby. I was just wanting to talk about everything. I'll try to come to one of your shows this weekend. Maybe we can talk after?" She was about to say more but that damn voice jumped in asking if her message was all right or if she wanted to redo it. Why? she asked herself in a fury. Why? That damn voice invariably happened whenever she didn't want it to. Cyber voice from hell, but she figured this time at least, she'd gotten the message across.

Glancing down at the notes she'd made for McKenna's comedy engagement, she decided to make an appearance at the club after she met with Danner.

Maybe he would even go with her.

* * *

Danner stepped into Rick's about six thirty and looked for Len, who turned out to be a tall, sandy-haired twentysomething with wire-rimmed glasses and a restless way of watching the crowd in the bar that spoke of experience with rabble-rousers.

Danner showed Len his ID and then asked if they could talk. The bar was in transition between the happy-hour crowd and the diners. Len said, "Ten minutes," and jerked his head to a side door that led to inner rooms. Danner ordered a beer, placed it on the end of the glossy wood bar, put his foot on the brass rail, and gave the room a once-over as well. The crowd was mostly fortysomething, at least for the women. The men were older, as a rule. The inebriation level was climbing and Danner could see why Len was vigilant; any one of the drinkers could tip over the edge from mildly drunk to wasted without some kind of watchdog.

After ten minutes and an exodus of businessmen, Danner watched a couple of nice-looking women go through the very door Len had pointed out to him. When Len gave him the high sign, he followed him through to a short hallway with several offices in the back. The two women were standing outside the door of the farthest office, smiling and talking to someone unseen. A man. Whose deep baritone sounded impatient, though the women didn't seem to care.

Len went into the first office and shut the door behind Danner. "You're here about the guy whose wife and daughter got killed last month. I got a call from Jimmy. You stopped by earlier."

"Has he been here before?" Danner asked, pulling out a picture of Jarvis Lloyd.

Len gave it a long, long look. "Yeah, maybe. You could ask one of Rick's girls."

"Rick's girls?"

He handed the picture back to Danner and gave him a sideways glance. "You saw a couple of 'em down the hall."

"Rick . . . like the owner Rick?"

He nodded. "Rick with a silent 'p' in front."

"Ahh."

"Yeah, he's my boss, but he kinda sees himself as a local Hugh Hefner. Has an apartment where they all stay. They hang around the bar a lot, but they're looking for something else."

"They might know Mr. Lloyd?" Danner lifted the photo.

"There was one chick . . ." Len frowned. "Didn't really fit in, but she got Rick's crank going for a while. Tough bitch, though. You could ask him."

"Would the other girls remember her?" Danner asked, sensing by the way Len talked that an interview with the owner might not get him the information he sought.

"Talk to Katrina. She knows everything about everything."

With that he opened the door and yelled down the hall, "Cat! Got a minute?"

One of the women straightened from her slouch outside Rick's door and came Len's way. As she approached, Danner raised his estimate of her age about five years. She looked good, but in that overly worn way that women on the prowl for a long time sometimes acquired. "Yeah?" she asked, sizing Danner up with interest.

"I'm Detective Lockwood with the Portland PD. We're looking for information on this man, Jarvis Lloyd." He handed her the picture, which she reluctantly accepted.

"What about him?"

"Jesus, Cat," Len said, annoyed. "He's the home invasion guy. The one whose wife and kid got killed!"

"Why should I know him? Fuck you, Len."

"What about that friend of Rick's, the one who talked like she wanted to screw on the top of the bar? The cold super-bitch?"

"Sheila? She left, thank God. I hated her. I think she stole from Rick, though he doesn't want to believe it."

"Where can I find her?" Danner asked, his interest quickening.

"Hell if I know. Check *America's Most Wanted*. That woman was looking for a big score. Thought she had it with Rick, but he's got more sense than that." She sniffed and pushed back a tress of super-held brunette hair, which scarcely moved at her touch. "She mighta hooked up with this guy," she said, glancing toward the photo. "He looks like a patsy."

"Is Sheila her real name?" Danner asked.

"Honey, nobody goes by their real name." She gave him a pitying glance. "So, what do you make a year, Detective? Fifty? Sheila was looking for the five hundred thousand and up crowd. Such a shame."

She sauntered off, and Danner wasn't sure whether she meant him or something else.

"Can I hook you up with our police artist?" Danner asked Len as they walked back into the bar. "I'd like a drawing of this Sheila."

"Tomorrow?" Len asked.

"Call me." He handed him a card and left Rick's and headed to the hospital where Jarvis Lloyd had recovered consciousness but had not yet been released, being held on a seventy-two-hour watch after his suicide attempt.

But Danner got nothing more out of Lloyd. The man had gone from crying to staring sightlessly at the ceiling, and he was deaf to Danner's request for more information about Sheila.

By the time he was on his way home it was after ten. He

wanted to stop by Coby's but knew he needed some sleep or he would just pass out on her couch. Wishing the Lloyd case would magically resolve itself and go away so he could spend some time on the Deneuve homicide, he drove to his apartment, dropped into bed, and fell into a coma-like sleep until morning.

Chapter 18

Friday night at Dooley's was crowded with young people surging into the city for the start of the weekend. They took the seats from the usual cops who frequented the place and when Coby walked through the door, she had to squeeze between two hard male bodies who barely noticed her as they were checking out their look in the mirror above the bar while exiting.

Inside, the place was semidark with lines of glowing green shamrock-shaped lights surrounding the mirrored bar. She saw Danner seated at a bar stool at the far end, holding on to another seat while several young women tried to edge their way in. One had a small section of butt cheek on the saved stool's leather top, but the woman obligingly moved on with a sniff and hair flounce when she recognized Coby as the seat's rightful owner.

"Hi," Coby said, sliding onto the stool. "Crowded."

"Wanna go someplace quieter?"

She shook her head, then told him about her plan to take in McKenna's comedy act later on. "You're welcome to join me, if you'd like. I thought we could catch some food here."

"Bar food," he said.

"I love bar food. Fried goodness."

He smiled. His dark hair was wet from a quick spate of rain that had pounded Coby's umbrella, and she had to force herself not to brush a couple of sparkling drops from his suede jacket before they melted into the fabric. She was leery of intimacy of any kind. She wanted him to take the lead.

As if the Fates were against them, Danner's cell phone started buzzing, a low sound meant to keep from drawing too much attention. "Lockwood," he answered, then listened for several moments, his face giving nothing away.

"What?" Coby asked when he hung up.

For an answer he shook his head. "Damn," he said softly. "Gonna have to take a rain check."

"Work?"

"We've been putting the pressure on this guy whose wife and daughter were killed." He quickly filled her in on Jarvis Lloyd's suicide attempt. "Looks like he's finally cracking, and I need to be there."

"A rain check," Coby said.

"If Metzger was around I could rely on her, but it's Celek." He was talking to himself and not liking what he was saying. His blue eyes suddenly captured hers. "Tomorrow night? Tentatively, depending how this goes? My brother's band's playing at a nightclub in Laurelton."

"The Cellar. Right."

The bartender reached them at that moment. "What can I get for you?" he asked over the noise.

Danner placed two twenties on the bar. "Some bar food. Whatever she wants." Then he turned to Coby and gave her a quick but warm kiss right on the lips in front of the whole room. No one paid the least bit of attention, but Coby was slightly breathless as she plopped back down on the stool. "Fries," she told the waiting bartender, who didn't bat an eyelash. "And do you have some of those sliders? And a glass of red wine?"

Forty-five minutes later Coby stepped out of Dooley's into a rain-washed street, streetlights glimmering in zigzagged streaks in the standing water. But the precipitation itself had stopped and she stepped cautiously through a shimmer of liquid on the way to her car. Traffic was heavy and she had to wait at a light, headlights white circles that half blinded her as she crossed hurriedly in front of a pile of cars to where her own vehicle waited.

She eased into traffic and felt that clunk again under the right front tire. *Gotta get that looked at*, she told herself again. She hadn't noticed it since the trip to the beach. One of those problems that didn't completely immobilize her, which made it easy to put off fixing it.

She had time to kill, so she drove slowly toward the comedy club, which was on the east side of the Willamette River while she was on the west. Crossing the Steel Bridge, she meandered through areas of Portland she normally never saw. The downtown area stood on the west bank of the river, the Pearl District/Nob Hill/Alphabet District stretching west; her condo was located on Eighteenth, eighteen blocks west of the Willamette.

The Joker was located in a converted warehouse about five blocks off Burnside Street. It had a parking lot that wrapped around the building on all three sides, which kept the street, dotted with parking meters, void of cars other than those passing on the roadway. There were a couple of scraggly-looking pines in a narrow bed near the front door; the club's answer to landscaping. A marquis read: WANNA LAUGH? GET YOUR A** IN HERE! Coby wondered if the neighbors had forced the PG version. Judging by the renovated older homes and maple-lined streets stretching eastward, she would give that a yes.

She paid a cover fee and walked inside. Like many of

the cabaret-type clubs she'd been to, it smelled faintly of beer, popcorn, and cooking oil. The patterned carpet was beaten down by a deluge of tromping feet and when she got to her assigned seat, a theater chair that was meant for singles or those who didn't want the café tables and wooden chairs on the main floor, she noticed the stitching was ripping and soon the cushioned seat would be detached from the sides. She sat down carefully, wondering when she'd become so . . . old. The place felt like a college hangout, even though the patrons were all ages, and she couldn't help feeling like an uninvited guest.

The first act was a guy who could juggle anything . . . badly. His schtick was making his ineptitude funny, which it almost was, but not quite. But McKenna came on next, wearing a backward baseball cap and a smirk. She told stories from her own life that were downright funny; Coby found herself grinning and laughing. If McKenna had been unclear about her sexual orientation in high school, she'd gotten over that now. A lot of her humor came from being gay and dealing with straights. Someone had once told Coby that comedy was derived from truth and pain: a true story that was painful was the source of some of the best material. McKenna made Coby a believer with her uncomfortable tales that were filled with humor.

There was another act after McKenna, but Coby had no interest in anyone else. As soon as McKenna said good night and the crowd broke into enthusiastic applause, Coby hurried back to the lobby and told the guy behind the counter that she was a personal friend of McKenna's and gave her name.

The guy regarded her skeptically. He had sleeve tattoos and several painful-looking plugs in his ears, a Rod Stewart haircut, and a severe case of black eyeliner. She had a mental image of herself: tan slacks, tan linen blouse, tan jacket, light makeup, straight light brown hair cut by a professional, and decided she couldn't look more suburban/bland.

"You're a friend of McKenna's?" he repeated with just the right amount of disbelief.

"We were high school classmates. Tell her my name and she'll know me. I have her cell number plugged into my call list." She pulled out her phone, called up McKenna's number, showed him.

That finally convinced him and he directed her outside the building to a side door with several concrete steps and a red awning. She nodded. She'd seen it on the way in, and now she walked out the front door and around the building to the steps where another couple was already waiting, shivering a little, the man holding the woman close.

Coby blinked in shock, seeing the woman's profile.

"Ellen?" she asked in disbelief. "Ellen Marshall?"

She turned and eyed Coby critically, and said, with the same amount of amazement, "Coby?"

"What are you doing here?" they asked each other in unison.

The guy she was with suddenly grinned, a white slash of straight teeth, and Coby dragged her eyes from Ellen to finally look at him . . . and got her second shock. "Theo? Good God. You're *together*?"

Jarvis Lloyd was like a fountain, overflowing with thoughts and feelings and guilt and remorse and sheer misery, but in the way of real information, he was a bust. Danner listened for about twenty minutes before pulling Celek away from the guy and asking, "Aren't you on robbery?"

"I was helping you," he protested.

"I know. Thank you. But . . . nothing's happening here," he pointed out, irritated that Celek had dragged him away from Coby and from McKenna Forrester's comedy act for one more sloppy round with Lloyd, for whom Danner was fast losing any kind of sympathy.

"Tell me where to find Sheila," Danner said to the shattered man in the hospital bed. He felt like he'd asked him the same question a thousand times.

"I don't know. . . . She took me over."

Jesus H. Christ. If he heard that one more time, he thought he might pick up the man's bedpan and hit him over the head with it.

"We have an artist's rendition of her," Danner said. "The bartender at Rick's gave it to us this morning. Someone will recognize her." He'd tried to take a copy of the artist's sketch to Rick, the man, himself earlier in the day and see what else he could learn, but Rick was nowhere to be found and hadn't called the station, though Danner had left his card and been very specific about what he wanted. No doubt about it, Rick, of Rick's, was avoiding him.

Jarvis Lloyd scarcely heard him. "She found me," he said again. "I couldn't help myself. I thought . . . with Bethy so ill . . ."

"You thought she might be a replacement?" Danner guessed, trying hard to keep the censure from his voice.

"I didn't know. I didn't know she would . . . hurt Angie. . . ."

"Kill Angie," Danner reminded him. Maybe he was being brutal, but he didn't much care. The bastard had set up his family to be murdered, whether he meant to or not.

"I had a number for her, but it was a prepaid cell phone and it's gone." He looked woeful.

"Tell me everything you remember about her," Danner said, taking out his notebook. "We need to find her."

"I met her at a different bar first—not Rick's. She was so fascinating. . . ." A sad smile touched Lloyd's lips as he thought back.

Danner set his jaw and wrote "predatory" in lieu of "fascinating" into his book.

Ellen and Coby could scarcely stop talking long enough to absorb what the other was saying. They hadn't seen each other since Ellen had left Rutherford High.

"You're with Theo?" Coby said again, scarcely able to credit it. She flashed on them as their younger selves, humping and gasping and thrusting away in the sand. Wow. They'd stayed together? Hadn't she heard that Theo got back with his Gresham girlfriend, the one rumored to be pregnant?

"I'm sorry about Annette," Ellen said. "So shocking. McKenna told us. How's your dad?"

"Coping," Coby said.

"Do the police have any clues?" Theo asked.

"It's an ongoing investigation."

Ellen looked much the same as she had when they were seventeen except her blond hair was shorter now and streaked by design. Her eyes seemed larger, but that might have been because she was wearing more makeup. She'd gained a little bit of weight, but she'd been so small and thin in high school that it looked good on her.

Theo looked like he had in high school, too: a lean, muscular hard body–type who must work out regularly. His hair was shorter but still thick and dark, not a shade of gray. He flashed Coby that white smile again; he'd always been a bit of a charmer.

Which reminded her of Lucas.

"I've been kind of following up on our group," Coby said. "Annette's death brought back Lucas's like it happened yesterday."

"Hasn't it?" Ellen drew in her shoulders. "I thought we were all over that, but when McKenna told me what happened to Annette, and then I told Theo, we just . . . well, we couldn't believe it."

"You've kept in close touch with McKenna."

Ellen looked at Theo, then at Coby. He shrugged, answering some unspoken question, and as if a decision had been made, Ellen turned to Coby. "I left high school because I was in love with Theo. After the campout, we didn't really talk about what happened. Because of Lucas's accident, and then Theo was . . . we weren't clear . . . about things."

Theo put in, "Ellen was afraid she was pregnant. She wasn't," he added quickly. "But, well, you know what she went through before, and she wasn't going to go through that again, and I was stupid and freaked out and we broke up."

"I was heartbroken," Ellen took up the story. "I could barely make myself go to school, and my dad had an opportunity for a job in California and we up and moved to Sacramento. It didn't work out for my dad and he and my mom moved back, but I stayed. I just had some stuff to work through."

"Like me being such an asshole," Theo said with a smile. A moment later that smile left his face as if someone had stolen it away. "I suppose you heard I went back to my ex-girlfriend, Heather."

"The one from Gresham?" Coby asked.

"I was screwing with no consequences then. She *was* pregnant, but she had a miscarriage, which I just thought was lucky at the time, though she didn't feel the same way. We just sort of stayed together because we were a couple, and it was high school, and it seemed like the thing to do, y'know? We were long broken up by the time of the accident, though."

Coby was lost. "What accident?"

"Yeah, I guess you don't know," Theo said. "Heather got

to be a gym rat. She was working out with weights, lifting them up, and the bar fell on her neck and killed her."

"That was your girlfriend?" Coby said, incredulous. "I remember when that happened. It was all over the news. My God."

"Let's go inside," Ellen said with a shiver.

"Have to wait till they open it," Theo said. "It's locked."

Coby shook her head, absorbing this latest bit of startling news. "We've had a lot of deaths of younger people associated with our group. What are the chances?"

"Guess we're just unlucky," Theo said.

Ellen dismissed that. "Lucas Moore fell because he was drunk and stumbling around in the dark. Rhiannon fell because it was around Christmastime and there was ice. I don't know about Heather. I didn't ever know her. But Theo said she was kind of a risk taker. Maybe she just put on too many weights."

"You said you weren't dating her then?" Coby asked.

"Nah, she was with some other gym rat. Had a couple of first names. I saw him at Heather's memorial service. Edward something? No, Jerry."

"Edward Gerald," Ellen put in.

"That's it. Ed Gerald." Theo gave her a nod.

"Sometime after that Theo and I found each other on Facebook," Ellen said, trying to right the conversation. "We just started corresponding. McKenna found me that way, too. Are you on Facebook?"

"I'm . . . I think I'm signed up for a few social networks, but I'm only so-so about keeping up on them. What's Heather's full name?" she asked.

"Heather McCrae. Why?" Theo gave her a hard look. "You're not going to make something weird of this, are you?"

Coby shook her head. "I don't want to sound like a conspiracy theorist, but it makes you wonder if there's something behind it all, doesn't it? I mean, can it all just really be bad karma?"

"You do kind of sound like a conspiracy theorist," Theo said with that smile.

Maybe she did. "Well . . ."

The back door suddenly opened and McKenna stuck her head out, baseball cap still in place. "Good God. Get in here before y'all freeze your asses off." She waved them inside and the conversation ended.

In the green room where McKenna was hanging out with some of the backstage staff, Coby found a seat on a beat-up couch where she could feel the springs poking through. McKenna paced around the room, asking what they thought of her routine. Ellen and Theo sat on another couch and held hands and told McKenna how great it all was. Coby felt like a wet blanket but couldn't join in the fun with much enthusiasm.

Was she wrong? Was this just all the coincidence of life?

Maybe.

Or maybe not.

Finally, McKenna wound down a bit and came over to Coby. "Glad you came. I heard you're investigating Annette's death with Danner Lockwood. Got something going with him?"

"Well . . ."

"Yeah. It's all over you." She grinned, then immediately sobered. "Who do you think killed Annette?"

"I don't know."

McKenna scooted a stool up to Coby. "You think it's connected to Lucas's death, don't you? I heard about his lock of hair being found. Creepy. Sorry. Who would hang on to a dead person's hair?"

"What are you talking about?" Ellen asked, looking repulsed.

Coby brought them up to date on everything Danner

had discussed with the others at Annette's memorial service. There was a long stretch of silence after she finished while they all absorbed the information.

"No wonder you think there's some connection," Ellen murmured. "I don't mean Heather, but Lucas and Annette . . . it seems weird."

"Rhiannon died, too," McKenna said.

"I think back on that campout and what we all said—" Ellen broke off.

"Well, it didn't have anything to do with that," McKenna answered promptly.

"You said everybody got notes, later on," Ellen reminded her.

"Yeah, but, they weren't all that bad. They were just stupid."

Coby looked at McKenna. "Mine was kind of pointed about my father, which was the lie I told that night."

"So, you *were* lying." She smiled. "I wasn't. I really did wreck my parents' car and my brother covered for me. But the note wasn't about that. It just called me a lesbo. I figured it was Vic just being the ass he is. And Genevieve's was almost complimentary."

"You're kidding," Coby said.

"No." McKenna shook her head. "Like the note writer was a secret admirer almost. You know Gen was screwing Lucas Moore that night, right? Well, whoever wrote Gen's note saw her with Lucas and thought it was really sexy. Probably Vic. He'd be the kind to secretly watch somebody getting it on."

Coby hadn't known Gen and Lucas actually had sex and planned to ask more, like how McKenna knew so much, but Theo broke in.

"You guys don't know Vic at all," he protested vehemently. "He didn't write those notes. He didn't! He's not sneaky like that. It wouldn't be him."

"You saying he wouldn't watch people having sex?" McKenna challenged.

"I'm saying, if he'd seen Genevieve with Lucas, he would have crowed about it," Theo told her flatly. "Even with Lucas dead, Genevieve would have never heard the end of doing the horizontal in the sand. That's Vic. That's what he would do. But this note stuff . . . it's more a girl thing, if you ask me."

Danner had said the notes seemed "girly" as well, Coby recalled.

"But Lucas was Rhiannon's boyfriend," Ellen protested. "Who would side with Genevieve screwing around with Lucas behind Rhiannon's back? None of us."

Coby felt the weight of her own interest in Lucas back then like a stone around her neck now. "I kissed Lucas that night, too," she admitted, slightly embarrassed.

"Yeah, but you just kissed him," McKenna said. "Right?"

Coby nodded. "Yep."

"Well, then, that doesn't really count. Not like Gen," she stated flatly.

"You kinda blame her, don't you?" Theo said, gazing at McKenna with a faint smile, needling her a little. "For being a man-stealer."

She gave him a hard look. "Pay attention. I'm not into guys."

"Okay, a *lover*-stealer, then," Theo said.

"What about Yvette?" Ellen asked, pulling the conversation back to the previous issue. "She said she was Lucas's secret lover."

"You believed her?" McKenna tossed back at her.

"No . . . but why did she say it?"

McKenna looked at Coby, then Theo. "Did anyone believe her?"

"At the time, I might have. Maybe. At least I entertained the idea. She was so adamant," Coby reminded them. "But not anymore. She told me at the beach house that Lucas definitely wasn't Benedict's father."

"I'm surprised she admitted that much," McKenna said with a sniff.

"Who is his father, then?" Theo asked. "It wasn't any of us guys. That woulda come out long ago."

"I bet Annette knew," Ellen said. "Maybe all the Ettes know."

"I don't know why it's such a secret," Theo said with a shrug. "You all told a lot worse things at the campout."

"Hey." Ellen looked upset.

"I'm just saying," Theo pointed out. "Why is it such a big secret? Still now? The kid's, like, almost in junior high."

"Yvette's like that," Coby said. "Secretive and . . . fierce. Wynona is convinced she had something to do with Annette's death."

"Maybe over Benedict's 'secret dad'?" McKenna looked skeptical.

"Any DNA test would prove who the kid's dad is," Theo said.

"As long as there's a match," Ellen agreed.

"Well, it wasn't any of us guys who were there," Theo said. "Nobody wanted to touch Yvette. She's such a bitch."

"Maybe someone did, though," Ellen said with a shrug.

"Maybe Lucas mighta taken a bite there," Theo said, sounding skeptical, "but Yvette already said he's not the father, and I don't get why she'd lie about that now. The next one most likely woulda been . . . probably me." He held up his hands in surrender. "But the other guys—Paul, Vic—Yvette wouldn't even look at 'em. And Galen, he's always been shy and pulled back."

"What about Kirk?" McKenna asked.

Theo shook his head slowly. "The kid doesn't look anything like him, and Kirk's pickier about women than you might think. That leaves Jarrod. He could be the father, I suppose. Except he liked Coby back then, and when he wasn't with her he was with Genevieve. I'm telling ya, it's none of us. You know what I think? I think Yvette was already pregnant at the campout, and she used Lucas's death as a means to pretend he was the father. Kept everyone from looking at anyone else."

"But now she doesn't want that myth to go on," Coby said. "She wants us to know Lucas isn't Benedict's father."

"Maybe she's ready to reveal who he is," Ellen said.

"Probably a goddamn paternity test in the wings," Theo said. "It always comes down to money."

"You're a real cynic," McKenna told him, and he just nodded.

Paternity test. Something niggled at Coby's brain. She tried to grab it but couldn't quite, and then suddenly it was there.

"Oh, my God. Dana was right," she said. "I did get it wrong."

Danner punched the button for the elevator and found Celek beside him. There was an officer assigned outside Lloyd's door, just in case he had some regrets about everything he'd admitted to Danner, though it wasn't much more than they'd already guessed. Lloyd had fallen for the mysterious Sheila and had been talked into putting his wife, Bethy, out of her misery; she was dying anyway was how Jarvis consoled himself. But then things had gone terribly awry.

Celek said, "I'm going over to that nightclub in Laurelton tonight. The one where your brother's playing."

Danner focused in on him. "Think something's going down there?"

"I don't know. But sometimes it seems like when certain groups are at a place, then that place gets targeted."

Danner, who'd been getting into the elevator, felt a cold finger trace down his spine. "Are you saying what I think you're saying?"

Celek's cherub face tightened up. "What do you think I'm saying?"

"That these burglaries have happened when Split Decision's at the venue?"

"After they play at a place. Yeah. I guess that is what I'm saying. Those places then get knocked over."

They stared at each other, and at the main floor Celek stepped out, but Danner stayed inside the car.

"You coming?" Celek asked, slightly uneasy.

"You go ahead," Danner said. "I've got a few phone calls to make."

When Celek, after a moment's hesitation, headed for the front entrance, Danner exited the elevator car and stood in the hospital foyer, standing by a spiky rhapis plant and placing a call to Jarrod's cell. When he failed to pick up, Danner called the Knapp/Lockwood house phone because he didn't have Genevieve's cell, readying to leave a message when Gen herself picked up.

"Jarrod's with the band," she said with a sniff and in a tone that suggested Danner should know that, too. "They're playing at the Cellar in Laurelton this weekend."

"I'm going to see them tomorrow night. Why aren't you there?"

"'Cause I hate the band," she stated bluntly. "Why're you so all-fired eager to talk to Jarrod?"

"Who said I was?"

"You just sound like it. What's wrong? What did he do?"

"Nothing, that I know of," Danner said.

"So this is about Annette, then? Come on over. I've got a few things to say about her. I just need somebody to really listen to me, okay?"

Danner checked the time. Nine thirty. All week he'd

wanted back on the Deneuve case but hadn't found the time. And now Genevieve was offering him a one-on-one without Jarrod even around, an opportunity that might, or might not, bear some kind of informational fruit.

Either way, it was a chance he wasn't going to squander. "I'll be there in twenty minutes."

Chapter 19

"What do you mean you got it wrong?" Ellen asked, frowning.

Coby shook her head. She needed to talk to Danner and she needed to do it tonight. "I've got to go. Could I get your cell numbers, so that we can talk some more later?"

Ellen, Theo, and McKenna all exchanged cell phone numbers with Coby, who tried to make a quick exit. They wanted to keep discussing Yvette, and Benedict's paternity, but for all intents and purposes the subject had been exhausted.

As Coby headed out the side door and toward her car, she punched in Danner's cell number, but the call went straight to voice mail.

"I could get a complex," she said aloud, though she knew he was on a job. When the beep sounded, she said, "Hey, there. I've left the Joker. McKenna was good. I was hoping I could see you tonight. Or talk to you? Give me a call."

She hung up and checked the time. Nearly ten.

She wondered exactly what his job entailed tonight.

* * *

The suburban house where Jarrod and Genevieve lived was a tan ranch with used brick running beneath Cinderella windowpanes, their diamond pattern sending out a retro message as clear as shag carpet, pet rocks, and disco music, though Danner tagged the actual age of the house somewhere in the early sixties.

As he pulled his Wrangler into the driveway, he realized the brown Toyota station wagon parked beside him was just pulling out. A woman with short, frosted hair gave him a wave and he waved back at Kathy Knapp who, though Gen and Jarrod had been married for years, was pretty much still a stranger to Danner. Not exactly the warm and fuzzy family, he and Jarrod. He loved his brother but they'd never been all that close in a friendship way. Jarrod was a musician and Danner was, well, not. There was a huge gap between their two worlds, and there was also Coby. Somehow Jarrod felt like she'd been his and Danner had taken her from him. He'd said as much, long ago, though it was a tacit thing between them now: understood, nearly forgotten . . . nearly.

Danner climbed out of the vehicle, pulled his cell phone from his pocket, and switched it off. He was long off duty and he didn't want any interruptions; he needed a night off from Jarvis Lloyd.

Someone had left a light on and he knocked on the door and looked around, glad the rain had stopped, feeling a cold breeze tuck its chilly fingers inside his jacket collar. Leaves blanketed the yard in an orange, yellow, and brown carpet. The lonely maple in the center of the yard was lopsided, and he could see the scar where a major branch had fallen from the other side. There was something forlorn about that, but Danner shook off the sensation as the door opened and Genevieve appeared, holding open the screen door.

"Mom's visiting a friend," she said by way of greeting. "A male friend. Ten o'clock at night. You have to wonder."

"Well, she's single," Danner said.

"Whatever." She waved him inside, as if it were the most natural thing and she didn't give a rat's ass about it anyway.

Danner stepped into the living room. The carpet had been replaced at some point and looked like someone took great care with it. A row of lighted vanilla candles sat atop a dark wood mantel, their tiny flames flickering, sending out an aroma that Danner inhaled deep into his lungs.

"They say vanilla is a woman's fragrance," Genevieve said. "Men like musk or something citrus or woodsy, I guess. Women like vanilla. I like vanilla."

She was standing in the center of the room, her arms crossed over her chest. She meant business. "Jarrod really has a hard-on for that band of his," she said, as if they were in the middle of a conversation. "Nothing stops him from being with them. Kinda like having a third partner in this marriage. And fourth and fifth, if you count the other two idiots besides Kirk: Spence and Ryan. But then there's Kirk." She rolled her eyes. "I've threatened to leave Jarrod more than once but he just smiles and kisses me and tells me I'm a liar, which I am. I would never leave him."

This was said with an underlying edge of steel that made Danner glad it was his brother, not himself, wrapped into this strange marriage. Danner had his own worries about Jarrod and his band, and he made a mental note about Spence and Ryan. When he went to see Jarrod's band tomorrow night, he would see what he thought of them as well.

"You wanted to talk about Annette," Genevieve reminded Danner, though he had mostly just agreed that was his purpose. Genevieve had been the one to really orchestrate this meeting.

"You thought Annette's death was a homicide before anyone else," Danner said.

"That's right." She was gratified that he remembered. "Annette was my friend," she began, then for a moment he thought she was going to actually break down. But Genevieve's emotional armor was fairly awesome; he'd seen that in her over the years, and she pulled herself together. "I was there, too, you know."

"I know."

"So, fire away, Mr. Detective. What do you want to know? Who I think killed her? Yvette, of course. Come into the kitchen and I'll see if I can dig out some wine and cheese. I'm starving. How about you?"

"I could eat," he admitted, thinking back regretfully to his aborted meal and evening with Coby.

He followed Genevieve into a galley kitchen with cherrywood cabinets that had been lovingly taken care of over the years, though a few scars were still visible, and took a seat at the nearby pedestal table, which had a white Formica top nestled into a wood frame. The chairs were wood with spoked backs. They looked uncomfortable but weren't.

"I really liked Annette," Gen began as if she were about to launch into full narrative, which would be fine with Danner. He was a listener by nature. "I don't like that many women, but I liked her. She was . . . brutally honest. She wanted a baby, did you know that?" she asked as she dug into the cupboards, coming up with a green marble cheese board and matching knife.

"With Dave Rendell," Danner said.

"Yup." She pulled a block of cheddar and another one of something whiter, Monterey jack, maybe, and quickly sliced them and fanned them onto the marble board. Then she dug out several boxes of crackers and put them in a bowl, placing everything on the table beside Danner's elbow. Lastly, she opened the refrigerator again and discovered a bottle of white wine, already opened. Pouring two glasses, she slid one to Danner. "You're not on duty, right?"

"I can have a drink," he said, munching on some cheddar and crackers.

"Good." She tipped her glass back, and something about the way she gulped her drink and then stopped, deliberately, as if she were forcing herself to take a break before another swallow, made him think she might be on the verge of a problem.

"Someone killed Annette while we were all there," Danner said. "A fairly bold move, considering any of us could have caught them in the act."

She shook her head. "Annette didn't have enemies. She was *liked*."

"I don't get the feeling that it was a premeditated act."

She thought that over. "Okay. I'd agree to that."

"So, it seems like it might have been a crime of opportunity. It doesn't feel like a crime of passion, either."

"Yvette would kill for passion." Danner waited. He'd mentally catalogued Yvette as the main suspect among Coby's friends, but he wanted to hear whatever else they had to say. When he didn't react, Genevieve went on, "But apart from her . . . well, maybe not. Annette was happy in her life. She probably would've had a baby, if someone hadn't killed her first. It would've happened for her. She was kind of *blessed* that way, you know? She got what she wanted." She took another long swallow from her glass, nearly finishing it. "So, if you cancel out Yvette, then yeah, it probably was a crime of opportunity."

"Our killer's an opportunist," Danner said. "He or she took advantage of the hot tub."

"Think he or she killed Lucas, too?"

"I don't know," Danner admitted. "Moore's death was ruled an accident."

"But *you* think the deaths are linked," she pressed. "I

mean, come on. There's that lock of hair somebody's been hanging on to. Annette told her dad it was Lucas's."

"I know."

"You don't believe it?" She gazed at him in surprise.

"I don't know. But let's go with your theory: that Yvette killed her. Out of passion and opportunity? Why? Over this lock of hair? Something else? Annette was her sister."

"Yvette's impulsive," Gen responded, eyeing her now-empty drink. "And unstable. She really resented the fact that Annette had everything: a loving husband, a comfortable lifestyle, a baby planned for the future. Or maybe Annette was already pregnant."

"She wasn't. Per the autopsy."

"Okay, but that was only because Dave was dragging his feet. Annette would've talked him into it eventually. She really had the most perfect life of all her sisters. I know Suzette's engaged to Galen, but seriously? Galen acts like he's a landscaper, but he's basically menial labor for his dad's company along with his millions of other brothers. Nicholette's got a good job but she's divorced and has a sketchy boyfriend. That Ekhardt guy looks at you like he wants to undress you, especially if you're, like, really young and pretty. Juliet's just a wannabe . . . who's slept with every guy she's dated. She's sure cut a path through our guy group, and now she's pinned her hopes on Kirk, and that's like the kiss of death for a guy like him. And, well, Yvette, we all know what she's like." She turned back to the refrigerator and rummaged around for another bottle of wine.

How much wine had she consumed before he'd arrived? he wondered as she gave a hoot of discovery and pulled out a second bottle. She seemed okay. She was certainly tracking, at least for the moment. But at this rate the alcohol was bound to get her.

"My mom tried to hide it in the vegetable bin behind

the romaine. She knows I want to get pregnant and she thinks she's helping me."

"You and Jarrod are planning to have kids?" Danner asked, wondering if Jarrod was on board with that. His brother didn't seem to have any serious interest in anything beyond the band these days.

"Well . . . yeah." Her lips trembled and she pressed them together, hard. A moment later she shook her head as if physically throwing off whatever she'd been thinking about. "All this conjecture . . . who cares. Yvette probably killed Annette. She's your likely suspect. They were fighting. Maybe Yvette pushed her into the hot tub and then Annette banged her head and drowned. Yvette's just so . . . angry all the time. No moment of opportunity for her. Flat-out rage. If Annette was going to tell something about Yvette, something she didn't want told, well, hey, Yvette would just take care of it."

"Someone held her head underwater," Danner reminded her. He thought about eating another cracker but had already consumed a third of the tray. He wondered if Coby had gotten her bar food.

"Yvette. She would jump in and hold her forcibly under. I could see that. That's just her style."

"No one was in wet clothes," he said.

"Then she didn't jump in. She did it from outside the tub. What do you want me to say? That's it's not Yvette? Who do you want it to be, then? Jesus." She was working a corkscrew with an effort. Danner was about to offer help when it finally released with a soft pop. "Kirk was in wet clothes," she reminded him. "Once he put them back on, anyway."

"Timing-wise, he wasn't by the hot tub at the time of Annette's death. He was getting dressed."

"How do you know?"

"I was there, too. I remember where certain people were, right before Annette was found. Kirk's one of them."

"Your own personal litmus test, huh? Too bad. If it's not Yvette, he'd be my second choice," she admitted. "No more band. Maybe we could concentrate on some other things then, like our own family. You want kids, Danner?"

"Someday."

"I want 'em. But I'm not like Annette. I'm not blessed. The more I want something, the harder it is to get. Do you feel that way?"

"I've had it happen." He'd made a mistake in coming here tonight. Genevieve wasn't really interested in offering any information or insights into Annette's death, she was too wrapped up in her own problems. She was offering up the people she wanted the killer to be, that was all.

"Jarrod and I have fertility problems," she said now, apparently finally getting onto the subject that absorbed her most. "It's the problem du jour for anybody who's anybody these days, right? Hurray for us." She'd refilled her glass and now lifted it high in a mock toast. "All the really important people are doing it, don't you know." Bringing the glass to her lips, she looked across the rim at Danner. "You know how much it costs? For each implant attempt? Fifteen, twenty thousand. Just to get started. We don't even have enough for one try. Goddamn economy. And then my husband wants to quit his day job and just be with the *band*."

"Jarrod wants to quit?" Danner hadn't heard that.

"He hates his job. Always has. But hey, who doesn't? I just wish I had one . . . sort of. Got my teaching degree but never went back for my master's. Didn't want to. But then my dad died and everything went to shit, so here we are." She glanced at his glass and asked, "Want a refill?" before she even noticed his was still full.

"No, thanks."

"Okay, okay." She waved a languid hand. "You wanted to talk about Annette. Or, no, actually you wanted to talk to Jarrod. You think he knows something?"

"I just want to talk to him. Not about Annette."

"Yeah, well, good. 'Cause he doesn't know or care really about what happened to her anyway. It's like sort of interesting to him, but not really. He's, like, living on the moon or something." She looked momentarily forlorn, then shook that off. "So, who else do you know it's *not*, besides Kirk?" she questioned.

"Pretty sure it's not Jean-Paul and it's not Benedict. And it's not Coby Rendell."

Genevieve's ears pricked up. "Oh?"

"I was watching Coby," Danner said neutrally. "I was with her the half hour before Suzette found Annette. Before that, Annette was alive."

"What about me?" she asked. "You think I could've done it?"

"Last time I saw you, you were with Jarrod."

She snorted. "Well, sure. He was playing at being attentive that night. Guess we're each other's alibi." She sighed and sank into the chair next to Danner's. Her blue eyes were beginning to haze over a bit. "I would have never hurt Annette," she said. Then, "Yvette . . . that's another story. I don't like her. She didn't like Annette. Well, she doesn't like anybody, really. She got in a fight with Annette, and she's the one with the secret, isn't she? I mean, who is Benedict's daddy, right? Did Annette know? Did anyone? I bet Jean-Claude knows, and I know it's not Lucas."

"What was Yvette and Annette's fight about?"

"They were snipping at each other all night. It was always that way with Annette and Yvette. Snip, snip, snip."

"How do you know Lucas isn't Benedict's father?"

"Because Yvette started saying so. The night of the campout, Yvette wanted us all to believe she and Lucas were lovers. She insisted they were, but they weren't. It was all a lie to cover up something else. So, where was Yvette that night? Was she with someone else? She wasn't with Lucas."

"You know this for a fact?" Danner asked.

"I can't account for every minute of Lucas's time, but most of it." She ran her tongue around her lips, frowning, deep in concentration. "We all kind of had a thing for Lucas, you know. He was like this major make-out king, but not with Yvette."

"But there are a lot of hours unaccounted for after everyone fell asleep."

"Not so many . . . I snuck away with Lucas for a while," she admitted with a faint smile. "So did Coby, first, though it was just a warmup. Some making out. But later, when he and I were alone . . ."

Danner was aware she was needling him a bit and kept his face expressionless. "Maybe Yvette snuck away with him, too."

"Nope. I think she met someone else," Genevieve stated clearly. "Someone she doesn't want us to know about. Bet it was Benedict's father."

Her words were slurring just a tiny bit. As if hearing herself, she got to her feet, then had to grab for the counter for support, hanging on to the edge.

"Maybe they were fighting over something else entirely," Danner said. "She had the envelope with the lock of hair in her hands."

"But that was new. Something she found that night. She and Yvette were arguing earlier, just like always." She refilled her glass, but her aim wasn't on the mark and she slopped a bit of wine onto the counter. "Oops."

Danner decided it was maybe time to make an exit, before Genevieve became falling-down drunk. She'd held it together at Annette's party, but then she'd been with Jarrod and maybe he'd kept her from going too far.

"Tell Jarrod I'll see him tomorrow," Danner said, setting his barely touched glass near the kitchen sink.

"You're going . . . to the club . . . the Cellar . . . ?"

"That's right."

She seemed to have a little bit of trouble focusing on him. "Maybe I'll go, too . . . then . . . as long as you're gonna be there."

Danner said good-bye, realizing on the way out that she hadn't eaten one piece of cheese or a cracker the entire night.

Coby was in bed when her cell phone buzzed on her nightstand. Fumbling for the switch, she snatched up the phone and saw it was Danner. "Hi," she greeted him. "You got my message?"

"Yeah. Did I wake you?"

"No, no. I was waiting for your call. Listen, I thought of something. I went to see McKenna's act and believe it or not, Ellen Marshall and Theo Rivers showed up."

"Ellen . . . from the night at the beach?"

"She's back with Theo again." Coby could hear the bit of incredulity still filling her voice. "Did I tell you about them? Well, never mind, I'll fill you in tomorrow." She stopped herself. "Are we still going to the Cellar to see Jarrod's band?"

"You bet," he said emphatically.

"Good. Anyway, I was talking to McKenna and Ellen and Theo about Annette's death, and we got onto Yvette and Annette's fight, and who Benedict's father might be . . ." She heard his sound of surprise and asked, "What?"

"I had a similar talk with Genevieve tonight. Go on."

"Anyway, then I thought about how when I called Dana

and asked if she knew why Annette demanded, 'And what about Dana?' to Yvette, and Dana told me I must have got it wrong." She paused. "Tonight I realized I *did* get it wrong."

"What?"

"It wasn't 'what about Dana,' it was 'what about DNA?' because the next thing Annette said was, 'The truth's going to come out.'"

"So you think they were talking about a paternity test for Benedict."

"I do. And I think they were talking about a paternity test that had already happened," Coby agreed. "They were fighting about it."

"So the boy's paternity's still a secret. I wonder why."

"Yvette let me know that it wasn't Lucas, but that's all she said. When she and Annette were fighting, she told Annette to keep her mouth shut, and then said that Annette was only eighteen when she first got involved with my dad. And Annette told her it wasn't about her, and Yvette said it was always about her."

Danner mulled that over a moment, then said, "You know what it sounds like?"

"Yeah. Like Yvette was involved with someone older than she was, because she was only seventeen when she got pregnant. If Benedict's father was her same age, it wouldn't really be the same issue. But if he's older . . . like one of the dads, even . . ."

"Who?"

Coby had been thinking about it ever since she'd understood what she'd overheard. "Hank Sainer," she said.

"Why Sainer?"

"Because he stopped me just before I left Annette's memorial service and asked to meet me at my office on Monday."

"Ahh." Coby could practically hear the wheels turning in his brain. "He didn't say why?"

"No. But I got the impression he wanted to talk about Annette's death."

"If what you're suggesting is true, it would ruin him politically," Danner said. "People might get over the fact that Yvette was underage because she was seventeen, but this secret paternity for all these years. . . . That smacks of cover-up."

"He's never acknowledged he's the father," Coby said. "Maybe he didn't know. Maybe he just found out."

"There's Lucas Moore's death wrapped into that, too. It was ruled an accident, but now with Annette's death, there are questions."

"Danner, I know we're just speculating, but . . ." She could feel her heart pounding.

"But?"

"What if Yvette was meeting Hank Sainer the night of the campout? What if that's who she was with, and she just said she was with Lucas to hide her affair with Hank?"

"Then I'd say your Monday meeting is going to be very interesting."

Chapter 20

Charisse Werner called Danner at 10 A.M. the next morning as he was making himself a cup of coffee. Instant. Starbucks Via.

The ADA didn't mince words. "You read him his Miranda, right?"

"If you mean Lloyd, no. I told him to tell me everything about Sheila and he just started talking."

"I just spoke with Lieutenant Draden. According to what *you* told him, Lloyd implicated himself in a double homicide last night," she said in a voice that could cut glass.

Danner stated tightly, "He's on a seventy-two-hour hold. If you want him arrested, I'll go down and read him his rights right now."

"You should have done it last night," she insisted.

"If I'd planned to arrest him, I would've," he shot back.

"Yeah, well, now we're gonna have a bitch of a time in court, if he gets any kind of defense attorney. Remind me to send you a bowl of fruit and say thanks."

Danner held back a smart remark. Charisse was known for borrowing trouble and tossing around blame long before it ever became a problem. "I'm going to do my damnedest to track down the woman who killed Beth and

Angie Lloyd," he told her. "Jarvis said she just took him over. About a thousand times. I don't care whether you can use that in court or not. I'm going to find Sheila, and when I do, I'll read her her goddamn rights."

"Do that, cowboy." She clicked off in a huff.

Danner ran through the shower to cool off. Lawyers. Rules upon rules upon rules. Half the time the true issue got buried under layers of lawyer shit. He supposed he should be more concerned with an individual's rights, but when it came to spineless worms like Jarvis Lloyd, he really didn't care.

As he was getting dressed—blue jeans, black shirt, black jacket, and yes, cowboy boots, thank you, Charisse—his cell rang. Glancing at the number, he almost hooted with joy.

"Where the hell are you?" he demanded.

Detective Elaine Metzger drawled, "Well, by golly, sounds like you missed me."

He could picture her short and tough frame and pugnacious chin. Somewhere between forty-five and sixty—she was cagey about her age—she scared people with her glare, though there was almost always a twinkle in her eye; you just had to know.

"Are you back?" he asked.

"I'm in town. Wasn't planning on showing up for work yet, but from the sound of it, you might need a hand."

"I do. Come back early. Please."

"You know, I learned something about myself on this trip: I hate good weather. Hawaii . . . what a fucking waste of time. Everybody shows off their skin and guzzles fruit drinks with a squirt of alcohol and acts like they know how to party."

Elaine was a scotch drinker. She could nurse a glass all night, or gulp down three in succession; she never seemed to show the effects.

"I need help with the home invasion case," Danner said.

"Honey, that's what I'm here for."

Sending a thank-you to the gods, Danner brought her up to date on everything that had happened with Jarvis Lloyd since she went on vacation. He didn't say that he wanted her to take over as lead dog because he wanted to spend his time elsewhere; she could figure that out on her own. Probably already had.

In the end, she proved him right by saying, "I'll take the sketch of this Sheila to Mr. Prick . . . Rick . . . with the silent 'p' . . . whatever . . . and squeeze him. You go ahead and figure out what those bohunks in Tillamook are doing over the Deneuve murder. They need you more than they think they do."

"Not exactly bohunks at the sheriff's department."

"Bohunks," she insisted. "Anyone who lives at the coast . . . bohunk."

"Have an opinion, why don't you."

"I'll try. How's Celek been helping out?" she asked, almost as an afterthought.

"Fine. Working some burglaries."

"Off homicide? That your idea?"

Danner thought about the implications with his brother's band and the venues they played that had been burglarized. His gut tightened at the thought, and it took him a moment to drag his attention back. "Celek's a terrier. Grabs hold and won't let go, tail wagging all the way."

"You're actually giving him a compliment?" she asked, incredulous.

"Well, yeah. He's got his moments."

"You got time to go with me over to Prick's?" Metzger asked. "What the hell's his last name?"

"Wiis. Spelled with two i's."

"And a silent 'p'. Can't wait."

"I'll be at the station in about an hour."

"All right. Get your pretty on," she retorted. "We got work to do."

The JJ&R offices were closed for all intents and purposes on Saturdays, but like the week before, Coby found herself working anyway. This time she had no client to deal with; she'd just come in to give a glance over Shannon Pontifica's contract and another longer look at Rhys Webber's written refusal to open the pocketbook for his ex-wife. Already one of the man's numerous paramours had found her way to YouTube and had sent out a message about Rhys and his philandering ways in a both comical and scathing video that was enjoying thousands of hits. The ex-wife's lawyer had called Nicholette and said gleefully that they would see her and her client in court.

Rhys was said to be apoplectic. Coby had tried to warn him that when the shit hits the fan, it's stinky and messy, but he hadn't listened and now, well, it was stinky and messy.

Her cell phone rang and she saw it was her dad. "Hi there," she greeted him. "I'm at work, just kind of cleaning up and—"

"They're going through our bank records," her father burst in. "Mine and your mother's! And our phone records. All financials. It's invasive and makes me feel like a criminal!"

"Who?" she asked automatically, but she knew.

"The sheriff's department. I hear that your ex-boyfriend's working with them. When I saw him with Faith, I wondered what the hell. Now he's part of the investigation, for God's sake. Is she still seeing him?"

"Um . . . no."

"Good. I was afraid he was feeding them information about me."

"Dad . . ."

"Do I need a lawyer? I think I need a lawyer. And your mother, too."

"Dad, I'm . . ." She'd been about to tell him that she was the one seeing Danner Lockwood, but his words knocked it right out of her head. "Are you and Mom . . . together?" she asked instead, her voice just short of incredulous.

That stopped him. "How do you want me to answer that, Bug?"

"Honestly, would be a good start."

"We've been seeing each other," he admitted. "We understand each other. Always did."

"Good God." Coby got up from her desk and stared out the window at the skyline. It was clear that afternoon, the low sun slanting against the downtown buildings, creating dark shadows that swallowed the landscape on their other sides. "I need to ask you a question."

"All right," he said cautiously.

"Were you seeing Mom before Annette died?"

"No. Never. Not the way you mean," he said quickly. "I loved Annette. But you know your mom and I have always been friends."

Not always, Coby recalled very clearly. "Could the police make a case that you were thinking about leaving Annette for Mom?"

"No!"

"Dad, I'm not fooling around here. I know Annette wanted a baby and you were less than excited about the prospect. Add that to the fact that you were seeing Mom and it's a problem."

"It's not like that," he insisted.

"I don't care what it's like," Coby shot back at him.

"That's what it *looks* like. And that's what prosecutors go for, when they're making a case."

"I called you for some help," he said, his voice sounding uncertain, like he was losing control of it. "That's all I wanted."

"And I want to help you. One of the best ways I can is to point out reality. It doesn't look good. It doesn't. And if they're going through Mom's records, too, then they already know."

"Find out who killed Annette. It wasn't me, Bug!"

"I know, Dad. I know."

"Find him!"

Or her . . .

"Dad, Faith isn't seeing Danner Lockwood. I am," Coby admitted. "And Danner's already doing his best to find Annette's killer. Just be smart. Let the authorities do their job and stay calm." *And away from Mom.*

"You're seeing him?" he repeated, sounding dazed.

"Yes."

"What about Joe?"

"You know we've been through a long time. Danner's going to find out the truth, Dad. Don't worry."

His answer was a short, disbelieving bark of laughter, then a mumbled good-bye and a hang-up.

Coby replaced her receiver and wondered if interviewing her friends was a waste of time. Maybe she was making things too complicated. She wanted answers about Annette's death, and it might have nothing to do with Lucas Moore or her group of friends or anything that happened in the past.

Were her friends right? Was Yvette involved? Coby had resisted adopting their view for the very reason that Yvette felt like such an easy target. Too easy, maybe.

But maybe she should rethink that attitude, because she

was beginning to be worried sick about her father . . . and mother.

She was gathering her purse, laptop, and some papers when she heard a knock on her half-open door. She'd thought she was alone in the offices, and her pulse skyrocketed in tandem with her worried thoughts. "Yes?" she called.

Joe stuck his head inside. "Here you are on a Saturday again. Trying to get employee of the year?"

She exhaled hard, forcing herself to relax. "I see you're here, too."

"Yeah . . . about that . . ." He strode casually into her office, his hands in his pants pockets. "You know who Jarvis Lloyd is?" he asked.

"Um . . . yeah . . . he's the home invasion victim?" Coby wasn't about to tell him that Danner was investigating the crime, though as it turned out she needn't have worried about being so protective.

"You're looking at his new attorney," Joe said, pleased with himself.

Coby stopped in the act of zipping her laptop computer into its case. "Since when did you become a criminal defense attorney?" Coby asked, surprised, though she knew the answer only too well, which Joe immediately pointed out.

"Oh, come on. You know my background," he said.

"But you prefer divorce cases. You purposely gave up criminal law."

"Why do I get the feeling you're trying to talk me out of this? Is it because of your relationship with Detective Lockwood, who's been mercilessly dogging my innocent client, I might add?"

Coby stuffed papers into her briefcase, feeling pressure building on all sides. She wanted to scream at him. She wanted to deny, deny, deny. Instead, she counted mentally to five, then said in an even voice, "My dad's looking for a good attorney. He thinks the police suspect him of his wife's murder. Maybe you can fit him into your busy schedule."

Joe instantly dropped his act. "Jesus. Are you kidding?"

"Take it up with my father. He likes you. Tell him you talked to me and I thought it was a good idea." She brushed past him, then paused at the door. "And stop needling me. I thought we were over that."

"*Are* you dating Lockwood again?" he asked seriously.

"Working on it."

"I miss you, Coby."

"Oh, Joe . . ." She would have laughed if she hadn't been so worried about everything as she walked out of her office ahead of him. He didn't miss her. He was merely a master at rewriting the past and making it seem better than it was.

Punching the Down button on the elevator, she checked her watch. Almost one. She had the whole afternoon to catch up on work and then she would be seeing Danner.

The elevator doors opened and she hurried across the echoing concrete chamber of Parking Sublevel B, her heels tapping rapidly. There were only a smattering of vehicles this afternoon, though Sublevel A was public parking. Digging for her keys, she was halfway to the Sentra when she noticed something wrong.

Her steps slowed. The car's rear tires were flat. As she drew nearer she saw the same was true of the front two, as well. All four tires were flat, and as she bent down, she saw a series of slash marks against the nearest rear tire, as if someone had been in an awful hurry, or a blind rage, before it had been punctured.

And there was something on her windshield. A paper.

Heartbeat racing, she moved forward and carefully

grabbed the edge of the page. It was a piece of blank printer paper.

Scrawled in black marker, it read:

YOU DON'T BELONG, BITCH.

Coby's breath came in sharp gasps, matching her wildly beating pulse. She glanced around jerkily, certain someone was waiting for her behind the post, or the side of the elevator, or that huge black Tahoe.

With a shaking hand she unlocked the Sentra, sliding the paper onto the passenger seat. Then she pulled out her phone, her eyes darting to every darkened corner. She punched in Danner's number, and a heartbeat later clicked off. She waited. There were cameras, right? Maybe the perpetrator was on film.

She walked the length of the garage, her nerves screaming. But she was alone. Whoever had slashed her tires and left the note was long gone.

And there were no cameras apart from the ones at the entrance to Parking Sublevel A, which captured all the weekend shoppers who used the parking structure. The garage was ticket-accessed; no one on duty. She would have to pull the tapes if she wanted to find whoever did this. Unless they'd walked in . . .

And it could have been anybody, she realized. Maybe it wasn't even meant for her personally. JJ&R had their share of dissatisfied customers, Rhys Webber being a case in point. He sure as hell didn't like her.

Yet . . . the not belonging part . . .

In the end she punched in Faith's number and started counting in her head, distantly aware that her heartbeats were still fast and hard. When Faith hadn't picked up on the third ring, she almost chucked the whole idea and went back to her first thought. Danner. He would gladly help.

He was a cop. She just didn't want to be a damsel in distress, especially while he was working.

"Coby?" Faith finally answered.

And despite feeling in control, Coby could feel hot tears fill her throat. It took her a moment to say, "I . . . need help."

"What's wrong? Are you okay? Coby! Where's Danner?"

"I'm in the parking garage at work. Someone's slashed my tires. Can you come get me?"

A long moment as Faith assessed. Then, "I'm on my way."

Coby clicked off, calmly called a towing company, then leaned her back against her car and kept a wide-eyed vigil until Faith's BMW came down the ramp onto Sublevel B.

An hour and a half later, she told her sister, "I'm all right," for the umpteenth time, sitting on a plastic waiting room chair, having Faith pace around in front of her. It was a living nightmare. Coby realized she never should have called her.

"You're not all right," Faith snapped. "Stop saying that."

Faith had arrived just before the tow truck. They'd made plans to have the Nissan towed to Les Schwab Tires, and the towing man had winched the car up and onto a flatbed. She and Faith had followed the truck to the tire store and then Coby had picked out new tires.

"I needed new tires," she said to Faith, trying to make light. "Just hadn't gotten around to it yet." And to the employees at Les Schwab, "There's kind of a clunk under the right front tire."

Faith was having none of Coby's "I'm more than okay" attitude. "Somebody's out for you," she said in a whisper, as they were only a few feet from the counter. "What does that mean, you don't belong? Who've you pissed off?"

"Any number of people." Coby walked farther out of

earshot. Though she appreciated Faith helping her out, she now wanted to handle things herself.

"This has to do with Annette's murder, doesn't it? You've made somebody nervous."

"All I've done is talk to a few old classmates."

"You think one of them did it?"

"No." Coby gazed at Faith in frustration. "*No.*" She wasn't about to discuss her theories with her sister.

"Who, then?"

"I don't know."

"You have an idea who killed her, don't you? And somebody knows it."

Coby held up her hands and sidestepped her sister, going to a vending machine. She yanked her wallet from her purse and pulled out a five-dollar bill. "I need caffeine. You want anything?"

"No, thanks."

Coby inserted the bill and waited for her can of soda to drop, gathering her change and dropping it into her purse. Then she popped open the can and took a restorative swallow.

"Coby, c'mon," Faith said. "Stop being so strong. I get it. This is scary. I'd be out of my mind, considering someone killed our stepmother."

"Faith, thanks. Really. You've been great, but really—stop. You don't have to stay with me."

"I want to," she said, trying hard to read Coby's feelings and failing.

"No, really. Please."

The two sisters stared at each other a moment, then Faith sighed and asked, "You sure you're okay?"

"Yes."

"You're going to tell Danner about this, right?"

"Yes. Tonight."

"All right." She gave a quick little shrug of her shoulders. "One more thing: Mom and Dad. They really are together."

"Oh . . ." Coby sighed. "I keep hoping it's a bad dream."

"Don't you want them together?"

"Not *now.*"

"But after this is over?"

Coby stared at her older sister, who sometimes was so damned dense it made Coby want to bang her head against the wall. "What if this isn't over, Faith? What if Dad, or Mom, or someone else we care about is responsible? What if, in the end, we learn something we just don't want to know?"

Faith gazed at her steadily. "Maybe you should stop investigating with Danner. Maybe he could be . . . diverted."

"Diverted? Oh . . ." She felt like she'd been kicked in the stomach. "You really do think one of them did it!"

"No. No . . . no, I don't." She shook her head, trying to convince herself as she moved toward the door, not even looking up to say good-bye as she headed through the double glass doors and across the tire store's parking lot toward her vehicle, her hair blowing in the wind.

Coby thought about what she'd said, and the note on her windshield, and her slashed tires. Anger burned through her; her veins felt on fire. Whoever had tried to warn her off had scared her; that was true. But if they'd thought they would actually scare her off, they'd miscalculated: she was more determined than ever to learn the truth.

Danner walked into Rick's with Metzger at about three o'clock. The same bartender he'd met the first time he visited the nightclub was there. This time he gave his name—Charlie—but he looked nervous about talking to the cops.

"We need to see Rick," Danner told him.

His eyes rolled toward the door to the inner sanctum, then back to Danner. "He doesn't like to be disturbed in the afternoon."

Metzger leaned an elbow on the bar. "Call him."

Charlie sized her up. Elaine wore her dark hair short and didn't give a damn about the silvery strands of gray curling near her ears. He picked up his cell phone, punched in a number, and said nervously, "Mr. Wiis? The police are here." They heard squawking on the other end. "I told them, but . . ."

Elaine snatched the cell phone from his hand and said pleasantly into the receiver, "Mr. Wiis, we'll be coming into your back offices in one minute unless you'd care to meet us out here. We're investigating a murder and would prefer not to bully you. But if we have to, we will. Your choice." More squawking. Louder this time. Then she said, "We'll be right in." She hung up, looked at Danner, who couldn't quite smother a smile, and said, "He seems like a very engaging personality."

They left Charlie and pushed through the door to the inner hallway, which this time was void of hovering women. Danner led them to Rick's door and Elaine gave a light knock. A moment later the man himself answered in a burgundy smoking jacket and an expensive toupe that had tilted just a smidge.

"I was resting," he answered defensively to Metzger's narrowed assessment of him. It was clear he'd come up short.

"All we need to know is how to find Sheila," she said. Danner passed the man the artist's sketch.

Rick wanted to both rush them out the door and somehow defend himself, so he kept them standing by the door but started into a convoluted explanation about the women in his entourage and how sometimes he didn't know them that well, how he even had a few who just popped in for a bit and then left, not wanting to join the group, so to speak.

"Hard to believe," Metzger muttered to this last part.

"Tell us about Sheila," Danner said.

"Sheila was like that. Didn't want to join. She just sorta hung around, but she wasn't really Rick's material, if you know what I mean. She was better than Lucky, though. That girl was fucking weird." He kissed the tips of his fingers and touched the sandaled feet of a brass figurine on a nearby table that might've been Buddha but looked a lot like the character of George Costanza from *Seinfeld.*

"So Sheila moved on to Jarvis Lloyd," Danner prompted.

Rick shrugged. "She thought he was a patsy. She was looking for the big score."

"You kinda pick up stray women here, don't you?" Metzger said, glancing around at the black-and-white photos he had on the wall. New photos, Danner suspected, though the look hearkened back to the Rat Pack and the sixties.

"I run a nice place," he said.

"Uh-huh." She gave him another assessing look, her gaze lingering on the smoking jacket.

"We think this homicide was about Mrs. Lloyd," Danner told him. "But something went awry and the daughter got killed, too. Lloyd made himself believe he could put his dying wife out of her misery. An act of mercy, self-involved as it was, and stop the financial bleeding."

"Enter Sheila," Metzger said, picking up the narrative. "And Lloyd suddenly has a plan and a timetable. No sense waiting around. They set up a plan and Sheila kills the wife, wounds Jarvis Lloyd, and then is surprised by the daughter. Then mayhem."

"Suddenly, Jarvis Lloyd's plans to ride off into the

sunset with Sheila are scratched. He's seen her kill his own daughter," Danner said.

"And she's made a big mistake." Metzger paused, letting the scenario sink in.

"So, she takes off and now we're looking for her," Danner said after a moment. "What kind of person is Sheila?" he asked Wiis. "You think she has any remorse?"

Rick thought a moment. "No."

"She likes money?" Metzger asked.

Rick laughed without humor. "She would cut the ring off her dying grandmother's hand."

"She didn't get the big payoff from Lloyd," Danner said. "His financial records show he sold his stocks over the last few months. He says to pay for his wife's care. But it was a lot of money, and it's just waiting in a bank account now."

"Think she'd try to come back for it? Contact Lloyd? Maybe see if they can pick things up again?" Metzger posed.

"She's too smart," Rick said.

"It's a lot of money," Danner pressed.

Rick looked from one to the other of them. "Maybe . . . after a long time . . . but I saw where he got arrested."

"Good lawyer might get him off," Danner said, thinking of Charisse Werner and how pissed she'd been at him that morning. He didn't really believe Jarvis Lloyd had a snowball's chance in hell of getting out of this mess unscathed, but Rick Wiis didn't have to know that.

As if suddenly deciding it was time to cash in his chips, Wiis blurted, "She bunked with Magda for a while. On the east side."

"How do we get hold of this Magda?" Danner asked, but Rick was already turning to his desk and a black book.

As they left the place, Elaine said, "A smoking jacket and a little black book. Seriously?"

"He's living the dream," Danner said, and Metzger's snort was loud enough to cause a newly arriving male patron in a sharp gray suit to give her a look as he pushed into Rick's.

"Guess I'm not his type," she said.

"But he was yours," Danner responded, and the laugh he chased out of her nearly doubled her over.

Chapter 21

The Cellar was exactly as advertised: a cellar. The main entrance was down a flight of concrete steps painted red, the paint chipped off from many footsteps; the rail was a piece of gray metal pipe. At the base of the stairs was a door with a circular window that Danner pushed open. Inside stood a maître d's podium with a gaunt, tattooed, dark-haired man standing behind it whose hair flopped forward into a Flock of Seagulls wave over his eyes. He said, "Take a seat anywhere," and Danner, with Coby's hand tucked into his elbow, led the way into a dark, black hole with wooden chairs scattered around the perimeter of a dance floor, and a chain-link fence dividing the dance floor from the bar, which was decorated with multicolored Christmas lights that spilled onto the chain-link divider.

Danner had picked Coby up at her apartment at her request and they'd driven to a local burger joint called Shake It Up near the Cellar that Coby had heard had fabulous hamburgers. Shake It Up had come through as advertised, though its real specialty appeared to be shakes and malts. Coby and Danner had each ordered a burger, then shared an order of fries. Afterward, they drove to the Cellar, and by the time they were sliding several chairs around one of the tiny round tables it was after eight. Jarrod's band was the scheduled first act and were slated to appear on stage at nine.

As Coby and Danner sat down, angling their chairs toward the stage, a waitress in ripped jeans and a black midriff leather top took their order of two Coors Lights. Coby wasn't about to trust the wine in the place, but she also wasn't ready for hard liquor.

Now she slid a glance toward Danner, who was lost in his own thoughts, but she knew he was probably reviewing what she'd told him at Shake It Up about her slashed tires and threatening note. She'd put off telling him as long as she could, not wanting to travel down that road till she had to. But it hadn't gone particularly well.

The evening had started with Danner briefing her at Shake It Up on his meeting with Genevieve the night before. He'd told her all about it and Coby had listened attentively with one ear. Danner had ended his tale with, "Gen said she was probably going to be at the Cellar tonight."

Coby had surfaced enough to hear something unsaid in that statement, something uncertain. "What's wrong?"

"She just . . . lost a little bit of focus while I was there. From the wine."

Coby could easily read between those lines, but Genevieve was Danner's sister-in-law and she simply nodded and therefore glossed over Gen's obvious inebriation. She responded to the bulk of his narrative instead. "So, she blames Yvette, too."

"Maybe because she just doesn't like her," was Danner's response.

"Yvette's hard to like," Coby agreed.

"But it doesn't make her a killer."

"Are you going to interview her in person soon?"

"I was thinking Monday, after you talk to Hank Sainer,"

he said. "She works at Xavier's in Laurelton as a barmaid, so maybe Monday afternoon."

"If whatever Hank wants to talk to me about seems to have something to do with Annette's death, I'll urge him to take it up with you. I'm not a lawyer, so there's no expectation of attorney-client privilege, but if it has to do with Benedict's paternity, he might be afraid of letting it all out."

"Sounds good," Danner had said and they finished their meal and headed toward the Cellar.

Now Coby eyed him surreptitiously. She'd carefully kept the events of her afternoon from him for reasons she didn't quite understand until they were walking from the Wrangler toward the club's entrance, when she'd surprised herself, even, by bursting out with, "Someone slashed my tires today. All four of them. And left me a note on my windshield in black marker: 'You don't belong.'"

Danner had stopped short and stared at her. "What? Why didn't you tell me?"

"I . . . don't know. I guess I wanted it to be something else . . . but . . ."

While she stumbled around for an answer, he suddenly grabbed her arms and said, "Coby," in a voice that was like a slap of cold water.

She pulled herself together. "I know. I was afraid to say something." She told him about calling Faith and getting her tires replaced, finishing with, "I think I've made someone nervous."

"You shouldn't be a part of this investigation," was his flat response. "Christ, I'm an idiot!"

"No. Nope. This is what I was worried about!" she said. "Don't stop me. Don't get overprotective. I'm in this by choice. You're just helping out the TCSD, and it's not your call!"

"I want you safe!"

"I can take care of myself!"

They glared at each other for several tense moments, and then he added quietly, "I couldn't live with myself if anything happened to you."

She'd wanted to throw herself in his arms and wrap herself around him, drag him to bed and make love till the sun came up, but she knew better than to run on pure emotion. "Give me some credit," she told him. "I'm not putting myself in crazy danger here. This . . . message . . . is a warning, but so what? We're tweaking somebody's tail and that's what we need, isn't it? And besides, they're cowardly, otherwise you would have been their target, not me. They're afraid of you and so they sent the message to me."

"I don't like it," he stated emphatically.

"I'm okay. I'm right here. And on Monday, after I see Hank, maybe we'll know something more. We could even learn something tonight, depending on who shows up."

Danner had let the discussion die, but Coby knew he'd just put it on hold for a while. Now she turned to him and said, "Are we going to get past this, or do you want to leave?"

"Goddammit," he muttered.

"Danner, you're not my keeper."

"Somebody killed Annette," he reminded her tensely.

"And we're going to figure out who that is. Together."

He shook his head. "All I want is to get you as far out of harm's way as possible. I want to go back to your place. I want to drink wine and kiss you all over and get naked and fall in bed together."

Coby laughed, amused and relieved. "Well, join the club. We could go right now."

In the dim light his gaze captured hers and she felt her breath catch in her throat. Her pulse started to race. Then Danner groaned, closed his eyes, and muttered nearly unintelligible invectives before saying regretfully, "I have an issue with my brother that I have to take care of."

"Well, I'm free later," Coby said lightly.

His eyes opened and he finally relaxed a little. "That a promise?"

"Uh-huh."

He reached across the table and squeezed her hand. "I wish to hell this Deneuve case was resolved."

"And the Lloyd case."

"That one's coming along," Danner admitted, seeming glad to change the subject, which was fine with Coby. "My partner, Elaine Metzger, who's been on vacation, called today, and she and I went to interview a guy, show him a picture of our suspect. He's one of those guys who insulates himself with an entourage, though he's pretty penny-ante on the big-shot scale. But Metzger's a bulldog who doesn't give a shit. She's a tank, more in spirit than size, and she just barreled in and we managed to see this demigod without his entourage and he eventually coughed up a lead."

"To the killer?"

He nodded. "The woman we're looking for roomed with another woman named Magda for a short time. We contacted Magda and at first she swore she didn't know anything about Sheila, our suspect. Then later she said Sheila rented a car from Enterprise; Magda saw the sticker. A Toyota sedan. We've got dates around the time the car was rented and Metzger's on it, checking with every Enterprise car rental in the city. Sheila may not be her real name, but we've got the sketch. Just a matter of time, I think, till we find where she went."

"That's great," Coby said.

He nodded slowly. "If only the Deneuve case were so clear. On the trail of just one suspect."

She circled the bottom of her beer bottle along the

scarred tabletop, moving it through rings of condensation. She didn't want to wade back into the same dangerous waters, but she had other things to tell him, too. "We keep circling around Yvette, and next week you'll talk to her . . . and she is unlikable and she lied about Lucas being Benedict's father, though she was only seventeen at the time. . . ."

Danner waited for her to go on, but Coby had stopped. "And you're wondering if she's at the top of the suspect list for reasons that might have nothing to do with Annette," he finished.

"Exactly. Everybody thinks Yvette's involved in Annette's murder. Maybe accidentally, maybe not. Both Wynona and McKenna think she's capable of killing her sister. Maybe she is. How do you know?"

"You keep looking. Asking questions. Piecing everything together." He said it reluctantly, still not wanting her involved.

But she *was* involved. "Let me tell you about the rest of my evening with McKenna, Ellen, and Theo," she said, subtly reminding him, and then she related everything she could recall of what she'd talked with them about in the green room.

When she was finished, Danner picked out one point: "This death of Theo's ex-girlfriend. I think I remember it. A couple of years after I was out of high school. She died at her gym. Somewhere in Gresham. What's her name?"

"Heather McCrae. And the gym-rat boyfriend is Ed Gerald. I know it was an accident and unrelated to anything else, but all these deaths . . ." She shook her head.

"People die," Danner said.

She nodded.

"But it's just one death more attached to your group."

"Yes," Coby said. "It just feels like Heather's death should mean something, even if it doesn't. Like Rhiannon's."

"I can look up this Ed Gerald." He shrugged. "No stone unturned."

"Good."

The conversation lulled, and Coby took the opportunity to say, "I want to ask you a question, and maybe you can't answer it, but I have to ask."

"Shoot."

"Is my dad a suspect? Has anyone from the sheriff's department said anything to you? Can you tell me?"

He hesitated, then said, "Information is going mostly one way, from me to them."

"If you learn anything, could you warn me?" She knew she was walking a thin line, but she had to know. "He's my dad."

"I don't think the TCSD is anywhere near an arrest," was his careful answer. "That I would know."

"Okay." She felt herself blush, knowing she was putting him in a compromising position.

And then suddenly Genevieve trooped in, followed by Vic and Paul, and then Juliette, Suzette, and Galen. Spying Coby and Danner, they surged toward their table, grabbing chairs and another couple of tables, which were a hot commodity because there were so few of them. By the time they were all seated their group took up one corner of the dance floor.

Genevieve sank into a chair next to Coby. When the waitress cruised by, everyone ordered a drink with alcohol except Gen, who asked for a Diet Coke. She glanced around and, seeing Danner's gaze lingering on her, stated flatly, "I'm my own designated driver tonight."

Coby gazed from her to Danner, who said simply, "Good thinking."

"It's like a high school reunion around here," Vic observed. He'd lost weight since high school, and his hair had thinned, but overall, he looked better, Coby thought.

Suzette said, "Kirk told Juliet that you guys were coming tonight, so I told Vic and Paul."

"I mentioned it to McKenna last night after her show," Coby added. "But I think she's got another show tonight."

Gen gave her a hard look. "You saw McKenna's act? How was she?" she demanded.

"Great, actually. You know who else was there to see her? Ellen. And Theo."

"Together?" Juliet asked, startled.

"Surprising, huh?" Coby nodded. "And they're back together. A couple."

"When did that happen?" Suzette asked in surprise and Juliet appeared to be trying to ask the same, but Suzette beat her to it. "Another of us together," Suzette added, smiling beatifically at Galen.

Coby said, "You'd have to ask them. They seemed really happy."

"Theo's with Ellen again," Paul said slowly, shaking his head as if he couldn't believe it. "You know his ex-girlfriend died in that freak gym accident. Knocked the bar onto her neck and suffocated herself. Couldn't lift it up."

Coby sensed Danner's attention sharpening and made certain she did not exchange a look with him. "I remember that," she said.

"Well, sure. Every time Theo's name is mentioned one of you guys brings it up," Juliet complained. "Every time."

Paul shrugged, uncaring. "So?"

"It's annoying," Juliet snapped. Coby surreptitiously eyed the petite, dark-haired Juliet and wondered if what Gen had said to Danner about Juliet sleeping with all the guys was really true. Knowing Genevieve, it could just be hyperbole. And Juliet was now with Kirk, whose macho attitude wouldn't really be able to tolerate a relationship with someone who'd been with his friends.

Suzette observed, "None of you guys hang out with Theo much anymore."

"He's not around," Galen said.

"Yeah, it's not our fault," Vic added. "He's always too busy. One girl or another . . . and about that Gresham girl who died at the gym, where was her spotter? I always wanted to know."

"Somewhere else, obviously," Gen said, eyeing Juliet's glass of white wine.

"People don't always have spotters," Galen said, to which Paul grunted an agreement.

"It just seems strange, though," Vic muttered.

"What did Theo and Ellen have to say about Annette's death?" Galen asked Coby.

She gazed into his serious eyes. Suzette was clinging to his arm, all ears. "Like everyone else, they thought it was kind of strange that another death happened with our same group, or most of them, and at the same location."

"We're not all really a group," Vic said. "We just went to the same high school."

"That's the very definition of a group," Genevieve snapped. "Jesus." She seemed particularly testy tonight.

The note left on her windshield flashed on the screen of Coby's mind: You don't belong, bitch. Someone didn't think she was part of their group, and she had to figure it was one of her high school friends. Picking up her beer, she took a careful sip, wondering who had left the note. Maybe even someone in this room?

"The guys are a group," Juliet pointed out. "They were the cool group from high school."

"We're still cool," Vic said with a grin.

Suzette said admiringly to Gen, "You know everybody wanted to be you, don't you? You were like royalty. Princess or queen of everything."

Genevieve made a disparaging sound. "You just think

that 'cause you're younger. I was a homecoming queen one year. Lot of goddamned good that's done me."

"I am seriously gonna puke," Vic said, and made huge, ugly retching sounds while Paul grinned and slapped him on the back.

Coby realized Danner, though he was pretending to be somewhere else, was still actively listening. She thought about Jarrod a moment, wondering if she should say what she was about to in front of his brother, then mentally shrugged. Protecting people's feelings went against trying to flush out a murderer. Turning to Genevieve, she said, "McKenna said your note wasn't about stealing your stepsister's guy. It was about you and Lucas Moore together the night of the campout."

Gen straightened. "McKenna said that? How does she know? She never saw my note."

"Was that what it was about? You and Lucas?" Vic asked. "You don't even have a stepsister. We all knew you were lying when you were playing that stupid game."

"Pass the Candle," Gen said through tight lips. "Okay, so I don't have a stepsister. I made it up. So sue me."

Vic came back with, "You just wanted everybody else to spill their guts. You weren't going to give anything away about yourself."

"You did write those notes, didn't you?" Gen said to him. "You did!"

"No, I didn't!" He turned to Juliet, then, and snapped, "You never saw me put a note in anybody's locker. You made that up. Tell them!"

"I saw you put something in a locker!" she protested. "I did!"

"Well, get your fucking eyes checked, because I never did it. And I'm tired of having to keep saying it!"

Juliet lifted up her hands. "Okay, maybe you were just hanging there." But she didn't sound like she believed it.

"Whose locker was it?" Coby asked.

"I don't know. I didn't do it." Vic's jaw was taut.

"Yvette's," Juliet said cautiously, watching him.

"Okay, whatever. McKenna never saw my note," Gen insisted. "I never showed it to anyone and I never told anyone."

"Was your note about Lucas Moore?" Danner suddenly put in.

It was like they'd all forgotten he was there, and now they all snapped to attention as if being called to order. Gen didn't know how to answer him and, after blinking a few times, decided silence was the best defense.

Juliet said to her, "You and Lucas were the most popular."

"Yeah. Well. Things change," Gen said, then snapped her fingers at the barmaid and ordered a glass of white wine.

In a flash of insight Coby realized Gen's claim about stealing her stepsister's boyfriend had actually been a projection of what she was doing to Rhiannon with Lucas. She'd been harboring a thing for the deceased surfer-dude for all these years. And what did that mean for her marriage to Jarrod?

Suddenly the lights went down.

"Hey, everybody," a loud, disembodied voice announced over speakers mounted on the walls. "Split Decision!"

On cue the first notes to an original song by the band blasted through the room and then red spotlights came up to show Jarrod and Kirk in front, blasting away on guitars with the other two members of the band, on keyboards and drums, a few steps back. Jarrod moved to the mic and started singing and Genevieve turned her attention to him. Coby was surprised to see a tear slide down her cheek, glimmering in a red streak from the lights.

Hoots and whistles sounded from the audience, which had, while waiting for Split Decision to appear, definitely gotten its buzz going. The decibel level had risen and conversation had become difficult. With the first few loud notes from the electric guitars, it was pretty much a given that all talking must either cease until the band's set ended or be conducted at a full-volume yell, which still probably wouldn't be heard.

Her eyes on Jarrod, Coby paid attention to the band and settled in to wait till they were done before she even tried to say anything to Danner or anyone else.

She didn't know why she was crying and she absolutely hated it that Coby had seen! Damn. She shouldn't have come. She should have stayed home. Alone. As ever.

Seething, Genevieve sipped her glass of white wine, completely aware that Danner Lockwood was watching her though he pretended to be only interested in the band. Well, maybe he was interested in the band, but he had given her *that look*. The one that silently disparages.

She hated *that look*.

Jarrod had *that look* down pat and wasn't afraid to use it.

Sitting back in her chair in a black funk, she was still rattled over the revelation that McKenna knew her note had been about Lucas, not the stupid lie she'd told at Pass the Candle. What had she been thinking? Jesus Christ. Although she'd barely passed her seventeenth birthday at the time, that was no excuse for just how plain dumb she'd been. A *total* dumbass. And yeah, she'd been homecoming queen. And yeah, she'd known she'd had admirers. And yeah, she and Lucas were the most popular kids in their grade, possibly the whole school at that time.

So fucking what.

She half turned away from Danner Lockwood and took in a large swallow, letting it roll around in her mouth. Terrible stuff, but, oh well.

She thought back to high school, feeling the tightness

in her chest. Lucas hadn't even had to try. He was just cool. She, on the other hand, had carefully orchestrated her popularity, and though she'd been accused, once or twice, of being entitled and kind of grating, well, that was just envy on the part of the losers who tried to bring her down.

High school was great. Best time of her life. Things hadn't gone so well since, though. Everything had turned to crap.

She'd wanted Lucas so much, and that night she'd had him. He was hers! And then he was gone. *Gone.* She'd befriended Rhiannon just to be close to him, then after he was dead she morbidly kept that friendship alive, like it even mattered anymore. Like it would keep her close to him. Wow. She had really been a dumbass.

All Rhiannon did was cry, which was okay at first, but then, as word drifted to Rhiannon that Lucas had been something of a man-slut—thank God Rhee had never put that together with her!—she started whining about him. How untrue he'd been. How everyone had known but her. How unfaithful all her friends were. Some of them were even accused of making out with him!

Rhiannon's affront both scared and annoyed Genevieve. How Gen had wanted to slap the silly bitch's face a time or two! And that hiking . . . Gen had gone with her a time or two, but guess what? It was *dangerous* along those trails. Lethally dangerous, in Rhiannon's case.

But she didn't want to think about that now. Didn't want to ever again. She still felt guilty about it.

Gen sank deeper in her chair, growing morose. Then there was Coby. And Danner, Gen's handsome brother-in-law—who was nevertheless just as lame as Coby simply by virtue of the fact that he was all in love with her! They were both all hyped about finding who'd killed Annette—not that Gen didn't want to know, too; she did—but Gen couldn't stand the way they were running around and playing detective together like it was a game. They kept asking about Lucas and Rhiannon and Annette and that other girl who died in the gym and none of it was going to amount to jack shit because they didn't know anything about anything. Yvette had killed Annette. Gen believed it.

What about Lucas's hair? an inner voice taunted her. *Where did that come from? Who had it, and where is it now?*

Genevieve sucked down some more wine. Someone had cut a piece from his head after he fell, she'd determined. Had to be. His hair had been perfectly fine while they were making love. . . . *While we were making love. . . .*

Her hands clenched at the memory and she fought back a wave of misery.

"You okay?" Coby asked, having to half shout to be heard about the noise of Split Decision.

"Yeah, why?" Gen glared at her, hating her solicitousness. Coby was just too damn smart. Never spent enough time glamorizing herself. Was one of those natural beauties who were uninterested in enhancing what Mother Nature gave them. Focused on her brains ad nauseam.

It was so goddamned unfair.

"You made a sound," Coby yelled, dismissing it as she turned away.

A cry, Gen realized unhappily. A plaintive cry for the loss of the one man who was her equal, loud enough to be heard above this cacophony. God. Her life was in ruins.

I can't have Lucas, and I can't have a baby.

Jarrod was at the mic, singing in that kind of rough-edged way she liked, but Spence and Ryan, the two morons on drums and keyboards, were now drowning him out. Gen hated them all. And why wouldn't Jarrod grow his hair out? Why? Was it so much to ask? He knew she wanted him to. Why did he object so much?

Because he knows you're thinking of Lucas.

Another song began, this one with both Jarrod and Kirk on vocals.

When it ended, Kirk stepped up to the mic. Gen glared at him, then frowned, wondering if she could order another drink without too many raised eyebrows. She focused on Kirk. *Well, this ought to be interesting,* she thought, her eyes roaming the room, looking for the barmaid. Kirk always let Jarrod do the talking because Jarrod was good and people liked him and Kirk was such an asshole and pissed people off without even trying. Now even Jarrod was looking at him askance.

Kirk raised an arm and said, "Hey, people. Glad you came out tonight to witness the last time Split Decision is going to be together. We're . . . splitting."

Gen's gaze jerked to Jarrod, who wasn't hiding his shock. He hadn't known, either!

"I'm heading to Southern California," Kirk said with a wide grin. "Got a friend who needs a bass player, so I'm going. Bye bye, rain. Hello, Mr. Sun." He lifted his guitar off his shoulder and held it over his head. "But right now we got a couple more songs, so here we go. . . ." He looked to Jarrod, who stared back at him, his jaw hard.

Gen recognized *that look.* Jarrod was pissed.

But then Jarrod went back to the mic, started in on some vocals, and the show went on.

Gen felt almost gleeful. Maybe, just maybe, this time the band was over for good!

Danner's eyes followed his brother through the last several songs. He felt tense as a poised bear trap. He'd heard Split Decision a number of times and had always thought they were good for a garage band, not for the big time, maybe, but good enough to keep a crowd happy around the greater Portland area. He'd always suspected that Jarrod knew it, too, even though Jarrod loved the band.

But Kirk's shocking announcement had definitely come as a surprise to all of them, Jarrod included.

The set ended and Split Decision went backstage without much more than a couple of mumbled good-byes. Kirk's bald head shone red as he walked with a swagger across the stage and out of sight. Danner wondered if they were just on break; their time wasn't up yet, was it? Then he heard Genevieve say, "Who knew?" and the rest of her friends chimed in with surprised noises. A few minutes later another band came on and broke into their first set, clearly taking over.

Danner was on his feet. He needed to talk to Jarrod—about a lot of things, it seemed.

"Ready?" Coby asked, looking at him.

"I'm sorry. I want to find Jarrod. Mind waiting just a bit?"

"No problem."

Danner skirted the tables and around the apron of the stage to a side door marked "No Entrance," which he ignored. That's what he loved about Coby, he realized. Her ability to just get what was happening and know when to go with the flow and not get in the way. She was amazing that way. Surprisingly self-confident. Never needing the kind of soul-sucking, constant reassurance so often demanded by other women.

You're thinking in terms of love, he told himself.

He supposed that should bother him some, at least register at some deeper level, but all he felt was grateful for her, glad that she was in his life.

He walked around the back curtain and past a guy who said, "Hey!" which Danner also ignored, and found Split Decision squaring off behind a set of double doors, all of them facing each other across a room with a few of the scarred wooden chairs from the club and not much else. Jarrod actually looked like he wanted to take a swing at Kirk.

"What the fuck's your problem, man?" Kirk goaded him with a sneer, begging to be hit.

"Hey, dude," Spence greeted Danner, his eyes darting around the room like he was looking for an escape.

"You're my problem!" Jarrod snapped back, jabbing a finger at Kirk. "Always with the big deal. Always, always making some kind of stand. Gotta be about Kirk!"

"That sounds like something from Gen's mouth." Kirk was unfazed. Glancing at Danner, he also said, "Hey."

Jarrod slowly dragged his gaze from Kirk and glared blindly at Danner. "What are you doing here?" he demanded, fists clenched.

"Seeing the show." Danner was on the balls of his feet, recognizing the danger of things exploding from his experience on the job breaking up numerous fights.

"I know you've been asking around the clubs about us," Jarrod snarled at him. "You think we're some kind of thieves."

"Not me," Danner said. So, they knew about Celek's inquiries.

"Bull—fucking—shit. And Gen told me about your long talk with her. Coby not enough for you? You want my wife, too?"

"C'mon, Jarrod," Danner said quietly. He'd never seen his brother so furious.

"C'mon? C'mon?" He took a step toward Danner.

"Whoa, whoa." Kirk was holding up his hands. "You wanna hit me? Hit me. What the hell did he do?"

Jarrod wheeled around. "You can't just shit all over us, Kirk! That's what I'm saying."

"You're the one shitting all over your brother," Kirk pointed out.

Jarrod suddenly leapt forward and punched Kirk in the

face. A quick jab that was startling with its speed and intent. Kirk went down, bleeding hard. Spence and Ryan rushed forward, shouting, then stood around on one foot and the other, completely out of their comfort zone.

Danner growled, "Come'n get me," his fists lifted, needing to turn Jarrod's anger from Kirk before he did real damage.

But the punch had drained the fury from Jarrod and now he staggered to a chair, collapsed, and held his head in his hands. His whole body was racked by tremors, as if he were sobbing without sound.

Danner crouched next to him and asked softly, "What the hell's this all about, man? It's not just Kirk."

"No, it's not." He raised a drawn, pale face and said dully, "I'm leaving my wife. She's in love with a dead man. She's always been in love with him. And she's tried to turn me into him and I'm sick and tired of it. Sick and tired . . . I had the band . . . but now that's gone. There's just nothing left." Glancing over at Kirk, he said, "Sorry, man." To Danner, "It's over. It's all over."

Chapter 22

Yvette felt inside the depths of her coat pocket, her fingers sliding around the keys. She was cold through and through, and yet her conviction was strong. With care, she drove the vehicle back to its garage, down a long asphalt drive, very aware of the pole lights that lit up her progress as she made her way to the building with its four garage doors.

This was Don Laidlaw's house. Don Juan, as he was known at Xavier's. Don was in his sixties, thought he was in his forties. He was portly with a well-fed, too many steaks and not enough vegetables look about him. His eyes were large, kind of buggy, and his hands were a little grab-ass. He had an eye for all the barmaids and waitresses at Xavier's and a thick wallet that he was only too happy to open. His wife had left him to go live in a sunnier climate with one of their two daughters and her stick-up-his-butt husband, or so Don claimed.

Don owned a two-story renovated farmhouse built sometime in the forties that was down a long lane. He lived in the house during the spring, summer, and fall, and in the winters he took off for Palm Springs and played golf and probably hit on the women who worked in the bars nearby.

Don liked Yvette. Especially Yvette, because she didn't like him. She told him: "I've got an eleven-year-old son and a job that sucks up all my nights. I have no time for anything but Benedict and work. What the hell would I do with you?"

"I'll take you out. We'll take the Rolls through the wine country and end up at the coast. I'm a gentleman."

With grab-ass hands.

She'd put him off for two years but just recently, when all the shit started raining down, she saw the benefit of knowing him. She'd pretended to be weakening, had even sat at his booth one night, briefly. Not long enough to get fired. Just long enough to set the hook.

He'd gotten drunk and she'd pulled his keys from his coat, knowing about the garage and Don's love of vehicles, the Rolls being only one. She'd sent him home in a cab that night, taken the keys to a locksmith and made a copy of five of them, the ones that looked like they might open the door to his garage or house. The next day, when Don showed up, looking for his keys, she handed them to him and told him with a smile that she'd made copies and he'd better be careful, she might show up at his place one day and surprise him.

He told her she could come by any time. Use his house. Use his cars. Use him . . . please. . . .

She laughed it off and then Don stopped by Xavier's one last time before heading to Southern California until mid-March. He tried to kiss her, but she pulled away. She didn't want him thinking he could get lucky if he stuck around.

Reluctantly realizing she was still unattainable, he said good-bye, and from the moment he stepped out of sight, Yvette started plotting.

She had months before he would be back.

Tonight, all her planning had come to the end. She'd

taken a bus to the stop closest to Don's house and walked down the lane to the garage, unlocking the fourth bay, knowing the car inside was the only one that wasn't a collector's. It was his wife's six-year-old Acura sedan. It was perfect for her plans, and she unscrewed the back license plate and left it at the house.

She drove the Acura to her apartment, parking it on the street. She worked a couple hours at Xavier's and complained of a headache and possibly coming down with the flu and left her torked manager to cope without her. The bastard would probably actually have to do something, for once.

And then she'd called *him* and made the date. He'd refused, of course, but she'd been pretty insistent. He knew the place she wanted to meet. He knew the turn-off from Highway 26 that would wind through a dark, two-lane road and end up at the little inn where they used to meet.

She'd waited in Don Juan's car and watched as his Land Rover cruised by. Then she went after it, pacing herself, keeping back when he made the turn.

And when he'd reached the hairpin turn with a pond on one side and a ten-foot ditch on the other, she rammed him with everything she had, sending him spinning out of control and into the ditch with a slow tumble that ended in the field beyond.

Now she was shaking. Shaking so badly she could barely close the door on the garage, aware she was lucky the Acura had kept running although there was definitely some serious damage on the left front side.

She walked back toward the bus stop, aware that her left leg was aching badly. Something had rammed her upon impact. The dashboard? Steering column? Whatever it was, it hadn't affected the engine. Her leg had been pinned, though, something she hadn't messed with until she was back at Don's garage, and then she'd had to work herself free. Now her knee hurt like hell, but it was functioning and that's all that mattered.

After boarding the bus, she sank into a seat in the middle. Thirty minutes later the bus dropped her off and she half walked, half hobbled through a wisping fog to her apartment complex. Juanita was there, taking care of Benedict. She didn't know Yvette had left work as Yvette had parked her car down the street, changed into less noticeable clothes, then walked down the road to the bus stop. Now she did the reverse, circling the complex on the way to her car. She changed again, wincing in the cramped space. Her knee was swollen, she realized, and as she put back on the Xavier's uniform—black short skirt, form-fitting top, black tights—she wondered just how noticeable the swelling was.

She entered her apartment as if she were just getting off work. Juanita, who'd cleaned the kitchen and picked up the living room, was dozing on the couch. She awakened with a start when Yvette appeared, and then happily chattered on about Benedict and how he'd done all his homework, had actually shown his math paper to Juanita—such a smart boy!—who hadn't understood any of it.

As soon as Juanita was out the door Yvette moved to Benedict's room, switching off the hall lights and letting her eyes adjust to the dark. She cracked open the door and listened, hearing her son's even breathing. Then she walked to his bed and gazed down at him.

He was the most beautiful boy. Beautiful boy.

And he was all hers.

She retraced her steps to the kitchen and poured herself a glass of water, staring out the window to the parking lot below. Something was wrong with her. She was quivering like a palsy victim. Quivering all over.

Reaction. Closing her eyes, she tried to zen out.

She hoped to hell Hank Sainer was dead.

* * *

Coby watched Genevieve get to her feet and walk toward the Cellar's chain-link-fenced bar area. Danner had been gone about fifteen minutes and the party was breaking up even though the current band was energetically trying to keep the crowd happy. Suzette and Galen had followed Gen, and Paul, after a moment, headed their way as well. Juliet looked from Vic to Coby, then got up, said something about leaving, then strode out the door.

Vic gazed at Coby in a way that made her start to feel nervous. She thought of the slashed tires.

But what he said was: "Kirk Grassi's an asshole."

Though Coby wholeheartedly agreed, she said, "He's your friend."

"An asshole friend. We've all got 'em. You know why he's leaving, don't you?" he said. "He can't stand Jarrod. Resents him, his suburban life . . . everything about him and Genevieve. Kirk's glad they lost all their money on that house. They couldn't afford it but Genevieve is such a bitch with big plans, and Jarrod let her run all over him way too long. Kirk finally said fuck it, and that's what you saw tonight." He picked up his beer and drained the rest of the bottle.

Coby absorbed that, then asked, "What about Juliet? He said he was going to California. Didn't sound like he was taking her."

He barked out a nasty laugh. "Juliet? We've all had a piece of that. Kirk knows."

Just talking to Vic made Coby feel like she was going to need a cleansing shower. "I thought he was her boyfriend."

"What are you, still in high school? Boyfriend? She's a hookup, and she can call it any damn thing she wants, but Kirk's not into her. Not like that."

"Sounds like she's the last to know," Coby stated coolly.

"She knows. Don't feel sorry for Juliet, or Suzette, or any of those Ettes. They're all crazy, fuckin' bitches, if you ask me. Even their own dad said they were at Annette's party."

"Doesn't sound like Jean-Claude," Coby said tautly, gathering up her purse. She'd heard enough.

"Yeah? Suzette overheard him. You can ask her."

Coby left the table. She saw the rest of them through the black chain-link wall. Gen was just getting a glass of wine and Suzette and Galen were hanging around. Coby had a sudden memory of Jean-Claude saying, "All my daughters are smart and beautiful, but a little tweaked, eh?" to her when she'd first seen him at Annette's party. And she'd thought Suzette had been taking a nap, but maybe she wasn't asleep and had overheard.

But "a little tweaked" was a far cry from "they're all crazy, fuckin' bitches," Vic's own spin on Jean-Claude's comment.

Gen waved Coby to come inside the bar, and she reluctantly did so. Better than talking any more to Vic Franzen.

Jarrod was still sitting in his chair as Ryan and Spence helped Kirk to his feet. The left side of Grassi's face was swelling rapidly.

There was a strained silence in the room, broken when Jarrod said, "Spence, Ryan, if you've been lifting band equipment from our venues, better stop. The law is onto you."

Danner looked from Jarrod to Spence, Ryan, and Kirk who were all staring open-mouthed in Jarrod's direction.

"Huh?" Ryan asked, blinking rapidly.

"They'll find you on craigslist, or wherever you're selling the stuff," Jarrod said. "If you turn yourselves in, return the stuff, and make restitution, you might even get a pass," Jarrod added reasonably. He slid a look to his older brother for confirmation.

All Danner could feel was relief in being tacitly told that his brother wasn't involved in the burglaries. He nodded to both Spence and Ryan, whose faces were studies in panic.

"We didn't do anything wrong," Ryan protested.

"An investigation is under way and you have a limited time to get ahead of it," Danner told them. "You need a good criminal defense attorney."

"Are you deaf, man?" Spence yelled. "We're not going to jail for this! We weren't even there."

"Jesus, you guys are dopes," Kirk said in disgust.

The two accused men left in a rush then, grabbing their equipment and practically stumbling over each other on the way out.

Jarrod heaved a sigh and said, "They brought me some cash. I didn't take it. Told them if they were stealing to stop. They knew Gen wanted a baby and that we couldn't and how much it was going to take to have one . . . Gen talks and talks. They wanted to help pay for the IVF procedure."

"They're dumb bunnies," Kirk put in. "But they're not, like, criminals."

Danner looked at him and Jarrod rushed in. "I swear, Danner, if you say something like a crime's a crime, I'll punch you out, too!"

"Yeah?" Danner asked him.

"A crime's a crime," Kirk stated flatly.

Jarrod glared at him coldly a long moment, but Kirk merely sent him back a lopsided grin; he held no grudge. Finally Jarrod shook his head in disbelief, then gave a short, aborted bark of laughter. "Dumb bunnies," he repeated.

Danner said, "Tell them to get their lawyer to contact Joshua Celek at the Portland PD. Soon."

Jarrod stared at the floor a moment, then nodded and said, "Will do."

Danner turned to leave, but Jarrod asked, "Can you hold on a bit? I need a little time before I go and face her."

Her being Genevieve. Danner thought about Coby, then pulled out another chair and straddled it backward, wondering how long it took someone like Jarrod to grow some balls.

Coby was perched on a stool beside Genevieve, who'd finished her drink and was twisting the stem of the wine-glass between her fingers. Suzette and Galen had left and Paul was trying to talk Vic into going as well.

Vic seemed to want to hang around, and that finally decided Genevieve, who threw both Coby and Vic a dark look and seemed to want to say something else, then flounced away.

"So, have you learned anything about Annette's murder?" Vic asked as soon as he and Coby were alone again.

She found herself glancing at her watch for the umpteenth time. "Not really."

"Not really? Or you just don't want to say? Hey, I can keep a secret."

Coby had had enough. "Vic, is this some kind of learned behavior? This I'll just keep being annoying and maybe something'll happen attitude? It's why everyone wanted to blame you for leaving the notes. You know what mine said: 'You don't belong here.'"

He'd opened his mouth to protest, but now he slammed it shut. "No, it didn't. You said it was about your dad." He hesitated, as if unsure. "Didn't you?"

"Never mind." She'd just tossed that out to see what

happened, but Vic was clearly at sea. He might be odious, but he hadn't left her the note; ergo he hadn't slashed her tires. She hadn't really thought so.

And then she saw Danner weaving around the dancers who were swaying to a slower beat as he made his way to the bar. Vic followed her gaze and tossed down some money for his beer.

"Everybody gone?" Danner asked.

Vic said, "I'm the last. Are the guys really done?"

"They're packing up."

Vic shook his head and took off and Danner took his place at the bar by Coby.

"Everything okay?" she asked him.

"Yeah." A smile flirted at his lips, then disappeared. "Although I think my brother's marriage is about to end."

"Oh?"

"I wouldn't be surprised," he said.

"I'm sorry to hear that." He nodded in agreement, and after a moment Coby asked, "Is Kirk really leaving Split Decision?"

"What time is it?" he suddenly asked.

"Ten thirty. I just checked my watch."

"Is that all?"

She laughed. "Does the night feel interminable?"

"It has since we've been at the Cellar," he said, "but I have a feeling that's going to change."

"Yeah?"

He moved in closer to her, close enough that she caught a peek-a-boo view of the edge of the shoulder holster where he kept his gun. "I think there was a promise tossed out earlier that I want to make good on."

Coby swept up her purse and gave him a smile, then turned without a word to the exit. She was aware of him behind her as she hurried up the steps and outside to the street. The rain was on hold; there was an expectation in the air, as if something was pent-up and waiting to happen.

Danner caught her at the top of the stairs, before she turned to the parking lot. As if he felt the atmosphere, too, he suddenly pulled her close, melding her body to his, hands sliding to the small of her back, sliding her forward.

Coby was smiling. She opened her mouth to say something clever, she hoped, but the kiss his lips slammed onto hers left no doubt what was in his mind. And it ignited her. One moment she felt playful, the next she felt limp in his arms, which only fueled his desire. She ran her hands around his back as well, feeling the tense muscles beneath his shirt.

"PDA," she finally gasped out when she came up for air.

He lifted his head, gazing down at her hotly. "Let 'em look."

"In front of the Cellar? Take me home. Now."

He growled, then kissed her again, hard, before letting her go. She started laughing and his teeth were a slash of white in the darkness. Then he cupped her chin and brought her forward for a long, sweet, lingering kiss that promised what the rest of the night would hold.

I wait in my car, cracking the window in order to see and hear them, as the windows are fogged from rain and the warmth of my heater.

Coby Rendell is a cancer. She's spreading like an evil scourge.

But she's a cancer with intelligence. She's gathering information. She's drawing conclusions. She's everywhere. With her man, her lover, Detective Danner Lockwood.

I want them both dead.

Coby . . .

The circle was ruined long ago, but she should have never been there at all.

She doesn't understand.

And she won't stop.

Soon, soon, an opportunity will arise, a plan will form. Soon she'll be gone.

As I wait, Coby appears at the top of the steps and smiles into the night. She draws her coat close and looks back.

And then Danner Lockwood joins her, wrapping his arm around her, looking down at her with love, pulling her close, pressing her body to his in a way that leaves no room for doubt that he wants to fuck her.

My blood boils. I feel my breathing accelerate.

She's laughing, ducking her head, playing. But then she responds and he kisses her hard, like it's his last hour on earth. And she's bending to him like wax.

I want to pleasure myself at the sight of them, the way their hands ravage each other, their lips straining forward as soon as they part, their bodies ripe with wanting.

My hand drifts downward.

But I refuse. Turn my groping fingers into a fist of rage.

I watch as she laughingly tosses her head and says quietly, "In front of the Cellar? Take me home. Now."

He pulls her to him once more, then groans and complies, cupping her face and kissing her lightly before grabbing her hand as they hurry around small puddles in the tarmac to his car.

I slide down out of sight.

I feel physical pain.

My insides writhe.

I cannot let them live.

* * *

They were in his car and Coby couldn't think straight. She squeezed her eyes closed, filled with wanting him. And he definitely felt the same way. Opening her eyes, she stared through the windshield, but the word "sex" seemed to be glowing in red letters in front of her vision. S E X !

He half turned to her, his hand poised on his keys, ready to switch on the ignition. She saw the echo of what she wanted in his tense expression. "What are you thinking about?"

She moved her head helplessly. "I'd be embarrassed to say."

"Say it."

Instead, her gaze drifted down to the place between his legs, and his groan of desire made her cover her face with her hands and laugh softly. "I feel like I'm fourteen!"

"We've got to get to your place, and fast."

Danner was turning out of the parking lot, his jaw set, his expression hard. He muttered something about feeling like he was going to explode, which sent her into another fit of laughter.

"Stop it," he said, flashing her a smile. "I mean it."

Which made her laugh even harder.

Then his cell buzzed. He'd turned it off when they were at the club, only flipping it back on as they exited. He'd even grunted to himself in satisfaction that he'd had no calls.

Giving her a tense look, he hesitated a moment, then picked it up. "Lockwood." Coby could hear a male voice twanging away on the other end of the line, though she couldn't hear what was being said.

Oh, no, she thought as the Wrangler suddenly slowed and Danner pulled sharply over to the shoulder on Highway 26, not exactly the safest move. He put the vehicle in park and turned on the hazard lights as he listened intently. Then he said, "Okay. I'll head to the scene."

"What?" Coby asked, when he'd switched off.

He stared at her through the semidarkness of the vehicle. "There's been an accident not far from here, just outside Laurelton. Someone ran Hank Sainer off the road. His Land Rover rolled and he's being pulled out with the Jaws of Life."

"Oh, God . . . is he . . . alive?" she asked hopefully, fearfully.

"I'm going to find out. After I take you home."

Chapter 23

Danner's cell phone rang twice more before he pulled in front of Coby's building. The first time the message was that Hank Sainer had been life-flighted to Laurelton General Hospital, but it was the second call that caused him to sit up in his seat and freeze.

"What?" Coby asked, fear skittering down her spine.

He hung up after saying, "I'll be right there," and turned to her a bit blankly. "Jarvis Lloyd tried to leave his room and when the guard outside tried to stop him, Lloyd grabbed his gun, placed it under his own chin, and pulled the trigger. He's . . . dead."

"Oh, my God."

"I've got to meet my partner at Riverside West Hospital, where Lloyd is."

"Okay."

"Stay here," he said urgently. "Be safe."

Coby said, "I'm going to call my dad. Hank's a friend. If he wants to see Hank, I'll take him."

"Just be careful."

"Always."

She slid out of the Wrangler and lifted a hand in goodbye, watching his taillights disappear around the corner, realizing distantly that the rain might have stopped but fog was drifting around in feathery pieces, like props in the dance of the seven veils, teasing one moment, gone the next. Shivering, she pulled her coat closer to her neck and hurried up the two steps to the small stoop and her own front door. She let herself in and switched on the lights, feeling discombobulated. Had it really only been a few short hours since she and Danner left for dinner at Shake It Up? It seemed like a lifetime ago.

Crossing her living room, she switched on the television. The news was almost over but she had her television set to Channel Seven and she reversed her DVR as far as it would go and there, suddenly, was Pauline Kirby's narrow face and her dark cap of hair with its severe cut. The background was a hospital. Laurelton General, Coby realized as she turned up the volume.

"Appears to be a one-car accident," Pauline was saying, "although another driver came upon the scene a few moments later and was certain two cars pulled off Highway 26 in front of him, one closely following the other. The other driver did not stop, apparently. Mr. Sainer was life-flighted here, arriving just moments ago. He is undergoing surgery now."

The scene switched to the wreck of Hank Sainer's car, and Coby shuddered. It truly looked as if the Land Rover had been ripped apart by a giant can opener, which was kind of what the Jaws of Life were.

She lost the thread of Pauline's narrative, wondering about Hank. And then her thoughts turned to Jarvis Lloyd and Danner. The program went to commercial and Coby pressed the Forward button to catch up. Just before the program ended, the local anchors said there had been a shooting at Riverside West Hospital, a patient having taken their own life.

Picking up her cell, she phoned her father's condo.

When she got no answer, she tried his cell and wasn't all that surprised when her mother was the one who answered.

"Mom, it's Coby. Have you heard about Hank?"

"Your father and I are on our way to the hospital now," she said.

"I'm coming, too," Coby said, then snapped off before her mother could say anything, positive or negative, about that decision.

Riverside West was a madhouse, inside and out, when Danner arrived. The hospital was in lockdown mode after the shooting and Danner, who preferred to leave his gun in his car unless he was on active duty—mostly as a means to avoid the kind of tragedy that had just taken place—had done just that, tucking the Glock in his glove box. He'd hoped to avoid the security rigamarole he would encounter just trying to get inside, but that wasn't going well. His badge was being scrutinized as if he were a terrorist, and it was only when Metzger, who'd been waiting for him, cruised by the front of the hospital and saw him that his explanations were treated seriously and he was allowed inside.

And just as they were walking away, the news vans pulled up with a screech. Danner glanced back through the wall of security personnel and through the glass doors to see Pauline Kirby step out of a white van. They'd left Laurelton General and injured politico Hank Sainer for the even bigger story of Jarvis Lloyd's suicide.

Metzger caught his glance back. "Don't let the vultures get you."

"Hank Sainer was at the beach house the night Annette Deneuve was killed," Danner said. "It was a side note last week and would be a lead story if it weren't for Lloyd."

"You're involved with breaking news all around," she muttered. "Pauline's gonna be hunting for you."

"Lucky me."

Lloyd's body was already in the hospital morgue, and they took the elevator to the basement. The guard who'd had his piece stolen by Lloyd and witnessed the suicide was standing with a small crowd of hospital personnel when they entered. He looked sober but in control, except for the quiver that sporadically hit his knees.

"Hey, sit down," Danner said, pulling up a wheeled stool and easing the protesting man onto it. "What happened?"

In the automaton voice of a person who'd already told the tale too many times, Officer Rod Eyerlie recounted the events of the evening, which broke down to: 1) Lloyd called the nurse and asked for something to help him sleep; 2) a nurse brought him a sleep aid; 3) he pretended to take it; and 4) he walked out of the room and told Eyerlie he was sorry, then actually slammed himself into the surprised guard, lifted his gun, held Eyerlie at gunpoint for about ten seconds, ordering him to retreat, and when Eyerlie did so, he placed the barrel under his chin and fired.

Danner watched the man carefully as he recited the events. It wasn't easy witnessing a suicide. When Eyerlie finished, Danner put a hand on the man's shoulder and said, "Nothing you could do. Lloyd was intent on killing himself."

"We should've handcuffed him to the bed," Metzger said as they walked together out of earshot.

"Yeah." What Danner didn't add was that people bent on taking their own lives mostly found a way to do it. Maybe some could be convinced that life was worth living. In Jarvis Lloyd's case, with the blood of his daughter on his hands, Danner doubted that would be the case.

"Guess Charisse Werner won't have to be worrying

about whether Lloyd was Mirandized anymore," Elaine said dryly.

Danner didn't acknowledge her. There were a whole lot of new issues to contend with now.

The fog was still patchy as Coby nosed her Sentra around Laurelton General's front parking lot. The lot was nearly full, but there were scattered spots. She parked toward the street side of the lot, away from the center median with its covered roof where vehicles faced each other beneath the portico that ran from the parking lot and to the front doors.

She was surprised at how quiet it was, but then the media had probably been seduced by the Lloyd suicide. Hank Sainer was a politician whose name was known, but Jarvis Lloyd—he'd been traveling down the road of notoriety already and had just hit the wall of infamy head-on.

Entering the hospital, she turned to the reception desk, where a man in a dark blue blazer sat, wearing a headset. He regarded her approach with eyes that gave nothing away and a less than interested attitude that said if she wanted information, she was definitely going to have to ask the right questions and maybe, if she was lucky, she might actually get some answers.

"I'm a friend of Hank Sainer's," she said. "He was involved in an automobile accident this evening and is in surgery, I believe."

"There's a waiting room outside the OR," was his response. "Down that hall and around the corner, by the emergency room doors."

"Thank you."

She turned to follow his directions, and at that moment the front doors slid open and Yvette, wearing a short black dress with a Lycra bodysuit top, half stumbled through the front doors. Her hair, normally tied into a ponytail, was straight and disheveled and there was a wild look in her eyes.

"Hank?" she asked desperately, spying Coby.

If Coby hadn't already suspected Hank was Yvette's secret lover, the father of her child, she'd be getting a pretty good idea right about now. "Still in surgery."

"Is he awake? Has he said anything?"

"I just got here. I think my dad's here." She found she couldn't say "with my mom."

"Do they think he'll live?"

"Well, we're all hoping," Coby answered. "Come on, there's a waiting room outside the OR."

Coby started toward the hallway once more, but Yvette didn't move. She seemed paralyzed. Disoriented. Returning to her, Coby eyed her with concern. Yvette looked as if she were gazing at some horrible scene that only she could see.

"I can't," she said.

"You sure? You can come with me, if you want."

"No . . ."

Yvette's feet seemed stuck to the foor. It was as if there were a line drawn on the carpet that she couldn't cross.

"Did you know Hank was coming to see me on Monday?" Coby asked. "He caught up with me at the memorial service and made the appointment. I got the impression he wanted to talk about Annette's death."

Yvette reared back as if Coby had struck her. "*Monday?*"

"That's what he said."

She said in disbelief, "He was really going through with it."

Coby hadn't intended to ask Yvette about her suspicions regarding Benedict's paternity, but sometimes the opportunity just arose. "With . . . the DNA test?" she guessed.

Yvette's dark eyes were dull as they focused on

Coby. "You know about that. I thought so," she stated flatly. "Annette just couldn't keep her mouth shut about anything."

"Hank Sainer is Benedict's father," Coby clarified.

Yvette looked lost and disillusioned. She gave a curt nod. "We already had the DNA test done. Annette was on me about it. She wanted me to acknowledge Hank, or something, but he'd never wanted Benedict. Then all of a sudden, bam! He goes for full custody! He was taking me to court!" Yvette seemed to shake herself back to the present, and for a moment Coby thought she might break down and cry. "But he can't now, can he? Unless he recovers."

With that she turned on her heel and headed back outside, moving with a funny, limping gait. It was as if she'd made some kind of decision that had been up in the air before she'd entered the hospital, and now she was ready to act upon it.

Coby hesitated for half a beat, then hurried to catch up, heading through the glass doors after her. "Wait! Can we talk a minute?"

"Not interested." Yvette made a beeline for a car nosed into the center strip parked beneath the roof. A small compact. A black Ford Focus.

"Annette was going to tell everyone that Benedict was Hank's son. That was the secret she planned to tell."

"She was *siding* with Hank!" Yvette stopped at her car, frozen, keys in her hand though she didn't put them in the lock. Coby was only a couple of steps behind or she wouldn't have been able to see because of the fog. "You want me to say I killed her?" Yvette suddenly yelled, still turned away from Coby. "Is that what you want?"

"What happened that night? You were fighting with her about spilling your secret."

"You bet I was." Now Yvette turned, the planes of her face shadowed, her mouth grim. "Annette was a know-it-all bitch who had to meddle in my affairs. We fought. Yes.

And yeah, I pushed her into the hot tub. But it was a mistake. I was just so mad at her that I shoved her. She fell into the tub and then I rushed up but she was just sitting there, kinda dazed. I told her she was a bitch and I went inside. I left her there.

"She just wouldn't leave me and Benedict alone, you know? I hated her. All she ever did was mess things up! But then . . . then she was dead, but when I left her she was sitting up!" Yvette's voice had started to shake. She seemed to be unraveling right in front of Coby. "Somebody else held her under. It wasn't me, and it's not my fault that she died! Yes, I pushed her, but it was an accident. If she'd just left me alone . . ."

"What about the lock of hair?" Coby asked quickly as Yvette stabbed the key in the lock and twisted.

"I don't give a good goddamn about Lucas's hair. It wasn't my sick souvenir. I lied about him, okay? I admit that. We weren't lovers, but that's all I lied about."

"You were with Hank the night of the campout."

"Yes! Yes. I was with Hank, okay? But Lucas just *fell.*"

"You saw him fall?"

"*Yes*. He tripped and fell and it was *terrible*. Stop making a federal case out of it! It was an accident, too!" She jumped into her car and slammed the door behind her.

"Do you think I don't belong?" Coby yelled after her, which earned her a look that said Yvette thought she was completely nuts.

Yvette threw the car in reverse, nearly running over Coby, who moved a good ten feet away, then she jammed the car into gear and it leapt forward with a little *blurp* of tires.

Coby's breath was coming fast. She felt like she'd just run a marathon. Everyone had said Yvette had killed Annette, and now it looked like they'd been right. Except Yvette wouldn't cop to the fact she'd held her under. Not yet, anyway. Maybe in time. Maybe now she just couldn't accept that she'd killed her sister.

In a detached part of her mind, she heard an engine fire up. Someone leaving the hospital.

But her mind was making feverish connections. Yvette was with Hank and not Lucas. Lucas's death *was* an accident. He died of head trauma—no, wait—Danner had said he died from drowning, though from his injuries it looked like he'd hit the back of his head against the cliff or rocks or both, and then turned over later. Possibly by the waves. Or possibly by someone who'd taken a piece of his hair?

Yvette had kept the secret of Benedict's paternity for her own reasons. But Hank had been about to go for full custody, and Yvette clearly believed he had just cause or she wouldn't be so scared now. In a fit of anger, she'd shoved Annette, who then fell into the hot tub and drowned. But someone had held Annette under; there were marks on the back of her neck and she'd tried to claw her way free. Yvette wouldn't go so far as to accept blame for that, but then maybe she hadn't done it? Maybe it was just as she'd said: she had entered the house after pushing Annette. Maybe someone else seized the opportunity to get rid of Annette, who was all about divulging secrets and had found a lock of hair that she believed was Lucas Moore's.

The departing car's headlights swept the front of the hospital as it curved through the turnaround, its engine revving. Coby saw the flash of light, and a detached part of her brain knew she was in its path, so she moved to one side of the parking lot.

But what if Yvette was telling the truth about Annette? What if someone else—a true opportunist—had either seen or come upon Annette falling into the hot tub and simply finished what Yvette had begun? What if someone came upon Lucas Moore after he fell onto the rocks and clipped a swatch of his hair and then pushed his face in the water, making certain he drowned?

What if someone then followed Rhiannon onto a cliff trail and made certain she tumbled to her death?

"But why?" Coby said aloud.

The sudden loudness of the approaching car's engine. A high-pitched whine. A squeal of tires screeching against slippery pavement.

Coby jerked around, shocked. Headlights blinded her. Twin beams in gray fog. White and glaring.

The car shot forward. Spurting toward her. A sedan? her brain wondered as she leapt for the grass.

The car came right at her. *Smack!* She felt a jolt in her hip. She spun like a top, then went down. Facedown into mud and grass. She yanked up her knees in a move of automatic self-preservation, certain the car would run over her legs. But it tore past Coby, accelerating.

Groggily, she raised her head to try to read the license plate, but the fog obscured everything but the shape of the red taillights and a general idea that the vehicle was light-colored.

She laid her head back down. Afraid. Cold. Wondering if the driver would suddenly reverse and try for a second attempt at her. Fear shot a jolt of adrenaline through her system and she struggled to her feet.

She swayed, catching her breath.

She heard shouts. Coming from the hospital. Someone had seen the attack.

But the car was long gone, onto the highway, by the sound of the disappearing engine. Not interested in another swipe at Coby.

"Are you all right, miss?" It was an orderly, she thought, based on his white garb. He hadn't come from the front of the hospital but was apparently already outside, walking along one of the sidewalks from another wing.

"I think so." She slowly sat back down on the cold, wet ground.

"Are you sure? I can get a wheelchair or a gurney."

"No. Just give me a minute."

"I'll be right back," he said, running toward the front door, clearly not believing her.

But Coby knew she was basically unhurt. All she felt was reaction. From everything that had happened the whole day. She didn't know what it meant. She didn't know how much was fact and how much was conjecture on her part, but someone was out to get her.

And whoever that someone was, it wasn't Yvette Deneuve, because Yvette hadn't had time to drive out of sight, turn around, and circle the parking lot to attack Coby.

And the car that came after Coby was white, or tan, or maybe even light gray, hard to tell with the fog.

But it sure as hell wasn't a black Ford Focus.

I disappear into the blanket of the fog, uncertain. By all rights she should be dead but she darted at the last moment, spinning away. I think I may have just grazed her.

Did she know it was me?

A thrill shoots through me. Stimulating. Sexual. I hope she knows it was me!

No. I cannot think that way. Cannot let the desire that rules me overtake my planning.

I am a master at the art of planning and opportunity.

I killed Lucas.

I killed Annette.

I killed that bitch Heather.

I wanted Rhiannon dead, but I did not kill her, though I know who did. . . .

The time is coming.

If Coby Rendell is not dead, she will be soon. The minutes of her life are ticking down.

I will make sure of it.

Chapter 24

There was no escaping the hospital cavalry. Coby tried to make it to her own car, but the orderly who'd seen her came out of the hospital with a wheelchair and a real need to call 911 and the police, and the only way Coby could get him to hold off was to climb into the wheelchair and let him push her back inside.

"What's your name?" Coby asked him, half turning in the chair, as he was behind her and she had to admit that she did feel a bit weak. The hit-and-run had knocked the stuffing out of her temporarily.

"Tim."

"Well, Tim, if you would wheel me to the ladies' room, then I'll place a call to my boyfriend, Detective Danner Lockwood of the Portland PD. Thank you, but I don't need any more help. I know what this is about," she stated firmly, lying a little.

"I'm taking you to the emergency room—" he started, but Coby cut him off with, "No. I'm on my way there anyway, but I'm going to clean up first. You can wrestle me if you want, but that is the way it's going to be. You understand?"

For an answer he slowed the wheelchair to a stop. Coby

could see a restroom sign down the hall. Climbing from the chair, she ignored the feeling of her limbs being worked from some other place than her central brain. She didn't look back at Tim as she headed toward the restroom, but she was pretty sure he was eyeing her progress with laserlike intensity. Convincing hospital personnel that you didn't need help appeared to be about as easy as winning an argument with a TSA agent.

In the bathroom she stared at her image in the mirror. There wasn't as much mud on her face as she'd been afraid of, which was a plus. But in the negative column, her coat, blouse, and jeans were covered in splotches of mud and grass, and her eyes were huge, pupils dilated, her face drained of color. She splashed water on her face, and that helped.

She wasn't really going to call Danner. That was a lurking "I told you so" she didn't have time for. Carefully, she mentally checked herself over, and apart from some areas that were definitely going to be sporting bruises, she was unhurt. No broken bones, no lacerations apart from a scratch at her knee that was barely bleeding.

She was okay.

No thanks to the driver in the white car.

Rage flooded her and brought color back to her face. She was flat-out mad at her would-be killer. Who was it? Why? Because of her investigation?

"But you don't know anything," she told her reflection, perplexed. She'd thought it was all tumbling into place with Yvette's confession about Hank Sainer, but Yvette certainly hadn't aimed her vehicle at Coby.

Hank Sainer. Someone had run him off the road tonight, too.

The same person? Someone else?

Were there two people involved in these killings?

Who are they?

* * *

Yvette drove with controlled fury through a spotty fog that, as the temperature declined, was trying to freeze. Freezing fog. The kind of thing that put a sheen of ice over everything and sent cars spinning into ditches. All the way back to her apartment she kept her attention on her driving, but when she was safely parked, she stopped a moment and took a breath, her hands still on the wheel.

What the hell kind of game was Coby playing? Fishing around. Trying to win sympathy, encourage intimacy and the sharing of secrets. Bullshit. Coby Rendell's better-than-thou attitude hadn't changed one bit since high school. Maybe it was even worse.

A heaviness invaded Yvette's chest, making it hard for her to breathe. She remembered the screech of metal against metal. The strange whistling sound as Hank's Land Rover went airborne. The wrenching crash as the vehicle smashed down, turned over, and rolled.

Crossing to the refrigerator, Yvette pulled out a pitcher of water, poured herself a glass, and gulped water cold enough to make her teeth ache. She needed him dead. Dead and gone.

A strangled sob emanated from her throat. She hadn't meant for it to happen! She still loved Hank Sainer, had loved him since the first time she saw him, one afternoon when he'd picked Dana up from school. Dana had always been a true pain in the ass. Whining about her eating disorder, never letting anyone forget. But her dad . . . wow . . .

Yvette recalled seeing Hank that first time, a spring day her junior year. She locked eyes with him and he smiled, then looked away, then looked back, a line of consternation forming between his brows. He'd had no plan to get involved with a teenager—it was about the last thing an up-and-coming politician would choose, but then sex and politics, they kinda went together, didn't they?

Yvette sure didn't have the same reservations. She *wanted* him. One of those animal things that just was.

From that day forward Yvette had pursued him. She'd made herself available everywhere Dana was, going so far as to make Dana a friend for a brief couple of weeks, something no one remembered or thought maybe they'd misinterpreted. Yvette and Dana? Not a chance.

But by then Hank was hooked. She caught him alone on the back patio of his small, rented house, the place he'd lived after his divorce from Dana's mother. Nothing near as nice as that goddamned penthouse he lived in now.

She'd simply walked up to him that night and laid a hand on his chest. Tensions had been simmering between them for weeks. The moment was breathless and hot and Yvette had debated how to ask him to make love to her. Should she be all ballsy and just come out and say, "Let's make love"? Or should she play a little more coy and naive—guys just about shit themselves over a girl who could pull that off right—and stare at him with dark, liquid eyes and simply mold her body to his? She chose the latter, and it was the right move. With a groan he grabbed her hair, gazed back at her in mounting frustration, and muttered, "What the hell are you doing?"

"What we both want, Mr. Sainer."

"Hank," he said, then nearly swallowed her up with a kiss that felt like it was the end of the world.

Man.

Even now Yvette could get a little turned on by the memory. Jesus, she wished she had a man who could quench this desire, but hell . . . as soon as she got close to someone else—anyone else—the mood just evaporated with a *poof!* Nothing there. Not a god . . . damned . . . thing.

Her affair with Hank burned hot and liquid and out of

control for those few months. When the opportunity of the campout came along, it was like a sign from forces beyond their control. Yvette waited and suffered and waited some more through that interminable campout and ring of ridiculous confessions. She'd lied about herself, of course. She'd never had sex with anyone when she was thirteen! She just wanted to shock the socks off that stick-up-their butts group, although Ellen had certainly thrown a curveball with admission of an abortion. That was cause for a double take, all right. But then it was all Yvette could do not to break out laughing. Seriously? These losers were actually going to reveal deep and private things about themselves?

No, her secret was staying secret: She was having an underage affair with one of the dads! A political candidate who had his eye on the governor's office, although she hadn't known that last part at the time. And she wouldn't have cared anyway. She wanted him. Inside her. Sliding back and forth and moaning and telling her how beautiful she was and that someday, someway, they would be together.

They were deep into lovemaking the night of the campout, high atop Bancroft Bluff, wrapped together in a blanket on the dune, carefully out of sight from the rim of houses that made up that chichi cul-de-sac above the beach. The roar of the ocean was their music; overhead a waning moon gazed down upon them through drifting clouds.

Yvette was close to climaxing. "C'mon, c'mon, c'mon," she was chanting through clenched teeth. All Hank had to do was one of those last deep thrusts and she'd be *there*!

And then . . . and then . . . a voice. "Hey, man." A male voice. From just outside the circle of visibility on that dark night.

"Oh, Jesus . . ."

Lucas Moore practically tripped over them. He was staring down at Hank's bare butt. His long hair hung along the sides of his face and his lower jaw was slack with disbelief.

Hank pulled himself out of her so fast it caused Yvette to cry out. And that made Lucas stagger backward, away from them. One foot stepping back about a yard.

Hank charged Lucas, to what? Reason with him? Beg him to keep his mouth shut? Yvette would never know.

For Lucas just teetered a moment, arms pinwheeling, and then he was over the edge in silence as the scream in Yvette's throat was caught there in total horror.

Hank grabbed her hand, squeezing so hard there were bruises the next day. He snatched up her clothes, shoving them at her stomach. He was muttering, half crying, and Yvette, finally finding her voice, let out a loud mewl.

He clamped his hand over her mouth. "Get dressed. We have to get help. Nine-one-one. Oh, my, God . . . oh, God."

He let go of her long enough to yank on his own clothes, stumbling a little as he dragged on his pants. Yvette stood in unmoving silence, her lower jaw trembling. She knew Lucas was dead. She'd never seen anyone die before. But he had to be dead.

"We killed him," she said.

"No, we didn't! He's alive." Hank clenched his hands in his hair, breathing hard. "My phone . . ."

"You can't," Yvette said, struck with sudden clarity. "It will ruin you. And I can't have that."

He stared at her, slack-jawed. He wanted someone else to take the lead. He needed someone else to make decisions.

"You're supposed to be at the tavern, right?" Yvette reminded him. "You left the dads at the house for a while. That was what you told them. Go to the tavern. Get seen."

"But . . ."

"I'll go down the beach and stay out for the rest of the

night." She picked up the blanket, folding it over her arm, thinking hard. "I'll go back tomorrow and tell them something. But you go now."

"I'm not going to leave you out here alone."

"Yeah. You are."

She practically had to push him to walk out the access road to Bancroft Bluff to Highway 101, which would take him to the nearest town, Deception Bay. Yvette waited impatiently as he kept looking back, then she half climbed, half slid down the cliff to the beach and headed south, in the direction opposite the beach house and the other dads and girls.

She saw Lucas's body in the tide pools. He was lying on his back, looking for all the world as if he were stargazing.

A shiver spread through her and she ran down the beach as far as she could, until her lungs were on fire and her muscles shivering. Wrapping herself in the blanket, she lay down behind a huge piece of driftwood and stared at its rough and charred surface, the result of many campfires made behind its sheltering arm, until dawn broke. Then she stared at the ocean.

She returned to the house by going farther south, away from the cliffs, where the beach and Highway 101 were almost on the same elevation. She walked up a public path between some houses and then trekked north to the beach house, coming in on that melange of shock and misery that followed Lucas's death.

Hank was there, looking gaunt and wild-eyed. He'd gone to the tavern, hung out awhile, buying a couple of beers for a few of the regulars, just so they would remember him, then returned to the house. He shook his head ever so slightly when he saw Yvette, his eyes pleading. He wanted to tell. He wanted to confess. He wanted to lay it all out for them.

So she told them all that she and Lucas were lovers.

Rhiannon fainted and she made an enemy for life in Genevieve.

And then she found out she was pregnant.

And then Hank didn't want anything to do with her. . . .

Now Yvette gazed stonily at the refrigerator. The glass of ice water was empty, still in her hand; the pitcher sat on the counter, ice melting. She'd pleaded with him. Begged him to take care of her and her baby.

The memory made her close her eyes and shudder. How pathetic. How debasing. He'd just ignored her to death.

She kept thinking he would change his mind. As soon as the baby arrived, they would be a family. She kept the secret of its parentage to herself, but she wasn't going to give up the child. She was proud of her pregnancy and when, after Benedict was born, Hank still refused to see him, she was filled with fury and anguish.

And resolve.

She blackmailed him. Year upon year. And he paid. Maybe he thought it was a form of child support, maybe he just wanted to keep his past indiscretions hidden, especially when he was with that filthy, grasping whore, Geri? God, how Yvette hated her! She'd dreamed about how to break them up, but then it had happened all on its own without Yvette's intervention.

And then Annette, beautiful, social-climbing bitch that she was, overheard Yvette leaving Hank a somewhat pointed message, and she yanked the phone from Yvette's hand and saw whom it was to: Yvette had him listed as "Fucking Bastard," but Annette knew the number because Dave had it as well. Annette was vigilant about whom her husband called, and as soon as she saw the number on Yvette's cell she put two and two together. And then she couldn't keep her mouth shut! Nag, nag, nag! Threaten, threaten, threaten. Yvette wanted to kill the bitch!

Annette wanted Hank to take a DNA test, just to be

sure. Yvette didn't need it, nor did she want it. But lo and behold, Hank suddenly wanted it. All of a sudden, he decided it was time to be Benedict's father . . . and he planned to use Yvette's years of blackmail against her. He'd kept records for years of the blackmail payments and all her parental misdeeds, gleaned from her unwitting sisters, though Annette was the biggest contributor. Hank had friends in high places. They would forgive him an indiscretion from years earlier, or so he believed, or at the very least, they would consider him the better parent, because it sure as hell wasn't going to look good for Yvette.

Annette thought this was a grand idea. All of a sudden Yvette was either fighting with Annette or fighting with Hank. The night of Annette's party Yvette just wanted her to *shut the fuck up* and she pushed her into the hot tub. Had she killed her? She didn't think so. Had she wanted her dead? Well, maybe. But it didn't really matter, because the result was the same. Annette was dead and gone, and she hoped Hank was on his way to the great beyond as well.

Yvette's cell phone buzzed and she gazed at the screen. "What the hell do you want?" she demanded. She listened and felt herself move into a kind of alternative reality; she was being called to judgment. This was it. They knew. They knew already. Into the receiver, she said in a near monotone, "Listen, bitch. I *know* you. If I go down, so do you. I've got something of yours."

Then she slammed down the phone.

Coby walked into the ER waiting room and inwardly groaned when she saw not only her father and mother, but Donald and Wynona Greer as well. Jean-Claude was there, too, looking strained. Well, they all looked strained, and when they saw her appearance they just gaped.

"Coby!" Leta said.

"I fell, Mom," she said, easily brushing on the lie. "How's Hank? Any news?"

Her father couldn't seem to take his eyes off her mud-spattered clothes. "They haven't told us anything. Dana's been notified. She's flying here tomorrow."

"What happened?" Leta demanded.

Coby just shook her head. Jean-Claude's phone bleeped and he pulled it out and looked down at the screen. Wynona got up from her chair, her gaze on Coby, when one of the nurses came through a set of double doors that led to the operating rooms and came their way. Everyone waited tensely.

"Mr. Sainer is still in surgery to relieve pressure inside his skull. It will be awhile yet, and he'll be in recovery after that."

"You want us all to leave," Donald Greer said, reading between the lines.

She simply answered, "I'm just informing you of the time line."

Watching the nurse's retreating back, Wynona said, "Come on, Dad. We can come back in the morning."

"Who did this?" Donald questioned, staring at Coby. "Someone ran Hank off the road. Who did it?"

"Yvette," Wynona answered for her, also turning her gaze to Coby.

Coby didn't respond. She wasn't about to reveal what she knew without talking to Danner first. But Wynona's gaze scoured her.

"She did it. She ran him off the road. Why?" And then, answering her own question, she said in disbelief, "Oh, no. He's not Benedict's father, is he?"

Dave's head snapped up. "No."

Jean-Claude opened his mouth, closed it, blinked, and sat silent.

He knows, Coby realized. *He knows about Hank.*

Wynona saw his reaction, too. "Oh, my God. What did she do to Annette?"

"She would never hurt Annette!" Jean-Claude burst out, as if the words were torn from his chest. "She would never hurt her sister!"

"She ran the father of her child off the road," Wynona snapped. "You don't think she would harm anyone who got in her way?"

"Yvette would not hurt Annette or Hank," Jean-Claude insisted harshly. He was still gripping his phone tightly in his right hand. "She loves her son . . . and she loves Hank . . . and she loved Annette."

This last piece sounded tacked on and false, but Coby let it go.

Donald, who'd been sitting, now stood protectively by his daughter, as if he felt Jean-Claude and Wynona's argument would escalate into something ugly. "We're all upset," he began, but Wynona whirled on him.

"Stop it, Dad. Really. I can't do the whole school administrator thing right now. Yvette's gotten a pass way too long!"

Jean-Claude shook his head and said, "I have to go."

Wynona snapped, "I know it's tough to hear, but facts are facts. Yvette's behind Hank's accident. I'm sure of it."

"I saw Yvette. She was here," Coby said into the tense silence that followed. "She came into the reception area, but then left. She was scared for Hank, and I guess she decided waiting at the hospital wasn't going to help."

"Couldn't face what she's done," Wynona said, and Jean-Claude threw her a furious look and stalked away.

Donald chided, "Wynona . . ."

Her face burned with sudden color. "I'm not trying to be a mean bitch. It's just the truth. I've been around the Ettes a lot." She turned to Coby. "I was always dragged along with Dad every time Jean-Claude invited us to go somewhere. I know them. They're all fucked up."

"Wynona!" Donald was appalled.

"Tell Coby, Dad. Tell her what you know about the other Ettes. One of the other ones. Go on!"

"I'm not playing this game with you," he declared furiously, but Wynona was not to be stopped.

She turned to Coby. "He caught Juliet putting the notes in the lockers. Didn't think it was a big deal and he was kinda pissed off about how everyone at the campout treated me, so he let it go. He never even told me until after Annette died." She glared at him.

"You just keep slandering Yvette!" Donald was in a huff. "You need to stop making assumptions about her or anyone else. The notes were a school prank, and I caught Juliet and she was embarrassed and that's all. I wasn't going to turn it into a circus. Leave Juliet and Yvette alone."

"It is a circus, Dad. It *is* a circus! Don't you get it? And people have died!" She was disbelieving. "I'm no fan of Vic Franzen, believe me, but Juliet's maligned him for years. We all have. I don't care how embarrassed she was, it wasn't right that you kept this from me, from us."

"I was the vice principal, and I handled the situation the best way I knew how," he insisted.

Clearly Donald Greer thought he'd done the right thing, but it would have helped to have known anyway, Coby thought. And his silence sure hadn't helped Vic Franzen. And Wynona was right: people had died.

"Jean-Claude can't hear anything more about his daughters." Dave suddenly spoke up and they turned to Coby's dad. "He just lost one, and you're blaming another one for her death. And now you're attacking a third one, when this note business is just the kind of thing kids do."

Donald nodded emphatically, glad for the support.

"So Juliet gets a pass, too," Wynona said bitterly. "Fine.

I'm the aberration here!" With that she walked away, following the same route Jean-Claude had taken out of the hospital minutes before.

"She can't leave without me," Donald said. "I drove us." And with that he said good-bye to Dave and Leta, shaking Coby's dad's hand hard, a gesture of friendship in an uncertain world.

A few minutes later Coby left as well, and Dave and Leta were getting ready to depart; Coby watched as her father carefully helped her mother into her coat. Another time she would have felt happy at the sight, but now she just felt impatient with all of them.

Outside, Coby flipped up the collar of her jacket and looked cautiously from right to left, half expecting some mad villain to race around the circular drop-off and smack her down. She crossed quickly and then nearly jumped out of her skin when she heard, "Coby."

She whipped around, hand at her chest, as the voice registered: Wynona. She was standing outside her car, the driver's door open, and she gave Coby the high sign, silently asking her for a moment, before leaning in and telling her father, who was seated in the passenger seat, that she would be right back.

Coby waited and Wynona walked toward her, her expression grim. "What really happened to you?" she demanded. "You didn't just fall."

"I'm fine, Wynona."

"Somebody attack you or something?" She wasn't about to be put off.

"It wasn't Yvette," Coby stated firmly, then told her about the car that had grazed her and spun her to the ground.

"Maybe she came back around and—"

"*No.*" Coby cut her off. "It wasn't Yvette."

"But she has to be responsible!" she insisted. "She's the craziest of the Ettes."

"Wynona, just because you want it to be her doesn't make it so. It was someone else. And that's not all." In for a penny, in for a pound, Coby thought as she went on to tell Wynona what had happened in the parking garage earlier. "I'm on someone's radar, yes. But it's not Yvette's."

Wynona was shaking her head, struggling to believe whoever was after Coby wasn't Yvette. "There has to be some explanation."

"Maybe she's partly involved. I don't know. But she wasn't behind the wheel of that car. She left just minutes before in her black Ford Focus. She didn't have time to switch cars and circle around and come at me. This car was light-colored. I know that much."

Wynona's gaze was on her own vehicle with her waiting father. "But if it isn't Yvette, who is it?"

"Well, it's not you," Coby said with faint humor, "since you were inside with Jean-Claude and your dad and my dad and mom."

"Oh, God . . ." Wynona inhaled sharply. "It's Genevieve."

"No." Coby almost groaned at the way Wynona was switching allegiance.

"Yes," Wynona insisted, blinking as she came up with her new theory. "You're investigating. Everybody knows it. I still say Yvette tried to kill Hank, her lover, tonight, but it must have been Genevieve who killed Annette and Lucas."

"Lucas's death was an accident," Coby stated automatically. "And Annette was Gen's best friend."

"Lucas's death wasn't an accident. Someone cut a piece of his hair the night he died. After he died. Or one of us would have noticed! You know it and I know it. They took a piece of him as a trophy."

"Maybe they took a piece of his hair because they loved him," Coby said. "Whatever the case, he fell from Bancroft Bluff. It still could have been an accident."

"This person who loved him, they didn't report the accident and try to save him?" Wynona demanded.

"We were kids. Who says any of us would have automatically done the right thing?"

"I would have. You would have." Coby couldn't argue that, and Wynona went on, "Genevieve was in love with Lucas. She still is. And back in high school she was absolutely obsessed with him and their popularity. It's like she stopped maturing right then and there. She's never gotten past being homecoming queen.

"That's not just me being jealous, if that's what you're thinking. Sure, I've had my problems. Some really serious issues that I'm still working on. But you go and ask Gen about Lucas and how she worked on becoming Rhiannon's best friend, just so she could be tied in to the whole Lucas melodrama after he died. *Ask her*. Oh, and while you're at it, ask her about the time I caught her in the bathroom, crying over a picture of Lucas. You know what she told me that day? That she was so unlucky because she'd wanted to be pregnant with Lucas's child, but it was Yvette who'd gotten knocked up instead. She was just about undone over that."

"You caught her in the school bathroom crying over Lucas?"

She shook her head. "It was at the Knapps'. Our whole senior year, my dad spent a lot of time with Lawrence Knapp and Jean-Claude and some with your dad, too. I got to see a lot of the Ettes and Genevieve, though you weren't around much."

"I kind of tried to avoid anyone associated with the campout," Coby admitted.

"Yeah, well. I was just the opposite. I tried too hard to

be accepted by all of you! I might not have been cool enough to be anybody's BFF, but I was there, and I remember."

As illuminating as this was, Coby was starting to feel cold and shivery. All she wanted was to get clean in a nice hot shower. "You know, I'm freezing to death here."

"I know you don't believe me. And okay, I've been a broken record about Yvette. But it's Genevieve. I'm sure of it. Annette found that lock of hair. I don't know how come she knew it was Lucas's, but she did, and I bet she confronted Genevieve with it."

"We don't know the hair's Lucas's, and even if it is, and Genevieve took it, and Annette found it . . . it's not enough to kill someone over."

"That's what you think because you're rational," Wynona told her curtly. "Always, always rational. But if you think with your heart, instead of your head, crazy behavior can take over."

"Okay."

Realizing she was losing Coby to the cold, Wynona just lifted and dropped her hand in a universal gesture of "I give up." She gave a terse good-bye and headed back to her car.

Once safely ensconced in her Nissan, Coby let out a pent-up breath. Home. Shower. Bed. She wished Danner were a part of that prescription, but doubted he could get away from the Lloyd suicide.

Yvette sat at her small kitchen table, bathed in the light from the small lamp on the counter that served as a kind of kitchen night-light. She was exhausted. And gritty. And full of a sadness she couldn't even really fathom.

And fear. She'd taken drastic action to keep Benedict with her, but if the truth ever came out, she would go to jail for the bulk of her son's life, and what good would that do?

If Hank woke up . . . if he pointed the finger at her . . .

Maybe she should just leave. Right now. Just go away with Benedict and never look back.

A knock on the door caused her to chirp with fear. The next moment she knew who it was; she'd called him over, asked him to take Benedict. Her momentary flight of fancy was over. She had to wait . . . and hope Hank never woke up.

She opened the door to her father. "He's asleep in his bed," she told Jean-Claude. "Probably won't even wake up."

Jean-Claude gazed at her in concern. "I'll take him to my house. Where are you going? How long will you be gone?"

"I just need to get away for a while, Dad. That's all. Not long."

"With Hank in the hospital, fighting for his life?"

For an answer she kissed him on the cheek. A lifelong avoidance tactic of Yvette's that worked more often than not. Now her father gave her a searching look before heading into Benedict's room. A moment later Benedict stumbled out, in pajamas and a coat. Yvette had packed her son a bag as soon as she got back from the hospital. Now she gave it to Jean-Claude, then looked down at Benedict with love, holding his sweet face between her palms.

"Mommy loves you," she told him.

He just looked at her blankly, in the sleep zone.

Kissing the top of his head, she watched as Jean-Claude guided him out the door. Her father said to her, "If you've done something . . . if you need help . . ."

"No, Dad. Go. I'm okay."

As soon as he was gone, she sank back down at the table, wondering when he would find the gift she'd left them tucked in Benedict's backpack, among his things.

Chapter 25

As soon as Coby closed the door to her town house behind her, her cell phone buzzed. All she wanted was a hot shower. Some time to decompress and mentally put things in order. But she forced herself to see who was calling.

Danner.

Quickly she pressed the green button to answer. "Hi," she said, and heard how tired she sounded, though she tried to push some enthusiasm into her voice.

"You sound beat," he said, not bothering to hide the disappointment in his voice.

She glanced at her bedraggled reflection in the entry hall mirror and thought, *You have no idea.* "Are you . . . off duty, so to speak?"

"Yep. We're planning to put Sheila's sketch out to the media. Might as well let the public know. She's running already, but when the news of Lloyd's suicide hits, she could go into deep hiding. Wanna catch her first."

"Are you . . . heading home?"

"Are you up for a late-night visitor? One who's about two blocks away from your place?"

"I'll leave the light on."

* * *

Danner was there in ten minutes and Coby had barely had time to take off her coat and wipe off the excess mud. Her clothes were still spattered and stained, and for half a minute she thought about changing, but what good would that do? He was going to find out anyway, and she wanted to talk about the attack with him.

His dark brows slammed into a frown when he saw her. "What happened?"

"Sit down," Coby ordered, and when he was still standing, she added, "Please," which seemed to do the trick, as he slowly perched himself on the edge of her couch.

She told him the tale of her adventures since they'd split up. How she'd run into Yvette, who'd admitted that Hank Sainer was Benedict's father. How she'd been nearly run down by a speeding driver who she believed had definitely targeted her. How it couldn't have been Yvette behind the wheel, though Wynona Greer was sure that it was. How Wynona had also insisted that Yvette was involved in Hank's accident, and how then, also at Wynona's insistence, Donald Greer had admitted that he'd known it was Juliet Deneuve who'd left the notes in the girls' lockers all those years ago, but hadn't said anything until recently. How Wynona felt all the Ette sisters got passes while no one else did, and then how she'd finally turned her brain around to think beyond Yvette as the killer, only to land on Genevieve Knapp Lockwood.

Danner reacted several times during the narrative, but Coby kept putting up her hands and making him wait. A listener by nature, he normally could easily wait until someone was finished talking; he'd learned it was the best way to really hear what a suspect, person of interest, or eyewitness was trying to say. But with Coby it was different. Everything about her made his nerves raw in an undefinable way that he'd never felt before. He practically had to sit on his hands to keep himself from jumping up and grabbing her, holding her close.

"I was heading to the shower when you called," she finished. "But I didn't want to talk you out of coming over. Can you wait? I won't be long."

He had a few things to tell her himself. "A shower would be good," was his answer.

He saw the flash of understanding in her eyes and gave up sitting on the couch. In two strides he was across the room, dragging her into his arms.

"A shower *would* be good," she repeated a trifle breathlessly. They stared at each other, then she started backing down the short hallway toward her bedroom and master bath, Danner's arms still around her. He moved with her, kissing her neck and cheek and any other bit of skin he could find.

Urgently, they pulled off each other's clothes, and just as urgently scrambled into the shower beneath a cold spray that had them both jumping away before the temperature came up and filled the glass enclosure with hot water and steam.

"It's been too long," Danner muttered.

"Too long," she repeated.

"Too . . . long . . ."

His hands slid up her slick rib cage to capture her breasts. Coby moaned and ran her own hands down his muscled back to the curve at the base of his spine. For a brief moment she was transported back to that first time, when they'd stumbled into his apartment after making out in the car, yanked off each other's clothes much like now, then fallen into bed, Danner swearing a little at their awkwardness, Coby laughing.

And then she was naked and he was, too, and though he tried to slow it down she wouldn't let him. They'd made love with abandon, with more energy than finesse, and it had been glorious.

Now she didn't wait. She took him in her hands and caressed him and Danner sucked in a breath, muttered something impatiently, then lifted her up and pushed inside her and she was laughing again, then moaning, and they were hot and wet and slippery against the shower wall.

"Coby . . ." he groaned.

I've missed you, she thought, but her mind was fractured. *I love you.*

And then he was moving with deep strokes and she arched her neck and met his thrusts, sensations taking over in a burst of pleasure.

They slipped down the wall, coming back to earth, and Danner reluctantly pulled away and said with concern, "Your leg's bleeding."

She looked down. "It's a scratch. I'm not hurt. Don't stop . . ."

And she put her hands on his face and brought his mouth to hers again.

"We'll file a report tomorrow," he said, much later, after they were dried off and Coby had placed a bandage over the scratch on her knee. She looked across the expanse of her bed at Danner who, now in jeans but still bare-chested, a white terry-cloth towel slung around his neck, looked back at her.

Coby's mind was still pleasantly reviewing the lovemaking in the shower. She didn't want to come down to earth. She answered with a nod. He was a cop and that was never more evident than now, when he was picking up his shirt and the shoulder holster and gun he'd discarded on the floor outside the bathroom.

"What kind of car was it?" he asked, and with an

inward sigh, she knew this brief vacation from reality was about over. At least for now.

She didn't pretend to misunderstand. "I think I know the shape of the taillights. It was light-colored."

"No license plate?"

"I didn't get a look. Maybe it wasn't there? Or maybe it was. I just got a flash. I wasn't really thinking sharply."

"That's two attacks on you in one day," he pointed out grimly.

"I don't know why. I don't know anything," Coby admitted.

"Maybe you do," Danner said. "You just don't know that you know it. Yet."

"I know Yvette and Hank had an affair, that Benedict's Hank's son, and that she—probably they—saw Lucas fall. She said it was definitely an accident, and I believe her."

"How did he fall?"

"That she didn't say, but she was with Hank that night at Bancroft Bluff, and my guess is that Lucas just stumbled upon them. Maybe they tried to talk to him and he just lost his footing? That's the impression she gave. They didn't report his fall because Hank was with Yvette, who was underage."

"Maybe he would have lived, if they had." Danner was grim. "Do you believe Wynona that Yvette ran Hank off the road?"

"That's extreme, even for Yvette, but maybe. She was concerned about him. She came to the hospital."

"And then left before seeing him."

"She was . . . undone."

Danner grunted, picked up his shirt, and pulled it over his head. Then he slipped on his shoulder holster and the black rain jacket he'd worn the night before.

"Maybe Hank can tell us something when he comes to," she said.

"I'll get someone to pick up those security tapes of your building. See if any of the cars that went through the gate belong to someone we know."

She tried to think back to the vehicles that had been at the beach house. To remember what everyone drove, but she was too tired to think clearly.

Danner suddenly stopped short in the act of running his hands through his damp hair. "These attacks on you started after you went to see McKenna at the Joker Friday night," he said.

"Yeah. I guess so."

"What happened there? Anything unusual? Something you haven't really thought about yet?"

"Well, no. I didn't expect to see Ellen and Theo, of course, but other than that, we just discussed Annette's death, like I have with everyone else. I was giving them information, and they were mostly stunned."

Danner thought a minute, then said, "And they told you about the girl from Gresham who had the miscarriage. Heather something . . ."

"McCrae. Heather McCrae. And the gym-rat boyfriend had two first names."

"Ed Gerald," Danner said.

"That's right."

"I'll try to track him down tomorrow. What time is it?" He was heading out of the bedroom, getting ready to leave.

Coby glanced at the bedside clock. "About two." She followed him into the living room and to the front door.

He hesitated, his hand on the knob. "It's late. I should probably go and let you rest."

"Do you have to?"

Danner's gaze captured hers. He shook his head, then grabbed her and held her close, pushing her up against the wall. "I should leave right now," he said, his mouth hot against her arched throat.

"Don't you dare."

The knock on Yvette's door was soft, but it woke Yvette as if she'd been doused with a bucket of cold water. She jerked to full attention, her head coming up from the kitchen table where she'd laid her head on her forearms after her dad left. Now she sat up straight and alert.

Her gaze darted around the room. She needed a weapon. She'd poked a dangerous animal tonight. There was a good chance that animal had come to make her its prey.

All she saw was the lamp on the counter, but then she shook herself back to reality. There were knives handy. A butcher knife in the sink. She was being fanciful.

Still . . .

She crept forward and peered through the peephole, and her brows lifted in surprise and consternation.

Her heart seized. Did they know about tonight? What she'd done? Did they all know? The inn where she used to meet Hank had been a secret until Annette learned about her relationship with him. Annette had wormed information from Hank, and she hadn't been discreet about any of it.

Maybe it was common knowledge. Maybe the authorities were coming after her *right now*!

Except . . .

She opened the door and looked onto the darkened balcony that rimmed the parking lot below. "What do you want?"

Genevieve walked inside without being asked. Her face

was white. "I heard about Hank," she said. "Someone ran him off the road."

Yvette waited, tense inside. "Yeah?"

"Jarrod told me tonight that he's leaving me. He says I've never gotten over Lucas Moore. He said that's why he's leaving me."

Yvette's tension uncoiled a bit. This was about Genevieve. Everything was always about Genevieve. "It's after two," Yvette stated pointedly. She was still holding the door open, and cold and fog were wafting inside.

"I always thought you killed him . . . Lucas," Genevieve said conversationally. "And I'm pretty sure you ran Hank off the road tonight. Annette used to talk about that inn just past the curve. She said you were the one who mentioned it to her, and she and Dave used to go there. It was historic and had cozy bedrooms and it was off the beaten path."

That ratcheted her anxiety right back up. "I think you'd better leave."

Ignoring her, Genevieve sat down at the table and asked, "When Hank wakes up, will he tell everyone that you were meeting him there tonight?"

"Don't make this something it's not," Yvette said, feeling a noose tightening around her throat. "You're fucking nuts when it comes to anything about Lucas Moore."

"Am I?"

Her smile was a little left of crazy, and Yvette felt a shiver start at the top of her spine and shoot down to her tailbone. Genevieve Knapp was a danger she hadn't even seen coming.

Kirk Grassi scratched his bare chest and yawned, stumbling over the mattress he used as a bed and staggering to the bedroom window to look out at a gray dawn. He felt completely hungover and he hadn't had a goddamn thing to drink. Well, okay, there was that shot of bourbon when Juliet showed up screeching like a banshee. Jesus. So he hadn't warned her of his plans. So what? It wasn't like they were married or anything, and besides, he'd just kind of made the decision this last week since somebody offed Annette Deneuve. It wasn't like he'd been planning for months.

Women. They just didn't understand these things.

For reasons he couldn't explain, he thought back to the trashy girl with the eyeliner and the lollipops at the Seventh Heaven motel. She gave him the shivers, all right. Probably had six kinds of STDs, but truth to tell, Kirk was kinda jonesin' for her. She was invading his dreams, and twice over the course of this last week he'd woken up with a boner to end all boners thinking about her sucking on Mr. Happy the way she'd gone after that lollipop.

And things were crap with the band anyway. Jarrod was in a shithole of a marriage and though he wanted out, was that really gonna happen? Besides, Kirk had already made his plans before Jarrod's announcement that he and the Fucking Bitch were through, so . . . it was too bad, but it was what it was. Kirk was leaving. He'd paid the rent on this rathole through the month, so he could just go.

Except Juliet had practically ripped him a new one. So goddamn mad he thought she was going to foam at the mouth. He'd kinda gotten mad right back for a minute or two, but then he'd thought, fuck it. Let her scream. She was one whacked-out piece of tail, that was for sure. But she'd slept with every guy he could name except maybe Jarrod. She was a groupie's groupie. Did she really think any guy would take her seriously?

And Suzette . . . well, she wasn't the slut Juliet was, but she was weird city. Pasting on a sweet face while sinking the knife in your back. Honest to God, it made Kirk want to shudder all over. What the fuck was Galen thinking?

'Course, a guy could forgive a lot of things if the chick was good in the sack. Maybe Suzette knew more about sex than she let on.

But then, the heart wanted what the heart wanted, or so he'd been told. Mostly he kinda thought the dick wanted what the dick wanted, but that wasn't true for girls, so he'd allow the heart thing might be a better way to look at it. A more overall way.

Kirk headed to the living room, if it could be called that. Pretty much a place he just dumped stuff. His front door was wide open. Juliet hadn't even bothered to close it. "Well, shit." He closed it, but not before looking down at his 4x4 in the parking lot below.

His heart clutched and then he went hot, then cold.

That fucking bitch had scratched a line across his new paint job! Okay, four-year-old paint job. But she'd *ruined* it!

For a moment he couldn't decide what to do first. Go kill Juliet. Throw some things in his car and get the hell out of Dodge. Scrounge up some breakfast. Or go back to bed.

After a moment of serious reflection, he chose bed.

"I'll go see Yvette," Danner told Coby.

He was lazily drawing figure eights down her bare back as weak sunlight came through her bedroom blinds. Early morning. She felt like she hadn't slept at all, which was because she hadn't slept at all. Not that she was complaining.

"I'll get on those security tapes, but there's nothing to do on the Lloyd case but wait for someone to spot Sheila," he said. "At least I have time to concentrate on Annette's homicide."

"It's Sunday," Coby protested. "Don't you get any time off?"

"I've been off the last few days," he answered.

"Really. What it's like when you're on, then? Do you work double-speed?"

He was nuzzling her neck, just below her ear, sending shivers along her nerves. She could feel him smile. "Sometimes," he admitted. "And then sometimes I can do nothing for days."

"Let me know when one of those stretches pops up."

With that he reluctantly pulled away from her, got off the bed, and began searching for his clothes. "I'm going to try to see Yvette early," he said, pulling on his pants. "Sunday morning's a good time to find people home unless they're early churchgoers, but I just don't see Yvette fitting that mold."

Coby nodded. "Think she did kill Annette and she's just trying to excuse herself? Now I'm wondering if I was played a little by her last night."

"Maybe she'll say something to me that'll confirm her involvement one way or another."

"Want me to go with you?"

"No! I want you to stay right here and wait for me to get back."

"Sounds like a good idea," she said with a smile. "Not a practical one, but a good idea nonetheless."

"A great idea." He finished dressing and gazed at her in the bed. "I'll call Detective Clausen at the TCSD today, or maybe tomorrow. Monday. See what's gone down the last week."

"I can tell you. They're checking into my dad. He's their number one suspect." Coby struggled to her elbows, then swung her legs over the side of the bed and grabbed her robe, sliding her arms down the sleeves.

"That's routine. He's the husband." Danner headed out of the bedroom and Coby followed, leaning against the jamb between her bedroom and living space. She didn't want him to go.

"But for us, it's just been Yvette looking guiltier and guiltier," she said instead. "She probably is guilty. It just seemed like blaming Yvette was too easy. But if it walks like a duck and quacks like a duck, most often it's a duck. Yvette's been the most likely suspect in Annette's death all week. That hasn't changed."

"Let's hope she gives something away."

"Don't bet on it. We're talking about Yvette."

For an answer he crossed to her once more, pulling her into his arms. "And you're going to stay here and out of harm's way."

She was snuggled against his chest. "Nice try. But I'm going over to Lovejoy's. I want to talk to Jean-Claude, and maybe Juliet will be working in the tearoom. I want her to know that I know she was the note writer. See what she says."

She felt him tense. "It's all I can do not to tell you to be careful again."

"I'm fine. Good-bye," she said, kissing him.

"I'll call you later."

The door shut behind him. Coby went straight for the coffeemaker, putting it together, reluctantly setting aside her memories of the night before with Danner, memories that jolted her when she moved a certain way, reminding her at muscle level the extent of their lovemaking. And that made her smile.

An hour later she was showered once again, dressed, her hair dried, makeup applied. It was still too early to go to Lovejoy's, so she sat down at her kitchen table with sliced apples, cheese, and toast and thought about everything that had transpired the last week, starting with Annette's birthday party and murder, and ending with Hank's hit-and-run and trip to the hospital.

And twice someone had targeted Coby, first to warn her, second to do her serious harm.

What do I know that I don't know I know?

She'd been wrong when she'd believed Annette and Yvette were arguing over Dana; they'd been arguing over DNA. Hank Sainer's DNA. But that was almost common knowledge now, so it was unlikely someone was trying to stop Coby from revealing Hank was Benedict's father. And anyway, that someone wasn't Yvette. At least, she hadn't been the person who'd tried to run over Coby in the parking lot last night.

What about the envelope with the swatch of hair?

Yes, Coby had discovered it at the party, but it, too, was common knowledge now. And the prevailing theory—that it was Lucas's and someone had cut it from him after his fall—wasn't a reason to go after Coby, either.

Danner had posed that the attacks had started after her trip to the Joker to see McKenna's act, but maybe it was something else? Something she'd learned, seen, or knew from earlier in the week?

Or maybe it was simple craziness on the part of the attacker?

She shook her head, pushing those thoughts aside. Went back to the party. Who was there? And what were they driving?

Faith has a white BMW.

That thought sent a cold jolt through Coby's system. What did Faith's taillights look like? she wondered. She thought hard. She was so bad with cars, but no . . . no, they weren't from a BMW, she realized with relief. If her memory was correct. *If*. . . She knew as time passed, recall became corroded, which was why eyewitness testimony was so unreliable.

With that thought she grabbed pad and pen and sketched out what she remembered from the rear of the car that had tried to run her down. Looking at her crude drawing, she made a face, hoping it was accurate, hoping it was enough.

Chapter 26

Danner had run reports on all of the people who'd been at Annette's party, gathering as much information as he could on each and every one of them. He had most of those reports in a folder in his car; he certainly had Yvette's. After scanning it, he drove to her apartment building around nine o'clock, checked the plates on the black Ford Focus in the parking lot, saw it was hers, and was satisfied she was home.

He walked up an outside stairway desperately in need of some maintenance; the paint was worn off the steps and there was enough sway in the handrail for OSHA to issue a safety citation.

At Yvette's door, he knocked and waited. Knocked again. Nothing. He pressed the bell but no sound emanated from within. The doorbell was either unhooked or out of order for some other reason. When he'd given her enough time, he called her cell phone. He thought he heard it ringing inside the unit but no one picked up.

"Yvette, it's Danner Lockwood," he said to her voice mail. "I'm outside your door. Would you please call me?" He left his number, then hung up. After waiting around awhile longer, he reluctantly got back in his Wrangler. Not much more he could do legally.

Checking over his information, he realized he didn't have anything on Edward Gerald, so he headed back to the station, idly wondering if Yvette was actively avoiding him. As he walked to his desk he was surprised to see Metzger already there. "You really can't stay away," he said.

She snorted. "Just like you."

"Someone tried to run down Coby Rendell last night," he said.

That caught her attention and she gave him a hard look. "Another hit-and-run?"

"Mmm-hmm."

"Busy night. Lloyd's suicide . . . the Sainer hit-and-run . . . now your girlfriend."

There were no secrets between them, but he knew she was baiting him a little. Normally he would go back and forth with Elaine, but after last night, he didn't feel the need. "Yep," he said. "My girlfriend."

"My, my, my," Metzger muttered. Then: "Why are they after her?"

"Good question. One I plan to find an answer for."

"There are only three reasons for homicides," Elaine started, but Danner had heard her theories many, many times and knew where this was going.

"Money, sex, basic overall craziness," he said before she could.

"Sometimes I forget you're paying attention. So, which one is it in this case?"

Danner thought about that long and hard. "Not money . . . there's some sex involved . . . but it's kind of all out there now. Nothing that involves Coby."

"Uh-oh," Metzger said.

Danner didn't respond. He knew what she was thinking: that left overall craziness, and of the three, it was the least easiest to predict and understand, and more often than not, bad things happened before the suspect was found out and caught.

It was around noon when Coby showed up at Lovejoy's, parking her car in the lot across the street. She hurried up the steps to the hotel's front doors and recognized Nicholette behind the beveled glass panels, standing at the counter and talking to Jean-Claude.

"Nicholette," she greeted her as she entered.

Nicholette turned, and Jean-Claude glanced her way, looking drawn. Seeing it was Coby, Nicholette seemed to want to say something, but then she firmly locked her jaw, as if afraid of spilling more secrets.

"What's wrong?" Coby asked, picking up on it.

"What isn't?" Nicholette countered. "Hank Sainer's in a coma and the police are taking the Lovejoy's accounts apart, as if the hotel were the reason someone murdered my sister!"

"It's what they do," Coby said, hearing an echo of what Danner had said in her words.

Her answer did not appease Nicholette, who looked at Coby as if she were a traitor. The easy camaraderie they shared at work had all but disappeared. Lines were being drawn.

"I asked her to come over," Jean-Claude said abruptly. Then, "Thank you, Nikki."

It was her cue to leave and she took it, nodding curtly and walking away on stiff legs.

Coby glanced over to the tearoom. "Is Juliet working today?"

"Why?" Jean-Claude's dark eyes were shuttered.

"I'd like to talk to her."

"Suzette's there this morning. Juliet will be in later."

"Who was working last night?" Coby thought to ask. "We were all at the Cellar together," she explained, seeing Jean-Claude react as if she were interrogating him and his daughters.

"William filled in," he said, referring to the man whom she'd met the last time she'd been here, the assistant manager, William Johnson.

"Is he the manager now? At least temporarily?"

"He has been. . . ." Jean-Claude looked back uncertainly, toward the door to the inner offices, and Coby's gaze followed his.

And then Dave came through the door, followed by Faith, who, upon seeing Coby, said, "So, you heard, huh?"

"No," Dave said at the same time Coby asked, "About Hank?"

"No, no. That's a tragedy. I hope he's okay. I meant about me being the new manager," she said. "Or at least I'm training to be." She came around the counter and reminded her father, "I've got to give some notice, so it won't be this week. Probably late next week."

He nodded.

Coby looked from Faith to Dave, and then to Jean-Claude and back to Faith, who was now heading briskly toward the front doors, as if she couldn't wait to get away from her. But Coby was having none of that. She darted after Faith and caught her outside, on the hotel's front steps. Faith was looking toward the sky and said, "Maybe it's stopped raining for a while, though the fog hasn't helped."

"You're quitting your job to come work at Lovejoy's?"

Faith sighed and forced herself to meet Coby's accusing gaze. "Is that a problem for you?"

"It's just . . . so . . ."

"Say it," Faith told her, her expression tightening.

"I don't know. Fast. Wrong, maybe."

"You think I'm an opportunist, benefiting from Annette's death. Like I've been waiting and waiting for this job!"

"But you work at a title company. I thought you liked it there."

"I'm barely hanging on to my job," Faith stated flatly. "I know you're the wunderkind at your office, and all that, but this economy has shredded the real estate market, and guess what, they just don't need many of us anymore. I've had seniority, but the company's struggling. It's just a matter of time before we're all out of a job. So, yeah, I asked for the manager's position and Jean-Claude and Dad were only too happy to hire me."

"Okay . . ." Coby tried hard not to think about Faith's white BMW. *The shape of the taillights doesn't match,* she reminded herself. *People don't* kill *other people over a job. . . .*

"Stop being so tense. The police will figure out who murdered Annette and it won't be Mom or Dad, because they didn't do it. I've got to go." She gave Coby a quick hug and then hurried across the street to the parking lot.

Coby stayed on the hotel's front steps and watched as Faith backed out of a spot. The taillight shape *was* all wrong, she thought with relief. It wasn't Faith who'd run her down. Of course it wasn't Faith. Not Faith . . . not her sister . . .

She turned and pushed back through the doors to the Lovejoy's lobby. No one was visible at the counter now. Dave and Jean-Claude had clearly gone back to their inner sanctum, so she crossed to the tearoom, pausing at the wide aperture that could be closed off with sliding doors for privacy.

There were several guests seated at tables having coffee or tea and reading the paper. The teapots were wrapped in calico tea cozies, and baskets of scones, covered in matching patterned cloths, were placed in the centers of the tables. Suzette, in a conservative black dress with a white apron and sensible shoes, was wiping off a tabletop, clearing plates and yawning.

"Coby," she said, seeing her approach. She straightened and looked beyond her as if expecting someone else. "Where's Danner?"

"Probably off working."

She gave her a knowing look. "Oh, come on. You didn't spend the night together last night?"

Sidestepping, Coby said, "I just ran into Faith."

"Faith." Suzette's dark eyes flashed and her expression grew hard. No more sweetness and light. "You heard about her taking the manager job? Nobody even asked me or Juliet if we wanted it!"

This wasn't a subject Coby wanted to talk about either. "What time does Juliet come to work?"

"This afternoon. We usually wrap up the tearoom by three and start serving wine around four. She should be here then. What do you think about Faith coming to work here?"

"Well . . ." Coby's cell buzzed at that moment and she excused herself, glad for the distraction. She walked back into the hotel lobby and examined the number on her screen. It was from her caller list: Joe. Why was he calling her on a Sunday? "Joe?" she answered cautiously.

"I'm going to give your dad a call. Do you have his cell number? I've got the Lovejoy's number, but I wanted to call him personally."

Oh, that's right. She'd suggested her father as one of Joe's clients, more to needle him than because she'd really wanted him to take her father's case. Joe sounded businesslike to the extreme. "Sure." Coby gave him the number, then, remembering their last conversation, added, "Jarvis Lloyd's suicide was certainly a surprise."

"Harassment by the police. Pure harassment."

"More like a guilty conscience, I'd say."

"If it weren't for the police, Lloyd would still be alive."

"Oh, Joe, for God's sake. Don't play that game with me."

"Your boyfriend's right on the front lines, Coby!"

"Bullshit. You're just pissed 'cause you lost a client. What are you doing, Joe? You're a damn good divorce lawyer, but when it comes to criminal law you get all competitive and it doesn't help anyone. Don't call my dad. He doesn't need your kind of representation." She pressed the red button and dropped the phone into her purse, furious all over.

Everybody was pissing her off.

Danner failed at contacting Edward Gerald, though he learned Gerald worked at Pump Up, a small athletic club on the east side of the river, just inside the Gresham city limits. Danner gave the manager his number and was told by the very disinterested man that he would have Gerald call him. Time would tell.

He glanced at his watch. It was afternoon, growing later by the minute. Almost as soon as he'd left the station Metzger had called him. A tip had come in about Sheila. A gas station attendant along I-5 had seen her sketch on the news and was pretty sure he'd filled her tank and that she'd headed north. For a few minutes Danner and Elaine had discussed Sheila and where they thought she might be going, but there wasn't much more to say. It was depressing for both of them, in that "maybe I could have done something different" way, though Danner, and most probably Metzger, too, definitely felt Lloyd had saved the state a lot of money by taking his own life.

He tried calling Yvette again, but she still wasn't picking up. Around four he decided to take a trip to her place of work, Xavier's, a restaurant with an active bar scene.

He walked into the place and noted the blood-red

booths and dark hardwood floors and central bar. There were a few people sitting in the booths and a man in his sixties seated at the bar.

The bartender looked up when Danner approached. "Can I get you something?"

"I'm looking for Yvette Deneuve. I understand she works here." He held up his badge for the bartender to see, but it was the older man at the end of the bar who started making choking sounds.

"You, too? I've been waiting for her to show up."

Danner turned toward the man, whose eyes were on his credentials, so Danner brought his badge over for the man to get a closer look. "You're a cop," the guy said. "You think she tried to kill that politician, don't you? Ran him off the road."

Danner blinked. The older man was one step ahead of him in this conversation. "I don't have any evidence of that," he said cautiously.

"Yvette comes on at six," the bartender put in. "But she went home sick last night. The flu, she said." He shrugged, clearly thinking it was a scam.

Danner asked, "Has she called in today?"

"Not yet. She'd better damn well be here."

"I think I have your evidence," the older gentleman said to Danner, who swung back to him. He stuck out a hand, which Danner shook. "Don Laidlaw. I left for Palm Springs yesterday and I'm back today. My doctor doesn't like something he saw on some tests. Might have to have some surgery, so I had to come back. I have this garage with my cars. I'm a collector. But I got some for just using, too. They're all in the garage."

Danner waited, and Laidlaw went on, "One of 'em's front end is smacked up bad. I fired the engine and it runs, so I guess she got lucky, but I know it was Yvette. She said she was gonna use my cars."

"When?"

Laidlaw shrugged and Danner saw the bartender look over at him. More information there, Danner decided. But Laidlaw went on about how he and Yvette were friends, and he'd offered up his house and cars, and she'd been teasing, like she was going to use 'em, but he hadn't believed her, but now . . .

"I'd like to see the car," Danner said, and without further ado Laidlaw slid off his stool, gave Danner directions, and said he'd meet him there.

Danner turned to the bartender. "You had something to add?"

He lifted his chin in the direction of the departing man. "Don's known around here as Don Juan. He likes younger women with a bad vibe."

"Like Yvette."

"Yup. She's been his favorite for a while, but she's only shown him some interest back just recently."

"Thanks."

Danner hurried after Laidlaw. He hadn't expected to solve the Sainer hit-and-run so easily. But if what Laidlaw said was true, then Yvette had a lot of explaining to do, probably more than she would be able to handle.

Coby left Lovejoy's and drove aimlessly for a time. She felt frustrated, as if she just wasn't thinking hard enough about everything. As though if she put the pieces together in some new order they would suddenly make sense.

She returned to Lovejoy's around five and found Juliet in the tearoom/wine bar, in a tense discussion with Suzette. The guests who'd been at the tearoom earlier had left and been replaced by several young couples who were drinking red wine from large goblets and nibbling on terrines of goat cheese, pesto and sun-dried tomatoes, bowls of olives, and an assortment of crisp, thin crackers.

Spying Coby the two sisters broke apart and both, independently, gazed at her mutinously. "What did I do?" Coby asked with a smile, trying to lighten the mood.

"What do you want now?" Suzette snapped out. "Faith's your sister. Isn't that enough?"

"You're trying to pin something on us," Juliet added.

They were alike in coloring and size, small and dark, but Juliet's hair was a shade or two lighter, as was her skin tone. Coby suspected she looked a bit more like the Ettes' mother while her other sisters favored Jean-Claude. She wasn't going to like the questions Coby had for her.

"Do you mind if we talk?" Coby said to Juliet, implying she wanted to be alone with her, which caused Suzette to give her a wide-eyed look and Juliet to stare at her as if she were a poisonous snake.

"What about?" Juliet demanded.

"I spoke with Donald Greer last night at the hospital."

"Wynona *hates* Yvette," Suzette jumped in. "You can't listen to her. Her dad's just the same."

But Juliet's eyes had dilated; she knew where Coby was heading. To Suzette, she said, "Give me a minute." When her sister started to protest, Juliet said through her teeth, "I'll be right back! Stop being such a bitch!"

"Jesus . . ." Suzette muttered, stalking away.

Juliet wore a black tunic over black leggings and black boots. She guided Coby to the side of the hotel lobby, near several wingback chairs in an alcove, and crossed her arms. "So?"

"Donald told me he caught you putting the notes in the lockers. He just recently revealed what you'd done to Wynona and, kind of like Annette, I guess, Wynona doesn't want any more secrets." Juliet didn't say anything immediately, just glared down at the floor, and Coby added, "You blamed it on Vic Franzen. Even last night you acted like you'd seen him at the lockers, slipping a note inside. You've never let him off the hook."

"Vic's an ass. He deserves it," she said, shooting Coby a cool look. "They all do."

"Who?"

"The guys. All this time I thought they cared about me. None of them ever have. Even Kirk," she said bitterly.

"But this note thing, Juliet. It had a life of its own."

"Oh, who cares. It was just a prank. Even Mr. Greer saw that, although everybody just keeps talking and talking and talking about it. I don't care. I just don't fucking care."

"Did you know Hank was Benedict's father?"

"You mean before the party? Did you think you were the only one Annette wanted to tell secrets to? We all figured it out."

"You all?"

"Me and my sisters. The Ettes," she said with a trace of sarcasm. "Yvette was seventeen and Mr. Sainer was too old for her and he had a career that their affair would ruin. Yvette was stupid about him. Still is," she added as an afterthought. "You think she killed Annette, don't you?"

"Not necessarily. If you and your sisters knew about Hank Sainer being Benedict's father, I don't see the why in that. I mean, why? Why would Yvette murder Annette? Her own sister."

"We only found out in the last few weeks," Juliet defended. "After Annette started talking about it. We didn't know before."

"Still . . . the word was out by the time of the birthday party."

Juliet seemed to want to argue that point, but she'd already said differently. "Well, Yvette's not right," she finally announced. "Nobody in the family wants to talk about it, but it's the truth."

"So, *you* think she did it," Coby said.

Juliet's hands fluttered with stress. "I don't know. Sometimes I think it might be someone else."

"Like?"

"I don't know. Okay? I don't know. But there was an incident here, just before the party, that upset Annette."

Coby remembered her father saying something about Annette being bothered over something that happened at Lovejoy's. "You know what it was?"

Juliet threw a look over her shoulder toward the tearoom/wine bar. "It's no secret that Suzette wanted Annette's job. Me, I really don't care. I don't care if I ever work another day here. But Suzette sort of tried to get Annette fired. Annette caught her at it just before the party."

Coby absorbed this. She hadn't seen any overt tension between Annette and Suzette that night. As if reading her mind, Juliet said, "Oh, Suzette squeezed her way out of it, just like she always does. But ask her about it. She and Annette made up, but it wasn't going to last."

"Are you suggesting that Suzette killed Annette?"

"I'm just saying that Yvette's unstable and probably killed her, but Suzette had problems with her, too!" Abruptly, she added, "I don't want to explain anything to you anymore. Where do you get off acting like you're above us?" With that, she stalked back toward the wine bar.

Coby was rolling all that over, getting ready to leave, when Suzette came hurrying toward her. She braced herself for what was undoubtedly going to be round two.

"You really pissed Juliet off," Suzette stated flatly.

"Did she tell you why?"

"No, but I can guess. She's pissed because she slept with them all—all the guys in the group—even though she thinks some of them are beneath her, like Vic, for sure, and Paul, and maybe even Theo. Galen did *not* sleep with her."

"She slept with Theo?"

"Girl, everybody slept with Theo Rivers. Ellen's just one of 'em. And maybe he's changed his ways now, but there was a time when he was as much a man-slut as Lucas was, maybe even more."

"Who else slept with Theo?"

"Well, maybe no one else from your group," Suzette conceded, "but that girl from Gresham sure did. He got her pregnant, and she miscarried, as we all know. Lucky for Theo, huh? But she wasn't the only one he slept with in high school, from what I heard. Ellen's parents probably packed her off to California just to keep her from getting pregnant again."

Coby was a little uncomfortable, listening first to Juliet, and now Suzette. There was a gleefulness to Suzette's tale that was unseemly. She'd always thought the youngest Ette sister was the sweetest one of them, but that was apparently a complete fallacy.

Still, information was information. "Juliet said you and Annette were at odds over something that happened at work."

Suzette's mouth opened in shock, then snapped shut. "She's such a goddamn bitch!" she declared, then swept back to the tearoom/wine bar as if ready to get into it anew with Juliet.

Sisters, Coby thought as she walked toward the front doors. Feeling eyes on her, she turned to see Jean-Claude, who was watching her with what looked like trepidation. She felt bad. He'd been through hell this week and she appeared to be only adding to it.

And then the inner sanctum door opened and Benedict walked through, coming to stand behind the counter with his grandfather.

"Well, hi," Coby said, surprised, retracing her steps to where Jean-Claude and Benedict stood.

"Go on to the back," Jean-Claude urged the boy. "You know you're not supposed to be out front."

"Why not?" Benedict scowled.

"Because we're running a hotel." Jean-Claude's voice was clipped. "Go on now."

Benedict made a sound of disgust, then practically stomped back through the door.

"Babysitting," Coby observed.

"Your father said it was all right to bring Benedict to work." He sounded a bit defensive.

Coby raised her hands. "He seems like a great kid."

"Despite how Yvette raised him?" Now there definitely was a defensive tone to Jean-Claude's words.

"I think I'll be going," Coby answered neutrally. "Is my dad here, still?"

"He's with your mother," he said with a bit of relish.

Well, it couldn't get more pointed than that, Coby thought. This being an investigator had its drawbacks when it came to friends and family.

The vehicle in Don Laidlaw's garage was a mass of mangled, twisted metal on the front right side. It was indeed a miracle that the machine had kept running and made its way back to the garage after whatever it had been through.

"It wasn't this way when you left for Palm Springs?" Danner asked Don.

"Hell, no. I checked the cars before I left. I always check the cars."

"How long were you planning to be gone?"

"Till March, or thereabouts. I go every year."

Danner gazed at the wreckage and thought, *"probable cause."* If Yvette didn't open her door voluntarily, he would get a warrant.

"You think Yvette did this?" Don asked anxiously. "You think she's all right?"

Danner didn't say it, but he felt for certain that Yvette was not even close to all right, and maybe never had been.

Coby was thinking about calling Danner on her way home when her cell phone rang first. Her anticipation vanished when she looked at the number. She didn't recognize the area code, though it seemed familiar, and so she answered her Bluetooth cautiously, "Hello?"

"Coby! Oh, my God. Coby. He died. He just died. I barely got here and he . . . maybe he was waiting for me . . . because he just died!"

The wail that followed sent a shiver down Coby's spine. "Dana?"

"I took a cab from the airport. I just got here. I just got here!"

"I'll be at the hospital in twenty minutes," Coby assured her, calculating zero traffic since it was Sunday.

"Oh, God. He's gone . . . somebody killed him . . . somebody ran him down!"

"I'll be right there, Dana. I'm on my way. I'm on my way. . . ."

Danner called Metzger on his way back to Yvette's apartment. "I may need a warrant." He quickly brought her up to speed on the latest events. "I'm gonna say that's the vehicle that ran down Hank Sainer, and Yvette's one of the few people who had access to it."

"I thought you were calling about Hank Sainer," she said.

"Sainer?"

"We just got word from Laurelton General that he died about an hour ago. His daughter's with him."

Danner was shocked. Somehow he'd thought Hank would make it. "All the more reason to get the warrant."

"I'm on it," Elaine said, then clicked off.

Danner felt a buzzing urgency, the kind of thing that happened to him when things started falling into place. He kicked himself for not getting to Yvette sooner. Maybe this could have been prevented. Maybe Hank would still be alive.

Pulling into her parking lot with more speed than caution, he had to rein in his impulse to hurry.

As soon as he turned off the engine he heard a shrieking he'd only been distantly aware of. A woman's ululation was lifting to the heavens, filled with grief and agony. The hairs on his arms raised as he climbed from the cab, and he drew his Glock.

Above him Yvette's door was open. The shrieking was coming from inside. In five long steps he was at the stairway. Six more and he was on the second level, running toward the door. He paused before crossing in front of the open aperture and yelled, "Yvette! It's Danner Lockwood."

The wailing ceased abruptly. Danner was on the side of the door, poised, ready to give a quick peek inside when a woman suddenly tumbled onto the balcony. A Hispanic woman, her face screwed up in fear and pain. She fell at his feet and he crouched down and grabbed her by her shoulders, steadying her.

"Oh, Mama. Poor Mama." Her eyes rolled to the doorway. "*Dios . . . Dios.* She is gone. She is gone. . . ."

Danner gently released her, rose to his feet, and cautiously stepped into the apartment.

Yvette lay on the floor, eyes open, staring at the ceiling, a pool of blood spread around her like a red halo. Beside her lay a broken lamp and a butcher knife. The blade of the knife was covered with blood from the gaping wound at Yvette's neck.

Chapter 27

Coby reached the hospital in twenty-three minutes, feeling a slight shiver as she circled in front of the entrance portico and past the place the car had run at her the night before. There was still an indent in the mud and grass where she'd fallen that made her grimace.

Dana Sainer Bracco was in the hallway outside the room where Hank had been taken after surgery, though his body was now in the hospital morgue. Seeing Coby, she ran toward her as if they were old friends, and in a general sense, Coby guessed they were.

"I don't know anybody here anymore," she said, hugging Coby, her body quivering. "I left and I never looked back. I didn't visit my dad enough. I'm sorry . . . it's just that you called me the other day . . ."

"It's okay," Coby soothed, patting her on the back. "It's okay. I'm sorry, too. I thought Hank was stabilized."

Dana inhaled shakily and released her grip on Coby. "His injuries were too severe. He never woke up. I thought he would when I got here, but I barely was at his side before the monitor went flat. . . ."

"I'm sorry," Coby said again.

Dana fought to pull herself together. "But who would

run him off the road? Were they just stupid and reckless? He didn't have political enemies. He always laughed about being so middle-of-the-road that no one noticed him. Who would do this?"

Dana was still petite and birdlike, even after having children. She'd gained a bit of weight, but it worked for her as she no longer was such a waif. She'd said she had her eating disorder under control. Maybe a happy family life could do that for you.

But now she regarded Dana with a tense, drawn face.

Coby's phone buzzed. "Excuse me," she said, relieved to have an excuse not to answer her. She saw it was a text from Danner. She'd called and left a message on his voice mail about Hank, but he hadn't gotten back to her till now.

The text read: *coming to Laurelton G see u soon*

"Danner's on his way here," she said to Dana.

"Danner Lockwood?"

"He's helping the Tillamook County Sheriff's Department investigate Annette's death."

"Oh, right. He's a cop. I think you told me that. . . ." She turned her gaze away from Coby, retreating into her own grief.

Coby glanced down at the screen of her cell phone, thought a moment, then pulled up the number for her father's cell. If Hank's death hadn't hit the news yet, it soon would. She figured she might as well send out a warning.

Danner drove away from Yvette's apartment with a sense of being two steps behind a killer whose murderous plan seemed to have little rhyme or reason. Annette, then Hank, now *Yvette*? Maybe Lucas and maybe Rhiannon and maybe Heather McCrae? Could one person really be responsible for all those deaths? No. He didn't believe that. Some of them had to be accidents. Had to be. Unless there was more than one killer, an idea that kept cropping up and being dismissed again, mainly because he couldn't see the connections.

Why? he asked himself. *Who?*

He'd had his hands full at Yvette's apartment after discovering her body. First he had to make sure no one touched the body or screwed up the crime scene before the ME and CSI techs arrived. Secondly, he had to keep the traumatized babysitter, Juanita, from becoming completely hysterical, which proved the more difficult task. Apparently Juanita had shown up at her usual time to take care of Benedict while Yvette was at work and had used her own key to enter the apartment. She'd opened the door and seen Yvette's body on the floor. That had stopped her cold for a shocked moment, then she'd begun wailing. She hadn't had time to look for Benedict before Danner showed up. A quick check of the premises assured Danner the boy wasn't there, but then, where was he? The answer had been discovered fairly quickly after Danner placed a call to Lovejoy's to locate Jean-Claude and was informed by William Johnson, the assistant manager, that Mr. Deneuve had taken his grandson home with him and wasn't expected back for the rest of the day.

So, okay, Benedict was with Jean-Claude. That was good. Danner didn't want the kid traumatized. He debated heading over to Jean-Claude's house in the west hills to give the man the bad news himself, but then he listened to Coby's voice mail and sent her the text saying he would be there soon. He'd wanted to tell her about Yvette in person as well, but almost as soon as he sent the text he had to rethink that. Jean-Claude needed to be told before the ravenous media found out.

Danner dialed Coby's cell and she picked up as if she'd been just waiting for him to call. "I got your text. You're on your way?" she asked, and he could hear the eagerness in her voice. It bummed him out that he was going to have to put her off.

"Something's come up," he said, hearing the grimness in his own voice. "I was planning to come straight to the hospital, but I was at Yvette's . . ."

"You talked to her? What did she say?"

"Coby, Yvette's dead. Someone slit her throat."

There was a shocked pause, an intake of breath. "*What?*"

Briefly he recapped the scene he'd come across at Yvette's apartment, finishing with, "Benedict's with Jean-Claude, at his house. I'm on my way there now."

"But . . . how . . . when? She was at the hospital last night." Coby sounded completely discombobulated.

"I don't know how long I'll be," he said. "I'll call you when I'm finished."

"I want to be with you," she said suddenly. "Jean-Claude's a friend. He's my dad's best friend!"

"After Jean-Claude's been given the news, I'll call you," Danner promised. He could hear a woman's voice asking questions in the background and added, "Until then, keep this between us."

"Of course. Yes. Absolutely." She was distracted.

"Coby . . ."

"Hmm?"

"I love you," he said. He clicked off, surprised at how much he'd needed to say that right then. Then he steeled himself for the job ahead.

Coby was in a numb fog. She was pretty sure he'd told her he loved her, but he'd also told her that Yvette was dead. Murdered. Strange, beautiful, mercurial Yvette Deneuve had been killed. Someone had sliced her throat.

Dana was talking but she couldn't hear her. Coby felt

like she was walking through a thick substance that robbed her of hearing except for the painfully hard beats of her heart.

Coby had dismissed last night's attack. Had made light of it. She hadn't truly believed that someone had been trying to kill her. She'd thought it was a message, maybe a warning. Now, though . . .

"What is it?" Dana was demanding. Her shrill voice finally penetrated Coby's cotton-stuffed ears. "You were talking about Jean-Claude."

"He's my dad's best friend," she said woodenly.

"That's what you said." Dana was impatient. "What is it? You're scaring me," she added, her sharp eyes scouring Coby's face. "What happened?"

Coby couldn't tell her about Yvette. She didn't want to tell her about Yvette. She was struggling to even comprehend what had happened to Yvette. "I need something to eat," she said flatly, as a diversion, realizing as she said it that it was the absolute truth. It was dinnertime and she hadn't had anything since her makeshift breakfast.

Without another word she headed for the cafeteria with Dana hurrying to keep up with her.

Jean-Claude's house sat on a ridge overlooking the city. Danner drove up the narrow, winding street and parked in the driveway of the daylight basement home next to a black Mercedes SUV. He walked up a curving stone path to the front door, which was surrounded by overgrown bushes that nearly swallowed the porch. He rang the bell, hearing the deep tolling sounds within, reminding Danner of a funeral dirge.

It was Benedict who answered the door. The boy looked a bit crestfallen upon seeing Danner. "It's a man," he yelled over his shoulder.

"I told you your mother would still be at work," Jean-Claude called back, his voice echoing from the floor below. Directly ahead of Danner was a wrought-iron rail that wrapped around the hole that was the stairs to the basement level. Jean-Claude's head appeared behind the rail as he ascended the stairs to the main level. Behind him, through huge glass windows, was a staggering view of Portland, the city lights winking on as night approached.

"Detective Lockwood," he said cautiously, upon seeing Danner in the doorway.

Danner's gaze flicked to Benedict, and Jean-Claude picked up on the unspoken comment. "Go on downstairs and play that terrible video game while I talk to the detective," he told his grandson.

Benedict didn't have to be asked twice. He gave a whoop of joy and jumped down the stairs and out of sight.

"You and Coby are both all over the place, eh?" Jean-Claude stated flatly.

"Mr. Deneuve, I have something to tell you," Danner began, searching for the right words. There was a protocol for delivering this kind of news, but he'd found he was no good at that kind of rote delivery.

But Jean-Claude was nothing if not perceptive. "Oh, Jesus. Oh, Lord. What's happened?"

"I'm sorry to inform you that your daughter, Yvette, is dead."

He blinked in shock, then backed away as if Danner had hit him. "No."

"I was the one who discovered her body," Danner said.

"What? How? Where?"

"Her apartment."

"An accident?"

"A homicide," Danner said.

Jean-Claude staggered back farther, holding on to the rail. "She was fine! She gave me Benedict last night! She was fine when I left her. This is a mistake!" He gazed at Danner pleadingly, but the truth was self-evident.

"I'm sorry," Danner said, and Jean-Claude buried his face in his hands and shuddered violently.

Five minutes later Danner and Jean-Claude were in the kitchen and Jean-Claude was muttering, "I knew something would happen. I knew it. She was so impulsive. Oh, my daughters . . . my daughters . . ." He pulled out a bottle of scotch, poured himself a drink, then sat down hard at the kitchen table. He stared at the drink but didn't pick it up.

Danner asked, "Would you like to call someone?"

"Yes . . . yes . . . Dave . . ." He picked up his cell phone from the counter and in a voice full of shock and disbelief baldly told Coby's father what had happened. He hung up and told Danner in a strangled tone, "He's coming over. He is at the hospital. Did you know Hank died tonight?" His voice cracked with disbelief. "They say things come in threes. That's three deaths in a week. Three deaths! Oh, my daughters . . . my daughters!"

And then he broke down and sobbed.

Coby bought herself a turkey sandwich and couldn't eat more than two bites. She turned instead to her black coffee, holding the cup for warmth and fortification as she felt her insides shudder uncontrollably. Yvette . . . she just couldn't be gone. It had been hard enough to believe that Annette was dead—murdered—but now Yvette, *too*?

Dana was picking at the salad she'd ordered and sniffling. Just as soon as she corralled her tears, they began again. "Who called?" she asked again. "You look like your best friend died. What happened to Jean-Claude?"

Coby was saved for an answer by the appearance of her father and mother entering the cafeteria together, Leta's arm clutched to Dave's. It pissed Coby off, and for a moment she gratefully stoked her anger at them. It was easier to be mad than confused and shocked. Dana greeted them, accepting their condolences, but a line slowly formed between her brows. When Dave and Leta went to find themselves something to eat as well, Dana hissed quietly, "Are your mom and dad back together?"

"You mean because it's barely been a week since Annette's death?"

"Well, yeah . . ."

"I know," Coby said flatly.

Across the room Coby heard a cell phone jingle and looked up to see her father reaching in his pocket. He pulled out the phone and the ringing got louder before he answered. He and Leta were standing in the cafeteria line, but Coby could see her father's expression and body language. One moment he was standing there, the next he had staggered out of line. Leta rushed to him, but he was heading Coby's way, his eyes wild.

"That was Jean-Claude," he said hoarsely. "Yvette's been killed. He wants me to come to his house."

"I'll follow you," Coby said, and everyone was too shocked to notice that she'd already heard the news.

She was worried about her father's driving, but Dave, with Leta tucked into the passenger seat, drove with exceptional care. Coby followed just as carefully, and by the time they got to Jean-Claude's, she'd begun to accept that this was real, that Yvette was really dead. She'd left Dana gape-mouthed and lost, and upset that the focus had suddenly shifted from her own tragedy, and had driven after her father and mother, not caring whether she was invited or not.

Nicholette had arrived just ahead of them, looking

white-faced and undone. Spying Coby, she decided to take her shock out on her. "Don't start asking your questions! I'm advising my father to speak to me, as his attorney, and no one else!"

"No one thinks Jean-Claude has anything to do with Yvette's murder!" Coby said in horror. "Nicholette, please . . ."

Nicholette tossed her hands in the air and went inside. Coby followed on her heels with Dave and Leta bringing up the rear.

The Deneuve family was in the kitchen, Jean-Claude and now Nicholette, along with Coby's father and mother. Suzette and Juliet had been notified and were on their way, according to Jean-Claude. Leta stayed to one side, standing against the back wall as Dave sat down next to Jean-Claude; she was the odd woman out. Danner, too, was several paces back.

Coby said to him, "My mother shouldn't be here."

"I'm about ready to leave myself," he told her.

"Let's connect later?" she asked and he nodded. Then she moved close to Leta and said in her ear, "Let me take you home."

"I'm here for your father."

"Mom, catch a clue. You shouldn't be here."

Leta's chin jutted mutinously. Her eyes warred with Coby's but Coby just held her gaze. Finally, she sighed and announced, "Coby's going to take me home now, Dave. Jean-Claude, I'm so sorry."

Both men nodded vacantly and Leta, seeing how little they noticed, preceded Coby from the house, her back stiff. Danner followed them to the door. "I'm right behind you," he said. "I'll come to your town house."

"Okay."

The whole night was surreal. Leta climbed into the passenger seat of Coby's Nissan and pulled the seat belt across her body, eyes straight ahead. She was afraid of losing the slightest influence over Coby's father, Coby realized, also seeing for the first time how weak her father was. He couldn't be without a woman, a forceful woman. Yvette was right about that; Annette would have gotten her way eventually, had she lived, and there would have been a new baby, Coby's half brother or sister.

"Hey . . ." A voice came out of the darkness, from somewhere near the bushes that were trying to overtake the front porch.

Coby whipped around, terror slicing through her before her brain registered that the voice was young and male. She couldn't see anything. It was too dark. "Benedict?" she asked cautiously.

He materialized from the darkness, all angles and limbs and big eyes. "Is my mom all right?" he squeaked out.

Coby's shoulders dropped. "Oh, Benedict. This is something you need to talk to your grandfather about." Coby wanted to grab him and hug him and comfort him, but he stayed back, just out of range.

"She's dead," he stated flatly. "I heard them. Somebody killed her."

"You really need to go back inside and talk to Jean-Claude. He'll be looking for you."

"Here."

He suddenly held out his hand. Dangling from it was something small and chainlike. A necklace. *The* necklace, Coby realized with a start. The sapphire pendant.

Benedict took it?

"My mom put it in my backpack," he explained. "She wanted me to find it. It's Aunt Annette's."

She lifted her hand to take the necklace, which Benedict pooled into her palm. "Does anyone know about this?"

"Grandpa. He thinks Mom left it for him, but it's for me." He started to cry. "Take it. I don't want it anymore."

He ran to the front door and yanked it open. Nicholette was standing on the other side and he barreled into her arms, surprising her. Through the aperture she saw Coby holding the necklace and she shook her head, as if she didn't want to talk about it. Then she shut the door.

Coby stared down at the sapphire necklace in her hand. Its appearance wasn't a surprise to Nicholette, so Jean-Claude must have told her about finding it. They were both protecting Yvette. Except now Yvette was dead, and Nicholette had warned her father not to talk to the authorities without a lawyer present. She was protecting him as well.

Or . . . ?

"Coby!" Leta rolled down the window and regarded her impatiently.

She should give the necklace to Danner. She shouldn't keep it. What did it mean? Yvette had taken it? So was she Annette's killer after all? Had she altered her story to protect herself, claiming she'd walked away from the hot tub when she'd really held Annette's head under in a fit of rage?

Stuffing the necklace in her pocket, Coby walked to her car on wooden legs.

"What did that boy give you?" Leta demanded.

"A lot more questions than answers," Coby responded, then drove her mother back to the Portland house where Coby had grown up.

It's all getting smaller and smaller around me.

Yvette stole the necklace from me. Stole it! My souvenir! She said that she and I were the same, but she's wrong. She said she's always known about me, but she doesn't know anything!

We're not the same. We've never been the same.

She took the necklace and thought she had the upper hand.

She slammed the lamp at me but only grazed my shoulder.

She's not like me. She's nothing like me! I found the knife and I stabbed her in the throat and pulled with everything I had.

I told her I was sorry, but she was already gone.

I am sorry.

But she's never done what she's supposed to do. She doesn't belong!

None of them belong anymore. They ruined it.

They were the queens and kings and now they're nothing.

I've done so much for them . . . and they don't appreciate it.

I have to make them see! Do something . . . something to make it all matter.

I've made mistakes. I failed to kill Coby last night, and she's getting closer to the truth. I can feel it.

She doesn't belong. She's never belonged.

Chapter 28

Dave called Coby just after she dropped off Leta. "I hate to ask you, but can you stop by Lovejoy's? Juliet left in a panic when she heard about Yvette, and I'm afraid William's overloaded. Suzette's already here at Jean-Claude's."

"Sure. What do you want me to do?"

"Ask William. Maybe close down the wine bar. Thanks, Bug. I really appreciate it."

She changed course from her town house to Lovejoy's. She'd called Danner and left him a voice mail, telling him about the necklace and Benedict and Nicholette. Though it hadn't occurred to her in the moment, she wondered if she should have gone back inside and handed the necklace over to her father, or to Danner, like she'd intended.

Instead she'd just stuck the necklace in her pocket, a kind of rote security measure, like stowing her car keys. Now the necklace felt heavy. A mental trick. Some huge onus.

She punched in her contact list and hit the button for Danner but was sent to voice mail. "I'm at Lovejoy's," she told him. "Can you meet me here? I've been called into active duty."

Just before she pulled into the parking lot across the street from the hotel, her cell rang back at her. Assuming it was Danner, she didn't look at the number as she clicked on. "Hey, did you get my message?"

Silence.

Coby's attention sharpened. Maybe a bad connection—maybe something else. "Hello?" she said loudly. "Danner?"

"I didn't kill her," the female voice responded. Unrecognizable.

"Who is this?" Coby demanded.

"Genevieve."

"Gen?" Coby repeated; there was some familiarity to the tone now, though her voice was strangled.

"I didn't kill Yvette. I saw it on the news . . . her apartment complex . . . I knew it was Yvette's. They said there was a female homicide victim. It's Yvette, isn't it? That was her door they focused on. I know it was! And I was there last night. I don't know when she died, but she was alive when I left her. I swear it! I don't think Jarrod believes me! He stormed out of here and he's probably calling Danner now, but I didn't do it!" Her voice was rising with hysteria.

"Calm down." Because of a special event in the area the garage attendant was waiting for her to pay in advance, so Coby said, "Just a minute. Genevieve. Hold on, just a minute." She tried to hold the cell with her shoulder and ear, dicey at the best of times, and open her purse at the same time. The attendant took her cash and said he'd bring change. "Genevieve? Are you still there?"

"I accused her of running down Hank Sainer. I was mad at her. She wanted me to leave. We argued some, but it was just words! Oh, my God. Oh, my God."

"Gen, just hold on." Frustrated, Coby curtly thanked the attendant for her change, then wanted to scream while he scratched his neck and told her there might be a place to park at the far end, and if not, come on back and he'd hold her car until a spot opened up.

Coby drove forward, searching for a parking place.

"We were talking about Lucas," Gen choked out. "I just wanted to blame her, but it was . . . I don't know. It's over! It's so over, and it's just been like this piece of me died with him, you know? She stood up there that day and swore she and Lucas were lovers and I knew it wasn't true. I knew it. I told Rhiannon it wasn't true, and she believed me at first. But then she realized Lucas had been unfaithful and . . . oh . . . it's never been right."

"Gen, I've got to put down the phone while I park." Coby set the cell on the seat and maneuvered into a spot. The place was packed and she remembered distantly that there was some wine-tasting thing going on in Nob Hill tonight. She switched off the ignition and picked up the cell. "Gen?" she said urgently as she squeezed from the driver's side.

"Yvette's dead, isn't she?"

"Genevieve—"

"*She's dead, isn't she!*"

"Yes," Coby said.

"I didn't do it. Honest to God, Coby. It's not my fault."

"No one's accusing you of killing Yvette."

"They will. I can see it coming. Jarrod's livid. He thinks I did it!"

Coby glanced both ways as she crossed the street and headed up the steps to the front doors of Lovejoy's. The lobby lights had been lowered some and no one was behind the counter.

"It doesn't matter what Jarrod thinks, if it's not true. What time were you at her apartment?" Coby asked. "Maybe you can help the police figure out who did kill her. Talk to Danner."

"I didn't kill her," she repeated, like a mantra.

"Call Danner," Coby repeated. "Let me give you his number." She rattled it off, unsure whether Genevieve was even listening any longer. "Gen, I'm at Lovejoy's. They're short-staffed and I'm just covering until they can get someone to fill in."

"Can I come be with you?" Her voice was small.

"Sure," Coby said, though a bit of warning slid along her nerves.

"I'll be right there!"

As soon as Gen ended the call, Coby phoned Danner, and it went straight to voice mail yet again. She told him about Genevieve coming to Lovejoy's, then said, "Call me," wondering why he wasn't picking up.

Coby headed toward the tearoom/wine bar and saw it was dark and looked closed. She was thinking maybe there wasn't that much for her to do when Juliet suddenly came through the door from the inner sanctum. "Oh, there you are," she said with relief. "I don't know where William is. Just didn't feel like I could leave."

"I'm so sorry, Juliet," Coby said, meaning it.

Juliet held up her hands, unable to talk for a moment. "Do you mind coming behind the counter?"

"What if somebody wants to check in or out? I don't know the first thing."

"Just give me a minute. I'll find William." With that she went back through the door and Coby stepped behind the counter and hoped to hell nothing would happen.

All day Kirk had thought about what he was going to do to Juliet when he got a hold of her. She was just like the little bitch in that Carrie Underwood song, "Before He Cheats," who trashed her ex-boyfriend's car. Kirk supposed he was lucky Juliet hadn't done all the things to his car that the cute little bitch Carrie sang about had done to that car in the song—with a Louisville Slugger, among other things. Juliet had only keyed the side of the 4x4, but that sure as hell was enough.

Now it was night and he'd decided on a course of action. Earlier he'd gone into a hardware store and purchased one of those bug bombs that killed everything from bees to spiders to probably Komodo dragons. All he had to do was get into her Mercedes, which was no problem because the relic had a loose window on one side that could be pulled down by simple pressure—damn thing was gonna fall into the door one of these days and shatter into a billion pieces—so all he had to do was slide it over, reach in, pop the lock. Then he could snap open the top on the spray can and get the damn poison started. The damn Mercedes would be, like, radioactive for hours, days, weeks!

Fuck her.

Juliet always parked in that lot across from Lovejoy's; everybody did. Yeah, there was an attendant there, Steve something-or-other, but he was a total tool who spent most of his time texting friends and looking for a drug score. A major pill popper was our man, Steve. It amazed Kirk he'd lasted this long at the job. Kirk had befriended the guy out of necessity; he really needed a place to park anytime Juliet wheedled him to come to Lovejoy's, which wasn't that often 'cause Kirk just wasn't interested, but on the rare occasion he said he would go there, there was never one goddamned parking spot for miles and miles around fucking Nob Hill Portland. As ever, Kirk had found his own means to have things work for him. For a couple of comped tickets to a Split Decision show, and the knowledge that lots of druggies loved to hang out at rock and roll concerts, Steve would let Kirk roll his 4x4 inside and pretend he just didn't see.

So it was a simple matter to access Juliet's car with no suspicions. Steve knew Kirk and Juliet were friends, anyway. The only problem would be if Steve wasn't on duty, and well, then Kirk would have to be all stealth and sneaky. An added hurdle, but not insurmountable.

Now there was a smile on Kirk's face as he looked at himself in the mirror. His bald head shone under the lights and he took a moment to play air guitar, watching how he looked. He was moving on from Split Decision. It felt right. Karma, man.

Five minutes later he was driving toward Nob Hill, lost in thought to his planning, when his cell rang. Kirk looked down at the screen. It was Jarrod. He almost answered, then thought, fuck it. What had Jarrod ever done for him really? They were supposed to be best friends and all, but that was all bullshit. Somehow Jarrod was the front man in this relationship as well as the band, and Kirk was, well, the horse's ass.

Jarrod called a second time as Kirk was turning into the lot, but Kirk ignored it again, relieved to see that Steve was indeed working tonight. "Hey, dude," Kirk greeted Steve as he pulled up.

"Hey, dude." Steve sounded worried. "We're really full, man. I don't think I got a place for you tonight. There's some big wine-tasting deal over on Twenty-third."

"I won't be long," Kirk said. "Just gotta check on Juliet's car for her. She pay this month's rent?"

"Her old man's hotel picks it up," Steve said, which Kirk well knew.

"Maybe you can put mine on the Lovejoy's tab, too."

"Ahh, man . . ."

"Forget it." Kirk laughed. "Just give me a few minutes. I gotta go see Juliet at work, but I'll be right back."

Kirk drove on before Steve could offer up any more whining. It wouldn't take him even that long, once he found a place to stow his own car. He'd already seen Juliet's silver Mercedes, parked nose-in, along the wall.

Another car was pulling into the lot and Steve got

distracted. Good. Kirk couldn't find a free spot, so he simply parked sideways behind Juliet's car for the moment. There was just enough room for that other car to pass by him. Sodium vapor lights illuminated the lot, but he thought he could slide the right back window down without being seen if he was quick.

Switching off his engine, he grabbed the can of bug killer from the passenger seat, then slid out of his car. He was to Juliet's back window in a couple of strides and he pressed his hands to the glass and pushed. Not too hard. Just enough to get it out of the track. Just enough to slide it around a little.

He felt the window give and smiled. He didn't even think Juliet knew about her vehicle's unusual flaw. He'd come across it by accident one day, leaning against the Mercedes.

A moment later he had the lock popped, and then he carefully slid the window back up into place. It was probably precariously hanging there, but if it only held for tonight he'd be okay.

He put the bug spray in the backseat foot well, was about to pop it open, then thought about it. Better hidden under the seat. It would still spray its noxious killer gas everywhere but wouldn't be so easy to see.

He bent over and reached under the passenger seat to make sure the space was empty. His hand encountered a piece of paper, some kind of tag hanging from under the seat. Grabbing it, he gave it a yank, and it fell into his hands with a release of strapping tape.

He gazed at it. A plain white envelope.

Reaching inside, he pulled out a swatch of blond-brown hair.

"Fuck me," Kirk whispered.

"What are you doing?" a voice behind him demanded. A male voice. Kirk jumped about a foot and turned around to see Danner Lockwood standing there, his expression cold, hard, and accusing.

For an answer Kirk simply handed over the envelope.

Danner stared down at the swatch of hair and felt the muscles of his stomach contract. "You had Lucas's hair?" he asked Kirk.

"Hell, no. This is Juliet's car."

Danner swung around to his Wrangler, which he'd simply thrown into park and left running when he'd seen someone breaking into a car. He switched off the ignition and left the keys where they were.

Kirk said, "Hey, man," when he headed across the street, horns blasting as he dodged traffic. "Hey, man! Where ya goin'?"

But Danner didn't answer. On his way to Coby's he'd gotten a call from Ed Gerald that had left him filled with dread. The gym rat had said, "You called me?" and Danner had explained who he was and that he wanted to revisit anything Ed could tell him about his girlfriend's death. Gerald had been reluctant to talk and Danner had missed three calls from Coby while he'd tried to conduct the interview, which had made him impatient. He was already distracted with driving; traffic was slow and sticky. He was fairly sure Ed Gerald was just a dead end anyway, but then Gerald said something that made the hairs on Danner's arms lift.

"She was hanging out with that friend of her old boyfriend's. That's who I thought she was gonna be with that day, but she went to the gym by herself and, well, the whole thing totally sucks. It shouldn't have happened that way. She was a great girl."

"Who was the friend?" Danner asked.

"I never met her."

"Do you mean she was a friend of Theo Rivers?"

"Yeah. That was his name. She dated him before me."

"And you don't remember anything about the girlfriend?"

"Nah . . . except that Heather said she called herself an Ent, like in the *Lord of the Rings*? I figured she was really tall, or something. I don't know. I didn't pay attention."

"Could she have said 'Ette'?"

"Well, yeah, but that doesn't make any sense, does it?"

Danner had immediately hung up, his mind spinning. Heather McCrae was friends with one of the Ettes? He'd listened to his messages and learned Coby was at Lovejoy's, so he'd changed his destination, wondering just which Ette had struck up a friendship with Theo Rivers' ex-girlfriend.

And then he'd run across Kirk . . . and then the envelope in Juliet's car . . .

Kirk sucked in a breath watching Danner dodge traffic. Steve appeared, in a huff. "Whose goddamn Wrangler is this?" he demanded, looking inside the vehicle. "He left the keys."

"It's the police, man," Kirk said, tearing after Danner. "Just park the fucker, okay?"

What the fuck was up with Juliet?

At first when Juliet returned with a handgun, Coby hadn't taken in the significance; she thought Juliet had armed herself as a safety precaution since Yvette's death. But the pistol was aimed at Coby's heart, and it didn't move.

Coby simply did not know what to say, and so they stared at each other in silence for a moment.

"Aren't you going to ask any questions?" Juliet finally demanded, motioning Coby toward the door to the inner sanctum. "All you've done is talk, talk, talk. Now you have nothing to say?"

"Why?" Coby asked.

"Move," Juliet ordered tersely when Coby just stood there. Though the gun was below the counter level, it wouldn't pay to have a guest suddenly come into the hotel.

"Where's William?"

"Sent him on an errand. If I'm not here when he gets back, he'll just think I took off irresponsibly. That's me. The irresponsible one." She took a step forward and Coby finally got her feet moving, into the back room, which was really a hallway with three offices jutting off it and, at the far end of the hall, the small kitchen that serviced the tearoom/wine bar.

"You killed Yvette?" Coby asked.

"I was there, at the campout, listening to all of you," Juliet revealed with a thin smile. "Genevieve was so popular, and she got you all to tell your secrets. And the guys were playing guitar. It was so perfect, you know. I wanted all of it."

Coby stared at her. Her memories of that night were vastly different.

"You kissed Lucas, and Genevieve had sex with him. I watched. And then he walked off and I saw him start to head up to Bancroft Bluff. I almost followed him, but I just stayed on the beach for a while and watched the waves come in.

"And then they were yelling—Yvette and Hank, though I didn't know it at the time—and then Lucas came tumbling over the cliff and just bounced on the rocks of the tide pools. He was staring at the sky when I came up to him. He couldn't talk. He was broken. So I turned him over and helped him die in dignity. I had a penknife and I saved some of his hair.

"But none of you stayed with the guys in your group. Even Genevieve didn't get with Jarrod till college. So I left you the notes. But you didn't belong. I didn't know that then."

Coby stayed perfectly still. Juliet sounded so rational, laying down the events as she viewed them, the reasons for her behavior, in a voice that was cool and collected. She believed what she was saying had meaning when it was all some world she'd made up in her head.

"Then Yvette was pregnant and I thought it was Lucas's baby. That made a kind of sense, you know?"

Coby carefully said, "Then you learned Benedict was Hank Sainer's," when Juliet paused.

"Annette learned. She started blabbing away and I wanted to kill her for destroying everything. Then she found Lucas's hair. Yvette was fighting with her and I just had my moment. So I drowned her and took her necklace. Yvette suspected it was me, I guess, because she grabbed my purse one day and dumped it on one of the tables at the wine bar. She snatched up the necklace before anyone saw. I hadn't wanted to put it away yet. Then she held it over my head, and after she ran Hank off the road, she planned to use it to keep me from saying anything, I know she did. I went over there to talk to her and she attacked me! I didn't really intend to kill her, but she threatened me. She said if I told about Hank, she would tell about Annette. I didn't have a choice after that."

"What about Rhiannon?" Coby asked, her eyes on the gun, her thoughts on the necklace in her pocket. Could she use it as a distraction of some kind?

"I didn't kill Rhiannon, but I know who did."

"Who?"

Juliet shook her head. "Oh, come on, Coby. You're so smart. You can figure that one out."

"Is the reason you've been with all the guys in the group

because they're special?" Coby asked, trying to keep the conversation going, seeking to stay with Juliet's logic.

"I wanted them to love me, too. Like they loved all of you." Her face darkened. "Vic's an ass. Paul's not much better, as it turns out. And if I'd known Theo was such a man-slut I wouldn't have bothered to take out his big-lipped whore."

Coby carefully asked, "Heather?"

"She thought she was such a physical specimen. It was easy to rip the bar from her hands and drop it on her throat."

"But you were never with Theo."

She tilted her head and smiled. "Not yet."

"What about Kirk?"

It was the wrong thing to say. Juliet's carefully constructed script couldn't stand rewrites. "That fucker! I hope he burns in hell!"

The hallway door suddenly burst open. Danner stood there, gun aimed. Juliet spun around wildly and fired a shot. It whizzed past Danner and slammed into the door. Bits of wood flew out.

But Juliet didn't wait. She tore down the hallway in the opposite direction, toward the kitchen.

And Kirk stepped into her path.

She lifted the gun and fired but he came at her in a flying tackle. She was spitting and screaming and fighting like a wild woman, scrabbling for the gun that had bounced from her hand.

Kirk hauled his fist back and punched her in the face. Hard.

She gave up instantly, crying and mewling and swearing she would see him in hell.

"You first," he told her.

Danner grabbed Coby and hauled her close. She could feel how much he was trembling. Or maybe that was her.

A moment later he released her and pulled out a pair of cuffs, then headed down the hall to where Kirk was sitting on Juliet, keeping her pinned down.

Ten days later they were seated around the small table at Coby's town house, sharing dinner with Jarrod, Genevieve, and Kirk, who'd had a change of plans and was now thinking he was meant for the police academy. Coby had her doubts on that one, as did Danner, but Jarrod had been encouraging. Maybe because he still wanted Kirk around for the band, even if Ryan and Spence were working their way through the legal problems resulting from their thievery.

Jarrod had left Genevieve, but she'd beseeched him to return. She needed him. She loved him. And she assured him she was over all that history with Lucas Moore. He'd been like an idol to her. Had he lived, she probably would have gotten over him sooner, but he died right at the height of her obsession and it took her till now to put it behind her.

Was it over, really? Coby wasn't completely certain, and neither was Jarrod. But he was coping, so Coby decided to hope for the best.

They'd had their own little Thanksgiving dinner, and as Coby carried plates to the kitchen, she felt Danner come up behind her and put his arms around her. "If you're not going to help, you have to let me go. There's work to be done."

"Sure thing," he said lazily, kissing her temple before reluctantly releasing her. "They caught Sheila just outside Seattle."

"I heard you on the phone with your partner," Coby said, rinsing the plates before putting them in the dishwasher.

"She was trying to ditch the gun, but they got it. Pretty sure it's the same one that she used to kill Beth and Angie Lloyd."

"You know Juliet told my father to send me to help out

at Lovejoy's that night," Coby said conversationally. "When my dad realized it, he just about had a heart attack, thinking he unwittingly set me up."

"Juliet's a certified fruitcake."

"She had her own construct. It just wasn't reality."

"Don't even think about excusing her."

"I'm not," Coby said. "But she's unwell. Jean-Claude did say his daughters were all a little tweaked."

"Two out of five are bona fide killers. That's more than a little."

"Okay." She laughed.

Jarrod brought in some of the flatware and the basket used for bread. "Dana still around?" he asked.

"She flew home, but she's coming back soon," Coby said.

Dana, after learning the whole truth about Yvette, Hank, and Benedict, had shown surprising maturity, or maybe it was her natural maternal instinct, by asking to be a part of her half brother's life. Jean-Claude had agreed, and they were working out plans for Benedict to visit Dana and her family soon.

Danner opened a second bottle of red wine and refilled his glass, Coby's, Jarrod's, and Kirk's. Genevieve demurred, though Coby wondered if it was just that she preferred white. She came into the kitchen and stood beside Coby while Danner took the glasses to the other two men.

"I was kinda nuts when I called you that night. I really thought I was going to get blamed for Yvette's death," Genevieve said.

Coby filled one of the pots in the sink with water and added some dish soap. "You were pretty adamant," she admitted.

"That's 'cause I'd just been there. I told you that." Genevieve gave her a studied look.

"Juliet said something to me that night in the hallway. She said she hadn't killed Rhiannon, but she knew who did."

"Oh?"

"She said I was smart enough to figure it out."

"And have you? Figured it out?" Genevieve brushed imaginary crumbs from the counter into the sink.

"Not completely. But your mom said you took up hiking for a while after high school. She was trying to remember when but wasn't really sure. She thought maybe you'd gone hiking a time or two with Rhiannon, Lucas Moore's real girlfriend."

Genevieve looked like she was going to deny it. She started to change the subject, then said suddenly, "I didn't kill her, but I was there. We got in a fight. She'd gotten so mean about Lucas, calling him names after she learned he wasn't faithful. I pushed her and yelled at her, and she pushed me back. We were standing there, furious with each other, probably a lot like Lucas at Bancroft Bluff." Her voice caught. "And then she fell, and I started to fall, but I caught a limb and hung on. I didn't kill her. I didn't."

"Does Jarrod know?" Coby asked.

"Nobody does. Except you."

"And me," Danner said quietly.

Gen looked from Coby to Danner and back again, correctly assuming they were going to expect her to tell her husband. "It's just not fair!" she cried. "I could've died, too!"

"But you didn't . . . and if you want to make a life for yourself . . ." Coby inclined her head in Jarrod's direction. Jarrod, who was seated on the couch with Kirk, running over some imaginary guitar chords with him, looked up at that moment.

Genevieve closed her eyes, then opened them, then walked over to her husband and asked Kirk if she could talk to Jarrod alone.

Danner slid an arm around Coby, and they both turned to watch them.

"It's hell being the 'It' couple," he observed.

Kirk joined them, turning back to see what they were looking at, then shrugging it off. "It won't last," he predicted.

Danner drawled, "I wouldn't be so sure. Sometimes it just takes a while to get right."

"That's romantic crap," Kirk said.

Danner and Coby looked at each other, then broke into laughter. Danner pushed her hair back and pressed a kiss on her forehead and Coby closed her eyes, still smiling.

"It's all good," he said.

"Yep. It's all good," she agreed.

GREAT BOOKS, GREAT SAVINGS!

When You Visit Our Website:

www.kensingtonbooks.com

You Can Save Money Off The Retail Price

Of Any Book You Purchase!

- **All Your Favorite Kensington Authors**
- **New Releases & Timeless Classics**
- **Overnight Shipping Available**
- **eBooks Available For Many Titles**
- **All Major Credit Cards Accepted**

Visit Us Today To Start Saving!

www.kensingtonbooks.com

All Orders Are Subject To Availability.
Shipping and Handling Charges Apply.
Offers and Prices Subject To Change Without Notice.

Romantic Suspense from **Lisa Jackson**

See How She Dies	0-8217-7605-3	$6.99US/$9.99CAN
Final Scream	0-8217-7712-2	$7.99US/$10.99CAN
Wishes	0-8217-6309-1	$5.99US/$7.99CAN
Whispers	0-8217-7603-7	$6.99US/$9.99CAN
Twice Kissed	0-8217-6038-6	$5.99US/$7.99CAN
Unspoken	0-8217-6402-0	$6.50US/$8.50CAN
If She Only Knew	0-8217-6708-9	$6.50US/$8.50CAN
Hot Blooded	0-8217-6841-7	$6.99US/$9.99CAN
Cold Blooded	0-8217-6934-0	$6.99US/$9.99CAN
The Night Before	0-8217-6936-7	$6.99US/$9.99CAN
The Morning After	0-8217-7295-3	$6.99US/$9.99CAN
Deep Freeze	0-8217-7296-1	$7.99US/$10.99CAN
Fatal Burn	0-8217-7577-4	$7.99US/$10.99CAN
Shiver	0-8217-7578-2	$7.99US/$10.99CAN
Most Likely to Die	0-8217-7576-6	$7.99US/$10.99CAN
Absolute Fear	0-8217-7936-2	$7.99US/$9.49CAN
Almost Dead	0-8217-7579-0	$7.99US/$10.99CAN
Lost Souls	0-8217-7938-9	$7.99US/$10.99CAN
Left to Die	1-4201-0276-1	$7.99US/$10.99CAN
Wicked Game	1-4201-0338-5	$7.99US/$9.99CAN
Malice	0-8217-7940-0	$7.99US/$9.49CAN

Available Wherever Books Are Sold!

Visit our website at **www.kensingtonbooks.com**